Sophie's Fire

The Story of
Saint Madeleine Sophie Barat

Constance Solari

Dear Siana,

Happy almost-Spring! This has been an amazing year and I want to thank you so so much for all of your help, support, ideas, enthusiasm and FUN! I hope you enjoy this book about our role model who would Love founded the Society for the sake of one child!

Love you always,
Donna XOXO

ISBN: 0615621457
ISBN-13: 9780615621456

A Raimondo ~
il mio cuore e il mio sostegno

Acknowledgments

THIS BOOK WOULD NEVER HAVE BEEN POSSIBLE WITHOUT THE SAB-
batical given me by Sacred Heart Schools, Atherton. In particular, I
wish to thank Rich Dioli, whose magical ways of conjuring money not
only sent me on sabbatical in 2010, but also sent me with sixteen colleagues to Joigny in the spring of 2006—a trip that fueled my interest in
Sophie's life. To him and to whatever philanthropic angels were behind
it all, thank you.

I have no words to express my gratitude to the Religious of the
Sacred Heart, who have kept Sophie's vision alive for over two hundred years. Throughout this process, I have never ceased to be amazed
at their generous and enthusiastic encouragement of a layperson from
California who wished to novelize the story of their founder. In particular, I thank Sister Kathleen Hughes, whose endless support of the
project extends back to 2008, and who has done much to help me
understand Sophie and her spirituality. Her insightful responses to the
manuscript's opening chapters freed me to exercise my imagination in
ways that allowed my Sophie to emerge. I thank the following RSCJ in
Joigny for receiving me into their community for a month in the spring
of 2010 and for allowing me to live next to the room where Sophie
was born: Sisters Doreen Boland, Chantal DeJonghe, Marie-Josèphe

Desclos le Peley, Isabelle Lagneau, Ysabel Lorthiois, and Maria Pasquier. I thank Sister Maryvonne Duclaux and her community for their hospitality in Poitiers, Sister Anne-Marie de Guillebon for our lovely walking tour of Sainte-Marie d'en-Haut in Grenoble, and Sister Marie-France Carreel for lunch with her community in Paris and a memorable walk through the gardens of the Hôtel Biron. In Rome, I thank Sister Margaret Phelan, archivist, for guiding me through the Villa Lante and for inviting me to the rededication of the RSCJ archives. Thanks also go to Sister Phil Kilroy, the Irish historian whose monumental biography of Sophie, published in 2000, provided a critical source of information. Her encouragement meant the world to me. Finally, to all the RSCJ who have encouraged me along the way, especially Sisters Suzanne Cooke, Frances de la Chapelle, Frances Gimber, Sharon Karam, Nancy Morris, Clare Pratt, and Sara Ann Rude. Sophie could not ask for more wonderful daughters.

Milles mercis to Michele Baschet for inviting me into Sophie's home in the Marais; and to Gilles Renaux, *tonnelier extraordinaire*, who shared the mysteries of making wine barrels in the old Burgundian style.

Eternal thanks to those who read the manuscript in its various stages. In particular, to Carol Schaffer, who read each chapter as it emerged from my printer, and whose eagle eye let me get away with little sentimentality, inaccuracy, or sloppy thinking. To Jennifer Ciucki, Hannah Doyle, Lynn Hillman, Jillian Manus, Juana Mikkelsen, Robin Stroll, and Marcia Wolf for their enthusiastic responses to Sophie and for their insightful comments. To Aimée Squires, my new friend from San Diego, for helping me get the publication ball rolling and advising me on some of the business angles of publication. To Vanessa Woods for creating the map of Sophie's France. To Julie Horvath for help with the website. And to Robert Harrison, Kathleen Hughes, and Cokie Roberts for their generous comments.

Finally, to my children, Antonia and Christopher, whose ongoing love and support in all things keep me strong and willing to take risks. And most of all, to my husband of forty years, who so graciously allowed Sophie to move into our home and take over our life together for months and months, and whose patience, support, optimism, enthusiasm, humor, and belief in my life as a writer has never flagged for a moment.

Introduction

WRITING A BIOGRAPHICAL OR HISTORICAL NOVEL POSES A UNIQUE set of challenges. One is faced not only with breathing life into a central character, but also with resurrecting an entire period of history and a particular place or set of places. In the case of Madeleine Sophie Barat, the task is daunting. Sophie lived through the French Revolution, the reign of Napoleon Bonaparte, the Restoration of the Bourbon kings, the French Revolutions of 1830 and 1848, the Second Empire, and the great unrest taking place in larger Europe as old kingdoms and princi-palities gave way to nation states, and absolute monarchies gave way to constitutional monarchies and republics. Sophie was also enmeshed in a labyrinth of Church politics as she maneuvered her way through the centuries-old power struggle between Rome and the French king and his bishops.

I have attempted to bring to life this historical backdrop so that the reader might more fully understand the world that shaped Sophie Barat. To do so, I have invented two families (friends of the Barats from the town of Joigny) who eventually move within this larger world and allow the reader access to its inner workings. But while Célestine Lorrain and Denis Marmaton may not actually have existed, they surely *could* have, and I have linked them with historical figures whose factual bases I have tried in all cases to preserve. Similarly, while Sophie obviously never engaged in conversation with Marmatons and Lorrains, the words she speaks when she is with them derive from her letters, her conferences, and the statements recorded about her. The same is true for conversations she has with her family, her religious sisters, and those historical figures (popes, cardinals, priests, etc.) whom she *did* engage directly. I obviously don't know in every case what words she used or what phrases she inspired in her interlocutors, but the conversations are "true" to the characters' historical selves—to the extent that the biographies and histories I have consulted are, themselves, "truthful."

In this same vein, I have included words or expressions that may seem anachronistic: people in eighteenth- and nineteenth-century France clearly did not, for example, use terms such as *micromanage* and *surreal*. I have selected modern terms in an attempt to convey the kind of expressions they *might* have used in their conversation and narration, had they spoken English today.

I have done all of this, of course, with the intent of bringing to life a woman of extraordinary gifts whose story deserves to be told. A genius, a mystic, an educator, and a highly successful entrepreneur, Sophie Barat was a woman who would have thrived anywhere and anytime. The educational philosophy that she developed is as relevant today as it was in 1800. Her concerns mirror those of us living in the twenty-first century as we stumble through history and continue to make the same mistakes and dream the same dreams. Her yearning for a life of connectedness to God is that of every human being who senses his or her own existential loneliness and seeks the transcendent. Her desire for justice and peace in the midst of violence, cruelty, and injustice is our own. Her global vision, in particular, is one that few can argue with today as we shrink the distances that separate us and become increasingly interdependent. She understood the essential interdependence of us all, wherever we reside on the planet. And her hope was to infuse this world with the love of what she called the Sacred Heart of Jesus, the symbol and source of God's love and compassion for this world.

Novels are not histories, and what Aristotle said in his *Poetics* about poetry's being a "better thing than history" (I, ix) might surely apply to fiction. While history must adhere to specific facts and events, the novel, in its quest for more general truths, can focus on what *might* have happened—the kinds of things that certain kinds of people would probably or inevitably have said.

I hope that readers find my Sophie compelling, and that those of you who already know her will find what I have written to convey the kinds of things she would probably or inevitably have said or done.

Table of Contents

Map of Modern France

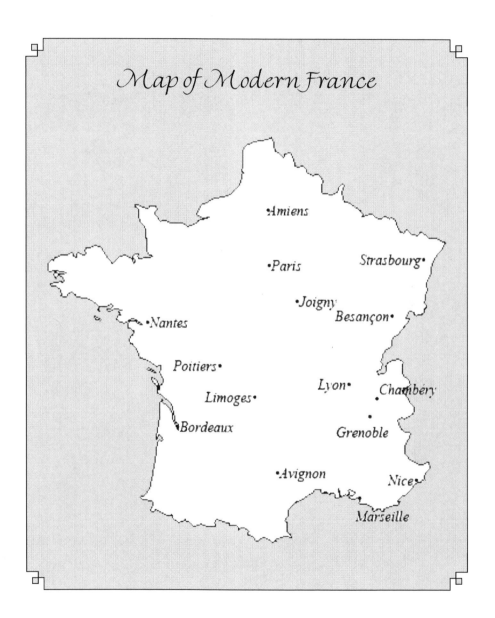

Part 1

Joigny

Fire

Winter, 1779

No one knows how the fire started. one rumor has it that Madame Marmaton, enraged at her husband's latest infidelity, hurled an oil lamp at him across their bedroom. Another version claims that Alain Guillot—a bookworm already at age eleven—fell asleep while reading La Fontaine by candlelight beneath his bedcovers. An unlikely story, but one that the Marmaton family preferred to put about the town.

What everyone *did* know by the end of the next day was that Marie Madeleine Barat was sent into a premature labor by the walls of flame and panic that were sweeping toward her home. The blaze started somewhere in the rue Neuve, and by the time people realized what was happening, the fire had engulfed several homes and was racing down the rue du Puits Chardon. The roar and crackle of flame, coupled with the wind generated by the intense heat, blew sparks and burning debris from roof to roof, quickly destroying the half-timbered structures and sending families into the street. When the fire took another turn down a narrow lane that paralleled the rue Neuve, the Barat home and several others were trapped between two sheets of fire. Men's and women's

voices mingled with screams and cries as mothers gathered their children and scrambled out of their disintegrating homes. When Madame Barat's water broke suddenly, all her husband could do was move her into a back bedroom and rush back outside to help his neighbors try to contain the blaze. It stopped three houses short of their home. Amidst the chaos and terror, Marie Madeleine delivered a baby girl very late in the evening of December 12, a full two months early.

I saw them all early the next morning—Marie-Louise, Louis, and Monsieur Barat, along with Louise-Sophie Cédor—as they scurried down the hill to baptize the infant at St. Thibault. Young Louis, who had appointed himself godfather, held the tiny bundle that was Sophie in his arms. They were certain she would die before the day was out, and probably her mother as well. The ten-year-old Louis was taking no chances with his sister's soul.

It was the feast of St. Lucie, and my grandmother from Sweden was still living with us. Despite the fire, my sister Véronique had awakened us very early, according to Swedish custom (which we observed in honor of *Grandmère*), with café au lait and saffron buns. She was wearing the obligatory white dress with crimson sash, but—in deference to the conflagration of the night before—the candles in her crown were unlit.

I watched the Barat family out my window as I sipped my café au lait.

~

The people of Joigny are terrified of fire. In 1530, the town was nearly destroyed by an inferno that swept through its narrow streets. If you walk partway down the hill from the Barat home and turn to the left, you come upon the House of the Tree of Jesse. With its twisted timbers and steeply pitched gable, it looks like something out of a Grimm's fairytale. In a niche is a statue of Mary with the infant Jesus in her arms. I don't know whether the statue was placed there before or after the fire of 1530—whether it was offered as talisman or token of thanksgiving. But my grandfather Lorrain remembers the religious processions that wound through the town to commemorate the fire and to pray for the town's preservation from similar calamity. I guess they ended their rituals too soon.

Sophie's brother and I used to pretend that the house was inhabited by an Alsatian witch who cast spells on young boys and changed them into geese. She would blind them, nail their feet to a board, force-feed them, and then cut out their livers and send them off to the king and Marie-Antoinette. Louis and I also liked to gather with Denis Marmaton, Alain and Jean-Marc Guillot, and Germont Fouffé, Louis' cousin, up in the vineyards above the town. From the top of the Côte de St-Jacques, we could see for miles beyond the Yonne River, which ambles its way through Joigny on its way to Paris. One of our favorite games was to reenact the slaughter of Count Guy de la Tremouille, who according to local legend was beaten to death by disgruntled citizens in 1438. Burgundians have a highly developed sense of justice. To this day, the fatal weapon—a cooper's wooden mallet—is the centerpiece of the Joigny coat of arms. A gentle reminder.

But all of this was before Louis became so serious.

Barrels

Fall, 1787

It is november 13, two days after the feast of st. martin, and the timbered, white-plastered home in the rue du Puits-Chardon is dark except for the lights flickering on the first floor. Madame Barat is in the kitchen with four women from the neighborhood. They are discussing Jean-Jacques Rousseau's *La Nouvelle Héloïse*.

In his atelier next door, Jacques Barat is making a wine barrel. He is surrounded by several men from the village who sip some of his new *vin gris*, just drawn from the lees and poured into small tumblers. They discuss the latest political developments in Paris as Jacques works his magic before them.

"The king will have to call a session of the Estates General now," growls Hubert Lorrain, a lawyer who has helped Jacques Barat buy and sell small plots of land in the region. He holds his glass up to the firelight to assess its pale apricot color before continuing. Monsieur Lorrain is the citizen most connected to the current intrigues of Paris. "The Assembly demanded it of him last summer, and the people are pushing de Brienne to force his hand."

Jacques has carefully selected the oaken staves earlier this afternoon and lined them up on a long table. The oak was felled in the forest of Othe, just outside Joigny, and the wood—first quartered, and then split and planed—has aged in the open air for three years. Cut into equal lengths of precisely 1.2 meters, tapered, and then hollowed out slightly on the inside, they are now ready for that transfiguration of wood and metal into a perfectly sealed and seasoned barrel.

"Bah, Brienne is *foutu*, like Calonne before him," counters Olivier Marmaton, who spits on the earthen floor to punctuate his disgust. Marmaton, a winegrower, has met with less success than his friends and is more bitter than they toward the government that continues to raise taxes as France falls ever more deeply into debt. "He'll be gone as finance minister before another year is out, mark my words." He spits again and brusquely empties his glass.

"Nevertheless de Brienne has convinced Louis to call a Royal Session this month," Lorrain continues evenly. "The Parliament will be allowed to vote on any fiscal reforms, and this latest crisis will be averted—or at least deferred." The quiet force of his words temporarily dispels Marmaton's anger, and the men suspend their conversation entirely as Jacques Barat begins to raise the barrel.

He arranges the narrow staves upright within a metal hoop so that, splayed at the bottom and hooped at the top, they are held in place by the force of their own tension. He readjusts the final stave several times until he finds one that fits perfectly into the last gap and then stands back to look at his work, taking a small sip of *vin gris* in the process. The rest of the men hold their breath, as if another remark will set the whole structure crashing to the ground.

"*Et voilà*," Jacques exhales quietly, inviting the men to continue their discussion. As they continue their debate as to the likelihood of Louis XVI calling the first Estates General in almost two hundred years, Jacques picks up another hoop, slightly larger in diameter than the first, and slips it over the top. With a wooden mallet and the wedge-shaped *chasse*, he hammers the hoop into place about a third of the way down the staves, moving briskly around the barrel as the men nod their approval. After pounding the staves back down into precise alignment,

he moves over to his tool shelf and pulls out the *batissoire*, a strong cord attached to a vise that will serve to pull the barrel into its finished shape.

"You watch," Marmaton responds, "Louis will figure out a way around the Parliament, and Brienne will raise taxes again. *Le salaud.*"

The rest of the men, not certain whether he has addressed his epithet to the king or His Majesty's latest finance minister, defer to Marmaton's temper as they have since they were children. Jacques Barat, who as a rule steers clear of discussing politics or anything else that might interfere with his visceral connection to the vine and the barrel, raises a dark eyebrow in response to Marmaton's rough language.

As the conversation heats up, so does the ritual. Jacques throws open the door of the atelier, lights a small brazier filled with oak chips in the doorway, and lifts the partially hooped barrel over the fire. He leaves it there for several minutes, spraying the interior occasionally with water. The heat and moisture render the wood supple, allowing the final shaping to occur. Moving quickly, Jacques lifts the barrel from the flame, places it on the floor, and loops the cord of the *batissoire* around its base. He tightens the vise, and the cord begins to pull the staves together. When the barrel has acquired its final shape, he flips it upside down, hammers two more hoops around the newly tightened circumference, and removes the cord. Now begins the crucial step of "toasting" the barrel. Placing it once again over the fire, he covers the top with a large piece of metal, lifting it occasionally to check the color of the interior and feeling the outside with his hands to measure the heat. An oaky steam has invaded the room, and the men watch as sparks emerge and the firelight shimmers on the ceiling, casting strange and beautiful shadows.

It is Hubert Lorrain who notices the bright eyes staring out from the corner of the atelier. Without having to look further, he knows it is the tiny Sophie, whose quick wit and irrepressible spirit have already charmed him entirely, though she is only seven. Her eyes have locked into the flame, and he remembers again the ominous circumstances of her birth.

"Your son, Louis," Marmaton is now readjusting the focus of his rage, and Lorrain notices a tightening of Jacques' facial muscles. The cooper refills his guests' glasses. Then he throws a few more chips onto the fire and waits for Marmaton's next strike.

"He has finished at the Seminary, my son Denis tells me. And so he will join the First Estate and become one of the bloody aristocrats himself."

People in the village whisper that Marmaton is a Freemason.

Jacques remains silent. His son has always baffled him, allying himself with his highly educated mother and showing no interest in the land. A sin in Jacques' holy book. He has watched the boy turn inward on himself for the last several years, spending all his time with his books and his gloomy prayers, and annihilating whatever grain of joy might have glimmered within him as a child.

Aware of Sophie's presence, Hubert Lorrain tries to short-circuit the new topic of conversation. "Come on, *mon vieux*, let's leave the boy out of it. The church would do well to have a Barat within its ranks."

Lorrain is wary of Louis, believing him to be jealous of the little sister whose intelligence eclipses his own. But he sees no need for Sophie to witness her brother's vilification. Louis has been teaching at the Collège St. Jacques in Joigny for the past several months, too young yet to be ordained as a priest but highly regarded for his learning and austere piety.

Lorrain shifts the conversation back to the looming financial crisis, and the men return to their assessment of Loménie de Brienne, the archbishop of Toulouse who once enjoyed an incongruous friendship with Voltaire and has recently angled his way into Louis XVI's cabinet. They debate his effect on Louis' policy-making as the ceremony of the toasting comes to an end and the *vin gris* exerts its soporific effect. The woody aroma of the charred barrel hangs heavily in the air. At some point, Jacques notices his daughter asleep in the corner and carries her up two floors to the small bedroom she shares with her sister, Marie-Louise.

He is certain she has followed every nuance of the men's conversation.

Célestine Lorrain

Spring, 1790

My mother always felt that Madame Barat was a social climber.

"Madeleine Barat would like to preside over a literary salon in Paris," she complained one evening as we sat over dinner, "not be stuck here in the provinces with a husband whose muddy boots offend her."

My father, who had a soft spot for Madame Barat as well as for Sophie, defended her. "She keeps the accounts for Jacques. She is a good Christian wife and mother."

"She spoils her children, especially *la petite Sophie*," my mother countered, cutting her fish with more energy than required.

"The child is frail, Loulou," my father countered. When he used *maman*'s nickname, we knew he was maneuvering her around to his point of view. "Look at how tiny she is; she never should have survived the night of her birth."

"Frail perhaps, but strong in her passions." This from my sister Véronique, who had watched the child grow up from our house several doors down the street. "And with a will to match!" Véronique had just turned nineteen and tended—like our mother—to judge people harshly.

"And an intellect that exceeds even that!" my father snapped, though he must have anticipated that this remark would return *maman* to her opening theme.

"Exactly my point, Hubert. She raises a girl to know things far above her station." The town knew that Louis had taken his sister's education in hand—and that she was already surpassing his own students at the collège. "What does a cooper's daughter need to know about Latin and mathematics?" As the daughter and wife of lawyers, my mother had an exaggerated sense of her social class and expected her fellow Joviniens to observe their own.

"That is not Madame Barat's desire. That is Louis," my father's voice cut across the table. "And it's not the *only* way that he usurps her parents' position."

I myself had witnessed Louis react to his mother's enduring patience with Sophie's willful temperament. On this occasion, he had commanded Madame Barat to slap the child for refusing to obey, but Madame had refused. Louis had turned white and left the room, forgetting about me completely. He seemed obsessed with the child, and I worried that his punitive character would do her great and lasting harm.

I mark that moment now as the end of our boyhood friendship. I often wonder if it was also the moment I first began to love his dark-eyed little sister.

"I *adore* Sophie!" My youngest sister Célestine, the one *grandmère* called the "changeling," accented her remark by slamming her fist onto the table and bursting into tears.

We knew better than to cross her when she got like this. *Maman* looked at father, and the rest of us concentrated on the pattern of the tablecloth. It was perfectly quiet for a minute except for Célestine's sobbing, and then she picked up her fork and began to eat as if nothing had happened.

The two girls had been inseparable until Louis' iron regimen of study had curtailed Sophie's childhood. But even now, they found moments to play together and exercise their vivid imaginations. Depending on the day, they were princesses of medieval Burgundy or penitent pilgrims wending their way from the streets of Provence to the abbey at Vézelay in order to worship the relics of Mary Magdalene. (The saint's corporal

proximity has resulted in half the women of our region's bearing the name Madeleine.)

Sophie had an ardent religious streak that appealed to Célestine's quixotic spirit. I once overheard her telling my sister the story of Abélard and Héloïse, and I confess I could not stop listening. Her voice vibrated with something between desire and despair as she moved the doomed lovers' tale from Paris to Argenteuil to the Oratory of the Paraclete near Troyes, not far from Joigny.

"*Paraclete* means 'the one who consoles' in Greek," Sophie whispered rapturously to Célestine. "But it *really* means the Holy Spirit. Abélard eventually *gives* the oratory to Héloïse, and they are both buried there now. *Together*. You and I will make a pilgrimage there one day, my darling Célestine."

At this point, she leaned over and solemnly kissed her friend on the mouth. As if a spell had been broken, the two girls burst out laughing and ran shrieking up the hill to the vineyards. They flew up the rue du Puits Chardon and were immediately joined by several others, as if the Pied Piper had sidled his way into Joigny, taking all the young girls of the village with him.

La Vendange

Fall, 1791

SOPHIE AWAKENS IN THE SMALL BEDROOM THAT LOOKS OUT ONTO the street. Her sister is still asleep in the other bed and breathing deeply. The weak October sunlight filters its way through the curtains, and Sophie's body is already quivering with the excitement of the first day of the *vendange*: that moment of perfect communion when all the men, women and children of the village—the very young, the very old and even the infirm—make their way up into the vineyards and harvest the grape crop on which the town's economy largely depends. The sun glints off the small crucifix on the wall beside her bed, and Sophie closes her eyes and runs through the litany of prayers that begin her day. Since Louis has been teaching at the collège, she joins his students every morning for early mass. But today he has suspended her obligation.

She jumps out of bed and dresses hurriedly, for there is no fireplace in the upstairs bedroom, and the weather has suddenly turned cold. After splashing her face with the frigid water she has poured into an earthenware bowl, she begins her simple toilette. Over a long-sleeved chemise, she pulls a brightly colored full skirt that reaches almost to her ankles. She slides wooden *sabots* over a pair of heavy sox, then adds a long white

apron, a white blouse, and the simple cotton *fichu* that finishes every Burgundian woman's ensemble. She brushes her thick brown hair, twists it up into a knot with her right hand, and then pulls a white muslin cap over her head with her left, hiding all but one curl that escapes over her left eye. She readjusts her *fichu* to cover both of her shoulders, decides to leave the curl free of her cap, crosses herself one more time as she runs out of her room, and dashes down the spiral staircase.

Her father is already loading baskets and buckets into a wheelbarrow just outside the front door. Her mother is in the kitchen preparing the elaborate lunch that the family will share after the morning's work is done. They will dine up in the vineyard with her Fouffé grandparents, her Barat cousins, and—this year—the Dusaussoy family. Her sister Marie-Louise, still sleeping upstairs, is all but engaged to their oldest son, Étienne.

"*Allez*, Sophie! Not so fast, *ma cocotte*!" Madeleine Barat worries about her daughter's excess energy and wags a finger at her, even as she pulls her close for a morning kiss. Sophie responds in kind and then pulls herself away, her brown eyes sparkling with excitement.

"What can I do to help you, *maman*? We must be the *first* ones on the hill today, before even the mayor and his family!" She hops back and forth from one foot to the other as her mother shakes her head with mock despair, clearly in thrall to her last-born.

"Where is Louis?" Jacques Barat has entered the kitchen with a heavy tread. His face breaks into a smile at the sight of Sophie, who throws herself into his arms. Then he asks again why his son isn't downstairs helping to load the wagon.

"But papa, he has left again for Paris! More courses at the University. He will be back at the end of the *vendange*. I know he told you last night at dinner!"

Jacques, whose mind for days has been entirely focused on the harvest, exhales an expression Sophie can't fully discern and turns angrily on his heel to continue the loading by himself. She runs after him, detouring briefly upstairs to awaken Marie-Louise so that she might help their mother.

"Only healthy bunches into *mon panier*," Sophie sings softly to herself as she travels down the row, pulling the small purple clusters from the vine and placing them gently into the conical basket that is strapped to her back. She has a habit of turning her thoughts into songs, and as she fills her *panier*, she weaves her father's careful instructions into an old Burgundian melody.

She reaches the end of the row and looks up. The Yonne is silver in the late morning light, and the hills to the west are hung with low clouds that lend the entire landscape a mystical veneer. The old chateau wall gives way to the steeple of St. Jean, recently renamed the Temple of Reason. Bright red tile roofs catch the autumn sunlight. The allée of linden trees leading down the hill seems an entryway to the entire world, beyond Paris, beyond even France. Sophie imagines a world where violence and terror don't threaten to overturn everything that she knows and loves.

There is talk now that even the calendar will change.

"So finally I find you, *ma petite PhiePhie!!*"

She spins around to find Célestine Lorrain hurtling across the vineyard, her cap flying off her shining mane of blond hair as she pirouettes in front of her friend. The child's striking beauty and unconventional behavior are the subject of considerable conversation in Joigny. Sophie whoops with laughter, unhooks her basket from her shoulders, carefully leans it against the vine, and the two of them race down the allée, leaving the rest of the Barat family shaking their heads. It is Sophie who reaches the bottom first, and the two girls join hands and indulge in a mock quadrille.

Two minutes later they are confronted by a pair of young men just coming up the hill to help with the picking. One of them is Denis Marmaton, Olivier's son. He has just been voted the youngest Joigny delegate to the new Legislative Assembly in Paris. Louis is certain that he's a Jacobin.

"*Et voilà!* The Madwoman and the Scholar-Maiden!" Denis laughs as he speaks, but something in his laughter, coupled with the way he looks at Célestine, makes Sophie uncomfortable.

Célestine gives him a pouty look, tossing her hair, but Sophie pulls her small body up to its full height and grabs her friend's hand, as if to steer her back up the path.

"We must go back to the vines, Célestine," she says gravely, and the golden-haired changeling accedes to her friend's request, albeit reluctantly. She turns around several times to look at Denis, who is already back in conversation with his companion—another young delegate from a neighboring village, who sports the new tricolor cockade on his hat.

"The little one's brother is a priest," Denis murmurs derisively, "and, you can bet, will retract his signature before the spring has come and gone."

He refers to the new loyalty oath that all priests must now swear to the revolutionary government. Louis has signed, after much agonizing and at the urging of his archbishop—none other than King Louis' former finance minister, Loménie de Brienne. But the pope has condemned the new Civil Constitution, which places control of the Church and its vast properties under the French government. De Brienne has been stripped of his cardinal status, and priests are beginning to retract the oath. At their political peril.

~

Madame Barat has uncovered her specialty, a *ragoût à la Bourgogne*. The group sitting around the makeshift table murmurs reverently as the pork, carrots, onions, mushrooms, sage, and thyme—allowed to commingle over the past twenty-four hours—exude their pent-up fragrance. Old Madame Fouffé distributes small round loaves of bread and watches as each person cuts a large circle in the top, pulls off the top crust, and removes the bread in the center. Sophie helps her mother ladle ragoût into the empty rounds, and Madame Fouffé removes a baguette from the large picnic basket, ripping the end off with a flourish and passing the loaf to her right. She seems twenty years younger in the brisk autumn air. Grandfather Fouffé opens a bottle of wine. When everyone is served and Sophie takes her seat, she notices Étienne nuzzling Marie-Louise's neck at the end of the table. She averts her gaze, but not in time

14

to miss the way Marie-Louise presses her head into his, or the strange energy that almost crackles around the two of them.

The only one who fails to notice is Madame Dusaussoy, who is still grieving.

"Come come, madame!" Madeleine Barat defers to Geneviève Dusaussoy's elevated position in the town, though she was raised in the same milieu. "You must eat!" She dips her spoon into the ragoût and holds it up in order to tempt her, but Madame Dusaussoy is unmoved. Sophie, who knows this is the woman's first outing since the death of her daughter in August, winces at her mother's obvious if well-intentioned gesture. She reaches under the table and squeezes one of Madame Dusaussoy's hands, which lie listlessly in her lap. She has eaten nothing.

Sophie can still hear Marie-Claire's agonized screams as she underwent the thirty-seven-hour labor that eventually killed her. Her infant son died several hours later. For many nights after, Sophie lay awake in her bed, re-envisioning the chaos on the ground floor of the Dusaussoy home. The towels going up and down the stairs—a pristine white as they went up, a terrifying crimson as they came down. The image will haunt her for the rest of her life.

Étienne's brother Jules Dusaussoy, home from law school in Paris, cuts the awkward silence. "They are discussing a new order for *émigrés* in the Legislative Assembly. Under its terms, the nobility must return to France under penalty of death."

It is hard to tell what Jules thinks about this latest move. He has advocated for the monarchy until their bungled flight to Varennes in June, and many of his classmates are highly supportive of the new revolutionary government.

"Bah! They're a bunch of mindless young radicals. Idiots on parade! You *see* who represents us from Joigny!" It is old Monsieur Fouffé, himself a retired solicitor and loyal subject of Louis XVI, despite the profligate spending of his Austrian queen and the lascivious rumors that swirl about her. The latest pamphlets in Paris claim she is a lesbian whore. Because of their attempted escape in June, the royal family is now under house arrest in the Tuileries Palace.

Fouffé has nothing but disdain for young Denis Marmaton and the new municipal government in Joigny. It is Denis who has begun calling

town meetings in St. Thibault; Denis who has led the successful move to convert St. Jean into a Temple of Reason—after first hammering the heads off most of the Romanesque sculptures that line the nave.

Madame Fouffé waves another baguette at her husband, warning him to lower his voice. "The Marmaton family is sitting just across the field, Henri," she hisses. "*Be quiet!*" While her husband understands much about the political situation, she fears that he doesn't comprehend the dangers ahead for those who speak out against the Revolution.

As if in response to this anxiety, a group of children comes sweeping down the main path, heading toward the allée.

"Onward to Versailles!" shrieks Marie Marmaton, the youngest of the Marmaton brood. She holds a stick above her head, shaking it with feigned menace. "We'll cut out the bitch's entrails and fashion them into a cockade!"

"Off with her head!" screams another as two boys swoop past, waving loaves of *pain de campagne* affixed to stakes. Sophie knows they mimic the heads of the palace bodyguards, carried on pikes by the crowd that had accompanied the royal coach from Versailles to Paris.

"Down with the King!"

"Down with the Dauphin!"

"Down with tyranny!"

"Bread for our families!"

The children's voices, echoing those of the working-class women who marched on Versailles in October of 1789, mingle strangely with the air of well-being in the vineyard.

Sophie watches it all with a sort of wonder, horrified by the violence of the scene. She is deeply aware of a world that is slowly unraveling around her, of forces gathering on the horizon to sweep away not only France's most basic social, political, and religious institutions, but the assumptions that lie behind them. While this awareness terrifies her, she also remembers Olivier Marmaton ranting in her father's atelier. Something about the queen's buying a two-million-franc necklace while the peasants were screaming for bread. And the French treasury's being empty.

~

They have spent hours since lunch harvesting the grapes and watching them, loaded into small horse-drawn carts, roll down to the village where they will be sorted and pressed. Sophie's upper arms and neck have begun to ache, and she is now humming a melody to accompany her favorite Bible passage: *Je suis la Vigne, et vous les sarments.* I am the Vine, you are the branches.

From several rows over, she hears a chorus of men singing loudly:
We have only one life to live,
So friends, let's pass it gaily!
Whatever is coming after it
Let's not worry ourselves about it.
What good is it to learn history,
Isn't it the same everywhere?
Let's just learn to drink—
When you know how to drink, you know it all.

She smiles for a moment at their hymn to drink and pleasure. Then her expression turns serious, and she resumes her soft humming, imagining now that the vine and branches can hear her, and that the health of the clusters depends on her song.

Jacques Barat is directing the placement of the final baskets of grapes into a wooden wheelbarrow before sending Jean-Pierre and Jean-Marie Barat, the twelve-year-old twins of his first cousin Jean, down the hill. The boys begin their careful descent, balancing the barrow on its wooden wheel and watching to see that none of the bunches tumble into the dirt. Sophie sees Célestine's older brother, Guy Lorrain, approach her father, stop to exchange a few words, and then move toward where she is bending in the vineyard.

"So who are you today, Mademoiselle Sophie?"

Guy, who is studying law in Paris with Jules Dusaussoy, delights in her imagination and worries that Louis' severe methods will have by now completely squelched the child's fanciful inclinations. He has not seen her for many months.

"I am the Countess Marie de Champagne, dressed like a *paysanne* and sublimating her great passions in the fields," Sophie responds, breaking into the smile that has dazzled Joigny since her earliest childhood.

"Then I shall be your chaplain and we shall recite your rules of Courtly Love!" Guy responds. "Where shall we begin?"

Sophie knows he is referencing *De Amore*. She and Célestine have recently found a copy of the book in Monsieur Lorrain's library—the provocative text that lays out the precise manner in which a courtly lover was to comport himself at Marie de Champagne's palace. "Rule number thirteen," she says without hesitation.

"Rule number thirteen," Guy answers with mock gravity, bowing in Sophie's direction. "*Public revelation of love is deadly to love in most instances.*"

"Rule number eighteen," Sophie quips back, her eyes sparkling and her color rising. "*Good character is the one real requirement for worthiness of love.*"

"Rule twenty-six," Guy counters. "*Love is powerless to hold anything from love.*" The two of them start laughing, though even the nonchalant observer would have noticed something slightly pained in the young man's facial expression.

Germont Fouffé, Madame Barat's nephew, appears from nowhere and checks the status of Sophie's *panier*. "Almost filled, *ma petite cousine*?" He smiles indulgently at the eleven-year-old child who barely reaches his waist and marvels at the speed with which she has filled yet another basket. "You were born to work the vineyard, *ma puce*. Why you spend all your time locked up with books I'll never understand!"

Germont works closely with Jacques and will probably take over the Barat wine operation one day. He, too, is concerned about Louis' rigid ways with his little sister and has heard unsettling rumors of the severity with which he punishes students at the Collège. Germont wouldn't be surprised to find a knotted *discipline* hidden somewhere in his bedroom.

The two men take the loaded *panier* from Sophie and carry the grapes over to a horse-drawn cart. They add the clusters to those which have just been emptied into the cart, return the empty basket to her, and then move across to another section of the vineyard, where they will complete the same task.

Sophie watches them walk away, hooks the basket straps over her shoulders once again, and then continues her way down the row. In another hour she has filled it. Most of the other workers have already gone down the hill to participate in the crush. Madame Barat and Marie-Louise have returned home to begin preparing a late-night supper for the extended family.

The sun is going down over the western hills, and Sophie moves almost like a sleepwalker toward the allée. She is tired to the bone with the delicious fatigue that accompanies a full day's physical exertion. But something else is pulling her toward this spot, and she moves in obedience to the call.

As she stares through the trees, the rose and gold of the sunset seem to pulsate and throb over the distant hills. She suddenly remembers the Italian word for sunset she has learned that week. *Tramonto.* Across the mountain. She looks out over the valley and thinks again of the vastness of the world beyond Joigny. She feels something move within her that she cannot identify. A warm glow that increases as it moves up her spine and then through the rest of her body, making her almost swoon. She falls on her knees and closes her eyes, which have inexplicably filled with tears.

"I love you," she whispers. Not knowing whom or what she addresses.

Terror

Fall, 1793

"THEY'VE GUILLOTINED MARIE-ANTOINETTE!"

We were all gathered at the Café du Pont (recently renamed the Café du Citoyen), and it was Alain Guillot who brought us the news, having ridden hard all night to deliver this latest bulletin.

His message, shouted into the smoky interior where men of every class and political disposition gathered in the evening, generated a variety of reactions. Some maintained a shocked silence. Others nodded approvingly and knocked their glasses together. Those sitting at our table, holding a mix of political opinions, kept our eyes down, studying the wine in our earthenware tumblers.

The king had lost his head in January to Dr. Guillotine's newly invented device—already an emblem of the Republic's egalitarian spirit. King or peasant, priest or fishwife, it didn't matter. All classes benefited from this efficient and "humane" method of disposing of the regime's enemies.

"*Les salauds.*" It was Germont Fouffé. Of us all, he was the most conservative, an earthbound feudalist born three hundred years too late.

But at this moment, even those of us supportive of the Revolution felt a measure of horror.

"If she goes, Barat and his type shouldn't be far behind," Alain Guillot reasoned, pulling a chair up to the table.

Louis Barat had been imprisoned in Paris since May. No one knew exactly where, but Denis Marmaton—whom we all suspected of putting him there—had been overheard to say that he was in the Conciergerie.

As Denis Marmaton had predicted, Louis did retract his oath to the new Civil Constitution. After the brutal murder of several non-juror priests in nearby Auxerre, he left his job at the Collège, hid in the family attic for several months, and then, heavily disguised, took off for Paris where he hoped to support himself as a teacher.

"My God, the goodwife Barat will have another seizure when she hears this," I responded. My sister Célestine had been with Sophie just two days before and witnessed Madame Barat fall into convulsions brought on by a lengthy crying jag. She had been refusing to eat for days, and Sophie had only gotten her to take food through her culinary skill and unparalleled powers of persuasion. Célestine claimed that Sophie had now become the parent to her mother.

"Have you seen what Madame now has hanging on the wall in their house?" Alain continued. He was Madame Barat's nephew, and the Fouffé women were strict Jansenists, whose religious austerity was typical of the region.

I knew what he referred to, for Célestine had told me. But I waited to hear Alain's description. "Two etchings of the Sacred Heart," he spat out incredulously, "one of Jesus and one of Mary. She actually paid to have them framed! *Maman* says her sister is becoming a screaming *Cordicole!*"

"If they're not careful, the Jacobins will have them all in prison," Alain continued with an exasperated air. "Doesn't she realize the Sacred Heart is the symbol for the counter-revolution?" We all knew that Louis XVI had gone to the scaffold wearing a badge depicting the Sacred Heart.

No one at the table believed she understood the pictures' political significance. They were a gift from Louis and undoubtedly on view as a reminder of her absent son.

But there was no doubt that the Barat family was being watched. The commune of Joigny had sequestered their goods for the past several months, ever since Louis had retracted his oath; and more than one citizen said the entire family was lucky not to have been thrown in prison. It took far less than kinship with a Vatican-friendly priest to fall into the righteous maw of Maximilien Robespierre.

"What would they do without the girl?" Germont mused as he pulled on his pipe. I knew he didn't mean Marie-Louise, and not just because she no longer lived at home. That spring, she had married Étienne Dusaussoy.

Germont was right. Madame Barat seemed to have lost touch with reality since she'd heard about her son's imprisonment. Jacques had become even more silent, spending endless hours in the vineyards and avoiding many of the men he had grown up with.

"Father claims that Sophie's far quicker than her mother at negotiating the ins and outs of Jacques' finances," I added.

Since finishing law school, I'd been helping my father with his business and become familiar with the Barat accounts. With the current surveillance, it was more important than ever that the family maneuver its way through the labyrinthine tax system without error. Attempting to defraud the government of its due was now a capital offense—and the regulations seemed to change hourly.

"You're right, Guy. She's good with the accounts," Germont added, a bit too gruffly. "And since Louis has been gone, she's not locked up all day with books, paper and pens. Good thing. She has plenty to keep her busy."

We all thought Germont would have liked to marry his young cousin. In addition to managing the finances, she continued to help her father in the vineyard and was also contributing to the family coffers through her skill as a dressmaker. But her studies of Homer and Virgil and Dante were taking her further and further away from Germont's circumscribed world, and I sometimes wondered if he wouldn't like to see Louis' stay in prison be a long one.

"Nevertheless," Jules Dusaussoy spoke up sharply, "the family should be more careful. Especially now that they've killed the queen."

"She was an Austrian *bitch*!" Olivier Marmaton, showing the effects of hours at the café, had staggered over to our table and leaned the bulk of his heavy body into my shoulder. The smell of alcohol, garlic and a rotting tooth blew itself across our table, and he gave Jules a menacing smile.

"She may have been an Austrian bitch, but she was the Queen of France," Germont retorted from his end of the table and made a move to rise.

As Jules and I pulled him back into his seat, Marmaton gulped down the wine in his tumbler, waved the empty glass around his head, and snarled, "We call her *Citizen Capet*" with as much disdain as he could muster. "There *is* no Queen of France." He turned on his heel and lurched back toward the bar.

~

It did seem as if Sophie was reasserting her connection with the life of the village. Since Louis' departure, we saw her more frequently in the hills and in the town. And she went back to spending time at our house with Célestine, doing what young girls do at age thirteen or fourteen. I'd caught them reading *Clarissa* together one afternoon, exclaiming over the poor young woman's trials and tribulations at the hands of the roguish Lovelace. And Madame Barat had recently asked Sophie to read one of Marmontel's more risqué stories aloud at her literary gatherings—much to Sophie's embarrassment.

But I often watched the girl walk down the hill to the river, where the market still functioned along the quay three days a week as though the world weren't falling down around us. She was sometimes taunted by those who, because of her brother's imprisonment, allied the Barat family with the aristocracy. But the epithets never fazed her. She seemed to live in some space that was once removed from the rest of us. Full of laughter and passion, yes; but possessed of a fundamental equanimity that transposed her into a slightly different key. If she heard the remarks, there was no evidence of it. I suspect she simply folded them into a large mental tapestry she was constantly weaving of the world she observed around her. A world where pain and joy coexisted as part of some invisible design to which she alone had access.

Part 2

Joigny and Paris

Return

Early Spring, 1795

I WAS DINING AT THE BARAT HOUSE WHEN LOUIS SHOWED UP ON the doorstep like Lazarus returning from the dead. I hardly would have recognized him, but Sophie—who ran to the door when she heard her mother's cry—knew him at once, throwing herself into his arms as Madame Barat sobbed and Jacques and Marie-Louise hurried over to keep her from swooning onto the earthen floor.

He was beyond haggard—his hair reduced to thin wisps from the many months in prison, his skin a mottled yellow and pockmarked with scabs. He was hunched over and walked with a slight limp. Whatever gleam might have been in his eye when he set out for Paris in 1793 had gone out. There was only wariness.

"*Sophie*! Get your mother a chair!" Jacques shouted as he helped Louis to the large oak table where the Dusaussoy family and I had been invited to celebrate the first birthday of Marie-Louise's little son. Louis-Étienne had begun to cry loudly at all the commotion, and his grandmother Dusaussoy was attempting to quiet him by rattling her amber beads.

Sophie did as she was told but kept her eyes riveted on her brother as Jacques helped him across the room and lowered him into his own chair

at the head of the table. When she was sure her mother wasn't going to slide into unconsciousness, she poured him a glass of wine. Amidst the baby's cries and Madame Barat's sobbing, everyone else maintained a stupefied silence.

"*Voilà*, Louis. A good glass of the local *vin gris!*" She smiled at him but was met with a vacant stare.

Jacques threw another log on the fire.

~

That night, she awakened to Louis' screams. She ran from her attic loft down to the second-floor bedroom. She found him tossing within drenched sheets, muttering fragments she could barely discern—fragments that rang with terror and delirium.

"Louis, *réveille-toi!*" She shook him gently by the shoulders and tried to awaken him from the dark place into which he'd fallen. "Wake up!"

His eyes widened at the sight of her, and his first response was to grab her wildly, holding on as if she were a life preserver. She felt his fingers dig deeply into her shoulder blades. A moment later he pushed her away, and she saw the wariness return to his eyes. When she tried to stroke his hair, he cut her off sharply.

"Stop it, Sophie. Don't touch me." His tone was more frightening than the look in his eyes. Shaking, she moved toward the pitcher on the commode in the corner and poured him a glass of water.

He drank it greedily, and Sophie seated herself in the small rush chair across the room. She waited.

"You cannot imagine, Sophie." When his voice finally came, it was stripped of emotion. "The blood. The screaming. The drums. The rats. The filth. The stink of misery and fear and tyranny reeking through the cells and corridors." He paused for a moment, staring at the glass and frowning, as if trying to resurrect an image.

"I met a young girl at the Conciergerie. Her name was Clothilde, and she looked just like you. Your eyes, your hair, even some of your expressions." Louis shifted his gaze to his sister and then quickly turned it away. "Her only crime was to have embroidered badges with the symbol of the Sacred Heart. . . . They loaded her into a tumbrel on her nineteenth birthday, calling her things I wouldn't repeat, and fed her to Madame Guillotine."

He finished the water and placed the empty glass on the floor, as if he didn't quite believe any of this—the bed, the glass, the table, the girl sitting near him—existed.

"We were sure you had died," Sophie finally spoke, her voice quavering. "We heard that thousands were taken to the guillotine. *Thousands*, Louis. Many of them priests and religious. We waited every day for someone to bring us the terrible news."

After a minute of silence, Louis replied softly. "It was my old schoolmaster who saved me. He was in prison, too. Because of his beautiful penmanship, the Committee for Public Safety"—here he smiled wanly and repeated the ironic designation—"the Committee for Public Safety forced him to copy out the death lists every morning. He saw my name and kept moving me down the list. I didn't understand either. And I was *so ready* to die." He rubbed his hand across his forehead and looked directly at some invisible point across the room. A righteous fervor had crept into his expression, dispelling the wariness but suggesting to Sophie a kind of madness. "Almost all my friends are *gone*, Sophie. They are all martyrs now. *Holy martyrs*."

She heard the note of regret in his voice, as if he'd missed life's great opportunity and would forever wander the highways and byways of France, looking for the shining destiny that had eluded him.

"But Louis, you are alive!"

He ignored her. "My only hope now is to go to Russia. The Jesuits are thriving there."

Sophie looked at him quizzically, but he had thrown himself down on the bed and turned his back to her. She waited for him to speak, but realized after several minutes that he'd fallen back to sleep. She tiptoed over to his bedside, pulled the quilt over his thin shoulders and returned to her upstairs garret.

⁓

Sophie told me all of this as we sat together on a fallen log atop the Colline de Larry. What struck me most was the robotic quality of her

29

voice—as if Louis' psychological defenses had embedded themselves in her own consciousness and forbidden her emotions to engage with the events she narrated. She never stopped looking at the river as she spoke, and when her voice fell silent at the end, she continued to gaze into the valley.

After several minutes, she turned and stared deeply into my eyes. "I'm afraid for him, Guy. Louis may have escaped the guillotine, but something within him has died. His vitality or his hope or whatever it is that keeps us fully—" Here she stopped herself.

"Human?" I offered.

She nodded, and something in her expression appeared relieved that I had said it for her.

I refrained from sharing my view that these qualities had withered within Louis well before the Revolution, offering instead the rosy cliché that time would heal his wounded spirit. It was Sophie, not Louis, whom I was worried about.

~

Before the year ended, I learned that he had taken her off to Paris.

Le Café Olympe

Late Spring, 1796

IT IS ONE OF THE FIRST DAYS THAT REALLY FEEL LIKE SPRING, AND Sophie has been up since well before sunrise.

Her days follow the same early routine: morning prayer, mass, and then a breakfast of dried bread and water. She sometimes wonders if Louis has discovered a special method of desiccating bread so that every molecule of water is sucked up into the Parisian atmosphere. She and Octavie sleep on pallets in the attic of the dark, cheerless structure owned by old Mademoiselle Duval. It is what Louis calls a "safe house." She has been here since November.

"So*phie!*" Mademoiselle Duval's voice comes from the front door, where someone has come to deliver a message. In the adjoining parlor, Sophie is finishing a shirt for her brother—something she has tailored from an elegant length of cotton that her mother sent from Joigny. She plans to give it to him for his feast day.

"*Oui, madame!*" she replies, jumping up to respond. She looks across at Octavie, who is embroidering an altar cloth, and runs out of the room. She smiles, thinking of the endless stories she has read of women and their needles, women and their looms, women and their

distaffs—women and their endless ways of stitching and weaving and spinning the world back together.

Sunlight floods into the room from the doorway, and Sophie looks longingly out the door. The visitor has disappeared.

"Sophie, *chérie*, someone has brought an important message that must be delivered to a house in the rue du Temple. Father Barat is not here, so you must take it!" Mademoiselle is flushed with excitement, and Sophie knows she is seeking reassurance. "He doesn't like for you to go out unless there is a very good reason, but –"

"Of course I must go, madame. Louis will approve." Pulling a light shawl off the hall rack, she takes the message—knowing better than to ask what it contains—, kisses the old woman goodbye, and steps into the rue de Touraine.

The street is dark and narrow and typical of this section of Paris, where some of the bloodiest street fighting of the Revolution occurred. Mademoiselle Duval often prays aloud for the souls of those butchered outside her door during the September Massacres three and a half years before. Sophie, once outside her prison, thrills at the sight of daffodils blooming in a window box and hurries toward the boulevard du Temple, worried that Louis might appear at any moment and send her back into the house.

She veers left and travels two or three blocks before turning into the rue du Temple. She finds the number, rings the bell, and hands the note to a woman who opens, explaining that it comes from Mademoiselle Duval. The woman takes the note without speaking, nods, and closes the door. Wanting to defer her return, Sophie continues down the street.

"*PhiePhie!*" The words cut across the narrow road and into Sophie's consciousness like a second source of sunlight. It is a moment before she fully recognizes the young woman running toward her. Wheat-colored curls tumble from ribbons that cross her head in several places, keeping her hair up off her neck and enhancing the décolletage of her sheer muslin dress.

"Célestine! You are a veritable Aphrodite, *ma petite!*" Sophie shrieks, running to meet her in the middle of the rue du Temple. "*Qu'est-ce que tu es belle!*"

"And you, my darling, are also *belle*—but still far too small!" Célestine, who towers over her friend by a full head, sweeps Sophie into her arms.

The two girls hug each other tightly and then reenact the quadrille they danced in the vineyard four years before. Now, however, they dance in the incongruous shadow of the Temple's medieval towers—towers that housed Louis XVI and Marie Antoinette in the months before they were taken to the guillotine.

"What are you doing here?" Célestine, laughing and pushing Sophie away, looks her up and down. "And what in the world are you *wearing?*" Sophie still dresses in the costume of a Burgundian peasant, and Célestine snatches the cap off her head, releasing the abundant brown hair that falls almost to her waist.

Sophie relents and puts the cap into her apron, sliding her arm through Célestine's. "I made myself a dress like yours, but Louis threw it in the fire!" She laughs awkwardly, even as she remembers the anguish and shame that she felt staring at the fabric going up in flames and listening to Louis rebuke her vanity. Her brother has discovered countless ways to make her feel unworthy.

When Sophie fails to elaborate, Célestine snorts with contempt. "So tell me!" she insists. "*What* are you doing here?"

Sophie hesitates before answering. "I'm really not quite sure. Louis convinced my parents that I should not stay in Joigny. That it was not safe for me to remain in the countryside."

Here, she looks meaningfully at Célestine, one of hundreds of young women who have come to Paris to work in the military sweatshops. Many have been taken by force from small villages and towns, among them Marie Marmaton, whose family has fallen from favor since the demise of the Jacobins and the execution of Robespierre. Célestine has come to Paris voluntarily—in solidarity with Marie, but in absolute defiance of her family's wishes. The young women make uniforms for the French army, now at war with Austria and the Kingdom of Sardinia. A young Corsican general named Bonaparte is beginning to make a name for himself.

They have returned to the Boulevard du Temple. "You can imagine how my mother fought it," Sophie went on, "but Louis convinced her. He's a full priest now, you know, and his word is law for all of us."

"But how, a *full* priest? He could be deported—or sent back to prison! And what's he doing right here in Paris?"

"There are secret chapels everywhere, Célestine. A non-juror bishop ordained him last September." She pauses a moment before adding, "We have a secret chapel in our house." She doesn't mention the exorcisms that seem to be Louis' special gift. He has forced her to witness them on several occasions, despite the terror they inspire in her.

Célestine stops and stares at Sophie as if she were a relic from another time. Then another thought creeps in. "But that puts you in danger as well, PhiePhie!"

They are approaching the rue de Touraine and Sophie makes an instinctive move to turn right. Célestine restrains her.

"We must keep walking," she says gently. "I have things to show you."

Curiosity and the joy of staying outside in the sunlight with her friend trump Sophie's knowledge of what such a decision will eventually cost her. She squeezes Célestine's arm, and the two young women continue walking toward the river, oblivious to the stares that follow them.

"But you, Célestine! What about you? We hear horrible things about the workhouses." Sophie knows that Marie almost died after an illness contracted in the cramped living quarters. She has heard other, more disturbing things as well. Of abuse and rape and suicide.

"Horrible and wonderful, like everything else in the world," Célestine responds lightly. Too lightly, Sophie thinks. "Like this place here." The two have stopped at a large plaza. A fountain plays in the center, and Sophie gasps at the beauty of the open space.

"This is the site of the Bastille prison," Célestine says quietly. "Many died here in the name of liberty. Now the prison has been demolished, and the blood has turned to water." They dip their hands into the basin, and Sophie crosses herself and solemnly marks her friend's forehead with the sign of the cross. Célestine stares at her again, pauses to touch the water on her brow, and then continues, as if her friend's gesture were a perfectly conventional response to her surroundings. "Soon they will erect a monument here to the Revolution."

Sophie gazes in silent fascination. Louis has restricted her movements to the immediate neighborhood and to occasional pilgrimages to the Temple. The rest of Paris is a mystery to her.

"Many things change their names in this city," Célestine says with more than a hint of irony. "Just two miles down the river was once Place Louis XV. Then it became Place de la Revolution. During the Terror the *tricoteuses* named it Place de la Guillotine as they sat there knitting and watching the heads roll. And now they call it Place de la Concorde. Imagine, Sophie—the Plaza of Peace."

They shift onto the Boulevard Henri IV, leading toward the Seine. The street traffic has increased. A pair of women ride by on horseback, flourishing sequined crops and wearing jackets that are cut like a man's.

When they reach the river, they sit on the stone wall bordering the quai and look across at the Île St. Louis.

"You still haven't told me what you're doing," Célestine says gently.

Sophie looks at the silent grey buildings on the small island. "Our life is a life of secrets, Célestine. But I don't really know what most of them are."

They watch a barge pass under the Pont de Sully.

"Louis has his ministry, and we study and teach and pray and sew. And he tries to make us remain quiet. That is all. But I don't know why. Sometimes I don't know if Louis himself knows."

Célestine looks at her intently, narrowing her eyes. "Who are 'we'?"

"Mademoiselle Duval. She owns the house. And her maid Marguérite, and Octavie Bailly. She is my friend. And Mademoiselle Loquet. She writes pious novels." Here the two young women laugh, knowing the genre well. Feeling guilty at this small betrayal, Sophie continues. "And there are people who come for the mass. And others who come for religious instruction. I work with the little ones."

"And does your brother feed you? You look as if you could blow into the river!"

When Sophie fails to answer, Célestine snorts again and then continues, "And what does Louis have you studying now?"

Sophie hears the derision in her friend's voice and smiles in spite of it. "Mathematics and the Church Fathers." Célestine frowns. "And more Latin. And of course the Bible."

Célestine purses her lips and expels a scornful breath. "And I presume he keeps you locked up in this sinister house?" Hearing no reply, Célestine jumps off the wall. "Come with me, Sophie. There are people I want you to meet!"

The two travel quickly up the Boulevard Henri IV, almost jogging through the labyrinthine streets of the Marais, until they come into the spacious grandeur of the Place des Vosges.

"*Oh la la!* I had no idea a city could contain such beauty!" Sophie gasps.

Célestine leads her under the arcade that encircles the entire plaza until they arrive at a small, unmarked door. It lies between a butcher shop and a vendor of ribbons and hats. The windows are completely shuttered.

"Now you shall meet my friends!" Célestine exults as she pushes Sophie over the threshold.

Sophie is accosted by the smell of coffee, chocolate and smoke. When her eyes get used to the dim light, she sees several tables, all of them frequented by women. Most are dressed like Célestine, but when one of them steps out from behind the bar to greet them, Sophie sees that she wears Turkish pants and a tightly fitted jacket. She looks to be about forty. Her hair is swept up violently in back with combs, and a thin red ribbon winds around her neck: a stylistic offering to those who have perished on the guillotine.

"Welcome to the Café Olympe!" Her voice is low, but it shimmers with a note of expectancy, as if untold excitement lies within each new acquaintance.

"Pauline, this is Sophie Barat, a friend from Joigny," Célestine exclaims. "Sophie, meet Pauline Léon, the most famous chocolatière in Paris!"

Pauline embraces Sophie, kissing her on both cheeks, and then repeats the salutation with Célestine.

"You must hurry to the table in the corner. Claire is here and she will be delighted to see you!" Pauline leads them past several tables—one filled with girls from Célestine's factory.

"Pauline and Claire founded the Society of Republican Revolutionary Women," Célestine whispers." When Sophie fails to react, she adds,

"You have much to learn, *ma cocotte*. They have both spent time in prison."

"Sophie Barat, Claire Lacombe." Pauline makes the introduction and then scurries back to the bar.

"I see I shock your friend, Celestina." Claire's rich voice emanates from a place deep within her body, and she pronounces Célestine's name as if it were Italian: *Chay-lay-steena*. Sophie averts her eyes from the deep décolletage that vies with Claire's voice for attention, and feels the blood rush to her face. The woman's ample breasts are framed with a brocade fabric the likes of which Sophie has never seen.

"She's probably never met an actress before—much less one who's spent time in the Conciergerie!" Claire Lacombe, like Célestine earlier, assesses Sophie's peasant garb, and Sophie's humiliation is complete.

"*Viens*, Celestina. Sit by me!" Claire motions to the seat next to her. "I have missed you, my little seamstress. Tell me what new intrigue is unfolding in the uniform factory."

As Célestine regales her with the politics and gossip of the workhouse, Sophie looks around the room. She notes three framed prints hanging over the bar, all of them portraits of women, and is surprised to recognize one of them as Marie Antoinette. The other two she does not know. The conversations at the tables are animated, and several of the women smoke clay pipes.

When Claire leans over to speak with a new visitor to their table, Sophie whispers, "Célestine where *are* we? What is this place?"

"It's a women's club, *chérie*."

"Pauline said it was a café!"

"But we are not *allowed* in cafés, my darling. In fact, the women's clubs are now repressed as well. But oh well, here we are!" The irony in Célestine's voice gives way to delight, and Sophie giggles.

"So it's a revolutionary café?"

"You might call it that."

"But why is the queen's picture on the wall?"

"Because, my darling, she is one of us, *non*?"

Sophie looks at Célestine for clarification but receives none. Pauline has arrived at their table with two cups of steaming hot chocolate, and Sophie's eyes widen. She has had nothing hot to eat or drink in several

days—one of the various fasting regimens that Louis has instituted at the house.

"Who are the others?"

"The large one in the gold frame is Olympe de Gouges. You have heard of her, *non?*"

"Never. Did she found the café?"

"No, we just call it after her. She was one of us as well."

"What did she do?"

"She lost her head, like Marie Antoinette. But for different reasons." She pauses briefly and squints across the room at the portraits. "No, that's not quite right. For some of the same reasons."

"I don't understand."

"You will one day, my little one. Olympe wrote the *Declaration of the Rights of Woman and Citizen*. Two years later she lost her head. She was a Girondine, and the Jacobin men were terrified of the women by then."

Sophie is disturbed by the glibness of Célestine's conversation.

"The other portrait is of Emilie du Chatelet. Perhaps Louis has had you read her? She translated Newton's *Principia* into French and had an affair with Voltaire."

The two women lock eyes and raise their eyebrows in mock horror, a ritual of their childhood.

"She once sneaked into a café dressed like a man. This was decades ago, of course. She was born too early to lose her head." At this point Célestine pulls out a pipe. She fills the small white bowl with tobacco and tamps it down, then lights it using the taper on the table.

"*Et voilà!*" Célestine exhales gloriously and uses the long stem of the pipe to point out a table next to them. "Those women next to us, they are some of the *amazones*—and I don't mean Hippolyta and her friends!"

When Sophie shakes her head, she explains. "They fought with the men in '91. In men's clothing. The next year they fought for the right of women to wear pants, bear arms and join the army." She takes another long drag on the pipe before finishing her thought. "They were denied."

At this point the visitor to their table has risen, and Claire stands up as well. "Thérezia and I must go to Thériogne. She is raving again." Claire inclines her head to each of the women—"Sophie, *enchantée*.

Celestina, *à bientôt.*"—and sweeps out of the room as if she is making a stage exit.

Sophie takes a deep breath.

Before she can ask the question, Célestine explains, "Thérezia is a Thermidorean." When Sophie looks puzzled, she shakes her head and clucks disapproval at her friend's ignorance of politics. "The ones who are now in power, PhiePhie. They took over after the Jacobins. Thérezia writes all of her husband's political speeches."

Sophie picks up her cup of hot chocolate but finds she cannot drink it; the days of enforced fasting have taken their toll on her system, and she fears she'll vomit if she takes another sip.

"Célestine," Sophie finally exclaims, setting the cup reluctantly back on the table, "this is a whole world in here. Just like our house on rue de Touraine."

Célestine laughs at the comparison, but Sophie shakes her head. "No, it's true, Célestine. People trying to make a life for themselves. Trying to find the center." After a moment, she adds, "Who is Thériogne?"

"Thériogne de Méricourt. Perhaps the most dazzling of us all." Here, Célestine takes another long draw on her pipe. Sophie inhales the second-hand smoke and finds it strangely pleasant. "A seamstress, a courtesan, a concert singer, a *salonnière*. A speaker at the National Assembly. She would often appear in public with a plume in her hat and a pistol and sword dangling from her golden belt. They called her the Fury of the Gironde." She stops and sips her chocolate.

"She was stripped naked and flogged in the Tuileries gardens by the Jacobins when she spoke out at a rally. She's gone mad as a result, and now many of us take care of her in a house here in the Marais."

The sudden lack of feeling in her voice reminds Sophie of Louis.

"A safe house," Sophie says softly.

"If you will, PhiePhie, but safe from different things."

"Perhaps. I'm not so sure."

Célestine looks at her quizzically but fails to ask her for clarification. She is still in awe of Sophie's erudition and senses that she wouldn't understand her friend's meaning, even if she explained it.

When the two women walk back out into the Place des Vosges, the sun hangs low in the sky and Sophie shudders. Célestine fails to notice.

"So, do you like my friends?"

"They are fascinating, Célestine. But I don't think Louis would approve."

The two of them burst into laughter, feeling like co-conspirators and separately imagining the ludicrous presence of Louis Barat in the Café Olympe. They lock arms and find their way back to the rue de Touraine.

"What I *haven't* told you," Célestine says with a meaningful look, "is that Pauline and Claire both fell in love with the same man. He died, and now the two of them are lovers."

~

When they arrive in front of #2 rue de Touraine, Sophie embraces her friend, sensing that she may never see her again. She walks in the door and is greeted by the joyful cries of Octavie and Mademoiselle Duval.

"Sophie, my darling girl!" the old woman exclaims through her tears. "We thought you'd been arrested!" As she hugs her close, Sophie is aware of the tall, spare form of her brother moving across the room.

"Where have you been, Sophie?" Louis' voice is even—that of a confessor. It's not so much a question as a command.

"I saw my friend Célestine Lorrain in the rue du Temple. You remember her, no? Guy's younger sister? She took me on a walk."

"She took you on a walk." The voice echoes her words but reveals nothing. Its emotional emptiness terrifies her.

When Sophie fails to respond further, he inhales deeply. The next thing she feels is a heavy slap across her face. The force of it makes her knees buckle, and only Octavie keeps her from falling to the ground.

She raises her left hand to her jaw, which is vibrating with pain, and senses the walls spinning around her. Octavie helps her into a chair as Louis moves angrily out of the room and Mademoiselle Duval hovers helplessly in the corner. When the room begins to settle around her, Sophie places her face in her hands and squeezes her eyes shut, as if to block her tears as well as the reality around her.

She wonders again what she is doing in this vast, bloodstained city. She knows there is something deeply disturbed in her brother's behavior, an unresolved rage that informs his view of both God and humanity. His power over her is absolute, and in her darkest moments she fears what it is, exactly, that her brother has singled her out to do.

That night she dreams she has escaped from the house and found her way onto a water taxi headed toward Burgundy. She dreams that the madwoman Thériogne de Méricourt is with her, and that she has bundled the broken woman in her own traveling cloak and rocked her all the way from Paris to Joigny.

Flowers

Late Spring, 1798

"Sophie!" madame barat's high-pitched voice sliced through the house like a scimitar, causing Jacques Barat to wince in his cellar and Sophie to spill some of the powder she was dusting onto her hair.

"We are to be at the Guillots in less than an hour, *ma fille*, and we must not be late! Guy is here, and Alain is outside in the carriage waiting for you!"

We were headed into the country to visit distant cousins of Alain Guillot. "The well-heeled branch of the family," Alain liked to call them. "My father owns a tenth of the land they possess, and Cousin Jean's wine is the most highly prized in the region."

I had tasted Jean Guillot's *Vin de Roses*, and there was good reason for its reputation.

Since we had business to transact with Jean that afternoon, Alain and I had offered to drive the Barat women. When Sophie walked into the room, even Madame Barat was speechless. The young woman who was known for the simplicity of her toilette was wearing one of the fashionable new empire-style dresses. Her hair was gathered up with ribbons and dusted with a liberal amount of powder, giving her the look of a Parisian demoiselle.

I caught my breath and stepped forward to greet her. "Sophie, how wonderful to see you!"

I'd been working in Paris for the past year and not seen her in many months. She had returned to Joigny when political events had once again sent Louis into hiding: non-juror priests were being arrested and deported to the Island of Cayenne, a penal colony off the coast of South America. I kissed her hand with exaggerated gallantry, and she offered me a modified curtsy. We both laughed and gave each other a hug.

"Allons! Allons, mes enfants!" Madame Barat hurried us out the door with some vague swishing motions, and Alain and I helped the women into the carriage.

The Guillots lived roughly eight kilometers southeast of Joigny, on the road to Beaune. The house sat amidst acres of rolling vineyards, and the vines were just beginning to sprout with leaves, giving a greenish glow to the entire setting. There were three boys in the family, all of them now in their late teens or early twenties, and Madame Guillot had been heard to say that she would trade them all for one Sophie Barat. She and the boys rushed out the door when they heard our carriage arrive, and there was a near tussle to see who was going to help Sophie down.

"Ah, there she is!" Madame Guillot exclaimed as Sophie descended, and I noticed a meaningful look pass between the two older women. They embraced warmly and hurried into the house ahead of us. All of a sudden Nicolas Guillot, the middle son, rushed up to Sophie and awkwardly thrust a small bouquet of pink and white roses in her direction. When she refused it, he tried to force them into her hand, at which point she threw the bouquet to the ground with a violence I'd never seen in her before.

"I shall *never* accept such a present from you—or from anyone!" she cried, a note of panic rising in her voice. *"Never*, do you hear me? From *anyone!"* Tears welled in her eyes, and she ran into the house.

The rest of us remained behind to console Nicolas, who looked as panicked and bewildered as Sophie.

When Alain and I emerged an hour or so later from Monsieur Guillot's library, she had regained her self-possession. Madame Guillot was clearing teacups and dessert plates, and seeing us, proposed a walk through the vineyards before we returned to Joigny. She seemed oblivious to the scene that had transpired on her doorstep.

Sophie and I walked together, several steps behind the rest of the group.

"They are not subtle," she said, nodding toward her mother and Madame Guillot as we neared the top of a rise, and I chuckled in agreement. The sun was high overhead and the emerald glow had increased, rendering the scene almost unreal. Even the Yonne, meandering its way across the valley, had a viridian cast.

"You cannot be angry with Nicolas for what he tried to do, Sophie."

"I know. I don't understand what came over me. I've apologized." The color had risen in her cheeks and she wouldn't look at me. "But I also know what *maman* is trying to do," she continued. "She'll do *anything* to keep me in Joigny now. Louis is in hiding once again, Marie Louise is busy with her children, and she is lonely with just papa, who never speaks."

"You cannot blame her either, Sophie," I chided gently. "She loves you like her life."

"But I don't *want* her life, or the life of Madame Guillot, or the life of my sister!"

The Dusaussoy marriage was proving fertile if not idyllic. Marie Louise had been delivered of her third child—a daughter—the month before. This brought her total number of pregnancies to five in five years; two had ended in miscarriages. Étienne spent most of his time at the café when he wasn't at his haberdashery shop in the Grande Rue. Sophie spent many hours soothing her sister's nerves and helping her care for the children.

"*Why* did I ever put on this dress and this absurd hairdo?" She shook her head, trying but failing to dislodge some of the powder.

"So what *do* you want, Sophie?" My question hovered in the air and hung suspended, like a piece of glass. When her answer came, I heard it shatter into thousands of tiny pieces.

"I want to join the Carmelites."

"*Sophie!*" She might as well have said she wanted to join Napoleon's army. "Then I suppose you have plans to leave the country? There are surely no Carmelite convents welcoming new members in France!"

She turned to look at me, her eyes filled with a quiet resolve.

"When I was a child, Guy, I used to pretend, you know. I made a Carmelite dollhouse out of a wooden box. An entire cell, complete with the little bed and the crucifix on the wall. And I made a doll out of wood and linen and called her Sister Madeleine." When she saw the look on my face, she smiled and said, "Don't laugh. It's perfectly true.

"All of the books Louis has made me read, all of the books I have read on my own—they suggest something so much bigger out there in the world. And yet it's all so very fragile."

After a pause she added, "You know, when I was in Paris, I saw Célestine." She chose her words carefully. "I met some of her friends. Amazing women, all of them. They've suffered such degradation—and such anguish. And they cover it all with a lightness that is more terrifying than the things they have endured."

I didn't respond, but I knew she was gauging my reaction. None of our family had seen or heard from my sister in two years.

"It made me believe that it's all as Louis says. Everything here is nothing. We are all *nothing*. There is only loss and grief. And sometimes worse." I took this as an oblique reference to the latest rumors about Célestine, but she tumbled on, the words now spilling out of her like running water. "I see only one way to live, and it involves separating myself from everything I might lose. The people I love, the places I love, the very feeling of love itself. Look at my sister and Étienne—they were *full* of love for each other. Now it is gone—*pouf!* Like a bubble."

"This is all so negative, Sophie. Where's your spirit? Your joy? This is *Louis* talking, not you!" Part of me wanted to shake her, and I could feel my anger rising at the thought of her locked away in a cloister. "You don't just cut yourself off from everything you love to avoid pain and disappointment!"

"Yes. Of course. It's more than that. I'm sorry, Guy—I'm not expressing myself well." She stopped speaking for a moment, and I could see the struggle going on inside her as she tried to find the language to convey her next thoughts.

"I am also falling in love, but I can't explain to you what that means, or what I'm falling in love with, and love may not even be the right word." Her voice was barely audible but gathered force as she continued to speak. "Yet I feel this intuition. That there's something constant that burns in our hearts, something that desires to be joined to the source of that burning. A desire to connect ourselves to something indescribable that I call God. It might be linked to those pictures that Louis sent us before he was arrested, those images of the hearts of Jesus and Mary. When I think of that heat and all-encompassing compassion, I am in love. Desperately, passionately in love."

She looked at me with something in her eyes that blended self-assurance with a fervent desire for me to understand. The little pieces of glass were beginning to reassemble themselves, and I looked with renewed awe and unspeakable despair at the young woman before me.

Butterfly

Spring, 1798

"LOOK, AUNT SOPHIE!" THE CHILD SCREAMS WITH DELIGHT. "A butterfly!"

He detaches himself from her hand and runs after it, following the creature as it darts among the low-lying bushes that grow along the riverbank. When it changes directions, Louis-Étienne chases it away from the water, across the path, and into a small meadow ringed with oaks, poplars, and lilac hedges. Sophie runs after him and then suddenly stops, unfurling a small picnic blanket and seating herself in its center. She unwraps the baguette she and Louis-Étienne have just purchased at the bakery. It is still warm, and Sophie smells the sweetness of the bread mingle with the lilacs. She fashions the paper wrapper into a cornucopia, creates a few small openings with her fingernails, and then runs over to help the child chase down his prey.

It is a peacock butterfly: the wings are a rust-red, each one tipped with a brilliant eye of blue, yellow and black. Louis-Étienne's eyes widen as Sophie gently scoops the insect into her makeshift cage, folds down the top edge to trap it there, and then hands the trophy off to him.

"Now pay attention, Louis-Étienne, so that it does not fly away!"

The child grasps the cage more tightly, and the two of them walk back to the blanket.

They are in the shade of a large oak tree, and the meadow throbs with spring. Bees hum in the lilac, birds call out to one another from the surrounding branches, a cow lows in the distance, and Sophie throws herself down on her back, staring through the branches at a sky the color of sapphire.

"Tell me the story of the Dairywoman and the Pot of Milk!" Louis-Étienne's dark eyes sparkle.

"All right, *mon chou.*" She sits up and opens the basket. "But first let's take out our lunch." She unwraps the Époisses cheese that they have bought at the little market near the bridge, and Louis-Étienne wrinkles his nose. "*C'est bon, l'Époisse!*" Sophie laughs and then takes out some olives and fruit that she has brought from home. They bless the simple meal, and she spreads some cheese on a piece of baguette and hands it across to her nephew.

"And now I shall tell you about the dairywoman who counts her chickens before they hatch!"

As she recites the tale from La Fontaine, the boy is mesmerized by her voice—low and soft but with a resonance that belies her tiny frame. Its cadences rise and fall with the dairywoman's daydreams, and all of it—the voice, the bees and birdsong, the perfumed air, and the slight breeze that is blowing in off the Yonne—assumes the cast of some softly diffused dreamscape.

When the tale ends, Sophie begins to eat a piece of the bread herself but finds it impossible to swallow. Her return from Paris has been accompanied by serious digestive problems brought on by Louis' enforced fasting regimens. She discreetly removes the bread from her mouth and wraps it in her napkin.

"Tell me another, Aunt Sophie!" the boy cries, oblivious to her discomfort.

"All right, my angel. Listen very carefully because today I have a new story for you!" The excitement in her voice causes him to sit up straighter. He checks to see that the butterfly is safe within its confines and nods his head, beckoning her to go on.

"It is the story of Athalie. A queen of Judah who has lost her husband and her sons and *all* of her grandsons." She deliberately omits mention of Athalie's mother, Jezebel. "Or she *thinks* she has lost them all." Here she widens her eyes at the child, suggesting untold dramatic surprises just around the corner. "She has fallen back into the worship of Baal, and the Jewish priests are angry with her. She does not know that the High Priest is hiding her last grandson, a child named Joaz."

"A child like me, Aunt Sophie?"

"Yes, Louis-Étienne. A child just like you. Maybe just a little bit older, but a good boy, just like you." Louis-Étienne is four.

She spreads some cheese on another piece of bread and hands it to the child. "So Athalie sees the boy one day at the temple and falls in love with him and wants to take him back to her palace."

"Just like Moses, right Aunt Sophie?"

"Yes, *mon chou*, very much like Moses. Little boys are very hard to resist."

He smiles at her and wonders why his mother doesn't speak to him this way. And why she spends most of her days crying.

At this point, Sophie suspends the narrative and leans back against the oak tree. Her eyes lose their focus and she stares at something Louis-Étienne cannot see. Moments later, her voice spills the poetry of Racine into the meadow, the hypnotic alexandrine lines blending themselves into the beauty of the May afternoon:

Mais d'où vient que mon Coeur frémit d'un saint effroi?
Est-ce l'esprit divin qui s'empare de moi?
C'est lui-meme, il m'échauffe, il parle, mes yeux s'ouvrent,
Et les siècles obscures devant moi se découvrent.

Louis-Étienne is frozen, knowing at some primal level that he will never forget this moment. His aunt seems to have left him, and he hovers somewhere between ecstasy and panic. Suddenly, the butterfly escapes.

"Aunt So*phie*!" She doesn't need to look to know what has happened, and she sweeps the boy into her arms and hugs him when he begins to cry.

"It's all right, my darling! The butterfly is much happier out of the cage! See how he flies up into the sky? Up to join the angels! Look!" The child's sobbing stops, and the two of them watch the brilliant wings circle overhead and then soar back toward the river. When it has disappeared, she pulls a piece of chocolate out of her apron pocket with a sly

smile and offers it to him. He snatches it from her hand and races to the other side of the meadow, where a calico cat has just emerged from the hedge.

Sophie thinks about Athalie and her love for Joaz, the grandson she almost kills. Another detail she has spared Louis-Étienne. She wonders at Racine's characterization of her, a woman so much more complex and engaging than her biblical source.

As she packs up the remains of the picnic, another series of verses bleeds its way into her memory: lines she has recently learned by heart and—just as she did as a child—attached to an old folk melody.

The flowers appear on the earth;
the time of singing has come,
and the voice of the turtledove
is heard in our land.
The fig tree puts forth its figs,
and the vines are in blossom;
they give forth fragrance.
Arise, my love, my fair one,
and come away.

As she puts the remnants of cheese and bread back into the small basket, she sings the last two lines over and over again, and looks across the clearing at the tow-headed child who is haloed by sunlight.

Chevalier

Autumn, 1800

I FIRST MET JOSEPH VARIN AT THE HOUSE IN THE MARAIS. LOUIS
had come out of hiding and returned to Paris when the establishment of the Consulate government stabilized the political situation.
He had met Varin shortly after his return. With Louis' permission,
I was there to visit Sophie, who had returned to Paris after the *vendange.*

Varin seemed something out of another century—a swashbuckling
adventurer with a fervent religious streak. Wiry, magnetic, and seething
with energy, he had been a soldier with the counter-revolutionary army
before committing himself to the priesthood. He still exuded the aura
of an officer of the dragoons and had reputedly just walked all the way
from Vienna to Paris.

I arrived at an inopportune moment. He was addressing a small
group of women. Sophie, sitting among them, her color high and her
mouth partly open, seemed particularly rapt. Varin, it must be said,
seemed equally rapt with her, and I could feel the charged particles spinning around the room. A small fire burned in a grate, faintly illuminating the religious images that hung on the walls.

"Sorry," I apologized as I crossed into the parlor. Sophie forced her attention away from Varin and rose to greet me, almost as if she were in a trance.

"Father Varin, it is an old friend from Joigny. Monsieur Guy Lorrain." Varin hid his annoyance at the interruption beneath the smooth veneer of a courtier. I was to learn that he derived from an old aristocratic family and bore the full name Joseph-Désiré Varin d'Ainville. He bowed slightly in my direction and motioned to the women that their time together was at its end.

"*Enchanté*, monsieur. Please," he motioned for me to sit down. "We were just finishing our session for this afternoon. Louis told me to expect your visit. He is away at the moment."

What I needed to discuss with Sophie was a private matter, and ten minutes later the two of us were walking toward the Seine.

"Do you know where she is? Alain and I have tried, but—"

"No, I haven't seen her. All I know is what she wrote to me last year, when I was home."

"That's not a full answer to my question."

"I don't know where she is. I would tell you, I promise." The dark eyes looked straight into mine.

"Do you know what she's doing?"

She pulled her cloak more tightly around her and looked down at the cobblestones, still wet from an afternoon shower.

"What do *you* think she's doing?" Her voice echoed with the gravity I remembered from her childhood. I thought of the afternoon I'd overheard her solemnly explain the meaning of *paraclete* to my sister and suddenly realized that I'd come expecting Sophie to fulfill this role.

We had heard rumors during the summer that Célestine was living with a former mistress of Napoleon in a mansion he'd bought her on the outskirts of Paris. A woman he called "Cleopatra," in honor of their amorous liaison in Egypt.

"We hear she's being groomed to become —" I was unsure how to finish my sentence before this young woman whose head was filled with visions of chastity.

"A *courtesane*?" She finished it for me.

I exhaled deeply and squeezed my eyes shut as if to block out the shame. "Yes. A courtesan. And that she is perhaps already meeting with some—"

"Success?"

This wasn't the word I would have used, but I was grateful to her for once again ending my sentence. We were approaching the quai. A pair of gulls swooped toward the river, cawing loudly as they trolled for fish.

"We must at least try to stop her."

"You won't stop her." Sophie's voice was gentle but firm. "She has made up her mind. And there is nothing any of us can do except love her and try to understand her—and help her to heal."

"*Heal!* What do you mean *heal?*" I hated the sound of my voice.

"To come back from the place where she is struggling, Guy." She gave me a look that begged for my understanding. "She is deeply wounded."

I checked my anger, wanting to hurl my own woundedness in her face and wondering how she could be so oblivious to it. When I failed to respond, she added, "Do you not struggle?"

"Yes, of course I struggle. We all struggle."

"No, I mean *truly* struggle. With what life we are to lead. With how we are to find meaning in all of life's contradictory messages. With how we are to redress the horror that we've all lived through for the past ten years."

"I thought you had it all figured out, Sophie. You're entering Carmel, *non?*" I could feel my vocal cords turning to steel. "Though I fail to see how that will help 'redress the horror.' And this *hardly* has anything to do with Célestine!"

"Doesn't it?" She smiled slightly. We walked over the bridge onto the Île Saint Louis and sat on a bench.

"I cannot presume to know all that Célestine is thinking," she went on, "and while I might be tempted to judge her behavior, I dare not. How can I possibly know all that has gone into making her do what she is doing? We know that she has a good heart, do we not? We can only love her and pray that she will eventually come home to the family that loves her."

I didn't know how to respond. I watched as another gull dove into the dark water and came up with a small, wriggling fish.

"You know," she continued, "in some strange way Célestine and I are very much alike."

I turned and looked at her incredulously.

"My mother and father feel abandoned. My sister thinks I don't care about her or her children. None of them understands what I'm doing with my life or why I have chosen to do it."

"And what *have* you finally chosen to do, Sophie?" I knew that the Carmelite houses were still closed to new members, and after watching her with Varin, I sensed that something had shifted.

She paused for a long minute before responding, but when she spoke, her voice had changed. "We are forming a new community with Father Varin as our guide."

"A new community? You mean some kind of *cult*?" I had heard of small groups of men and women beginning to form now that some of the strictures against religious life seemed to be loosening.

She laughed softly. "I don't expect an atheistic property lawyer to understand, my old friend. But he has an idea—an idea that fills me with the greatest joy I've felt since I was a child."

For the next five minutes she spoke of Varin's friendship with a group of priests in Venloo, some of whom he had known at the seminary in Paris before the war. They were setting up small teaching communities in France, and at the center of their work was that symbol of the Sacred Heart which had cost many their lives during the Terror.

"But it has *nothing* to do with politics," she insisted.

When I objected, stating that people wouldn't see it that way, her eyes shot sparks in my direction. "Margaret Mary Alacoque was *hardly* a counter-revolutionary! If the royal family chooses to use it as their emblem, that doesn't shut the rest of us out of the devotion."

"OK, Sophie, so explain to me what this 'devotion,' as you call it, means. Though I still think it's a cult."

"Love."

"Love? That's a rather cryptic response." My voice dripped with cynicism, but she was undaunted.

"Unconditional, never-ending love. *Agape*." She was staring at the river, as if to plumb its depths for some secret treasure buried there centuries before, undoubtedly by sirens or mermaids.

"Love for *what*?"

"For everyone. For everything. For God. For all who suffer." After a moment she looked away from the river and fixed her eyes on mine. "For Célestine."

Bridegroom

November 21, 1800

IT IS TOO EARLY FOR LIGHT TO ENTER THROUGH THE CHAPEL'S mansard windows. Candles flicker on the altar, and the four women assembled there stare at the painting of a Madonna that hangs above it. The virgin mother of God wears a flaming crimson gown, lending an incarnadine glow to the walls and ceiling.

Octavie Bailly is remembering her tendency as a child to weep because she could not be an angel.

Mademoiselle Loquet imagines the opening lines for her next allegorical novel. She believes she will call it *The Journey of Sophie and Eulalia to the Palace of True Happiness*.

Marguerite Mailleau wonders at Mary's audacious toilette.

Sophie thinks of nothing, but a rhythm is pounding its way through her body, and the reddish light is making her dizzy.

Father Varin is preaching on generosity—the spirit that will infuse this new community of women. They will be called the *Dilette di Jesu*—Christ's Beloveds. At the pope's suggestion, Varin has attached them to a small religious community of women in Rome under the protection of a priest named Paccanari. Any title mentioning the Sacred Heart is still far too risky in France, though devotion to it will constitute the community's very center.

"The building of a new social order will be, *must* be, the work of women," Varin thunders. One can almost hear the clatter of a saber and the jangle of spurs. "We have all seen the fruits of men's attempts to do so."

Sophie has learned that Varin's mother died on the guillotine the very day he joined the Fathers of the Faith in Venloo.

"Our devotion will be to the Sacred Heart of Jesus. A most perfect image of God's endless love for his suffering people. It is appropriate that your consecration occurs on the Feast of the Presentation—the day Mary was presented at the Temple to be *educated*."

Sophie tunes in long enough to think absently of Athalie and then lets herself fall into the seductive emptiness that often leaves her breathless. Without warning, the inner rhythms reveal their source and she is transported.

Let him kiss me with the kisses of his mouth:
For thy love is better than wine.
Because of the savour of thy good ointments
Thy name is as ointment poured forth,
Therefore do the virgins love thee.
A bundle of myrrh is my well-belovèd unto me;
He shall lie all night betwixt my breasts.
Behold, thou art fair, my love;
Behold thou art fair; thou hast doves' eyes.
Behold, thou art fair my belovèd, yea, pleasant:
Also our bed is green.
The beams of our house are cedar,
and our rafters are of fir.

"Intrepidity, strength, gentleness," Varin's voice hums in the background, but his words cannot compete with Sophie's vision.

Part 3

Amiens

Napoleon's Henchman

March, 1802

DENIS MARMATON HAD RISEN QUICKLY IN THE RANKS OF NAPO-leon's secret police. With the fall of the Jacobins in 1794, he slipped out of Paris to avoid being swept away in the final throes of the Reign of Terror. He learned of Robespierre's guillotining while quietly biding his time in a small town near the Loire River. By the time the Directoire had assumed political power, he was involved in the military arms trade. In 1797 he made the acquaintance of another arms dealer, Joseph Fouché, and when the Directoire appointed Fouché Minister of Police, he offered Marmaton a minor post. Soon after Napoleon had seized control of the government, Marmaton was asked to go undercover, posing as a member of the diplomatic corps, but serving as part of the vast network of spies working for the man who would soon be named Consul for Life.

He was in Amiens as part of Joseph Bonaparte's entourage; Napoleon's brother had arrived only days before to sign a treaty with the British. I was passing through Amiens on my way back to Paris. My grandmother had died, and I'd been in Sweden to settle her estate. We bumped into each other in a bar on the avenue Hottoie.

"Napoleon will sign the treaty, but it will all fall apart before the next year is out, just watch." Denis Marmaton spoke with the implacable self-assurance of a man ensconced in Power's inner circle. Back home in Joigny, we marveled at his uncanny ability to fall squarely on the victor's side, whatever philosophy that victor might espouse. He was dressed in the full regalia of an ambassadorial envoy, and the gold braid on his cuffs and collar vied with his teeth for their power to dazzle. He twirled his glass of brandy on the bar, as if to give me time to appreciate this revelation. "A key problem will be Malta. The British will never withdraw."

I'd read the editorials on the treaty's probable terms, including those concerning Malta, and I was unsurprised by his assertions. It seemed a delicate truce at best, and the upcoming months would in fact be the last peaceful stretch between France and England for many years to come.

"I hear you're now working for Fouché?"

"I work for the Consul," he countered quickly, letting me know by his inflection that this topic of conversation was off limits.

I didn't wonder at his reluctance to admit a direct relationship with Joseph Fouché. Known as "The Executioner of Lyons," Fouché had been responsible for the death of almost two thousand men, women and children during the Terror. One of my clients had given me a first-hand account of the Massacre of Broteaux Field, in which groups of people were handcuffed together, marched into a field, and sprayed with grapeshot. Their inconsiderate failure to die quickly resulted in the soldiers' having to wade through the heaps of screaming victims and kill them, one by one, with sabers and muskets. Among them had been my client's sister and her fifteen-year-old daughter.

I turned the conversation to Joigny.

"So how are the newlyweds?" I had attended Marie Marmaton's wedding in Paris the summer before. It was an occasion befitting the arriviste aesthetic of the new regime, and Denis had engineered it all: the marriage contract, the wedding—and the political appointment of the groom. Marie had told Véronique that he'd even selected her dress.

"He will do well, the young de Beixedon." Again the ring of self-importance. Marie's husband was a recently returned émigré, one of many aristocrats whom Napoleon was seducing into his camp. "The Consul will soon appoint him ambassador to the Cisalpine Republic, and we'll all be able to visit them in Milan." He said nothing about Marie.

"And your sister Véronique does well with the up-and-coming Civil Notary?" Veronique had married Alain Guillot in the spring.

"The match seems to agree with both of them," I responded. "There will be a little Guillot in the spring. And you, Denis? Has Napoleon found you a suitable spouse, or are you wedded to your job?"

"The two need not be mutually exclusive," he responded with a cynical grin. "I do what the Consul tells me, and if that includes marriage, so be it." Seemingly uncomfortable with this topic as well, he switched gears. "You've undoubtedly heard that your friend Louis Barat has joined the Jesuits-in-waiting?"

"Yes. I saw him in Paris at the time he was making his decision. In fact, I have met the formidable Varin."

Here Denis perked up, as I suspected he might at the mention of Joseph Varin. While Napoleon had recently signed a Concordat with the Vatican, reestablishing the Roman Catholic religion in France and restoring some of its property, the clergy still swore allegiance to the French government. And was paid by it. Distrust of the Jesuits—suppressed by the pope in 1773 and operating exclusively in Russia since then—still ran high. There was no doubt that Varin's Fathers of the Faith counted many Jesuit sympathizers among them, and Napoleon was watching them closely.

"The Consul will *never* allow them back in France. Varin had best operate with extreme caution." The tone of his last words suggested that something personal was at stake, though I couldn't attach to it anything more than Marmaton's visceral dislike for Louis Barat. "Napoleon sees the Church as a useful tool, nothing more. Religion keeps the people meek and pliant—and signing the Concordat has cemented his popularity."

"Don't forget that he desperately needs teachers and nurses in this brave new world he is building," I reminded him. "Pacifying non-juror priests and former religious is an efficient way to acquire them." While I shared Marmaton's religious skepticism and appreciated Napoleon's

utilitarian motives, I wondered whether he had correctly gauged the ultramontane currents that still ran strong in France. For many of its citizens, there was a higher law to be followed, and the earthly arbiter of that law lived in Rome.

"And what of the Saintly Sophie? Did you see her as well?" Hearing her name in his mouth made my skin crawl. "My father hears she's gone off the religious deep-end as well. Not with the Carmelites, but with some unruly group of females who are running a coven somewhere in France. Two hundred years ago, we'd have burned them all at the stake."

Apparently unbeknownst to Marmaton, the "coven" was operating here in Amiens. Jacques Barat had informed my father that Sophie was teaching in a school in the rue Martin-Bleu-Dieu, and this was another reason I was traveling through Amiens. Varin had found his *Dilette di Gesù* a setting for their work, and the boarding school had over twenty students. A free school for poor children had just been established as well, numbering over a hundred and fifty girls.

Our conversation had broken down again, and in obeisance to whatever malevolent spirit drove him, Marmaton raised his glass, looked me coldly in the eye, and said, "Fouché, you know—he's seeing a great deal of Célestine."

Mademoiselle Joquet's Delights

Spring, 1802

THEY MOVE THROUGH THE STREETS OF AMIENS, APPARENT DEVO-
tees of the God of Sartorial Absurdity. Three young women and a gag-
gle of disorderly children. The little girls are in matching smocks. The
women wear hats and dresses unlike any ever witnessed in the region
of Picardy. Probably in all of Europe. Exuberant globes of white fabric
burgeon around their heads, suggesting chef's hats that have inflated
to two or three times their normal size. On windy days, they threaten
to carry the women off, particularly Sophie, who is not even five feet
tall; one would take her for a student were it not for her ungainly attire.
Their dresses are black and strangely cut, suggesting a fractious marriage
between the frock of a Brittany milkmaid and the mourning of a Paris
widow. Both are of Mademoiselle Loquet's design.

The women have been awake since three in the morning. They sleep
together in the attic and arise when Mademoiselle Loquet, who occupies a private room beneath, raps her ceiling with a stick. The "alarm" is

supposed to sound at five, but the young women often imagine that they hear her rapping earlier and then must shiver in the cold until Mademoiselle arises from her bed and summons them to mass.

Suddenly three of the children make a break for the canal.

"Ama*lie*! Marie-Jo*seph*! Ni*cole*!" Sophie runs after them, but they ignore her, whooping with laughter and provoking the attention of the passers-by. The citizens of Amiens shake their heads and wonder again at these strange new residents. But several have not hesitated to entrust them with their daughters.

When the little girls tire of the chase, they rejoin their waiting classmates and the other woman in charge. She holds them there by virtue of her size—and a look that could wither a raisin.

Amalie is Mademoiselle Loquet's niece and can do no wrong. Tonight she has thrown another tantrum at dinner, tossing water glasses up in the air and laughing as they shatter on the refectory floor. When Mademoiselle Loquet does nothing to intervene, the other children laugh as well. The younger women defer to Mademoiselle's authority.

It is quite clear that their superior, like her niece, is in one of her moods. Tonight she will read to them from her latest novel, *Conversations with Clothilde, Designed to Inspire in Young Ladies the Practice of Virtue.*

After the reading is over and the girls and Mademoiselle have gone to bed, Sophie sits before the fire in the kitchen with Geneviève Deshayes and Henriette Grosier, young activists from Amiens who have risked prison to hide priests, and whom Varin has convinced to join the small band of *Dilette*. Geneviève plays the harp; Sophie and Henriette are doing the needlework that allows the school to meet its expenses. One of Mademoiselle Loquet's many cats has found its way into the room and jumps into Sophie's lap, purring. She laughs as the animal knocks her sewing to the floor and then lifts the animal up close to her face, nuzzling his soft fur.

"You seem to be feeling better, *ma chère Sophie*," Geneviève says with some relief. She worries that Sophie doesn't eat enough and spends too much time with her head in the clouds. "I saw the way you ran after Amalie today. You almost *caught* her!"

Sophie raises her head and rolls exasperated eyes at her two friends, who respond in kind. "There are days when I still dream of Carmel," she says, resuming her work, but allowing the cat to stay in her lap. In fact, there are many days when she questions the decision she has made to follow Varin. She smiles coyly and adds, "Our dear little Amalie often reawakens that dream!"

"Octavie will return soon from Rome," Henriette reassures her. "Then we will be four, and things won't be so difficult." Varin has sent Octavie Bailly to the Mother House of the *Dilette di Gesù* in Rome. Sophie misses her desperately.

Geneviève resumes playing the harp, and the women sew quietly, the only other sounds being the cat's purring and the occasional crackle of the fire.

"I sometimes think I'd like to go to the missions in Canada," Henriette breaks the silence. "Or travel *somewhere* beyond France."

Sophie nods her head in agreement. She has been reading about St. Francis Xavier's work in Asia and remembers the feeling she had as a child standing in the vineyards and imagining the world beyond Joigny. "But how can I want to become a Carmelite and wish to see the world at the same time? I make no sense at all!" She laughs in self-mockery, a musical sound that fills the room and causes the others to laugh with her. Then her voice turns serious. "And besides, God wants us to be here, at least for now." She stops her sewing to twirl the gold band on her right hand, and her gaze becomes unfocused.

She has just that day received another letter from Varin, to whom she writes frequently of her self-doubts. Her tendency to see herself in the worst possible light—a tendency nurtured by Louis and fed by the punitive practices he forced her to endure in Paris—borders at times on obsession, and Varin has written to her at length on the power of discernment. "Whatever your brother might have said to you, Sophie, these feelings of inadequacy are the enemy of your Beloved. Anything that fills you with such sadness and discouragement is the working of something absolutely counter to His love. I deny *completely* anything that does not express joy, happiness and encouragement, and so must you."

She smiles at the memory of his words, and for the moment her sense of unworthiness blends with a belief that somehow all is possible; that the brutality of the past ten years can be transcended; that rebuilding a society based on generosity is a reasonable prospect; and that teaching is the key.

"*Courage et confidence!*" Varin tells her endlessly, and the words have become her mantra.

"I want only to stay in France," Geneviève responds softly, continuing to play her harp. The cat purrs. A child's dreaming voice filters down from upstairs. And Henriette and Sophie lean over their work, stitching the world together.

The Hazelnut Tree
Summer and Winter, 1802

It was varin who gave me the news of sophie's new role.

He'd asked me in late spring to handle the legal details for a property transaction: the *Dilette* were to move in June from the rue Martin-Bleu-Dieu to a larger house on the rue Neuve. There were now over forty boarding students, and the fledgling society of women had three new members as well.

I had gathered when I visited Sophie in March that Mademoiselle Loquet was less than the ideal superior. Not that Sophie said anything, for she didn't. But such a conclusion was easy to deduce from the distracted way in which Mademoiselle Loquet spoke to me of the accounts, peppering her comments with questions about Paris, my familiarity with her literary work, and the latest word on women's hats. I answered her as best I could while I unraveled her haphazard bookkeeping system.

Varin finally sent Louise Naudet, a *Diletta* from Rome, to investigate, and in December Mademoiselle acknowledged her heartfelt desire to return to Paris. In the wake of her departure, Varin called the small community together and questioned them on issues of faith. When he got to Sophie, he unleashed his bombshell.

"Why did God make you and place you in the world?"

"To know God, to love God, and to serve God."

"And what does that mean, Sophie, to serve God?"

"It means to do God's holy will."

"You say that to serve God is to do God's holy will. I hope that *you* wish to serve God?"

"Yes, Father."

"Very well. God's will is that you be Superior."

She threw herself at his feet in tears, begging him to change his mind. She was twenty-three years and eight days old.

Varin explained all of this to me in a letter. (Ours is an admittedly odd correspondence, with details of Sophie's spiritual journey sandwiched between questions of law and accounting.) I was not surprised at his decision to name her Superior, and in fact Louise Naudet had firmly seconded his choice. But what interested me far more was Varin's account of Sophie's behavior on the day of her final vows. It was the Monday after Pentecost, a day that believers connect with fire and flame and what they call the "breath of the Holy Spirit" descending from Heaven. The ceremony was to take place in the chapel of the boys school run by the Fathers of the Faith in the rue de l'Oratoire, but when it was time for the women to leave, no one could find Sophie. It was Geneviève who finally discovered her, sitting under the large hazelnut tree in the garden behind the house.

She was immovable, radiant, and failed to respond for several minutes, even when Geneviève called out her name.

As I read Varin's description, I remembered the look on her face when she'd tried to explain the object of her desire in the emerald glow of Jean Guillot's vineyards. There was no doubt that she had found it under the hazelnut tree. And though I didn't believe in any of it, I envied her the ecstasy she must have felt—and knew it would take her even farther away from me.

Amazones

Geneviève Deshayes IS GOLD. SHE SWEEPS THE STREET STAIRS IN the rue Martin-Bleu-Dieu and tries to ignore the two fashionably dressed young women across the way, who turn their heads away and whisper. They were once her friends. Some nights she dreams of her former life, one full of frills and flounces, dinners and social calls. She has sold her gowns and jewels to support this new work. When the children cry out from the rooms below her, she remembers orphans—dazed and frightened—who were brought into Amiens during the Revolution. She found them places to live. She says she has forgotten everything she ever learned in school, so she teaches the younger children to read. And takes care of the holy oils, the communion wafers, the altar linens, and the sanctuary light. And sweeps. She worries about Sophie, whose health is becoming increasingly precarious.

⁓

Henriette Grosier is unalloyed silver, and her aunt Hyacinth is a flower. They have tried with anemic success to run a school for girls in

Amiens. Joseph Varin has convinced Hyacinth to sign the establishment over to his *Dilette* and talks Henriette into joining herself to God's heart. Henriette, too, has dreamed of becoming a Carmelite. White cloak. Brown scapular. Unending hours of contemplative silence. Death in a state of grace. "It will be just like the Carmelites," Varin promises, "but you will also teach." She will end up running schools in Amiens and Poitiers and laughing at his words.

~

Adèle Jugon is a beam of light. She is young and strong, and she breezes from one thing to another with joy and laughter, illuminating darkness wherever she goes. She tells Sophie that *she* will chase the children from now on. And she does. She comes from the village of Etiole, where Joseph Varin has found her caring for those who have lost all hope. She will end up leaving the *Dilette* to marry the Count de la Rivière, and when he dies and leaves her a fortune, she will become misery's anodyne. She has heard the English tales of Robin Hood and dreams that she is the man himself, dressed in forest green and armed with a bow made of yew. She watches Mademoiselle Loquet and is confounded.

~

Anne Baudemont is galvanized steel. A Poor Clare with nothing poor about her spirit. She is a builder and has sought to revive her order in the wake of the Revolution—with key changes she deems to be necessary. She once threatened the chief member of the Revolutionary tribunal in Rheims. Publicly and with considerable success. Varin has tried to discourage her from joining: "There is a great difference between reforming a 600-year-old monastic order and being called to be a Beloved of Jesus," he counsels. But she has come, and Varin will admire her many gifts, even as she becomes an agent of discord. She dreams of being an Abbess under Louis XIII. Or Cardinal Richelieu.

~

Claude Capy is phosphorus. She has come with Anne from Rheims, another follower of Saint Clare. Her brilliance Sophie holds up to the light, seeing wondrous potential there. In Rheims, Claude would dream that she was Joan of Arc, standing by with her banner as Charles VII was anointed in the cathedral. Now she dreams of Francis and Clare. She will contract brain fever and go mad. When she runs through the streets of Amiens, creating scandal for the school and anguish for her sisters, she will think she is running with Francis and Clare in the hills of Assisi. She will run so fast that she'll become a bird and fly high into the heavens, returning to earth only to flutter above Francis and listen to him preach. When she is taken to the madhouse at Saltpiètre, Sophie will wonder whether Claude has not perhaps seen the face of God.

~

Cecile de Cassini is a carbon diamond. She has fallen from a shooting star. Her father, an astronomer, is a member of the Académie Francaise and was born in the Paris Observatory. Her brother has spent his youth climbing trees and dissecting flowers; he will become a famous botanist. Cecile loves astronomy the way Sophie loves her Bridegroom. "I can only give lessons in astronomy and geography," she insists. "I don't like any other subjects but those." She believes that girls should know more than poetry and music, and she waits for those students who will love the stars and the curve of the earth as she does. She threatens to throw intractable children out the window. If she dreams at all, she is a meteor hurtling through space.

~

Henriette Ducis is highly polished copper. Her uncle is a famous poet and playwright who now occupies Voltaire's chair at the Académie Française. She remembers as a child hearing the famous Talma declaim her uncle's verses—verses that derive from Shakespeare, Sophocles, and Euripides. She is vivacious and eloquent and loves the theater. Sometimes she dreams that she is Antigone or Cordelia. She will teach the

children to read poetry with "exquisite cadence." And to see poets as prophets. When she arrives in Amiens from Versailles, she is in such a hurry to meet Sophie Barat that the carriage driver thinks she is about to be married. Her cousin will paint Napoleon's portrait.

~

Catherine de Charbonnel is patinated bronze. She arrives on a broken-down white horse. Her calico dress and lace bonnet are sodden. She has ridden over 500 miles from Auvergne to become one of Christ's Beloveds, and when Sophie looks out the window, she thinks she is looking at a character from Don Quixote. Catherine stutters and is awkward. Some say ungainly. Varin believes she will fail; Sophie knows she is a *savante*. When she slides into a classroom to teach, she becomes a swan with a golden tongue, unveiling her elegant education and a brilliance that almost blinds her sisters. She draws huge geometric diagrams on the floor of the attic. She doesn't dream, believing it to be a waste of time.

~

Félicité Desmarquest is the earth itself. She is the daughter of a Picardy farmer, one of sixteen children. Until recently, she has split her time between keeping her father's house and visiting prisons. She sees nothing odd in this juxtaposition. She is modest and disinclined to speak, preferring to look after her new household quietly and discover what her sisters need before they know it themselves. Sophie sees in her manner a vestige of Nazareth and believes her to be in constant conversation with the heart of Jesus. Félicité, too, has dreamed of Carmel. There are those who will call her a saint, claiming to see a halo floating above the school in Cugnières that she will soon direct. She dreams that she is Martha and Mary, rolled into one.

~

Joseph Varin is a fisher of women. He finds another—someone Sophie doubts will fill the bill. When Varin insists, she gives in, quipping that the community now numbers nine and will soon be ten, so she expects they now need a zero.

~

Sophie Barat is molten metal. With a bit of an edge.

Cancer

Spring, 1804

GENEVIÈVE DESHAYES WAS RIGHT. SOPHIE WAS DESPERATELY ILL, and by the spring of 1804 she was bleeding almost constantly. She took it as a sign that she would soon be relieved of her worldly burden and united for eternity with her divine spouse.

Geneviève Deshayes would have none of it.

When Sophie locked herself into her room, Geneviève discovered a way to break in and insisted that she stop willing herself to die. Varin reprimanded her "want of docility." At the same time he called her self-indulgent and rallied her to "be a man": *Esto vir!* Sophie had read her Teresa of Avila and knew that Varin had it slightly confused. That gender, in point of medieval fact, emanates from the heart.

But she allowed herself to be taken to the Sisters of Charity in Paris, who were well versed in gynecological afflictions, and she began, slowly, to recover. When the growth had finally subsided and she had begun to eat again—albeit minimally, for Louis had instilled in her a contempt of the body that she would never completely overcome—she moved into the stylish home of Madame Bergeron, the mother of a boarding student at Amiens.

"I spend endless hours in her elegant drawing room," Sophie wrote home to the community. "I am told I must behave politely, but I am bored beyond description. The men in their high, stiff collars talk of nothing but Napoleon. The women sit there quietly in their Roman gowns and side-curls, fanning themselves and interjecting occasional pleasantries. I sit there as long as I can and then plead exhaustion and sneak off to my room."

She was equally bemused by the new Paris, with its streets named after patriots rather than saints.

But Sophie had come to Paris for reasons other than her health.

I received a letter from her just days after her release from the hospital. She was looking to start a new school in Paris, and Madame Bergeron had a property in mind.

"She is counseling us to buy the Abbaye-aux-Bois," she wrote. "Father Varin suggests that I enlist your legal expertise, my old friend. Will you help us?"

I appeared at the Bergeron home one afternoon in May. Sophie was excessively thin but as animated as ever. Our mutual delight in seeing each other was the source of amusement to our hostess.

"Our unworldly religious chooses her friends in a most worldly fashion," she teased Sophie. "How many other lawyers and bankers do you have lurking in the shadows?"

Sophie laughed and then turned to me and asked how well I knew the property Madame Bergeron was recommending.

"It's a beautiful old Cistercian abbey in the seventh arrondissement, Sophie. Not far from the Hôtel des Invalides," I responded. "I'm sure Madame has explained that it was a school for girls until the Revolution."

"When it became a *prison*!" Madame Bergeron interjected, shaking her sidecurls to indicate disapproval. "Now it is standing empty! It would be perfect! *Perfect*!" She was a woman in thrall to the exclamatory.

"It would indeed," I agreed, "but for one small detail. The Sisters of Notre Dame are also trying to buy it, and they've already made a substantial offer."

Madame Bergeron insisted there had to be a way to outbid them, and Sophie looked back at me as if to seek confirmation.

"Possibly," I responded. "Let me investigate."

We spent an hour conversing in Madame Bergeron's exquisitely appointed salon. I noted a small painting by Fragonard hanging above the pianoforte—a young woman sitting in a swing, flounced and draped in the style of the *Ancien Régime*. Several people came and went, including a pair of uniformed men, one of whom turned out to be her son. They burst into the room to share the latest political bulletin.

"Napoleon has just been proclaimed Emperor of France! It's official!"

I saw Sophie's shoulders fall slightly and an inscrutable look cross her features. Madame Bergeron, too, looked dumbfounded, but her son's enthusiasm eclipsed whatever judgment she was about to make.

The remainder of the drawing room conversation remains a blur to me now. What I do remember, aside from the property discussion, is the private exchange Sophie and I had as she walked me to the *porte cochère*, where my carriage was waiting.

Looking at me gravely with those eyes whose depths were impossible to plumb, she said, "I know what this means for you."

"What does it mean for me, *ma petite Sophie*?" I knew the answer but wanted to hear it from her, as if her phrasing would somehow lessen my confusion and shame.

"Your sister," she answered quietly. "Célestine is now maintained by the son of an Empress."

At my failure to respond, she added, "I have not seen her, but she writes me often, you know. And I write her back."

Célestine had met Eugène de Beauharnais shortly after her break with Joseph Fouché, whose predilection for cruelty apparently extended into the bedroom. I had finally sought my sister out after running into Denis Marmaton in Amiens, and my impromptu arrival at her apartments in the Faubourg St. Germain coincided with her realization that Fouché would probably one day kill her if she didn't leave him first. For the past eighteen months she had been the lover of Joséphine de Beauharnais' son by her first marriage.

"So you've followed my sister's sordid exploits."

"I follow her indeed, and I continue to marvel at the mysterious way in which we humans so often tend to love the wrong things." She smiled, and I knew she was reminding me of a philosophical conversation we'd engaged in years before. Under Louis' tutelage, she'd been reading *The Divine Comedy*, and we'd walked through the vineyards above Joigny for a full afternoon, probing Dante's assertion that hatred does not exist—only love of the wrong things.

"Né creator né creatura mai,"
Cominciò el, "figliuol, fu sanza amore,
O naturale o d'animo, e tu 'l sai."

The sound of her beautifully accented Italian echoed in the marble foyer, and I wondered if any element of her studies ever slipped out of her mind.

"No creature is without the tendency to love; we are all *beset* by love," she continued, her color rising as it did when she neared the topic of her Beloved. "*Beset*," she repeated. "And how can we not be? Our creator is the *essence* of love."

She paused, probably waiting for her words to create a chink in my atheistic armor. When I remained silent, she continued. "I believe that Célestine's brutal relationship with Fouché has helped her to recalibrate the objects of her love, but she's still on the path to understanding. What we *both* know is that she is capable of enormous affection."

"Fouché is the incarnation of evil," I hissed. "How could she ever attach her affection to such a monster?" I was remembering what she looked like the night her terrified maid brought me into the bedroom where she lay bleeding, swollen, and unconscious from the beating he had given her.

"Perhaps," Sophie replied. "But the issue remains for us to try to understand *why* your sister mistook evil for good, and to hope that the experience with Fouché has allowed her to grow in her recognition of the good."

"Whether it's Fouché or Beauharnais, she's living in sin. *You're* the one who should be pointing this out to *me*."

"She's living as she must live at this moment, Guy. You are her brother, yes, but even you have no real sense of what has led her to the decisions she has made. I have only *some* idea, for she's shared with me

only pieces of what her life has been since leaving home. But the beating Fouché gave her is not the first violence she has suffered. I am sure of that. And I trust her essential goodness."

I made a move to interrupt, but she raised her hand to signal that she had not yet finished. The young superior was clearly feeling her new authority. "It is impossible for you to understand what women in France have suffered over the past fifteen years, Guy. Célestine was there, at the very center. She has met the survivors. She *is* one of the survivors." She started to say something else but checked her impulse. "And she has no desire to return to the world she lived in before the Revolution. She couldn't if she wanted to. It doesn't exist. The girl she was in Joigny doesn't exist. She may be living in sin, as you put it, but she's living in a world over which she has *some* degree of power. We must respect that fact, even if the current means by which she accesses that power are imperfect."

Again, I saw my sister's battered body lying in her sumptuous bed. "I don't really know what power you refer to."

"I know you don't," Sophie smiled gently and delivered me to my carriage.

Violation

Summer and Autumn, 1804

DURING THE MONTHS AFTER SOPHIE'S RETURN TO AMIENS, SCANDAL and loss extend their fingers into the corners of the house on rue Neuve.

"Disastrous news from Rome," Varin writes her in June. "Paccanari has been sentenced for serious misconduct. I won't elaborate. Cardinal Spina has asked me to become sole superior of the Fathers of the Faith in France, and I've had to break all ties with the *Dilette di Gesu*. I'm so very sorry, Sophie." Her heart drops, remembering the wise and generous counsel of Louise Naudet. Varin's failure to consult her before making the decision rankles, but she partially forgives him when she hears the ring of self-recrimination in his words. Joseph Varin is not one who generally allows himself to be deceived. "Your community will change its name immediately to *Les Dames de la Foi*."

"*Les Dames de la Foi*," Sophie murmurs softly. Ladies of the Faith. Female appendage to the Fathers of That Same Name, who seem to be ever more present in their community of women. Still no mention of the Sacred Heart.

Father Sambucy de Saint-Estève, a priest whom Varin has sent to serve as her community's confessor, spends a growing amount of time sequestered with Anne Baudemont, the former Poor Clare. Sophie hears the whispers in the hallway and reads body language far better than either of them suspects. Geneviève warns her of their growing alliance, but Sophie trusts that all shall be well. Saint-Estève is accompanied by another confessor, Father Bruson, and at Varin's behest, they act as Sophie's advisors. Father Jean-Nicolas Loriquet, director of studies at the boys school, has been appointed to oversee the creation of a formal "Plan of Studies" for Amiens.

Octavie Bailly returns from Rome, reeling from the Paccanari scandal and its repercussions, and decides to leave Amiens and enter Carmel. She will become Sister Beatrice and live her life behind the high walls of the Carmelite convent in the rue d'Enfer in Paris. Sophie is bereft.

Napoleon, suspicious of their growing numbers and influence, issues an Order of Suppression against the Fathers of the Faith. Varin orders that the boys school move out of Amiens and into the suburbs, where they can maintain a lower profile. He writes Sophie that under these new circumstances, prudence dictates that her community change its name again, this time to *Dames de l'instruction Chrétienne*.

The property in Paris is, in fact, sold to the community of Notre Dame.

But the move of the boys school to the Faubourg Noyon allows Sophie to buy its former campus, the Oratory, a commanding brick and stone structure built in the seventeenth century, whose gardens extend almost to the walls of Amiens' towering cathedral.

They gather there in early October, Loriquet and Sophie's stalwart band of teachers, to consider final revisions to the curriculum. They ascend the narrow, twisting staircase that leads to the community room, where one of the religious has recently painted a mural: a bevy of flying nuns who float ecstatically about the Sacred Heart.

"It was done by one of ours without artistic talent," Sophie comments wryly to Father Loriquet, "but it edifies us."

He gazes at the painting and chuckles. His encyclopedic knowledge extends over many areas, including geometry, astronomy, mathematics, geography, physics, literature, music, and several languages, both ancient and modern. He does not consider himself an art historian but must concur with Sophie's aesthetic judgment.

Loriquet has spent the past twenty years studying, teaching, and traveling—rounding out his education with an enforced sabbatical in a Revolutionary prison. In the wake of his experience, he has formulated a pedagogical system of methods and content appropriate to a world ravaged by war and violence. He has read the *philosophes*, watched the attempts to institute public secondary schools during the Revolution, and monitored the current debate on education.

"Napoleon knows that education will be key to French dominance in Europe," he begins. "He recently articulated his vision of a centralized system of colleges whose central purpose will be the teaching of patriotism and civic virtue. There's even talk of his founding an Imperial University. This, of course, will mean the subjection of all schools, public or private, to a central authority."

"All of which means nothing to us, of course," snorts Catherine de Charbonnel, "since neither his university nor his *lycées* will be open to women." Catherine, with her intellectual acumen and fine Ursuline education, has been appointed Mistress of Studies.

"Not precisely," Loriquet answers. "He is considering the establishment of secondary schools that would be open to children, male or female, whose fathers have received the Legion of Honor."

"One can only imagine his curriculum for women," interjects Cécile de Cassini. "What was it he wrote recently? Ah yes, I remember. 'Only religion and those assorted domestic skills necessary for attracting husbands should be stressed at a secondary girls school.' And for *this* a Revolution was fought?"

"Which makes our work all the more important," Sophie responds, snapping her fingers and flashing her eyes at the circle of women. "Let's begin!"

Catherine takes out the notebook in which she has listed those subjects currently being taught at the school. The women nod their heads, listening for omissions or misleading titles as she reads them aloud: "Christian doctrine. Bible and Church history. French language and literature. World history. Astronomy. Geography. Latin. Domestic economy. Accounting. *Maintien*."

"Please define *maintien*," Loriquet requests.

"Deportment. Posture. Self-control," Geneviève Deshayes answers.

"When and for how long and how deeply to curtsy," comes the voice of Cécile de Cassini. "Which finger to raise when lifting a cup of tea to one's rosy lips."

"I see," Loriquet says sharply, preempting any further sarcasm from the young astronomer. He looks slowly around the room. "Your list of subjects seems complete. It is essentially what we are teaching our boys, aside from the domestic economy and the *maintien*." Here he smiles. "Our challenge, of course, is how to *convey* these subjects. How to make them agreeable to our students. How to make the children passionate about what they're learning."

"And all of this," Sophie adds, "when the class sitting before you might include everything from émigré princesses to farmers' daughters. We must find ways to engage and inspire them *all*, regardless of their differences of background and temperament."

"You're working in a culture that is redefining the role of women," Loriquet continues, a shade of warning in his voice. "A new image is being shaped for her in the political arena, and we have already seen her outline in Rousseau's *Emile*. She will be called an Angel of the Hearth. She will exist exclusively for the comfort and ease of her husband and children. It is within your enormous power as teachers to counter that vision or to support it."

Sophie finishes Loquet's last sentence in her head. "Or seem to do one while supporting the other. Or do both at the same time."

The circle of women falls silent, each doing whatever she can to keep from screaming. Cécile is seeing shooting stars; Catherine is calculating the volume of an imaginary tetrahedron; Anne de Baudemont is remembering Suetonius' *Twelve Caesars*; Henriette Ducis is mentally reciting lines from *Medea*. Geneviève is studying the cobweb she sees in the corner of the ceiling. Wishing she had her broom, she focuses and unfocuses her eyes; through this exercise she hopes to repress what she's heard about a proposed law that would forbid teaching girls to read.

When Sophie feels the required moment of contemplation has ended, she speaks. "We must never forget our mission. Whatever else we're doing, we're bringing children into relationship with the Sacred

Heart of Jesus. In other words, we are bringing young women into intimate relationship with the world and its fragility so they might move into that world and shape it. We must give them the tools to do so. The Emperor may have his own way of phrasing it, but if we consider the larger implications of his program, it may be less limiting than it sounds."

She waits a moment, looking deeply into the eyes of each woman before continuing, "This is a reformist discourse. The state is seeking new models of behavior. One can form an 'agreeable woman' who also thinks critically, reasons logically, and values serious study. There is, as we know from our own experience and observation, a powerful interplay between the private and the public spheres. And there will *always* be women who move beyond the domestic hearth and exert their influence directly."

Here she smiles almost conspiratorially at her audience and knows she need expand no further on her subject.

~

Célestine Lorrain's salon has become the most glittering in Paris. In less than five years, she has risen from anonymity to become the choreographer of gatherings where politicians, artists, and poets come to share ideas and exchange witticisms. She owns a magnificent establishment, close to the Tuileries Palace on the rue Saint-Honoré, which serves as the setting for her soirées. Eugène de Beauharnais has given it to her, complete with all of its furnishings, for her twenty-fifth birthday.

Tonight's star attendee is Jacques-Louis David. Napoleon's official court painter, he will soon create his monumental paean to the Emperor's coronation. But tonight he is intent on painting Célestine's portrait.

"Let me paint you as Diana, *ma belle*," he urges, reaching out toward her white neck and shoulders and inviting her to pirouette so that all might admire her from every angle. Despite the tumor on the left side of his face—the result of a youthful fencing accident that has rendered facial movements difficult and the pronunciation of certain consonants almost impossible—he has charmed the small circle that gathers around him.

Célestine turns in the direction he has indicated, revealing a coiffure that sparkles with diamonds and pearls. Her gown is embroidered with gold thread, and the overall effect is blinding. Rumor has it that Eugène de Beauharnais would die for her.

"But are you certain that the virginal Diana is the proper vehicle?" she teases him. "I don't know that the allusion would bear up under public scrutiny."

The group laughs at her implication, and David bows as if waiting for her counter suggestion.

"I believe I'd do better as one of your Sabine Women," she retorts. "Have you thought of doing a second version? Perhaps adding a few more of those splendid conciliatory females?"

It is David's *Intervention of the Sabine Women* that has brought him to Napoleon's attention. The emperor interprets the painting as an image of love prevailing over conflict. An allegory of France forgetting its wounds and moving into an age of true enlightenment. An age, it goes without saying, overseen by his benevolent rule.

"Indeed, *there* they are on the wall at the Louvre—harbingers of Napoleon's Angel of the Hearth. How very prescient of you, *mon cher* David." It is the faintly accusatory voice of Alex de Beixedon, husband of Marie Marmaton. Marie, forever grateful for Célestine's reckless loyalty, continues to see her privately, despite their vastly different social status. Her husband is now the primary liaison between Napoleon and the recently renamed Italian Republic.

"You know that I executed that painting for my wife," is David's swift reply. "If I happened to play into His Majesty's political imagery, all the better." The bulging scar twists his smile into something impossible to read.

"A clever maneuver indeed," de Beixedon parries, "converting victims of rape into docile guardians of their husbands, children, hearth and home." He holds to the feminist theories of Condorcet and has learned much from his young wife. "No wonder it took you so long to complete it."

"Abduction, not rape," David snaps back. "Reread your Livy."

"Whatever you choose to call it," Célestine intervenes sweetly, shaking her golden curls and allowing their cascading diamonds to refract light onto the mirrored walls, "the women seem to come out on the short end, *non*? Or do you think they were writhing with joy as they were thrown over the shoulders of those virile Romans?"

As if summoned to the conversation by her last words, Denis Marmaton appears out of the shadows.

"*Bon soir, ma beauté*," he breathes into Célestine's ear, seeming at the same time to inhale some indiscernible fragrance from her diamonds. "And what are we railing about this evening?"

"We're discussing the exquisite pliancy of the imperial woman," she responds, her smile turning to ice and her body recoiling. Tonight Marmaton wears the eagle badge of the Legion of Honor. He has just been named a *chevalier* of Napoleon's new order of men.

"You're unhappy with the reinstitution of male authority?" he counters, an ironic smile serving to finish his sentence. Napoleon's new Civil Code has obliterated most women's rights enacted during the Revolution—rights connected with divorce, inheritance, property and child custody. Article 213 is explicit about woman's absolute submission to the authority of her husband. "But this is where you miss the point, my dear. You're all so much more beautiful when kept within your domestic space, doing what you all do so well." Continuing to smile, he looks to David for amplification.

"You've all heard the Emperor's latest answer to Madame de Stael, *non*?" the painter sidles back into the conversation. "Just last week, at the reception for the Vatican Secretary of State, she asked Napoleon to name the most extraordinary woman in history."

"And his august answer?" de Beixedon asks wryly.

"'The one who has the most children,'" David responds with a click of his heels, deferring to his emperor's wit and solid sense of values.

"And how, pray tell, did that answer sit with the Empress?" Célestine asks, her eyes emitting a quiet fury.

Joséphine's failure to produce an heir is the subject of increasing conversation, especially now that Napoleon has proclaimed a hereditary monarchy.

Before either of the men can counter, Eugène de Beauharnais appears, leading a young boy dressed in the frilled attire of the *Ancien Régime*. He brushes his lips over Célestine's hair as if to remind all onlookers

that she is his, and then gently nudges the child into the center of the group. "This is Franz Brunsvik, from Vienna. He will be playing the pianoforte for us this evening. A new sonata by Beethoven."

The young prodigy speaks no French, but understands that he is being introduced. He bows stiffly to the group, which returns it with amused if hyperbolic deference, and then follows Eugène to the large Pleyel piano in the next room.

As she maneuvers her guests into the evening's musical interlude, Célestine glances back at the men who follow her. She turns her head in a way that emphasizes the length and curve of her swanlike neck, and gives them a look that suggests she is about to share a piece of classified information.

"Do you know the title Beethoven has given to his new symphony?" she asks, lowering her voice to heighten the suspense. Herr Brunsvick, who serves as his son's business manager, has negotiated the performance contract directly with Célestine and shared with her the rumor now buzzing about Vienna.

The men give a collective shrug as they move into the opulent salon.

"Bonaparte."

Part 4

Grenoble

Imperial Bells

Winter 1804

THE NEXT TIME I SAW SOPHIE WAS EARLY DECEMBER, 1804. SHE had stopped in Joigny while en route to Grenoble, and our families were gathering to celebrate her visit as well as the recent birth of my sister Véronique's son. She was also catching her first glimpse of Marie-Louise's sixth child, a daughter named Sophie born the previous March.

The first Sunday in Advent had delivered a day of crisp, cold sunshine, and the women and children had attended mass together at St. Thibault. Old Monsieur Barat was having difficulty walking and had stayed back with the rest of the men. When the congregation poured out of the church at noon, the bells all over Joigny began to ring. They were still ringing when Sophie skipped through the door of my father's home with six-year-old Thérèse Dussaussoy in one hand and her little sister Julie in the other.

"So it is done," my father said acidly as everyone paraded into the house, stamping the chill from their feet and hanging heavy coats and wraps in the entry hall. He steeled his abdomen as Marie-Claire Guillot, his two-year-old granddaughter, flew into his lap. "We now have an *emperor*." He softened his voice slightly and looked down at the

ringleted child. She was the very image of her aunt Célestine, "So what do you think, *ma petite*? You are now ruled by an emperor and will live by his whims like your grandpapa lived by those of Louis XVI. The more it changes, the more it stays the same, no?"

The child stared at him gravely with eyes the color of cobalt.

Thérèse and Julie were pulling at Sophie's skirts, begging her to continue singing what she'd sung to them all the way home from church, and the three of them tumbled into the adjoining parlor. Germont Fouffé watched Sophie go with an expression resembling that of a loyal hound, then sublimated his feelings by engaging in the political discussion.

"*Buonaparte*," he sneered, emphasizing with his pronunciation the Corsican origins of the man he now called the Usurper. "He will bring ruin on us all before it's over." He looked for affirmation to his uncle Jacques, who merely rubbed his aching knees, shook his head and stared into the fire.

Alain Guillot took his infant son from Véronique's arms and wondered aloud at the child's future in Napoleon's war economy.

"He's readying the French and Spanish fleets for a battle with the British navy," my father announced, echoing his son-in-law's sentiments. "And if my sources in Paris are correct, he's moving to have himself crowned King of Italy."

I confirmed his information. "You're right, Papa. I dined with Marie and Alex just before leaving Paris. Alex is negotiating some of the details of the coronation. It's to happen in May, and everyone is quite sure the Italians will offer no resistance." Alex was now Napoleon's imperial envoy to Milan.

"It's all semantics, no?" Alain cut in. "Whatever he calls it—the Cisalpine Republic, the Italian Republic, the Kingdom of Italy—the area's completely under his thumb."

"They see him as an Italian rather than a Frenchman anyway," I answered. "His mother's a full-blooded Tuscan, and his father—like most of them—is Genoese. They'd rather have a Bonaparte than a Hapsburg!"

My father's voice came sharply. "Just tell me *how*, exactly, he proposes to maintain French control over all of these newly acquired territories?"

Startled by her grandfather's anger, Marie-Claire frowned, jumped off his lap and toddled into the room where Sophie was still singing. I followed her. We found Sophie sitting on the floor, surrounded by her six nieces and nephews—including the baby Sophie, who had crawled into the room on her own. She looked up and smiled but continued with the song, an old *cantique* I remembered hearing as a child. Louis-Étienne, Stanislas, and Thérèse were singing along. When she finished, seven-year-old Stanislas begged her for a story.

"How about *The Lion and the Mouse*?" she offered, looking at me meaningfully.

The children nodded eagerly, their eyes fixed on her, and I stealthily pulled a handkerchief out of my pocket. As she elaborated on the lion's charity in sparing the life of a mouse that finds itself under his paw, I fashioned a mouse from the fabric square, freeing the tail and tying off the ears just as she came to the story's climax.

"So one day the lion went exploring in the land of men and had the ill fortune to fall into their nets. And *who* do you suppose arrived to gnaw him free?"

"The *mouse*!" A chorus of voices greeted her question, and as they shouted, I let fly my little creature, delighting the older children but terrifying the baby, who burst into tears.

Madame Barat and Marie-Louise appeared out of nowhere—Madame waving her hands and making vague clucking motions; Marie-Louise, heavily pregnant and trailing hysteria in her wake. She picked up the baby with a catatonic gesture, fixing us all with a faintly accusatory expression. Madame Barat informed us that dinner was served. We filed into the dining room, where my mother and Véronique had prepared a winter banquet of roast goose, turnips, red potatoes, and oyster mushrooms that I'd gathered early that morning. When grace was ended, wine was poured, and the subject of Napoleon Bonaparte exhausted, conversation turned to the purpose of Sophie's travel.

"Father Varin thinks he may have found us another school," she explained. "It's an old convent in Grenoble called Sainte-Marie d'en-Haut. The woman who now possesses it, a former Visitation sister, is interested in joining her small community to ours. Her name is Philippine Duchesne. Joseph calls her a woman 'worthy of travel to the very ends of the earth.' His very words."

"You *are* traveling to the very ends of the earth, *ma petite*!" Madame Barat lamented. "Only a few kilometers and you're in Switzerland!"

"First I must go to Lyon," Sophie continued, smiling indulgently at her mother, "where he wants me to interview some new postulants."

"So *many* kilometers in the dead of winter," Madame Barat went on petulantly. "It is *madness*, Sophie! *La folie*!" Still unreconciled to Sophie's absence, she seemed to believe that a never-ending fugue of negative observations would at some point jar her daughter back into her right mind.

"But this is incredibly exciting, Madame Barat!" Véronique interjected. "A second school! You must be *delighted*, Sophie!"

There were times when Véronique Guillot considered Sophie's life with a certain amount of envy. Alain's frequent absences from home left her lonely, and the birth of a second child had left her feeling overwhelmed. I knew that she feared falling into the same abyss that had swallowed her childhood friend: the recent death of two of Marie-Louise's children had intensified her bouts of depression, and Véronique could barely recognize the laughing girl she had once known.

Sophie, alert to her sister's sensibilities, demurred. "We'll see what happens. Our last attempt to open a new school failed, you know."

"Through no fault of her own," I intervened quickly. "The Notre Dame sisters simply bid on the property first." I still felt guilty at my failure to negotiate the transaction in Paris for her.

"The best recourse, I find, is to breathe deeply and leave the rest to the Sacred Heart," Sophie answered gaily. "In the meantime, I follow the lead of Joseph Varin. And at the moment he's leading me to the foot of the Alps!"

Jacques Barat remained silent, but the look he gave his younger daughter was one of immense pride.

After dinner, Sophie and I found an opportunity to speak privately. I had two pieces of information that I didn't want to trust to correspondence, one of which involved Varin.

"I know for a fact that Minister Fouché is having Varin's mail opened—even his private correspondence. Which means he's opening yours." She looked at me with disbelief. "There's no question, Sophie. Denis Marmaton told me himself—and I'd be frankly surprised if *he's* not the one delegated to open it!"

Varin and I were corresponding about the acquisition of Sainte-Marie d'en-Haut, and Marmaton had recently alluded to my "dealings with Grenoble" in an unguarded moment. We were in the habit of meeting for an occasional drink: he, undoubtedly, to keep tabs on me; I, from a voyeuristic desire to watch how the man's mind functioned.

"So be very careful," I cautioned her.

"I don't understand what interest Napoleon could have in our little Society," she responded. "What possible threat do we pose to his power?"

"You're hooked closely to the Fathers of the Faith, and Napoleon is certain that they're Jesuits operating under an assumed name. He's right on both of these points, as you surely must know."

"But what is it he fears so much about the Jesuits?"

"Their extensive networks, which he views as a threat to his own, both inside and outside of France. Their history of power plays. Their intellectual acumen. Their power as educators. He went to a Jesuit school himself, remember! But you know this already, Sophie. I mention it now simply to emphasize that you *must* take care with what you write to Varin—or to any of his fellows, your brother included. Napoleon is allowing your community to operate, but he could shut you down at any time."

"I thank you for the warning, *cher ami*," she responded. "And yes, I do of course understand. Now what is the other subject you wish to discuss?"

"Célestine is pregnant."

Grilles

Winter 1804 – 1805

SOPHIE BARAT HAS NEVER SEEN SUCH MOUNTAINS. AS THE PUBLIC coach climbs its way into the rugged country that serves as gateway to the Alps, she is struck by the wild beauty of the terrain, in particular the blinding white peak of Mont Blanc that hovers far in the background. Grenoble is an ancient city, noted for its fierce independence and chivalric past, and stone houses cling to the mountains as if challenging gravity to pull them into the valley below. The coach clatters along the cobblestones, crossing one of the two rivers that encircle the city and lumbering slowly up the hill. It pulls up at the foot of a sheer rampart, from whose summit looms a brooding structure. If Sophie were given over to the gothic, she would doubtless feel a portentous shudder.

When the coachman announces their arrival, Sophie and her two traveling companions grab their bags and descend from the coach, finding themselves at the foot of a steep stairway that winds its way up to the convent building. Already exhausted after hours of jostling in the coach, the women begin the climb. When they are almost at the top, they walk through an arch into a small graveled courtyard and find a doorway surmounted by a statue and a cross. They enter a low, damp corridor, and before Sophie has taken ten steps, Philippine Duchesne throws herself at her feet.

"How beautiful on the mountain are the feet of those who bring peace!" she cries, kissing her shoes. Sophie, stupefied, follows the woman into the chapel.

~

Philippine Duchesne is solid oak. A teenage girl so taken with the Visitation Sisters that she has run away at age fourteen to join them. Eventually—and as her family has predicted all along—the sisters are turned out by the Jacobins, and the convent turned into a prison. Philippine moves back home and works to hide priests and bring comfort to prisoners. When the government relaxes its restrictions against religious orders, members of the Duchesne family—being of a generous and plutocratic disposition—rent the building for Philippine, who hopes to resurrect her Visitation community. She is determined but not charismatic. When Joseph Varin finds her, her community, such as it is, totals five. Varin thinks Sophie and Philippine will love each other, and in this case his judgment is sound. Philippine dreams of going to North America and living with the Native Americans. Unbeknownst to both of them at this point, Sophie Barat will be the one to get her there.

~

Father Roger is leading the sisters in their first retreat. They have spent six weeks fighting the snow that blows in through broken windows, exchanging stories of their lives during the years of Revolution, and sharing their vision of a life lived as a community of women dedicated to the loving service of others. Sophie encourages them to believe that a major step forward in this endeavor is to free themselves from all worldly attachments, to discard anything that impedes a perfect union with the source of that love. By the time Father Roger begins, they have emptied themselves of all possessions besides their boundless faith, hope and generosity.

Roger is one of Varin's Fathers of the Faith. He is a stalwart and energetic preacher whose techniques work well with the young men at the school outside Amiens. He thunders. He exhorts. He shakes his fist. Sophie is not sure that his strident rhetorical style will appeal to her fledgling group of women and has deferred the retreat for as long as possible. When he begins his homiletic rant, the women begin to smile. Their mirth grows until, by the end of the exercise, they are all exploding with hilarity—Father Roger included.

Even the Gods of Laughter seem to be smiling on the endeavor.

Sophie's community will be radical. They are forging a mission that many think is madness. People are whispering in Grenoble, and the whispers are not kind.

"The Superior is far too young."

"Monastic practices are not being observed."

"Family visits to boarding students are allowed less frequently."

"Older postulants are not accepted."

"Our community will be wholly contemplative and wholly apostolic," Sophie explains to her sisters. "We must move about France as our work requires it. We cannot flourish in the world if we are locked away from it. We must share with the world a sense of our strength and then *embody* that strength for the young women we propose to educate.

"That being said, we will proceed in our work as if we were *mothers*. We must *burn* with love for those children entrusted to us. All of them, even the *insupportables*." Her eyes send off scintillations. Those who have heard the story of her birth are not surprised by her repeated allusions to fire, and there are times when Philippine almost expects her to burst into flame. "Father Varin, who was profoundly shaped by his own mother and understands the power of this metaphor, expresses our approach this way: 'Firmness sometimes, harshness never, gentleness everywhere and always.'"

She looks hard at Philippine, who holds stubbornly to the monastic practices she is used to. "In order to accomplish this paradox of open enclosure," she continues, "the grilles"—she motions to the wooden screens installed between the choir and the congregation—"must come down."

Philippine loves the grilles. A physical barrier that separates her from all but her sisters and her students. A constant and palpable reminder of all that she has given up.

"They are impossible, my darling Philippine," Sophie insists. "If this is too difficult, perhaps it would help for you to consider them a worldly attachment."

Philippine, who is beginning to understand that austerity can be an indulgence, finally relents.

~

The two women will, for the rest of their lives, consider these months on the mountain a kind of heaven on earth.

Ré d'Italia

Spring, 1805

By naming himself emperor, napoleon bonaparte had established a hereditary monarchy in France. In March of 1805, he had himself proclaimed king of the former Republic of Italy, an area comprising the duchies of Milan, Mantua and Modena, as well as parts of the Papal States in Romagna, the western portion of the Venetian Republic, and the province of Novara. A series of statutes, added to the former Republic's constitution, gave the emperor or his viceroy full power of state and made his sons—natural or adopted—heirs to the Italian throne.

The imperial entourage set out from Paris for Milan on March 31. It was a voyage designed to dazzle the consciousness of Europe and leave no doubt about Napoleon's desire to create an empire worthy of Caesar. For months Italy had been preparing for the event according to elaborate instructions given by Napoleon's Master of Ceremonies, Louis-Phillipe Ségur. In Bonaparte's honor, roads were renamed, busts erected, triumphal arches constructed. In Alessandria he and his fellow travelers were treated to a reenactment of the Battle of Marengo, that key victory over Austria five years before which had cemented his power in Paris. When they reached Pavia, the emperor and his glittering empress Joséphine were greeted by jubilant crowds who gathered in the streets, waving flags that bore the new royal coat of arms. They entered Milan on the eighth of May through the newly named Marengo Gate, where citizens and soldiers—both French and Italian—displayed unbridled joy at his arrival. Fireworks, military maneuvers, horse races and street fairs alternated with meetings of the legislature, official receptions for clergy, and the readying of the cathedral for the grand event on May twenty-sixth.

I was invited by Alex and Marie de Beixedon to attend one of the balls following the coronation. They had recently engaged me to purchase a villa for them at Lake Como, and I was in Milan to negotiate the final details. The three of us planned to spend a week together at the lake when Napoleon returned to Paris.

~

We were in the *Giardini Pubblici*, Milan's expansive Public Gardens, which had been etherealized by Ségur and his crew of Italian magicians. Architects had designed temporary triumphal monuments that asserted themselves within the park's illuminated acres of trees and flowerbeds. The ball was set in the courtyard of an imposing neoclassical building. Small lanterns hung from every archway, lending a supernal glow to those dancing or promenading there. An orchestra played at either end, and fireworks exploded periodically in the moonlit sky, flooding the space with light and lending a certain suspense to the occasion.

We had just sat down at a large table in the gallery when Denis Marmaton appeared, accompanied by an Italian woman whose bearing announced her pedigree even before he'd uttered her name.

"Allow me to present Beatrice Sforza," he opened. He pronounced her first name in Italian, using the requisite four syllables. "Beatrice, meet my sister Marie de Beixedon, her husband Alex, and their friend Guy Lorrain."

She gave an icy nod to the three of us and sat down; Denis positioned himself next to me. I had noted his final, exclusionary pronoun and greeted him with exaggerated deference.

"I hear you're in Milan making yourself useful to my sister and Alex," Denis opened. "How fortunate that your visit could coincide with these glorious events." He moved his hand vaguely over the crowd, as if he were personally responsible for the spectacle.

"Indeed," I responded with a wry smile, "how fortunate we *all* are to have an emperor who so enjoys being crowned that he must repeat the act every six months. He and Fouché must be keeping you inordinately busy."

"We are always very busy," he replied curtly. "Conspiracies abound in even the most unsuspected places, as you and I both know. Speaking of which"—his tone grew accusatory—"how are your Jesuitical lady-friends in Grenoble?"

"They do well, though I doubt they'd subscribe to your adjective."

"Don't be absurd. The school is *crawling* with those priests. The sanctimonious Father Barat was just there, in fact—the ever-hovering big brother."

At this, Marie shot Denis a withering look across the table.

I ignored them and continued blithely. "*Both* of Sophie's schools are thriving, in fact. And to further the cause, she's just scored a victory against the French military."

"What are you saying, Guy?" Marie cut in, her expression shifting from ice to puzzled incredulity. "What do you mean, 'scored a victory over the military'?"

Even the inscrutable Sforza seemed intrigued that a young woman could have taken on *la Grand Armée Française* and emerged the victor. Her eyes stopped sweeping the room, and she gave the vague impression of having acknowledged our presence.

"They wanted to take over the convent in Grenoble for use as a military barracks," I answered. "Sophie resisted and won, producing Napoleon's official written permission for her community to occupy the building." Here I looked directly at Denis. "You must thank him personally on our behalf."

Napoleon's agreement to allow the community to use Sainte-Marie d'en-Haut undoubtedly sprang from his conviction that Sophie was preparing women to be dutiful wives and fruitful mothers for his empire.

But the imperial approval had come as a pleasant surprise, and just in time.

"Your emperor's coronation festivities certainly reflect a newfound love of the Church, *non*?" I added, noting Denis' failure to parry my last remark. "I missed the show in Paris, but I've never seen so many clerics and cardinals assembled in one place as I did yesterday at the cathedral."

"He knows what the people will like," was Denis' response.

"Indeed. Did they also like the way he took the golden round from the pope's hands in Paris and crowned *himself*?"

"I suspect most patriotic Frenchmen loved it."

I could only imagine Pope Pius's reaction. No doubt the memory of his predecessor's imprisonment and death while in French captivity exerted a convincing pressure to bow to Napoleon's audacity.

"You know, I presume, that our Sophie met with the pope in Lyon, just after Easter."

"Of course," was his glacial reply, his disdain no doubt arising from my suggestion that any such meeting could escape his spies.

"She writes that he's given her work his particular blessing."

"Precisely the kind of thing that will get her into trouble," he shot back.

"I think what she's doing is wonderful," Marie interjected. "We can only hope that she'll soon be opening a school in Milan." Here, she looked at Alex and placed her hand gently on her swelling abdomen.

Alex, who was used to finding himself caught between his wife and his brother-in-law, suddenly waved his right hand and pointed to the dance floor. The music had stopped, a silence had dropped over the crowd, and people were moving back from the center of the floor to allow the passage of an elegant young couple.

"It is Eugène," he said quickly. "I believe he is with Hortense."

The two young people bowed to the orchestra, cuing them to play, and as the music filled the space, the Empress Joséphine's two children paraded gracefully across the floor, signaling other couples to join them in a contredanse.

"It must kill him not to be dancing with *la Célestine*," Denis sneered. "I was certain he would have bundled her up and brought her along."

Neither Marie nor I spoke.

"She seems to have quite evaporated from the stage these last two or three months," he prodded. "David is still counting on doing her portrait, and yet *no* one can find her."

"He and she are in touch," Marie responded quickly. "In fact, she told me they've settled on her posing as Hippolyta, and he hopes to start painting in the summer. David is quite busy now, as you can imagine, with the coronation portrait."

For me to speak of my sister in front of Denis Marmaton was to drive her further into the that dark place where I believed her to reside, but circumstances dictated that I speak up. "She's in the Yvelines, where Eugène has bought her a country home."

I'd negotiated the sale myself. While I firmly disapproved of my sister's conduct, I was advising her (at Eugène's request) on her financial decisions. I couldn't help marveling at the personal assets she was amassing, the latest being a small chateau near Paris. "She felt that Eugène's responsibilities in Italy would be such that she could retire from Paris for a few months and not be missed."

"My, my, but the woman lends the term 'gifted' so *many* new dimensions," Denis observed with a sardonic smile. "De Beauharnais has fallen harder than I thought. I wonder what'll happen when Napoleon finally finds him the right wife."

Eugène had been promoted to the position of Imperial Highness, Prince of France, just months before, and the expectation was that Napoleon would soon adopt him officially. Joséphine had still failed to produce an heir.

"There's no doubt that the Emperor will marry him off soon," Alex responded, "but I doubt that marriage will do much to affect the liaison. Marriages so seldom do—my own, of course, being the exception." Here he looked reassuringly at his wife.

Uncomfortable with the conversation, I returned to politics. "What I find infinitely more interesting is to imagine how much of the Italian peninsula will be under Eugène's control by the time his status as viceroy takes effect," I added.

Neither Alex nor Denis replied to my remark. I inferred from their silence that rumors about the impending annexation of Liguria were true. From the way her body suddenly stiffened under her silks and satins, I guessed that Beatrice Sforza was drawing the same conclusion.

The Snow Queen

Fall and Winter, 1805 – 1806

THE FATHERS OF THE FAITH HAVE COME AND GONE, THE BISHOP OF Grenoble has given his provisional approval to the new community, and the independent spirits at Sainte-Marie d'en-Haut have readied themselves to begin their new work. On November 21, Philippine Duchesne and four other women make their first vows. In addition to the boarding school, a free school is opened in Grenoble. Another boarding school is established in Belley, between Geneva and Lyon. Joseph Varin calls for an election to occur in Amiens in January. It is time to organize the expanding society, and the members must elect a Superior General.

Sophie has been away from Amiens for over a year, and Madame Anne Baudemont, the former Poor Clare, has been busy.

⌐

Sophie's coach arrives in front of the Oratory on a snowy mid-December afternoon. The greeting she receives wears a chill to match the weather. She dismounts from the carriage, picks up her travel bag, and rings the bell several times before it is answered. A young postulant

whom she does not know answers the door and asks for her name and her visit's purpose.

"I am Madeleine Sophie Barat, just arriving from Grenoble."

The postulant waves her inside, and Sophie follows her down a corridor, across a courtyard, and into a room far removed from the rest of the community. On some level, the greeting reassures her, strengthening her hopeful belief that another will be elected Superior General. She has told Philippine many times that she has been sent away from Amiens because she is expendable. The work of God's heart, she knows, will flourish quite easily without her.

Indeed, all looks to be in order. Impeccable order. Madame Baudemont has set her seal on both the community and the school, and her tastes and preferences are in evidence throughout the establishment. When Sophie gains an audience with her hours later, Baudemont is not alone.

"You of course remember Father de St. Estève," she says, tipping her chin slightly as Sophie walks into the room. The two of them tower over her, and their aristocratic origins inform both their body language and their speech. They stand on either side of a large credenza that displays ribbons, certificates, and crowns developed by St. Estève for distribution at the school's elaborate prize days. His brother Gaston, Sophie has learned, is Master of Ceremonies at Napoleon's imperial chapel.

"Of course. *Bonsoir, mon père*," Sophie responds, nodding to them both. "I see that all appears to be running smoothly."

They offer a silent bow in response, allowing an awkward silence to fill the room. Madame Baudemont finally breaks it with a question. "We hear from Varin that *your* house prospers as well."

Sophie discerns the underlying intent of her remark and smiles in spite of it. "Our new house does well, *oui*," she replies.

It is Anne Baudemont's conviction that because she is superior at Amiens, the school is effectively hers: an autonomous body operating under her dominion. Varin, trying not to provoke Napoleon's increasing suspicion of networked religious houses, has forbidden any direct communication between Grenoble and Amiens, so there is little cause for her to doubt her position. Varin has asked Baudemont to avoid direct contact with him or with Sophie and to use St. Estève as her advisor—a pairing that suits them both.

The two exchange a meaningful look, and then St. Estève asks after her health, his voice becoming unctuous. "Along with Father Varin and many others, we are so very concerned about how all of this travel affects your delicate health."

All three of them know that the new Superior General will be required to visit every house on a regular basis.

"It seems to agree with me," Sophie responds brightly, gently challenging their united front. In truth, symptoms of her illness remain, and she wonders if her health isn't but one more reason to withdraw her name.

As the election approaches, Sophie reads her surroundings. The community at Amiens, many of whom are strangers to her, have had to accede to Baudemont's imperious demeanor or risk being transferred. Geneviève Deshayes is now in Grenoble; Henriette Grosier, in Belley. It is clear that most of the community in Amiens will vote for Madame Baudemont.

"She has moments of absolute *lunacy!*" Cécile de Cassini confides to Sophie late one night. The two of them have run into each other in the courtyard. Cecile is gazing at the stars through her telescope, and Sophie is up walking because she cannot sleep. "You've heard her laugh, Sophie. You've seen what she does. Surely you must have wondered about her mental balance!"

Indeed, Sophie has witnessed moments when Baudemont will break into almost hysterical laughter, encouraging the assembled community to join her. Those who refuse the invitation do so at their own risk. The laughter once established, her face will suddenly shift into an expression of displeasure and thereby command those assembled to silence.

"She rules through caprice," Cecile continues, "and St. Estève is no better. The two of them together are an unholy alliance." Cecile will leave the community for a Trappistine monastery within weeks.

One of the students, an impressionable girl of twelve who remembers Sophie's kindness to her when she first arrived in Amiens as a boarding student, pulls her aside. "I am afraid of them." When Sophie inquires why, the child tells her of a retreat Baudemont and St. Estève have recently orchestrated. "They darkened a room, took out all the furniture, and placed *skulls* all over the floors and window ledges. Then Mother Baudemont told us stories about *demons* who ride out at night and possess the souls of disobedient girls," the child relates, her eyes wide with terror.

Sophie says nothing, but her heart begins knocking in her chest. Visions of an exorcism Louis forced her to witness when she was only ten years old assail her. The wasted body of the young woman writhing on the bed. The foam issuing from her mouth, along with screams, inarticulate babbling, and profanities such as Sophie had never heard in her life. The chilling look on Louis' face as he hurled pinches of salt and passages of scripture into the air and brandished a crucifix over the bed. At one point, the girl's body had pitched forward and a flailing arm had struck him in the face. Louis had smiled strangely, taken the vial of oil the terrified Sophie was holding, placed a drop of it on each of his hands, and then forced the young woman's shoulders back against the mattress, shouting something at her in Latin as a medal of St. Benedict swung wildly from his neck. The young woman died only a few days later after choking on her own vomit.

Sophie hugs the child, tells her not to worry, and hurries back to her room. If there are demons flying about Amiens at night, she mutters to herself as she lies down in her narrow bed, they reside within anyone who would so terrorize children.

Geneviève Deshayes has warned her about St. Estève. "He is a literary man with a brilliant imagination. Extraordinarily gifted. But always on the climb. Be careful. Sophie. He's an unquiet genius—and charming, so very charming, when it serves his ends." St. Estève and Baudemont have effectively driven Geneviève from Amiens.

Louis-Étienne Dussaussoy is now at the boys school near Amiens, and when he visits his aunt and attends mass with the community, Sophie places him where all can observe his poorly cut clothes and country manners. She speaks increasingly of her father's work as a barrel-maker, as if to highlight Baudemont's superior credentials and thereby spare herself a position for which she feels unworthy.

Then she thinks of skulls and ribbons and crowns and wonders what they can possibly have to do with the heart of Jesus.

She is elected Superior General for life on January 18, 1806, by a single vote. The election is witnessed by Fathers Varin, Roger and St. Esteve. The congregation's new name will be Daughters of the Sacred Heart of Jesus, but at present—for political safety's sake—they will keep the name *Dames de l'Instruction Chrétienne*.

~

Sophie stays at Amiens for several weeks. It is a kingdom of ice. Baudemont and and St. Estève continue as if nothing has changed and do whatever they can to increase her feelings of superfluity. The two of them are working on a constitution to fill the void left by the formal dissolution of the *Dilette*. They pointedly exclude Sophie from their discussions. Varin tells her repeatedly not to worry. "*Courage et confidence!*"

On certain days the newly chosen Superior General picks up the broom that Geneviève Deshayes has used before her and sweeps the front steps, losing herself in the simplicity of the task and longing for the peace of Sainte-Marie d'en-Haut.

Philippine writes that a great missionary has visited them at Epiphany and spoken of his work in Louisiana. Her desire to travel to the New World has been rekindled, and Sophie responds with a secret. "I once hoped to do so myself, you know," she writes. "St. Francis Xavier, if you remember, is my patron. With this election I am now nailed forever to France, but perhaps you will one day go for me, my dearest daughter. Know that at the *very* moment your longing was being reawakened, Joseph Varin and I were discussing such a project. For now, we must all exercise patience."

Joseph Varin writes that he will no longer serve as the ecclesial superior. Such a position, he explains, continues to put the Society at risk. Sophie is now on her own.

Célestine Lorrain writes news of her eight-month-old daughter. She has named her Madeleine Héloïse and calls her Héloïse. "She is beautiful beyond description, *ma chère PhiePhie*, and the greatest miracle I

have ever experienced, next to my friendship with you. She is not speaking yet, of course, but she understands everything I say. I have begun to tell her some of the stories you told me when we were both so very young. That world seems centuries away, does it not? I return to Paris next month and must decide where my little Héloïse will live. It will be agony, but if she is to have any future, she obviously cannot live with me. I'd give anything to see you, my dearest friend." She also writes that Marie de Beixedon's infant son has fallen ill in Milan and is fighting for his life.

She does not write that Eugène de Beauharnais, now Viceroy of Italy and the officially adopted son of Napoleon, is to be married in March to Princess Augusta Amalia of Bavaria, daughter of King Maximilian I.

Crosses

Spring, 1806

MARIE AND ALEX DE BEIXEDON'S INFANT SON SUCCUMBED TO A violent fever in late February. Marie left Milan immediately after the funeral and returned to their home in Paris, disconnecting herself from surroundings that only sharpened her grief. Just weeks after her arrival in Paris, she received word that her father, Olivier Marmaton, was dying.

Her arrival in Joigny coincided with that of Sophie, who had decided to spend a holiday with her family on her way back to Grenoble. I'd traveled down from Paris in order to obtain her signature on several legal documents and to visit with my family. My own father had not been well, and Olivier Marmaton's impending death had darkened his spirits. Véronique had begged me to stay for at least a week.

Marie, Sophie and I spent an entire afternoon in the middle of April walking up in the Clos St. Jacques. The severe pruning given the vines at the end of winter had left the vineyard a seeming graveyard of stark grey stumps. Their annual ability to burst forth in abundant greens and purples had been a constant source of mystery to me as a child, and despite my adult understanding of botanical hibernation, I found myself now marveling at it all over again. Perhaps it was Sophie's proximity.

Toward the end of the afternoon, we seated ourselves at a rough-hewn table that sat at the very summit of the hill.

"The only thing that saves me from madness is to walk," Marie confided. She was haggard from weeks of worry and grief, and this was the first direct reference she had made to the baby's death. "I now know every alleyway, park and courtyard in the Faubourg St. Germain, and it was the same in Milan. Alex, you know, barely made it home for the funeral." Napoleon had just named his older brother, Joseph Bonaparte, King of Naples, and the ceremonial machinery was revving up again. "They called him back to Naples only two days after we put our baby boy in the ground." Disbelief at both the child's passing and her husband's extended absence at such a moment still echoed in her voice.

Sophie reached out and took both of Marie's hands in her own. Her appearance was only slightly more robust than Marie's. Events in Amiens had taken their toll, and she was once again suffering symptoms of the illness that had landed her in the hospital four years before. "We cannot hope to comprehend the pattern of our life as we move through it, my darling Marie," she said softly. "We can only trust in the love of God, only try to see that there's some sense in all of this that we, with our limited vision, cannot understand."

"There can be *no* sense in this, Sophie." Marie's eyes began to fill with tears, and she yanked her hands away. "This is the very *absence* of sense, and you'll never convince me otherwise!"

"Of course it is," Sophie replied, taking her hands gently once again. "Death, suffering, especially that of children—it is the Cross. How can any of us be expected to survive such things, much less understand them? But to do so, or even just to *aspire* to do so, is at the very center of our belief. It can give us strength when we feel we are about to break."

"*Your* belief, Sophie," Marie interrupted angrily, but she left her hands in Sophie's. "Not *mine*. If ever I might have believed in your God, that chance dissolved when I saw the light fade out of my baby's eyes." A sob broke from her, and Sophie gathered her in her arms, rocking her back and forth as if she were a child. The only sound for the next few minutes was Marie's weeping and the shrieking of a bird that mocked her grief from a distant tree.

"And then there is our darling Célestine." Marie pulled away from Sophie's shoulder for a moment, her eyes deepening with accusation. "She has a beautiful, healthy little girl whom she must now send away! Please tell me how *this* fits into your God's benevolent plan."

Sophie maintained a respectful silence and began once again to rock her. The bird had ceased its screaming, and an unearthly calm settled over the scene.

I stared down at the Yonne and pondered my sister's predicament. Eugène de Beauharnais had acknowledged his paternity but, in a move that surprised all of us, had signed over full parental rights to Célestine—a move that flew directly in the face of the new Napoleonic Code. He would offer generous financial support to his Parisian family, but Célestine would have full decision-making power over the child, provided he had occasional access to her. It was obvious to both of them, however, that her home would not provide a suitable environment in which to raise a child.

We were all fully aware that at this very moment, Eugène was in Munich to marry his Bavarian princess.

~

The three of us spent several days together, during which time Sophie shared some of her own anxieties. The recent birth of her niece Zoe brought the number of little Dussaussoys up to six, and talk continued within the extended family as to where and how they would all be educated.

"Louis-Étienne and Stanislas are at the boys school near Amiens," she explained. "But there are four more already, and who knows if this is the end?" Marie-Thérèse's fecundity continued to astound the population of Joigny. "My sister and Étienne are asking when Thérèse and Julie might start classes at Amiens or Grenoble!" Thérèse Dussaussoy was eight and Julie six.

She said very little about her recent election, but what she didn't say allowed us to understand that events in Amiens had not been kind. She was eager to get back to Grenoble.

"So no more battles lately with Napoleon's army?" Marie asked with a slight grin. She had not returned to the subject of her son since our earlier walk, but she still seemed ready to break at any moment. This was the first time I'd heard such levity in her voice. "You're quite the topic of conversation, you know!"

I smiled in concert with Sophie's laughter, but I also knew that Napoleon's Minister Fouché was making a determined effort to shut down the Fathers of the Faith. It was certain that their days in France were numbered.

Marie and I had several opportunities to speak further about Célestine and her little Héloïse, and a plan was forming in both of our minds that lent credence to Sophie's hopeful words up in the vineyards. I wondered if she hadn't wordlessly planted the idea in our heads as she rocked the grieving young mother in her arms.

Before any of us left, Olivier Marmaton died peacefully in his sleep, an ironic finale to a life lived in a permanent state of anger. Denis, deeply involved with events in Bavaria and Naples, did not attend the funeral but paid for a marble monument that dwarfed all others in the Joigny cemetery.

Summons

Spring and Summer, 1806

IN MID-MAY, SOPHIE RETURNS TO SAINTE-MARIE D'EN-HAUT. AS the Alps come into view, she feels the tension of the past months begin to dissolve, and when the rattle of the coach on cobblestones signals that they have reached Grenoble, she feels a surge of joy. She is eager to embrace the simplicity of life on the windswept mountain, and she knows she will be safe among women of like minds and spirits.

She and Philippine spend the first night talking far into the early morning hours. Sophie relays details of the Amiens election in a way that does nothing to indict either Anne Baudemont or Sambucy de St. Estève. Philippine shares images of her reawakened desire to travel to North America. She now dreams of being surrounded by native children in the territories west of the Louisiana Purchase. Waves of occasional laughter season their conversation as Philippine reports on the antics of a new boarding student. They end the conversation by softly singing several verses of the *Song of Songs* that one of the community has set to music. Sophie knows she is home.

She makes a retreat in early July with the intention of strengthening her resolve to stop "trembling" (a behavior she often accuses herself of) and to accept her new position with grace and generosity. Three days into the retreat, however, she receives a letter from Varin. Politics have finally forced him to detach himself officially from the Society, but he will continue to write to her despite Napoleon's watchful eye.

"There is a new school to be founded at Poitiers!" the letter opens.

Part 5

Poitiers

Les Feuillants

Summer, 1806

A HEAT WAVE EXCEEDING ANY IN RECENT MEMORY CRUSHES SOPHIE with its weight as she climbs into the stagecoach in Grenoble. With her is Henriette Girard, a woman of forty who has made her first vows the previous November, and whom Sophie hopes will lend her a degree of respectability: reputable young women in Napoleon's France do not journey unaccompanied on the open roads. She is once again experiencing symptoms of her old illness, made worse by the weather, the dirty inns, and the unappetizing meals they encounter as their carriage lumbers its way toward Lyon. Embarrassed at her condition but powerless to do anything about it, she resorts to silent meditation, hoping her fellow passengers remain oblivious to her suffering.

When they leave Lyon after a two-day rest, both the abdominal pain and the bleeding have stopped. The tumor that has stalked her for four years has inexplicably left her body, never to return.

"You know how ill I was when I left you, _ma chère Samaritaine_," she writes Philippine. "I complained gently to God in my meditations, fearing the absence of your attentive and loving care. And then I felt my entire self quiet down—body, heart, and soul. We'd scarcely left

Lyon when I realized that every symptom had disappeared! If anything, with all the heat and travel, I should feel worse! My joy is increased by the beauty of the landscape in this part of France. Our beautiful mountains have given way to the most expansive and breathtaking plains. We can almost smell the Atlantic as the wind sweeps across from the west."

At Moulins, a small town in the Auvergne, Sophie must negotiate transportation for the two of them to continue on toward Poitiers. A mail driver agrees to transport them as far as Limoges, and the two women clamber up into his wagon. As they travel along the Allier River, passing through endless fields of lavender and sunflowers, Sophie eases herself into another meditation, this time one of gratitude. She breathes in the fragrance of the air and lifts her face toward the sun, whose blistering heat has finally abated. She closes her eyes and begins to hum a *Deo Gratias*.

Without warning, the driver pushes the horses into a full gallop, sending his two passengers crashing into each other.

"*Mais qu'est-ce que vous faîtes là, mon ami?*" Sophie asks, trying to curb the anxiety that wells within her as the coach rocks perilously from side to side.

"What are you *doing* in the name of *God?*" Henriette echoes her concern, quite literally holding onto her hat and looking back to see if they're being chased by a gang of ruffians.

The grin on the driver's face only widens. "But this is why I drive the highways, *mesdames!*" he responds, then lets out a whoop and lashes the horses to increase their speed. Henriette and Sophie grab the sides of the wagon and close their eyes as dust clouds mushroom behind them and the horses flare their nostrils and toss their heads. Sophie whispers a prayer to St. Michael, fully expecting they'll capsize at any moment. Henriette whimpers and squeezes her eyes more tightly shut.

Then, just as suddenly as he has sped them up, the driver slows the horses down. Laughing heartily at his passengers' agitation, he sets down his whip and slaps his knee. "You must see that this is what attracts me to the job, *mesdames!* A lifetime of adventure on the highways! All of France as my domain! Possible danger at every turn—loose wheels, snowdrifts, blocked roads, even a tumble now and then—*C'est formidable!*"

The two of them stare at him as if at a madman.

On the second day their reckless chauffeur complains of a sore back. "It's the only downside. Too much sitting on my weary bum. This sciatica will be the end of me one day." He rubs his lower back and winces. Henriette looks at Sophie, who nods a quick assent, and unpacks a flask of ratafia that Philippine has slipped into their luggage. When he insists that he doesn't drink alcohol, Henriette convinces him to take a small glass of the almond liqueur to ease his pain. The carriage ride for the next several kilometers is peaceful as their Phaeton eventually nods off and the horses trot their way, unsupervised, along familiar roads.

At Limoges, a helpful priest offers to arrange a carriage that will take the two women all the way to Poitiers. Sophie agrees, trusting him to select an appropriate conveyance. When it arrives for them the next morning, they are aghast to find an open wagon loaded with merchandise. Henriette refuses to get in.

"But my darling Henriette," Sophie counters with a ringing laugh, "how can we say no to such a dazzling equipage! And what better way for us to enter the legendary city of Poitiers!"

Henriette stares in disbelief at the makeshift tent the driver has constructed for his "lady passengers." Four poles suspend a canopy of dirty canvas over a bed of straw, allowing them a small sheltered space to sit among the bundles of dry goods. She looks at Sophie and shakes her head.

"I will climb into this rattletrap only when I'm beyond the city limits, and that is my final statement."

Cadence, their jovial driver, gestures with bright enthusiasm toward his magical pavilion. "If you place your traveling bags on the straw, *mesdames*, you will find that you have *most* comfortable seating for the duration of your voyage." A loud groaning noise announces the arrival of a second cart, this one more rickety than the first. It is piloted by his servant Jacques.

The two women throw their baggage onto the straw pallet Cadence has created for them, but Henriette holds firmly to her purpose. Sophie laughs again, reminding her companion of the priceless gifts of humility and poverty. But the two of them follow the carts on foot until they are beyond the view of the good citizens of Limoges. With considerable awkwardness, they scramble up into Cadence's wagon and settle themselves atop their travel bags in a way that promises at least a moderate degree of safety. The small caravan plods its way toward Poitiers, covering all of five kilometers by ten o'clock that night.

"We spent the night amidst a university of rats," Sophie writes Philippine. "The inn looked like something out of a most dismal fairytale, and all night long we heard the squeaking and rustling of our restless roommates. Oh how I long for the peace and fellowship of our beautiful mountain!"

Cadence's cart breaks down on the third day of the journey, and they have no choice but to mount Jacques' even less auspicious conveyance. When several days later they see the spires of Poitiers' cathedral emerge in the distance, the rains begin. By the time they arrive in the city, perched high atop their bundles and exposed to the incredulous eyes of strangers, the two women are soaked to the skin.

"We can only hope," Henriette gasps as she climbs down, "that no one who's seen us will connect us with our purpose here!" Even Sophie is a bit concerned, looking at her bedraggled companion and knowing she must appear equally disheveled. They pull their travel bags down after them, and as Jacques unloads the rest of his merchandise onto a large plaza in the center of town, the two stalwart travelers thank him and set out to find the woman who is eagerly awaiting Sophie's arrival.

They have been on the road for thirteen days.

⸾

The abbey called *Les Feuillants* is an old monastery built by Louis XIII for a community of Cistercians. For almost two hundred years it housed monks who observed the Rule of St. Benedict, cared for their shrines, and worked their vegetable gardens. The Revolution and its aftermath have reduced much of it to ruins. The church and priory have been destroyed, the altar and holy objects desecrated, the furnishings stripped away, and the empty shell left only with its architectural beauty—vaulted ceilings, a large quadrangular stone cloister, and windows giving onto terraced gardens that fall gracefully toward the river Clain.

Sophie and Henriette ring the bell and wait in the rain, which continues to fall in sheets. The door creaks open, and an old woman motions them into a large, empty room. The building seems deserted, but Sophie hears the silence of generations of monks filling the hushed space. She inhales deeply and feels as if her heart is quite literally expanding.

All she knows from Varin is that the ruined monastery is now owned by a woman named Lydia Chobelet. She—together with several other women, of whom only one remains—has been trying to run a boarding school for girls. At the moment, the school's total enrollment is two, and Mademoiselle Chobelet is ready to sign the building over to the bishop for use as a seminary. A visiting Father of the Faith, Louis Lambert, has convinced her to wait.

Lydia Chobelet arrives after several minutes, graciously refrains from commenting on her guests' appearance, and takes them to their rooms. From her window, Sophie hears the gentle tick and click of windmills and watches throngs of birds gathering in the poplar trees that grow along the river. The rain has stopped at last.

Father Lambert arrives for dinner, and the five of them talk far into the night about Sophie's new Society and how it might meet the needs of the young women of Poitiers. Lydia and her companion, Joséphine Bigeu, share stories of their own: Lydia and her sisters' narrow escape from La Vendée, a region of counterrevolutionary activity that erupted in 1793; their move to Poitiers, where they opened a school and risked their lives and freedom to hide non-juror priests; their eventual meeting with Joséphine, who joined them in their attempt to run a boarding school for girls.

"They killed half the population of La Vendée during those terrifying months," Lydia states. "Over four hundred thousand people."

Here Joséphine intervenes. "You must have heard of the *noyades*, Sophie?"

Sophie shakes her head.

"They happened in Nantes. The soldiers stripped the people naked and forced them onto flat-bottomed boats. Some of the young men and

women, especially priests and nuns, they would first tie together, back to back. They called it a 'republican marriage.' Then they would push the boat out into the Loire River and sink it. Thousands died this way."

They wait for Sophie to absorb this information, and then Lydia offers her personal narrative. "For my family it was different. My parents and my brothers fell victim to one of the 'infernal columns.' These men, Jacobin soldiers, were ordered to kill anyone in sight and scorch the earth behind them. They came and slaughtered everyone they could find—women, children, it didn't matter."

Here, Lydia begins to recite the words sent back to Paris by the Jacobin General Westermann and published by the Committee for Public Safety when the columns had finished their work. She has memorized them as a perverse litany to honor her three younger brothers. Her voice is robotic. "'There is no more Vendée. According to the orders you gave me, I crushed the children under the feet of the horses, massacred the women who, at least for these, will not give birth to any more brigands. I do not have a prisoner to reproach me. I have exterminated all. Mercy is not a revolutionary sentiment.'" After a moment's pause, Lydia continues in her own voice. "My youngest brother was only seven years old. I hid in the forest and watched it all."

Mercy is not a revolutionary sentiment. The words ring dread into Sophie's very bones. She bows her head in deference to Lydia's grief and wonders once again if France will ever heal from the wounds of civil war.

Acquisitions

Early August, 1806

WHEN I RECEIVED DENIS MARMATON'S INVITATION TO DINE, I hadn't spoken with him for months. We'd seen each other in Joigny the preceding Christmas when he and his sister had traveled down from Paris to be with their recently widowed mother. Marie, still grieving for her child, had not yet returned to Milan. At that time, all the talk was of Napoleon's recent victory at Austerlitz and its consequences for the balance of power in Europe.

Tonight, as I approached the gates of his compound on the rue Saint-Honoré, I suspected we would be talking of more personal subjects. I'd debated coming at all, but curiosity as to what he might want from me and a desire to see his recently purchased establishment near the Tuileries Palace trumped my better judgment. I always gleaned something of note from his conversation once the wine levels began to go down in our glasses, and I had no doubt that his wine would be of the highest quality.

A liveried porter greeted me at the gate.

"I am Guy Lorrain, here for dinner at the invitation of Monsieur Marmaton." I wondered as I said *monsieur* how much longer it would be before Denis was promoted into Napoleon's new aristocracy. Rumor had it that Minister Fouché would soon be receiving an Italian title and a duchy to go with it.

I was escorted across the courtyard to where two footmen opened a pair of bronze doors revealing a lobby that glistened with crystal, marble, and gilding. On the left, an armoire filled with antique snuffboxes supported a life-size bust of Napoleon. Balancing the effect on the right was a small landscape by Watteau that shimmered above a marquetry table. An enormous bouquet of peonies sat on a pedestal in the center of the room, directly below a chandelier whose pink and white crystals threw a rosy glow across the entire space.

"Ah, Guy, *soyez le bienvenu!*" Denis emerged out of the shadows, his face its usual mask of irony. He led me into a large salon where two more servants waited to pour us an aperitif.

When we'd reached the fourth of our seven-course meal—a cherry-glazed duck surrounded by shaved black truffles—our conversation moved to Napoleon's establishment of the Confederation of the Rhine.

"After a thousand years, he's dissolved the Holy Roman Empire, just like *that!*" Denis snapped his fingers in the air to punctuate his assertion. In the wake of the Austrian defeat at Austerlitz, Francis II had been forced to renounce his title of Holy Roman Emperor. "We'll soon have every Rhineland principality under our protection." Here he smiled, apparently recognizing the absurdity of the term even as he said it. To be under Napoleon's "protection" was to be shielded by the tail of a scorpion.

"And one of these principalities is, of course, Bavaria," I noted. "How convenient that Eugène de Beauharnais has already been so deeply thrust into its family bosom."

He smiled. "Indeed. I was just in Munich. Organizing our communications networks."

"*Communications networks,*" I responded sarcastically. "Exquisite phrasing, Denis. Your emperor is a master of semantics."

"There are *many* who would like to do us harm, Guy, as even *you* in your safe little world of contracts and property law must understand."

"You allude, I presume, to the new Coalition?" I asked, thinking he meant the latest group of countries who were attempting to check Napoleon's power. England, Prussia, Russia, Saxony, and Sweden were forming a powerful alliance that promised Europe yet another round of warfare. Napoleon would need the manpower of the Rhine to sustain his military machine.

"I allude to them in part, but there are threats that lie far closer to home," he responded.

I understood that I was about to earn my dinner.

"I hear that Mademoiselle Barat is now wandering about Poitiers and its environs. The woman is nothing if not peripatetic."

I swirled the wine in my glass, held it up to the candlelight, and took a leisurely sip, forcing him to steer the conversation.

"She and the good Father Varin no longer write to one another, you know," he continued, fixing his eyes on mine.

"I *didn't* know," I responded, "though it doesn't surprise me, given Minister Fouché's insatiable interest in their correspondence."

"The Fathers of the Faith have three or four more months before the emperor closes them down." Denis' voice hardened. "I suggest that you be wary of your own dealings with them. Varin in particular. He's a chameleon in priest's clothing."

I was aware of Varin's sometimes mercurial behavior, and I knew that even Sophie was often frustrated with his tendency to put trust in people of whom she was skeptical—Baudemont and St. Estève being two cases in point. But she and I both knew that he had invaluable services to offer her as the Society moved forward.

"I've told you already," Denis continued, "that the emperor distrusts networks. *Any* kind of networks. And my latest information is that her minions in Amiens are moving to establish more schools in the north even as she sniffs around Poitiers."

My last exchange with Varin had to do with Baudemont and St. Estève's desire to acquire a foothold outside Amiens where the community could go in the event that Napoleon shut down the Oratory. To this end, Baudemont was looking for a setting in Cuignières, in the diocese of Beauvais. Meanwhile, St. Estève was in negotiations with the bishop of Ghent, who had offered them an old abbey for yet another foundation.

"Your information is, as always, accurate," I responded, toasting him with my glass. "*Salut.* But I hardly think the emperor has much to fear from Sophie Barat."

"*Fool!*" Denis' voice echoed off the gilded walls, and one of the footmen jumped, rattling the crystal decanter on his tray. "You know the school in Amiens is a hotbed of Royalist sentiment. Those simpering Gramont girls have joined her little band of rebels, and it looks to me *and to others* as if battle lines are being drawn!"

Eugénie and Antoinette de Gramont's mother had served as lady-in-waiting to Marie Antoinette and was the widow of a French duke. Both girls had recently made their first vows, and the duchess had become Sophie's regular hostess when she traveled through Paris.

"The school is open to everyone, Denis," I replied evenly. "A family's political connections are not automatic grounds for rejection. If a Bonaparte niece from Ajaccio were to apply, I'm certain she'd be as welcome as a Bourbon princess or a dairy farmer's daughter from Picardy. Check the school rosters."

"You're being disingenuous." I could see Denis' color rising, but his voice had returned to its earlier dispassionate key. "Louis XVI, as everyone knows, went to the scaffold with a badge of the Sacred Heart on his sleeve."

"If a particular group wishes to adopt the symbol for its own purpose—political or otherwise—it is of course their privilege. Sophie's interests, you know as well as I, lie well beyond politics. And she's hardly an aristocrat."

"You live in a dream world, Guy. Between our enemies outside France and those who conspire within, there are powerful forces at work. Only months ago we broke open another plot to kidnap the emperor."

I nodded and took another sip of his exquisite Haut Brion. The plot to which he referred, the Cadoudal Plot, had ended with the arrest of large numbers of aristocrats. The ringleaders—including two of Napoleon's generals—had been guillotined and their heads displayed on pikes along the Seine. The crackdown that followed sent many Royalists back into exile.

"That was almost two years ago, Denis. I don't see that the emperor has much to fear since Austerlitz. The old aristocracy is shattered."

"For the moment." I detected a slight tremor in his voice, and he set his glass angrily on the table, leaning toward me with a face full of hatred. "But they're like *vermin*, hiding just over our borders and breeding the next generation. And the Jesuits are lying in wait with them, passing time and conspiring with one another until the pope reinstates them."

A pair of chocolate soufflés were sitting before us when Denis shifted the conversation into a more personal mode.

"By now you must have guessed why I brought you here," he said as he motioned a waiter to decant a vintage brandy.

"I thought I delivered what you wanted with the duck course."

"You merely verified what we suspected already. I'm speaking of Célestine."

I could feel a veil fall over my expression as he pronounced the syllables of her name. I waited to respond until the waiter had refilled our water glasses. "And what might my sister have to do with the security of Napoleon Bonaparte?"

Denis' expression became steely. He picked up a dinner knife and plunged it into his soufflé, releasing a spiral of steam and reducing its volume by a third. "I don't speak here of security. I speak of family matters, and I'd prefer it if you dropped the act."

I sampled the soufflé, leaving him to clarify his remark.

"You've been managing her legal affairs for over two years, monsieur, and while you and she are careful to leave no written record, our people have gleaned fragments of information, admittedly vague, that the emperor himself finds"—he paused to find the right word—"*provocative*."

"Does he?" I replied, swallowing the chocolate confection and pausing to assess its flavor and consistency. "And why should the activities of his stepson's mistress so provoke the curiosity of a man getting ready to fight five of Europe's most powerful countries?"

He banged his fist on the table, causing the candelabra to jump and the candles to flicker ominously off the mirrored walls. "The emperor's curiosity is *none* of your concern! My question remains: What is your sister preparing to do with Eugène de Beauharnais' daughter?" His voice had risen to a shriek.

I sampled another mouthful of the soufflé, complimenting his chef and watching the angry flush in his face deepen to vermilion.

"What do you *suppose* she's about to do, Denis?" I looked directly into his eyes as if to challenge his power and slowly put down my fork.

He met my gaze, and his mouth twisted into a cruel smile. "The child surely can't be raised in the household of a *whore*."

With his final word, I checked my rising fury and redoubled my resolution to withhold the information he so desperately wanted. I looked around the room, imagining the broken lives of those on whom his current lifestyle rested. Then I smiled at him with as much pity as I could muster, pushed myself back from the table, and stated coolly before turning to leave, "There are all kinds of prostitutes, my dear Marmaton. Some more noxious than others."

Artemis and her Maids

May through August, 1806

WHEN FATHER LOUIS ENFANTIN, ONE OF JOSEPH VARIN'S MOST charismatic missionary priests, arrives in Bordeaux in the spring of 1806, his effect is that of a seducer on the local population—especially its population of women. The dashing young prelate delivers such an inspiring series of homilies that girls by the dozen are seized with the desire to give themselves over to a life of prayer and penance. The town buzzes and hums with gossip and malaise, and Enfantin is given full blame for what the town elders call their "romantic hysteria." Families are outraged at the thought of their daughters' joining one of the religious communities now cropping up all over France. One especially fervent devotée, Elizabeth Maillucheau, decides after a single encounter with Enfantin's magnetic field to devote herself to a life of radical action and prayer. She ignites a similar spark within five friends, and—unable to find a religious community that will receive them—the women decide to forge their own.

An ethereal twenty-two-year-old—appropriately named Angèle—proposes that they take refuge in one of the vineyards just outside the city limits.

131

"There is a small hut hidden up in the hills beyond the river," she exclaims, her masses of curly dark hair flying about her face as if electrified by the idea. "I used to run off and play there alone when I was a child." Angèle's parents have been guillotined during Tallien's months of terror in Bordeaux, and she and her brother are now legal owners of several acres of fine sémillon grapes.

"*Magnifique!*" Elizabeth exclaims, clapping her hands, hugging Angèle, and then extending her arms toward the heavens, as if this is all part of some celestial plan. "When we attend services tomorrow, let's each bring with us a small packet of necessary items. Once the mass has ended, we'll wait until our families have left the church, detach ourselves from the crowd, and then fly up into the vineyards!"

The women embrace one another with conspiratorial zeal and return to their family homes for the last time.

When the sun rises over the vineyard the next morning, the six young apostles are already awake and praying. They have gathered in the darkness along a ridge just beyond their rustic cabin, and Elizabeth is leading them in a meditation on a passage from the gospel of Saint John: "I am the vine, you are the branches. Whoever abides in me and I in her, she it is that bears much fruit."

The women smile to hear her shift the final pronouns into the feminine. As they try to visualize the implications of John's words, Elizabeth pulls out a small harp and plays a series of slow arpeggios, modulating the chords from one key to another and setting a mood of reverent anticipation. They face due east, and as dawn's fingers of rose and coral give way to the fiery ball lifting itself over the horizon, the vineyard's budding fullness explodes in their direction. Everywhere there is green. Nascent leaves herald chartreuse clusters of infant grapes. The river below is the color of verdigris, wending its dark way into the Gironde Estuary. When the music ends, they make their way wordlessly down the hill.

As they enter the church, all eyes are upon them. Their mothers, eyes reddened from crying, and their fathers, faces reddened with fury, watch them walk single-file down the aisle. Their self-possession speaks for itself. Elizabeth leads them in as if she were the goddess Artemis herself, minus her bow and arrows. They make their way to an empty pew and sit attentively through the service, holding themselves slightly more erect than usual. When they exit the church, a gauntlet of young men has formed on either side of the door; they hurl insults on them as they emerge into the sunlight. The women remain imperturbable and return to their vineyard cabin, dancing their way up the hill in a fever of pride and hilarity once they are out of sight.

And there they stay for three full months.

Responsibility for the women's "outrageous" behavior continues to be heaped on Father Enfantin, and when the third month of the women's rustic idyll approaches, his thoughts turn to Sophie Barat—only two hundred kilometers away in Poitiers. He knows from Father Lambert that she is assembling a community for *Les Feuillants*, and he suspects that in Elizabeth and her disciples, Sophie might find her ideal postulants.

"They are perhaps overly impassioned," he writes, "but I sense that Elizabeth, in particular, is well fitted to give glory to the heart of Jesus. You must come to us."

Sophie arrives in Bordeaux on August 12 and manages within days to pacify the parents, calm the townspeople, and mollify even the archbishop. He is hopeful that she might open a school in Bordeaux. She asks Elizabeth to lead her out into the vineyards so that she might see for herself the famous hut. By the time they arrive, both of them are in gales of laughter. On their hike across the river and into the hills, Elizabeth summarizes the women's adventure, recognizing even as she speaks that their bucolic escapade has been possibly a bit histrionic. But when they reach the summit, she and Sophie kneel on the ground in wordless communion. After more than an hour, Sophie turns to her rapt companion and speaks the words of St. Augustine. "*Videbimus; laudabimus; amabimus*. We shall see; we shall praise; we shall love." As she approaches the last verb, she pauses briefly, looking at Elizabeth's expression and visibly struggling to speak. On their way down the hill, Elizabeth asks her why she has hesitated.

"Because I saw it in you," Sophie answers quietly. "Only those who have loved can speak of love."

Elizabeth smiles shyly and the two continue their walk in silence. Sophie feels an enormous sense of kinship with this young wood-nymph whose spiritual life is a palpable force, emanating from her like the fragrance of the vineyard in the August heat. A wave of gratitude sweeps through her: one of those rare moments when she stops second-guessing herself and her decisions, worrying that she has made some wrong turn along the way God has imagined for her. She pictures Philippine up on her mountain and the little girls who are assembling around her at the schools in Grenoble. She thinks of Lydia and Joséphine, working to transform horror and grief into a vision of education in Poitiers. She even thinks of Amiens with a degree of composure, believing that perhaps things will resolve themselves yet—that Madame Baudemont and Father Saint-Estève will find themselves taken unawares, suddenly filled with the love that she feels pulsing in the heart of the young woman walking beside her.

Sophie is by this time inundated with applicants for her society, but she leaves Bordeaux with only eight young women—including Elizabeth Maillucheau and her Arcadian entourage. She promises Archbishop d'Aviau, a kindly old man whom she has come to love and trust, that she will return to establish a school there one day.

With Madame de Gramont d'Aster

April, 1807

COUNTESS CHARLOTTE-EUGÉNIE DE BOISGELIN HAD ONCE PLAYED at being a milkmaid in Marie-Antoinette's gardens at Versailles. A lively girl, full of laughter and imaginative spirit, she had been considered one of the most dazzling of the young queen's companions. Ten years her junior, Charlotte eagerly gave herself over to the pastoral games which the queen and her attendants enacted in the manicured gardens of the Petit Trianon. At age twenty, she was married to the Duke of Gramont d'Aster. Eventually, within the precincts of Louis XVI's royal compound, she bore him two daughters, Eugénie and Antoinette,

That life ended when Louis and his family were escorted off to Paris by the crowd that stormed Versailles in 1789. The Duke and his own family managed to escape to England, leaving their titles and most of their riches behind. When he died in 1795, his young widow taught school to support her daughters and returned to France only when the Terror had come to its brutal end. She settled first in Amiens, then

135

moved back to Paris and enrolled the two girls as boarding students at the Oratory.

At present, she was living in Paris, renting a suite of rooms in the large convent belonging to the Sisters of St. Thomas de Villeneuve. Despite their vastly different backgrounds, Sophie Barat and Charlotte-Eugénie de Gramont d'Aster enjoyed an increasingly close friendship, each recognizing in the other something that rose far above politics or class. Sophie had made the former duchess's suite her home-away-from-home whenever she visited the capital.

Joseph Varin had summoned Sophie to Paris just after Easter, and he and I met with her and Madame de Gramont for afternoon tea in one of the convent's large parlors.

"First and most important," Varin exclaimed excitedly, "we have the emperor's formal approbation. Signed in a military tent in Osterode on March 10. Imagine!" A fair amount of Varin's youthful enthusiasm for the army still remained.

France was currently at war with Russia after annihilating the Prussian army and marching into Berlin. In February, Napoleon had pushed Russia northward out of Poland and was now engaged in a waiting game. Poised in Osterode, he was biding his time before making a decisive move against the Tsar's gathering army.

Sophie put down her cup of tea and looked at Charlotte. I knew exactly what she was thinking. The image of the emperor using his militaristic pen to sign off on the work of Christ's heart was one that even her inventive mind could not assemble. I could see Charlotte's face register a similar amazement.

"And who presented him with the request for approbation?" she finally asked. "I thought we had agreed to wait quietly and not yet risk placing our little Society before his eyes." Here she shifted her gaze away from Charlotte and looked directly at Varin, knowing the response but wanting to hear it from his lips.

"The Bishop of Metz presented it to Napoleon's Minister of Religion," he replied. "He passed it on to the Emperor."

"And who solicited the Bishop of Metz?" she asked, her eyes now sparking with anger, as much at Varin's dissimulation as at the inevitable answer.

"Saint Estève."

"But this is good news, Sophie!" I interrupted, reading her concern but wanting her to celebrate the obvious security Napoleon's signature would offer.

"To have the emperor's approbation in writing, yes—for as long as he deigns to honor it," she replied acerbically. "But I'm more interested to hear how Saint Estève has characterized us in his request."

Here I pulled out the document itself, given to me by Varin for safekeeping. I summarized its main points. "The community, called *Les Dames de l'Instruction Chrétienne,* to be composed of both lay women and former religious." Still no reference to the incendiary Sacred Heart. "The community to adopt the rule of the Association of Notre Dame or the Ursuline Sisters. The community to have no ties with the Fathers of the Faith. The community to operate from Amiens." Here I could feel her stiffen. "The community to be given permission to expand within France and her colonies."

There was no mention anywhere of the existence of a Superior General or of any other schools.

I refrained from repeating the words Napoleon had been overheard to speak as he signed the document: "I am happy to validate any institution that would help to form women who are believers, not reasoners. By that very fact they will be attractive women."

Charlotte, reading the tension in the room, moved to pour everyone more tea. "Perhaps it is wise that Napoleon *not* understand that there is a consortium of schools," she said softly. "He might have refused the request if he'd seen anything resembling an association." She, too, was well aware of the precarious position of the Fathers of the Faith.

"She's right, Sophie," Varin snapped, unhappy with his protégée's reaction. "Any whiff of the Jesuits and you'd be crushed. It was an astute political maneuver. You should be grateful."

Sophie, whose wariness of Baudemont and Saint Estève was only increasing as information filtered down to her from Amiens, refused to reply.

"You must learn to curb your will, *ma Sophie,*" Varin's voice softened even as his criticism of her became more direct. "There are those working for the Society whose intentions are generous, and you must show

more faith in their judgment—and in the Divine Heart that is moving to make our dream come true."

Charlotte, knowing the impact these words would have on her friend, again stepped into an awkward silence. "I'm eager for you to see my daughters when either of you next visits Amiens."

"Indeed, madame," was Varin's quick reply. "I hear from Anne Baudemont that Eugénie is already showing extraordinary signs of leadership."

Charlotte acknowledged his compliment with a gracious nod, aware of Sophie's barely detectable frisson at the mention of Baudemont's name. "Both Eugénie and Antoinette seem quite happy in the novitiate," she responded. "But I so look forward to their having more time to spend in the future with their Superior General."

Varin returned the nod, and I pulled out the sheaf of papers I'd brought for Sophie's signature. She may have been marginalized by the power structure in Amiens, but any legal document of the Society still required her imprimatur.

We spent the remainder of the afternoon going over documents connected with the foundation in Poitiers, discussing Baudemont and St. Estève's latest plans for schools in Cuignières and Ghent, and listening to Sophie reveal her latest dream for a free school and accompanying boarding school in Niort, a town not far from Poitiers.

When the conversation turned back to politics, I casually mentioned that the Empress Joséphine had accompanied Napoleon on the Prussian Campaign. Napoleon's mistress in Paris had become pregnant, and rumors of an imperial divorce were once again flying through the corridors and backrooms of France. We wondered how much longer Joséphine would wear the glittering crown her husband had placed on her brow less than four years before.

Honeymoon in Manresa

1807

Sophie's return to Poitiers resembles that of a long lost and very much loved mother. She arrives a day before she is expected. The religious have gathered for recreation, and when she appears at the door, the onrush almost topples her. She escapes into the chapel to give thanks for a safe return, and Elizabeth Maillucheau—now called Thérèse—leads the women in behind her. Once there, Thérèse intones a *Te Deum*, causing ten other voices to burst into the rhythmical fourth-century chant of thanksgiving. As the final notes fade into the recesses of the room, there to mingle with the silenced voices of the Cistercians, the women move into the garden.

It is the Friday before Pentecost, and the evening is warm with the promise of summer. A full moon filters its light through the leaves of an ancient walnut tree, and the women exchange stories until well past midnight. The soft rippling of the river below accompanies the gentle tick of windmills and the occasional call of a night owl. At a signal from Thérèse, who has brought out her harp, they sing a series of songs they have composed in honor of Sophie's return. The young superior breathes in the fullness of the night and looks around at the women's

faces, irradiated with moonlight and with something else that she can only call grace.

For these two years in Poitiers, she is lost in what she will call her Manresa: an allusion to the town in Catalonia where Ignatius Loyola, the Jesuit founder, conceived his spiritual exercises and clarified his personal vision of religious life. The women arise early and engage in a process of silent prayer and meditation. They eat simply and frugally. Because funds are low, what they have to eat is dependent on how well their *commissaire*, Marie, is able to haggle at the marketplace. In addition to teaching and study, they work to restore *Les Feuillants* to its former levels of beauty and order. Sophie herself is often seen polishing the floor with large brushes strapped to her feet, skating from one end of a room to the other. Out in the fields a little girl named Madeleine cares for their single cow. The novices become as adept at milking as they do at cutting hay. They study and they teach. And at night they gather in the community room by the light of a single candle. As they embroider altar cloths and mend the children's frocks and stockings, they share the stories of their vocations—the small miracles that have brought them together in this place. Sophie places a pin in the candle to establish the point at which each speaker must stop and give way to the next, but there are evenings when the speaker's story demands that the rule be relaxed. Many are still reliving the horror of the past years; others are still mourning loved ones; some are simply trying to find the language to describe what has catalyzed a vocation whose logic eludes them.

Twice a week, Sophie gives them formal instruction. "St. Augustine tells us that the whole labor of virtue is in humility, and the reward of humility is charity."

Thérèse Mailluchau looks down at the calluses on her hands. Joséphine Bigeu rubs her shin where the cow has kicked it the day before. A young novice from Poitiers who asks herself what mending endless piles of clothing can possibly have to do with developing an "interior life" stares at Sophie with a look of perplexed exhaustion.

"We must remember that spirituality is a way of life, lived in response to the divine. It is a pattern of becoming fully who God wishes us to be."

The young Angèle, her wild electric curls long since shorn away, wonders again who God wishes her to be and asks herself how a person is ever to know the answer to this great mystery. She is immersed in the reading of philosophy and theology and cannot find the key.

Sophie counsels the young women to be generous in their dealings with others. "We don't live with angels, my daughters. The issue is to put up with human nature and forgive it."

Thérèse Maillucheau thinks about the child who has spoken cruelly to a little girl with a speech impediment. Lydia Chobelet tries to forgive Madeleine for losing the cow for over a day and costing the children a day's worth of milk.

"Show by charity how to meet a crisis. Always charity, my daughters. *Always* charity. More is gained by indulgence than by severity."

Henriette Girard notices the fire emanating from Sophie's eyes and has no doubt that she has touched the center of some cosmic energy. Henriette suffers scruples about her own levels of generosity and wonders at how a series of seeming coincidences has brought her into Sophie's society of women.

"Coincidence," she remembers Sophie saying to her one day, "is God's way of staying anonymous."

~

In July, after defeating the Russians at the Battle of Friedland, Napoleon signs the Treaty of Tilsit. The secret terms of the treaty permit Russia to grab the Ottoman Empire and Finland in exchange for France's seizing of the Dalmatian Coast and the Ionian Islands. Most of what was Prussia is now subject to a new king—Jérome Bonaparte.

Historians will later christen this moment the zenith of Napoleon's power.

~

In November, Minister Joseph Fouché shuts down the Fathers of the Faith, threatening them with arrest and exile if they have not returned to their dioceses of origin within fifteen days. Denis Marmaton executes

the order, and Joseph Varin takes refuge in his sister's chateau in Besançon.

~

In December, *les Dames de l'Instruction Chretienne* open a free school in Poitiers. It will serve one hundred children.

~

The moon rises over the old Cistercian monastery in Poitiers and sheds its quiet light. Sophie's voice echoes somewhere in its darkened crannies: "God's work is done in the shade and slowly."

The Virgin, the Mother, and the Whore

1808

CÉLESTINE HAS AGED, BUT IN A WAY THAT ONLY MAKES HER MORE beautiful. As she steps over the threshold of Marie de Beixedon's home in Paris, she is the embodiment of a woman who has folded suffering into her heart and allowed its pain to etch an astonishing grace into her features. She is twenty-nine years old, and she and Sophie have not seen one another for over ten years.

She pauses in the doorway, not certain how to address her childhood friend. Not certain, in fact, if she should even be here.

"PhiePhie?" Her voice is tentative, interrogative, anxious that she might have overstepped the boundaries of good taste.

It takes Sophie a moment to recognize her, dressed as she is in the expansive finery that Eugène de Beauharnais' largesse permits.

"*Ma chère Célestine!*" Her response is immediate once she realizes who is standing before her, and she rushes up to embrace her. Célestine's reaction is to fall to her knees, an act that embarrasses Sophie and causes her to kneel beside her.

"I promised not to tell you she would be here," Marie interjects, feeling a stab of guilt at her deception. "She didn't know if you'd come."

"Of course I would have come," Sophie responds softly, her eyes fixed on Célestine. "Please, my darling, let's sit down." She and Marie help the young woman up off her knees and guide her to one of Marie's damask-upholstered sofas. Célestine sinks into it heavily and Sophie sits down beside her, the latter's simple black traveling dress providing stunning counterpoint to the other's fur-trimmed pelisse. Sophie reaches out and takes her hand, waiting for her to speak.

"I know what you must think of me," Célestine opens, any vestige of the shining salonnière now absent from her demeanor.

Before Sophie can respond, she continues, the words twisting out of her mouth with what seems to be physical pain. "But I needed to see you. To speak with you. To hear your beautiful voice." Here for the first time she looks directly into her friend's eyes, hardly believing she is there in the flesh. "And to share with you a plan that I've had in my head for a very long time. Something that might serve to make up for . . ." Her words trail off, and Marie steps in to help her.

"Perhaps Sophie needs to know more about what happened," she offers gently. Sophie and Célestine have exchanged many letters over their years of separation, but Marie is certain that Célestine has withheld information—information whose darkest particulars even she doesn't know or want to know, but whose effects she witnessed nine years before.

"I think I can guess what happened," is Sophie's quick response, imagining not for the first time the act of violation that might precipitate a woman's descent into self-destruction. "What's important, what ultimately matters, my dearest friend, is what transpires in the wake of whatever violence you have suffered."

Célestine looks at her with gratitude. She has no desire to re-conjure the sights and sounds and terror of that night—images which have finally begun to recede into a generalized horror that lurks in the margins of her consciousness.

"As you know from my letters, Sophie, it was Therezia Tallien who saved me. She took me in—just as she had Théroigne." Sophie remembers seeing Therezia at the Café Olympe that afternoon in Paris so many years ago. She and another woman were off to care for the Girondiste Thériogne de Méricourt, driven into madness by a public flogging.

"She's a very fine painter, Therezia," Célestine continues. "And she made me paint my despair. We never talked about it. I just painted. And then she started taking me to the museum at the Louvre. Later she began bringing me books—history and literature and philosophy. It was a bit like being with you, Sophie, except that she didn't recite the stories to me—I had to read them myself!" Here the first glimmer of a smile crosses her face.

"And how long did she care for you?" Sophie asks gently, never letting go of Célestine's hand.

"For many months. I really don't know how many, it's all still a blur. But at some point she started taking me out into society. Her husband, you know, was the politician Jean Tallien. He's the one who freed Therezia from prison."

"Yes, you wrote to me of her kindness. And I have heard of her."

Sophie has indeed heard stories of Jean Tallien around the candle in Poitiers: ghastly tales told by women whose families suffered from the Terror he wrought in Bordeaux. She has also heard that his wife Therezia personally saved many Bordelais from imprisonment or death, and that her influence eventually caused her husband to curb his revolutionary zeal.

"It was at a party with her that I first met Joseph Fouché." Here, Célestine drops her head and stops speaking.

"I know what happened with Fouché," Sophie's voice comes quickly. "Guy told me. There's no need to repeat it." Célestine has failed to share this information with Sophie as well, as if she feels she must spare her friend details that would shock her sensibilities. As if Sophie resides in some pure white space that has no room for violence. As if her own Beloved had never been stripped naked, whipped, pierced and violated until he hung dead on a cross. "What I *do* need to know is what you wish from me."

As she speaks, Sophie places her other hand under Célestine's chin and lifts her bowed head so she can meet her eyes. She is struck by their azure depths, now darkened and modulated with anguish.

"Eugène de Beauharnais has made me a wealthy woman," she begins. "I've never understood what I did to deserve his constancy. Sometimes I think

145

I'm a sort of touchstone for him—a way for him to make up for the unhappiness suffered by his sister and mother. Do you understand what I mean?"

Sophie nods in response. She knows that Hortense de Beauharnais has been married off to Napoleon's mentally unstable brother Louis. And all of Paris is now waiting for Napoleon to divorce the barren Joséphine and marry a woman who will give him a son.

"And I know that our relationship—yours and mine, I mean," Célestine continues, "transgresses certain boundaries." Here she looks down again and pauses to collect her thoughts.

Sophie shakes her head gently in disagreement, but she doesn't interrupt the flow of Célestine's words.

"I have no way of going back, but having to give up Héloïse has forced me to—" Here her voice breaks. Sophie and Marie know there is nothing they can say and wait for her to regain her self-possession. "Giving her up has forced me to think of other ways to love. Does that make sense to you, Sophie? My *God*, I sometimes don't know what I even *mean* when I use that word." She looks at Sophie as if she is the repository of all the world's wisdom.

Sophie, who is coming to fathom what St. Augustine meant when he spoke of the "abyss of the human heart," nods her head. Helen. Dido. Héloïse. Francesca. Even Dante, in all his judgmental fervor, didn't quite know what to do with his adulterous heroine except swoon at her lovely feet.

"Yes, my daughter. I understand." She notes with moderate surprise that she has slipped into the form of address she uses with her religious.

Célestine, filled with relief and gratitude, chooses her words carefully. "I know you wish to open a free school for poor children in Niort. Guy keeps me up to date on all your good work. I'd like to help you, Sophie, if you don't think that money from a harlot's purse is tainted."

Sophie winces at her friend's choice of words, but before she can answer, the door bursts open. A nurse, holding Marie's new infant son and accompanied by a three-year-old girl with tousled platinum curls and eyes of azure, stands at the door. When the child sees Marie, she runs toward her with a shriek, flying joyously into her lap.

"*Maman!*" she cries, burying her face in Marie's neck.

Part 6

Peripateia

Men at Work

1808 – 1810

IN THE WAKE OF THE TREATY OF TILSIT, NAPOLEON SET HIS SIGHTS on the Iberian Peninsula. After subjugating Portugal and seizing control of Lisbon—and on the pretext of reinforcing the Franco-Spanish army—he began sending troops into Spain. On February 29, 1808, Barcelona opened its gates to what was believed to be a convoy of wounded. The city instead found itself at the mercy of an invading French column. The Spanish Royal Army, many of its troops scattered about Europe in the service of their former ally, was powerless to prevent the occupation. A coup d'état instigated by the Emperor led to the king's abdication, and in May Joseph Bonaparte was crowned King of Spain.

Napoleon had boasted that 12,000 imperial troops could take over the peninsula, but popular uprisings resulted in his having to send in almost 200,000 men. Before the end of the year, France had lost 24,000 soldiers, the French commanders had ordered a general retreat, and His Precarious Majesty Joseph Bonaparte was left fighting guerilla warfare for the next five years.

All Europe watched as the invincible Napoleon was left licking his wounds.

The following February, his troops marched into Rome. By May, he had annexed those Papal States he hadn't already seized, and the Pontifical flag was lowered from its position over the Castel Sant'Angelo. When Pius VII retaliated with an Order of Excommunication, Napoleon had him kidnapped and imprisoned in France.

Soon after this, while once again battling Austria, Napoleon revealed his fallibility as a strategic commander when France suffered massive troop losses at the battles of Aspern and Wagram.

In December, he divorced Joséphine to marry the eighteen-year-old Hapsburg princess Marie Louise. Within a year of the marriage, she obligingly gave him a son.

~

In Amiens, Father Sambucy de Saint Estève was weaving his own tapestry of power and deceit, though its threads were of a slightly different cast.

In a rhapsodic display of self-deception, he was slowly but relentlessly proclaiming himself to be the inspirational founder of the *Dames de l'Instruction Chrétienne*. To fortify his position, he began to construct an official Rule by which the house at Amiens (and eventually all of Sophie's houses) were to function. With his faithful lieutenant Anne Baudemont, he methodically dismantled the simple spirit and practices that had been at the center of Varin and his early colleagues' vision— and that now characterized Sophie's five other communities of women.

In his conquistadorial zeal, Saint Estève also attempted to wrest control of the recently established Congregation of Notre Dame—a teaching order begun in Amiens by a woman named Julie Billiart. Its mission was to serve orphans and the poor. Billiart's resistance to his aggression led him to denounce her to the bishop, resulting in her exile from the diocese. All but two of her nuns followed her to Namur.

A Garden Enclosed

1808 – 1810

Father jean montaigne, an elderly man of great learning, is known for his capacious silences. When he does invoke language, it is often without having established a context for his remarks. But his words, from whatever source they arise, ring with ponderous authority. As Superior of the Seminary of Saint Sulpice in Paris, he wears a violet skullcap whose brilliant hue is enhanced by the shock of white hair that fringes its perimeter. His eyes are a deep green, and they seem to look through his listeners rather than at them.

At Joseph Varin's suggestion, Sophie has sought him out as a spiritual advisor.

When she presents herself, his opening words refer to a Holy Spirit that he knows to be leading her forward. The seeming optimism of this remark he soon counters with a dark warning. "There is a seed of destruction in the midst of your Society, Sophie Barat, but a soul very powerful with God has prayed for you." He repeats these words several times, and as Sophie heads out his door to Amiens, he gives her a final admonition: "Let yourself be *devoured* by Jesus Christ."

He will act as her spiritual advisor until his death. In her correspondence, which she knows is under surveillance, she refers to the old abbot as "*Gran'maman*."

⁓

When Sophie returns to Amiens in the fall of 1808, she is greeted by Felicité de Sambucy, Saint Estève's elder sister and a former Ursuline nun.

"Welcome back into our community, madame." Her frigid tone belies the greeting, and Sophie squares her narrow shoulders in a wordless attempt to assert her authority—if only to herself. She notes that de Sambucy, whom her brother has appointed Assistant Mistress of Novices, is wearing a new, more elaborate costume, different from the dress worn by the religious in her other houses.

"My brother is engaged in an important meeting with Madame Baudemont and begs your pardon. He asks that I settle you into your room." The voice is Saint Estève's, but with a gloss of unctuous condescension developed and perfected during years in Paris's wealthiest convent. Sophie has heard that in Amiens the feast of St. Ursula has taken precedence over that of the Sacred Heart.

She stays long enough to know that her work for now is to weave unity among her remaining houses. Like a small homing pigeon, she travels at once to Grenoble, arriving at Sainte-Marie d'en-Haut in the midst of a splendid autumn.

⁓

The three women sit in a grove of acacia trees. One has a book open in her lap; another embroiders an altar cloth; a third stares up into the branches of the trees, where pods the color of russet shimmer in the afternoon breeze.

"'My sister, my spouse, is a garden enclosed, a garden enclosed, a fountain sealed up,'" Sophie reads.

Thérèse Maillucheau turns her eyes away from the tree's fertile luster and looks at Sophie. "What does it mean?"

Philippine Duchesne rethreads her needle and offers an interpretation. "The garden is the church. An enclosure for the faithful who might drink from its graces."

"Perhaps," Sophie counters. She has turned her eyes away from the book and stares across the valley, thinking of flowers and unicorns, and of women sitting alone in walled gardens.

While Sophie has read of the unicorn in the Old Testament, the ever-imaginative Charlotte de Gramont d'Aster has regaled her with legends about the creature. That its horn has magical curative properties, leading French kings to eat with utensils of alicorn to guard against food poisoning. That since James I, the unicorn and the lion—symbolic, respectively, of harmony and might—appear in exquisite contraposition on the British coat of arms. That only a virgin can capture the unicorn, and that to do so she must sit in a garden and wait. That the unicorn is an avatar of Christ.

"Perhaps we ourselves are the garden," Sophie finally responds. "Just as we ourselves are the church." The unicorn has leapt out of her imagination but left behind a boundless sense of well-being that fills her chest cavity and causes her heart rate to speed up.

Thérèse notes the look that has crept into Sophie's eyes and shudders slightly with that simultaneous rush of emptiness and plenitude that frequently possesses her during prayer. A sensation of her very soul rushing out of her body, only to return to it as if on fire, rendering her breathless and dazed.

After a moment Sophie finishes her thought. "In this sense, the fountain lies within each of us, waiting only to be dispersed."

She is seeing an image from John's Gospel—blood and water flowing out of Christ's side in a message of endless love and salvation.

On another afternoon, this one overhung with low clouds that give the valley the look of a Watteau painting, they ponder the Book of Wisdom.

"Wisdom is more mobile than any motion," Philippine intones solemnly. Today it is she who holds the book. "Because of her pureness she pervades and penetrates all things."

Thérèse is stretched out on the grass, gazing through the acacia branches and chewing on a piece of clover. Sophie sits on a small stone bench, rocking slowly back and forth as if she holds a sleeping infant in her arms. When Philippine hears no response, she continues reading. "For she is a breath of the power of God, and a pure emanation of the glory of the Almighty; therefore nothing defiled gains entrance into her."

Here Sophie stops rocking, sits up straight, and recites from memory. "Although she is but one, she can do all things, and while remaining in herself, she renews all things. In every generation she passes into holy souls and makes them friends of God." Her voice rings into the vaporous atmosphere.

She gazes at her two companions and smiles. They return her smile and bow their heads, feeling themselves—at least for the moment—to be one of those holy souls.

The valley below steams with clouds, suggesting a landscape of myth. Mont Blanc lifts her snowy crown above it all, sending shards of reflected white light across the valley in a kind of benediction.

Forced March

1811 – 1812

"So our emperor finally has himself a son," I remarked, looking across the room at my host and hostess. Marie and Alex de Beixedon, just recalled to Paris from Milan, had invited me for luncheon. "All Frenchmen can now enjoy the knowledge that his dynasty will continue into the next generation. And you now have two fine sons of your own to feed to Napoleon's machine." Here I looked directly at Marie, who was staring at her husband with alarm.

Prince Napoléon Francois Joseph Charles, King of Rome and heir apparent to the imperial throne of France, had been born in Paris to Napoleon's young Empress Marie-Louise. Less than two months later, Marie had delivered a second son to the house of Beixedon.

Alex smiled wanly, a look of fatigue having taken up permanent residence in the corner of his eyes. Napoleon was reconfiguring his political hierarchies in the shadow of his military debacles, and after almost nine years in Italy, Alex was being asked to use his diplomatic skills to churn out propaganda. Growing antiwar sentiment was rocking the cafés and salons of France.

"Even as I work to calm the public fury," he said wearily, "he's talking of another major campaign. I sometimes wonder why I ever

returned from exile." I was sure he now wished that he'd followed other French émigrés—including his brother—to a new life in the United States. Marie had confided to me her worries about his health, and I could see despair beginning to etch itself into his handsome features.

"It seems that our old friend Denis has been busy silencing the press," I continued.

"Indeed," Alex replied, his expression darkening. Denis Marmaton was no longer received in his sister's home. He seemed to be sinking ever deeper into Joseph Fouché's world of espionage, and I hadn't seen him for many months. "Minister Fouché has just issued orders to shut down two more newspapers, and the editors of *Le Moniteur Français* have been in prison since speaking out against the slaughter at Wagram."

"We had *how* many newspapers in Paris ten years ago?" I snarled, not wanting to hear the answer. "And now we have only *six*—every one of them under government control."

"Did you hear what happened to Madame de Stael's new book?" Marie interjected.

"Oh yes," I replied acidly. The publication of Germaine de Stael's much anticipated analysis of German culture, after having made it past the censors, had been suddenly halted when Napoleon changed his mind. Ten thousand copies were destroyed when his Majesty termed the volume "un-French." "She'd better stay in Switzerland if she wants to stay out of prison herself. One doesn't speak well of the Germans and survive in this climate."

Marie's stony gaze gave way to one of joy when three-year-old Jean-Marie entered the room. The boy bore a stark likeness to his father, with the exception of his mother's wide-set hazel eyes. He was followed into the salon by Héloïse, whose resemblance to Célestine grew more pronounced with every passing day.

"*Maman*! *Papa*!" The children flew across the room, one heading toward Marie, the other toward his father. Alex swept the little boy up into his arms, tossing him high into the air as the child squealed with delight. Héloïse threw her arms around Marie's neck and covered her face with kisses.

Then she saw me.

"Uncle Guy!" she exclaimed and, with the solemn poise of a six-year-old in training at the Italian court, moved across the room to where I sat. She curtsied, landed a decorous kiss on each of my cheeks, and then scrambled into my lap.

"And how is your other favorite uncle, *ma puce*?" I asked, tweaking her nose with my fingers. "*Maman* tells me you've just returned from Milan!"

"He does well. And he sends you his most special greetings!" The child winked as if there were some special understanding between the two of us and then kissed me again. "*Voilà*!" Already she was an enchanting blend of my sister's impetuous warmth and her father's political acuity.

Héloïse had just returned from a two-month visit with Eugène de Beauharnais and his growing family. His Bavarian princess had already given him two daughters and would bear him a son later that year. Following the terms of the custody agreement, he personally transported Héloïse to and from Milan three times a year. Princess Augusta had been extraordinarily gracious about the frequent visits of Eugène's mysterious little niece, and the child was becoming fluent in German and a favorite with her younger Bavarian cousins.

I wondered when she would be told of her real parentage. Or if she would simply guess at the truth. Or if on some intuitive level she knew already.

What none of us knew was that Eugène, who still reigned as Viceroy of Italy and Arch-chancellor of State of the French Empire, was at that moment in Paris to discuss preliminary strategy for an invasion of Russia in the summer of 1812.

~

I saw Sophie in Paris only twice during this first round of her wanderings. For over two and a half years, since her autumnal idyll in Grenoble, she had been shuttling from one place to another in an attempt to sow unity and concord—a nineteenth-century Peîtho clothed in the mantle of a Burgundian widow.

Upon leaving Grenoble, she had travelled back to Amiens, then on to Ghent, Joigny, Poitiers and Niort. In Joigny, she had seen her father for the last time. Tiptoeing into his atelier to throw her arms around his neck in her customary greeting, she found it empty. Stacks of barrel staves and metal hoops lay about the shop; the old wine press stood ready for duty in its corner. But the worktable was empty, and Jacques Barat had retired for the last time to his bedroom upstairs. The faithful old cooper died in June of 1809, as quietly and unobtrusively as he had lived.

With his death Sophie lost a personal and vital link to the earth itself, and while we did not speak of it, I sensed that one of her own branches had been violently pruned away, never to grow back.

She eventually returned to Grenoble, where she spent almost a year. Then it was back to Lyon, Paris, Cuignières, Amiens, and Ghent. There, while she was recovering from a lengthy illness, Father Sambucy de Saint Estève finally threw down the gauntlet. A letter summoned her to Amiens "immediately" to discuss implementation of his newly revised version of the Society's Rule. Her odyssey was about to take on a new dimension.

A month later, just days after my visit with Alex and Marie, Sophie and I met for dinner at Madame de Gramont d'Aster's apartments in Paris. She held a copy of Saint Estève's Rule in her hands.

"They are attempting to return to a way of life that existed before the Revolution," she remarked quietly, but with a tone of voice indicating that the gauntlet had been seized, its holder ready to take on the challenge. "There were six of us at the table in Amiens—Monsieur de Saint Estève, Madame Baudemont, Madame de Sambucy, Madame Copina, Madame de Charbonnel, and I."

All but Catherine de Charbonnel, I knew, had been part of a monastic order prior to joining Sophie's, and she was utterly intimidated by Baudemont.

"The original inspiration is lost, Guy. Nowhere is there any mention of St. Ignatius. Nowhere is there any mention of the Sacred Heart." Here her voice came close to breaking, but she regained command of herself and continued on. "They've cobbled together fragments of the Rules of St. Basil, St. Ursula, and St. Clare, and they are encouraging as many former religious as possible to join."

"Of course," I responded. "To ensure the continuance of a monastic life."

"Yes. He has every angle covered. Under his plan, we'll be under the authority of the local bishop. Our ability to move about freely within a network of houses will no longer exist."

"And the role of Superior General?" I asked.

"The position of Superior for Life is to give way to a term of ten years," she responded evenly.

I knew that in addition to the freedom of movement within a large network, the symbolism of a Superior for Life—uniting all communities under one central, unwavering authority—was a key element of Varin's vision, one that he had pulled from the Jesuit Constitutions. It guaranteed the Society both a certain level of autonomy vis-à-vis the ecclesial authorities and a central spirituality that would not deviate from house to house.

"And the Superior of each house will have *full* authority to receive and prepare new applicants to the Society," she continued, now standing up and placing the document in my hands.

"Oh yes," she added after pacing a few steps. "One more thing. We are to be called *Apostolines.*"

We looked at each other for a moment without speaking. Dumbfounded.

I read the pages over as she moved about the room, pausing occasionally to stare out the window in what I could only assume was an act of prayer. When I had finished reading, I looked at her across the vast salon with an expression that needed no verbal accompaniment.

"So what's your next move?" I finally asked.

"The house in Amiens has already voted to adopt the Rule provisionally," she replied, again without emotion. "Saint Estève has asked me to take the document on the road and generate support for it among the other foundations."

We locked eyes once again as the irony of her mission spread itself across the room, lodging its invisible bulk somewhere amidst the Flemish wall tapestries.

On one of them a white unicorn stood in resolute opposition to a lion.

⁓

In June of 1812, Napoleon ordered his *Grande Armée* of over five hundred thousand men to mobilize along the Russian frontier. They crossed the River Niemen on the morning of June 24 and began a march across Russia that moved with relative ease as the Tsar's army played a tactical game that traded space for time. As they proceeded along the road to Moscow, General Mikhail Kutuzov was assembling a force of one hundred twenty thousand soldiers at Borodino, fortifying a defensive position the likes of which Napoleon had never encountered. On September 7, the Emperor arrived with his army of one hundred thirty-three thousand. Ignoring the advice of his generals, he threw the army directly into the face of the Russians in a blazing show of strength.

By the end of the day seventy-four thousand men were dead, missing or wounded, and Kutusov was regrouping his forces, pulling them back toward Moscow, knowing Napoleon would follow.

⁓

Early in the morning of October 15, Célestine sent me news that Alex de Beixedon had died suddenly the night before.

"What in God's name happened?" I asked when I arrived at their home in the Faubourg Saint Honoré.

"They're calling it brain fever," was her quick reply. "It's the term the doctors use when they don't know what else to call it."

"When did he become ill? I didn't know—"

"He's been ill ever since they returned from Milan, surely you knew that."

"Unhappy, yes. But I saw no sign of physical illness."

She gave me one of those looks she'd been giving me since childhood. The one that marveled at how such obtuseness could occupy headspace with an otherwise intelligent mind.

"Where's Marie?" I asked. "How is she taking it?"

"In her room. How do you think?" Again that look. "The doctor has given her a sedative. He'll return this afternoon and in the meantime has left a nurse to look after her. I must go back to her now. If you could please just be here for them when the children awaken. You're the only uncle I could find in Paris this morning." Here she offered a conciliatory smile and hugged me before going upstairs to attend to her childhood friend.

As we gathered several days later for Alex's funeral, Napoleon's army was beginning its catastrophic retreat from a Moscow that had gone up in flames. The Tsar had refused to surrender. The Russians had burned their city to the ground rather than leave their enemy in possession of food and shelter. Bands of Cossacks and Russian light cavalry attacked the exhausted columns. The first winter snows began in early November, and the French soldiers died in droves of typhus, exposure, and starvation—some eventually forced to eat their own horses; some, according to witnesses, their fallen comrades.

In December, Napoleon, fearful of a coup, dashed back to Paris in a sleigh. His top general, Murat, deserted shortly afterward to consolidate his fortunes in Naples. It was Eugène de Beauharnais who accompanied the bedraggled remains of *la Grande Armée* back across the Nieman River. The number of returning soldiers was put at somewhere around 23,000.

~

The community in Poitiers sat in stunned silence. Saint-Estève's new Rule lay on the table in front of Sophie, and the women eyed it as if Eden's serpent had slithered in the door and coiled itself on their recreation table.

It was Joséphine Bigeu who finally broke the silence. "But where is the Sacred Heart?" Her voice, shaking with alarm and anger, ignited sparks of dissension that glowed like hidden explosives around the table.

"What about our Superior for Life?" asked the lovely Angèle.

"What about our ability to move from school to school?" said a young novice who believed she had committed herself to a new and radical vision of apostolic life.

Sophie sat quietly, having read the Rule aloud to them with unimaginable dispassion. She had promised herself not to betray her feelings, knowing that her sisters would see the weaknesses of Saint Estève's handiwork on their own.

Similar scenes played themselves out in Ghent, Niort, Cuignières, and Grenoble, where Philippine Duchesne and Geneviève Deshayes voiced an outraged refusal to adopt Saint Estève's "neo-Napoleonic Code."

In June Saint Estève was arrested for interfering with affairs in his local diocese. Sophie took this opportunity to return to Amiens, stopping briefly in Besançon to seek counsel from the silenced Joseph Varin. When she returned to Grenoble, she collapsed from exhaustion and illness and would not leave her mountain for another fourteen months.

It was October 1812, and the remnants of Napoleon's Grand Army were just beginning their miserable trek home.

Besançon

October, 1813

THE CHILD STANDS IN THE WATCHTOWER OF A FIFTEENTH-CEN-
tury stronghold in the northern Jura. Just sixty kilometers from the
Swiss frontier, the turreted chateau has provided a suitable refuge for
Joseph Varin since the forced dissolution of his Fathers of the Faith
five years before. If he looks beyond the moat, out toward the road that
leads in from Strasbourg, the boy can sometimes discern small groups
of soldiers straggling back from the Russian war. They have been arriving for months. Many are limping; some, led along by more fortunate
comrades who have not lost their sight or the use of a limb. All bear the
marks of illness and malnutrition, and many have taken up refuge in
nearby Besançon.

If he looks within the chateau gardens, the boy sees a man and
woman who have been walking for hours along the wide allées of linden
and chestnut trees, their leaves now turning to voluptuous shades of
red and gold. The man is a priest, Madame de Chevroz's brother. The
woman is very small but emanates an energy he can feel even from his
lofty tower. She is dressed in black. The two of them amble the length
of the park in deep and animated conversation, then stop abruptly while

he writes something down. They meander down another pathway, pick up speed as their conversation recharges, and then stop again while he writes, then crosses something out, then writes again. The leaves flutter their October colors as a cool but gentle breeze blows down from the northeastern rim of the Alps.

In the evenings everyone gathers for dinner, residents and guests together. The little woman in black at times cannot be found, and when this happens, the boy is sent with a lantern into the chapel. It is only with difficulty that he finds her tiny frame hidden in the cavernous depths of a high-backed pew.

They call her *la femme qui fait la mort*. The woman who makes death. And indeed she does at times seem given over to a kind of death, lost entirely to the world around her. But the boy prefers to hear the final syllable pronounced differently. For him she is *la femme qui fait l'amour*. The woman who makes love.

When he is older, he will recognize what the Italians have known all along. That *la morte* frames *amor*. That to love, to really love, is to die to one's self and to the things of this world.

When she leaves the Chateau de Chevroz several weeks later, Sophie carries with her a sheaf of papers, the fruit of those long walks among the trees with Joseph Varin. After a brief stop in Joigny and a retreat in Paris, she will return to Amiens.

Restoration

1814

On april 11, 1814, with paris occupied by enemy coalition forces and his own generals in mutiny, Emperor Napoleon Bonaparte offered his unconditional abdication. The Treaty of Fontainebleau sent him into exile on the tiny Mediterranean island of Elba, not far from his native Corsica. His wife and son fled to Vienna.

On May 3, Louis Stanislas Xavier de France, scion of the House of Bourbon, returned to Paris as King Louis XVIII. His route from England, where he had lived in luxurious exile since 1808, included a stop in Amiens.

I arrived in Amiens just days before the royal party was to arrive. Sophie had called on my services to oversee an emergency transaction involving the dowry of a novice whose final vows needed to be expedited. When I arrived at the Oratory on April 23, I discovered the novice to be none other than Madame Charlotte-Eugénie de Gramont d'Aster. Fearing that Louis XVIII would recall her to court, Marie Antoinette's former lady-in-waiting was, at age forty-seven, seeking to position herself where the royal scepter could not touch her.

The anticipated regal summons arrived two days after she became Mother de Gramont d'Aster. Bearing the official seal of the Bourbon kings and delivered by royal courier, it had been redirected to Amiens from her address in Paris.

"He wishes me to be lady-in-waiting for the Duchess of Angoulême," she said, looking up from the document. Charlotte, Sophie and I had just finished signing a stack of papers in one of the parlors. Other than funds left in reserve to retain her apartments at the convent of St. Thomas Villeneuve, all that remained of the de Gramont d'Aster estate would go to the Society.

"You mean the Princesse Royale?" I asked, verifying that she meant the sole surviving child of Louis XVI and Marie-Antoinette.

"Indeed. Marie Thérèse. Her mother called her *Mousseline.*" She smiled a bit wistfully, but the smile was gone as quickly as it had appeared. "She was only eleven years old when I last saw her."

The three of us sat for a moment in silence, thinking of the little girl who had been carried off with her family from Versailles in October of 1789. She had spent six years imprisoned in Paris, watching as, one by one, her father, mother and little brother were taken off to die. Two by guillotine, one by methods that would never be fully discovered.

"*Pauvre petite,*" Sophie said softly.

I wondered whether she referred to the ten-year-old girl's imprisonment or the teenage girl's forced marriage to the Duke of Angoulême—a cousin rumored to suffer from impotence and nervous tics, and who would be named the King of France for the space of twenty minutes in 1830.

We saw each other just two months later in Paris, where Sophie had arrived for a series of urgent meetings with Joseph Varin. With the downfall of Napoleon, Varin was at last able to move freely about France. Pope Pius VII had just issued a papal bull reinstating the Jesuits, and almost all the Fathers of the Faith would begin their Jesuit noviceship in August, including Louis Barat. Saint Estève, however, would not be among them.

"He's off to Rome," Sophie said briskly as I seated myself on one of the divans. We were in Madame de Gramont d'Aster's apartments, and

I noted that the unicorn tapestry had been moved into her main salon, where it presided silently over our conversation.

"You told me this was his eventual plan," I replied. "I wasn't aware that he'd already left Paris."

Sophie and Father Montaigne had met with Saint Estève the preceding December, while he was still under house arrest in Paris, in order to discuss modifications to his proposed Rule. They had met again in June, this time with Varin, and Sophie had pressed for several key changes, among them her right to remain Superior for Life and to assume the position of local Superior in Amiens.

"It's been his plan for many months," she replied. "We all knew it was just a matter of waiting for political events in France to play themselves out."

"When did he leave?"

"Yesterday. He visited me the day before to deliver some final instructions." For a moment I thought I saw the unicorn flinch from the corner.

After his release from house arrest, Saint Estève had moved quickly. Knowing that the Bishop of Amiens would forbid his return to that diocese, he'd successfully negotiated an appointment as secretary to Louis XVIII's newly appointed ambassador to the Vatican.

"He's eager to present the Rule for approbation in Rome," Sophie continued, "and claims he will be well situated to do so. But he's agreed to wait until I've called a General Council so that *all* houses within the Society might be in agreement about what, precisely, he will present to the Vatican authorities."

"Is this really such a good idea, Sophie?"

"We are insisting that he wait, and he's promised to do so for a limited amount of time." She paused for a moment and then added, "But we know he's not a man to exercise a great deal of patience."

"You mean he's not the man to do *anything* other than further his own interests!" I snapped back.

She shrugged. There was, in fact, little she could do. I'd seen men operate like this all too often in the world of business. He would travel to Rome and ingratiate himself with the Vatican power brokers. He would use whatever tactics he could to convince the Roman hierarchy that Sophie Barat was a weak and indecisive woman who couldn't

possibly preside over a religious order. He would convince them, in short, that *he* was the man for the job.

"He was adamant during his last visit," she responded, "that neither the pope nor the Jesuits in Rome will ever allow a corresponding women's society to exist." Here her eyes flashed with a spark of outrage I remembered from her early childhood. "He insists that his Rule provides our *only* chance for official approval, and as he will undoubtedly claim to be our official representative to the Holy See, we have very little leverage."

She paused a moment and then added, almost as an afterthought, "And my own council in Amiens firmly believes him to be in the right."

Her recent months in Amiens, I knew, had been a colossal exercise in restraint and forgiveness. While she had reestablished herself there as titular Superior, virtually everyone on her leadership council was loyal to Saint Estève.

"But how could they *not* be loyal, Sophie, when he professes to know the express wishes of the Holy Father himself?" I asked, shooting her an ironic smile. For a moment, I imagined the two men cozying up under St. Peter's baldacchino, laying the groundwork for a complete Vatican takeover of the Society.

"He also claims to have the ear of several cardinals and bishops," she added, "and the support of the Jesuit Superior in Rome. He maintains that the hierarchy will never allow us to call ourselves the *Madames of the Sacred Heart*."

"So his *Apostolines* will carry the day?" My smile turned wicked. "Surely Pius has more taste than that!"

"But there's more, Guy." Here her voice became lower, and in the depths of her eyes I could see the enormous struggle going on within her.

"Joseph is finally beginning to understand that Saint Estève might not be the man he thought he was."

It's about time, I thought to myself. Joseph Varin's unwavering confidence in Saint Estève's integrity had never failed to amaze me. I only hoped his epiphany hadn't come too late.

"He and I met yesterday afternoon, as soon as Saint Estève left with the ambassador."

"And?"

"We went over the revisions for what Joseph thought would be the last time, and he finally realized that the document, even with all its changes, is completely alien to the initial spirit of our order."

"Perhaps his reconnection with the Jesuits has brought him a heightened degree of clarity," I responded.

"Whatever has inspired it, *cher ami*, he is convinced that Saint Estève's Rule must be radically altered. I of course agree with him, and we have been encouraged by the head of the French Jesuit community to begin our work immediately. But I fear we may be headed for a schism."

Pretenders

Late May, 1815

DENIS MARMATON HAS SPENT THE LAST TWENTY YEARS PERFECT-ing the fine art of survivalism. While anarchy is his preferred ambiance, long periods of stability have allowed him to amass a fortune: some acquired through the financial trickle-down of Napoleon's empire-building; some through extortion; and some through well-timed if irregular withdrawals from the coffers of the Ministry of Police. He has learned well from his mentor Joseph Fouché how to tap into the labyrinthine circuits of the national treasury, particularly when events are spinning out of control.

The last two months have proved anarchic enough even for Marmaton's tastes. Napoleon has swept back into France from exile. His dramatic reappearance on French soil has catalyzed the reconstitution of an imperial army, the flight of the Bourbon court, and another round of warfare—this time with a coalition of European forces determined to drive Napoleon forever off the map. While Fouché has been busy consolidating his own political power, Marmaton has been gathering information he knows will be useful, regardless of the war's outcome.

"The emperor has raised an army of almost 300,000 men and hopes to up his manpower to 450,000 within a month or two," Denis explains. He and Fouché are seated in a small restaurant on the Left Bank. "His strategy is to move quickly into Belgium and drive a wedge between the Prussians and the English before their armies gather any more strength."

Fouché nods his head in acknowledgment of the information, but his eyes are staring over his companion's shoulder. What Denis Marmaton does *not* know is that his boss is engaged in a delicate game of double espionage, conspiring with Napoleon's Coalition enemies even as he pretends to support the emperor's return to power.

"This coincides with my own information," he finally says, turning his cold eyes on his lieutenant.

"What are his chances?" Denis asks, wondering what Fouché's sources might have yielded.

"The emperor is not well," Fouché replies. "They say he cannot bear to sit on his horse for more than an hour at a time." He smiles with a look that mingles cruelty and disgust. "Hemorrhoids. This doesn't bode well for a general who relies on personal charisma to inspire his troops."

Denis returns his smile, the left side of his mouth twisting into a smirk. He has heard similar reports. That Bonaparte seems wistful, at times even confounded by the events of the past months. That defeat and exile have eaten away at his boundless bravado. That even he can no longer sustain the weight of his enormous ego.

"Where are they headed?" he asks.

"For a little town near Brussels called Waterloo."

~

A small group of women and children make their way along a narrow, shaded path that leads across meadows and wheat fields. They are watched by dairy cows whose languor matches the pace of the small caravan. Reassuring themselves that the intruders mean them no harm, the cows return to their silent grazing. One of the women sits on a grey donkey and is singing. The other women and children, who carry baskets and other items destined for a picnic, sing along with her. Eventually they reach a small pond overhung with willow branches. White swans and a multitude of ducks vie for whatever lives on or beneath the surface. It is August, but the heat is mild, tempered by the fresh air masses sifting down from the North Atlantic.

While one of the women helps three little girls open up a blanket, another assists the woman off the donkey. She moves slowly after months of illness, but there is a briskness to her movements, and she doesn't stop singing until she is comfortably settled on one edge of the blanket. The children rush up to sit beside her as the final notes drift up into the overhanging branches. She puts her finger to her lips, bidding them to remain silent for a moment. They hear only birdsong, the lowing of cattle, and an occasional slap of water as a duck returns to the surface of the pond.

"Let us see what our Mother Deshayes has packed for us to eat," she finally says, clapping her hands together with childlike anticipation and signaling the two other women to unpack the lunch.

"One of you must tell Mother Barat the story of the Rollot cheese!" Félicité Desmarquest says as they gather around to look at a heart-shaped cheese that she has unwrapped and placed on a large wooden board. Beside it are several pears and two crusty baguettes.

"I will! I will!" exclaims Célinie Trouvelot, jumping up and down with excitement. Her father is a dairy farmer in nearby Rollot, and her family has produced the local specialty for generations. Félicité, whose own father raises cows in the region, nods in encouragement, and Célinie continues. "When King Louis XIV visited our town and tasted it, he gave it the title *fromage royale!*"

"And royal it is, my sweet Célinie!" Geneviève Deshayes responds proudly, "and we shall all be God's royalty as we share this beautiful day with our guest!" She turns to look at Sophie, who has begun to sing again, this time in gratitude for the simple meal.

After they have eaten, the children run off to play hide-and-seek, allowing the women time to catch up on events of the last several months. It is the first time Sophie has been alone with Geneviève Deshayes and Félicité Desmarquet since their early days together in Amiens. Félicité has been head of the house in Cuignières for six years; Geneviève, who has been here with her for the past eighteen months, still considers Sophie's health her personal responsibility.

"You are warm enough?" Geneviève asks.

"*Mais oui, ma fille!*" Sophie responds, opening her arms to the summer sun as if to ask how she could be anything but comfortable. One would hardly guess that only months before she had come close to death. A fever, undoubtedly helped along by the political intrigue in Amiens, left her bedridden for many weeks, and she has been sent to the Picardy countryside to regain her strength.

"So we've truly lost the house in Ghent?" Félicité asks.

"Yes," Sophie replies sadly, seeing again the two carriages that had pulled up in front of the Oratory eight months before. Six weeping French nuns and little Sophie Dussaussoy, her niece, until that moment a student at the school in Ghent, had tumbled out into the December darkness. Sophie had collapsed the next morning. "They are convinced that I'm a shameless Gallican whose first loyalties are to France."

"One can almost forgive them," Geneviève says brusquely. "Napoleon *did* imprison their bishop for four years. Let's not even mention his treatment of Pope Pius."

"But surely they can't believe that Sophie is conspiring with the French bishops!" Félicité protests.

Sophie ignores the remark and continues. "There is enormous pressure on the house to become autonomous. The city of Ghent is now free from French control and about to become part of a new political alliance. It will undoubtedly become part of the Netherlands. At any rate, *c'est fait*. It's done. There's nothing we can do. But that makes our loss no less grievous, and I fear the loss of other houses now that we are so, shall we say"—she pauses a moment and raises a dark eyebrow—"embroiled."

The other two women know what she is referring to. Since his departure, Saint Estève has been spinning his web of deception, tightening his hold over the house at Amiens and doing whatever he can to discredit Sophie in France and in Rome. For months, a series of accusatory letters has been churning from his pen in Rome, setting off waves of collateral correspondence between and among Joseph Varin, the Jesuit Provincials in Paris and Rome, the Chaplain to King Louis XVIII, and Sophie herself. Sophie has been waiting eight months for a response from the Italian Jesuit Provincial regarding the official status of Saint Estève's Roman convent.

"So what's the latest news from Amiens?" Geneviève asks, remembering her last unhappy days there before being shunted off to Grenoble by Anne Baudemont.

"Charlotte writes that he hasn't given up luring her two daughters off to Rome. Eugénie tells her that Madame de Sambucy, Madame Copina, and Madame Baudemont plan to join him there soon, and that she won't be far behind. He's procured a house for them and promises that all is about to be resolved in his favor."

The other two women look at Sophie with growing horror.

In an effort to relieve their anxiety, she smiles coyly and adds, "Charlotte has told Eugénie that if she leaves, she'll follow her all the way to Rome and stay there until she comes to her senses."

The next morning a letter arrives bearing seals from the College of Rome. Sophie opens it quickly, hoping it is the response she's been waiting for from Father Panizonni, the Jesuit Provincial. She walks into the community room, where Geneviève Deshayes is mending a child's pinafore. Suddenly Geneviève hears her gasp and fall heavily into a chair.

"What is it, Sophie?" she asks, running to her side and feeling her forehead to determine if she has fallen into a fever.

Sophie pulls herself away and rescans the final page, gasping once again when she reads the signature. Then she looks up at the worried face above her own and simply shakes her head. Geneviève takes the letter and reads it through as Sophie stares at the brilliant sunlight streaming through the window.

"Please read the last paragraph aloud to me, *chère Geneviève*. Perhaps then I shall believe it."

Geneviève begins to read, her voice shaking with rage.

"'I warn you, madam, that you will incur the excommunication invoked by the Council of Trent upon the pernicious and detestable custom of certain women who, not living under an approved Rule, wish to pass as religious in the eyes of the public." She sputters for a moment, then recovers. "Your fate is in your own hands. Your submission and deference to the wishes of the Holy Father and your adherence to Monsieur de Saint Estève's convent in Rome will be pleasing to God and helpful for union and peace; it will edify your sisters and be appreciated by your friends.' It is signed Stephanelli, College of Rome, on behalf of his Excellency Father Panizonni."

The two women look at each other in shocked silence as the sunlight dances in mindless oblivion around them. "Excommunication." "Pernicious and detestable." "Certain women." After a moment, unable to find words to combat those that echo like the voice of doom off the walls of her heart, Sophie breaks down in tears.

During the days that follow, Sophie, now back in Paris, receives endless advice from Joseph Varin, Father de Montaigne, and the king's chaplain, Father Louis Perreau. Stephanelli, meanwhile, has sent copies of the damning letter to the houses in Amiens, Grenoble, Niort and Poitiers. In early September she receives a letter from Eugénie de Gramont that Madame de Sambucy and Madame Copina have left Amiens and joined Saint Estève in Rome.

But there are aspects of Stephanelli's letter that don't ring true.

All of Sophie's advisors have personal familiarity with conspiracy, both as its victim and as its agent, and they have little trouble recognizing its face when it appears. When one of them points out that Stephanelli has included no documentation in the letter to back up his claims, Sophie composes a strong letter demanding proof of its allegations. When another makes inquiries into the identity of Father Stephanelli, no one in Rome can verify the existence of any such person. Madame Charlotte de Gramont d'Aster, invoking the glamorous cachet of her aristocratic roots, writes a letter of her own to the French Ambassador.

In mid-September word arrives that Stephanelli's identity has finally been unveiled. The writer of the letter is none other than Father Sambucy de Saint Estève, who in an act of apparent desperation has Italianized his surname and resorted to counterfeit threats.

After relieving Saint Estève of his secretarial position, the French Ambassador writes an apologetic letter to Sophie, informing her that "Rome does not proceed so quickly; congregations are proved before they are approved."

$\mathcal{R}$esolution

Winter, 1815

WHEN THE STORM HAD FINALLY PASSED, SOPHIE HELD A SECOND General Council in Paris. Its purpose was the establishment of official Constitutions for the Society. Ten councilors, two from each school, met for a period of six weeks to discuss and amend what she and Joseph Varin had drafted two years earlier in Besançon. Varin and another Jesuit priest, Father Julien Duilhet, helped to direct the discussions.

I met with her for lunch on the day after the official signing of documents.

"*Salut, ma belle!*" I began, lifting a glass of the wine from Joigny I'd brought to celebrate the occasion. "To The Society of the Sacred Heart of Jesus!"

Among other resolutions, the Society was now to bear the name of its original impulse.

She lifted her glass to meet mine and smiled a smile that could have dazzled Jesus himself, had he been seated at our table.

"*À la Société du Sacré Coeur de Jésus!*" she replied, her eyes shining, and we ducked momentarily into our youth as the crisp, floral flavors of the *vin gris* mingled on our palates. We were back on the Côte de Saint Jacques before the world had shifted beneath our feet.

"I hear the great Monsignor de Talleyrand-Périgord is to be the Society's official protector," I said, with perhaps an ounce too much reverence.

Sophie chastened me with a raised eyebrow and then laughed. "Yes, though he's delegated his function to Father Perreau." Perreau had been instrumental in exposing the Stephanelli deception and was furthermore an old friend of Joseph Varin.

"Even better," I replied. "Louis must be pleased with his little sister."

"I don't know that Louis is ever truly 'pleased' with anything," she responded, laughing again. I knew what Sophie meant but would not say—that Louis found any kind of pleasure to be a sin. "But I know he's relieved that Saint Estève is out of the way," she continued.

"For the moment," I cautioned. "He's not the type to give up easily, but his wings have at least been clipped."

We went on to discuss her plans for bringing Amiens back into the fold. By now Anne Baudemont had flown south to join Saint Estève's community in Rome, and Sophie was engaged in the delicate process of winning Eugénie de Gramont over to her side. She had already named her to represent Amiens at the General Council.

"She has enormous potential to lead our little Society forward," she stated, "and with the most loyal of Saint Estève's followers now gone from Amiens, I believe she will be a force for unity there."

I nodded, though I wondered how this imperious young noblewoman would ever be able to fulfill Sophie's vision of humble service to the heart of God. Her readiness to betray Sophie in favor of Saint Estève did not bode well, but there was something in the young aristocrat that strongly appealed to Sophie, and I knew it was useless to question her decision.

"And when will you be moving to Paris?" I asked.

"As soon as we can find a suitable building," she replied. "We need room for both a novitiate and a school, and you know as well as I that finding property in Paris has become close to impossible!"

I remembered our thwarted attempt to buy l'Abbaye aux Bois eleven years earlier and shook my head. I still counted it one of my greatest failures. "Let me see what I can do," I replied. "There's a property near Saint Étienne du Mont coming available. It's small and needs lots of work, but there's a lovely courtyard with a large elder tree in the center. I can see you there with your rosary and your Beloved."

She smiled and looked down, embarrassed at my abrupt intrusion into her intimate life.

Ignoring my final remark, she added, "And Philippine is here now as part of the General Council, and *no* one wields a hammer or glazes a window better than our Mother Duchesne!" Sophie laughed gently, remembering her friend's tireless labors at Sainte-Marie d'en-Haut. "Perhaps she'll even paint us a mural or two!"

She took another sip of the wine and then looked at me solemnly. "Now please give me news of Célestine."

Sophie's lengthy illness, coupled with the Stephanelli crisis, had curtailed communication with her friends and family for many months. It had been over two years since she'd last seen either Célestine or Marie, and our own conversations during that time had been few, brief, and focused entirely on business.

"She is well," I replied, refilling my glass and wondering how to phrase my response. "But her life has changed dramatically as you might imagine."

"You refer, of course, to Eugène de Beauharnais," she answered quickly. "What has become of him?"

"His father-in-law advised him well. He returned to Munich after Napoleon's Kingdom of Italy collapsed and riots in Milan forced him out as Viceroy."

"And what was his response to Napoleon's coup?"

"He stayed out of it," I replied.

She nodded approvingly. "So where does that leave Célestine?" she finally asked, her voice taking on a certain anticipatory edge.

"Where do you think? There's no way for Eugène to return to France. Maximilian will award him a Bavarian duchy. And his wife is pregnant with their sixth child."

Sophie stared at me. Feeling momentarily out of my depth, I added, "But he's left Célestine a very rich woman."

Her expression deepened, and I guessed what she was thinking. I started to qualify my statement, but she interrupted me before I could open my mouth.

"A very rich woman, depending on how you define 'rich.' And *la petite* Héloïse? She'll remain with Marie, I hope?"

I nodded. "Of course. She'll stay in Paris, though it seems likely she'll continue visiting her cousins in Munich. She's very close to the two older girls."

"And when will she be told they are her sisters rather than her cousins?" Sophie's tone was slightly acerbic.

"That's for Marie and Eugène to decide, and I suspect it will be later rather than sooner. If ever."

Part 7

Paris

Departures and Returns

1816 – 1820

IN THE WAKE OF ITS SECOND GENERAL COUNCIL *The Society of the Sacred Heart of Jesus* blossoms like a rose, and Philippine Duchesne takes her first steps into missionary glory.

Invited to the Council as an official representative from Grenoble, Philippine is elected as the Society's first Secretary General. Shortly after assuming this exalted position, she can be found driving nails, glazing windows, and laying bricks at the new Mother House in the Faubourg Sainte-Geneviève. It is there that she meets Louis DuBourg, Bishop of Louisiana and Seeker of Missionaries, whom she recognizes as her angel of deliverance. When, in Sophie's presence, she throws herself quite literally at the good father's feet, Sophie knows she is vanquished.

Within eight months, Philippine is traveling south to Bordeaux with several companions. Among them are Octavie Berthold, a convert from Calvinism and the daughter of Voltaire's private secretary, and Eugénie Audé, a convert of a different stripe. A dazzling fixture of Napoleon's court when only in her teens, Eugénie stopped one night in her glorious finery to primp in front of a mirror and saw the face of Christ Crucified.

When the women reach Bordeaux, they must wait for the wind to rise. The day before the vernal equinox of 1818, they board a two-masted schooner called the *Rebecca*. The ship moves slowly down the Garonne and two days later opens sail on the Atlantic Ocean. Over seventy days of violent storms, seasickness, slowly rotting food, and general wretchedness will pass before they drop anchor in New Orleans. There, the women take temporary shelter with the Ursuline sisters. When Philippine recovers from the miseries of scurvy, the intrepid team of five begins a forty-day trip up the river to St. Louis, passing plantations, cotton fields, and scenes of a world none of them could have imagined. When they arrive, they are greeted by a frontier town boasting four streets and a bustling fur trade.

It will be another twenty-three years before Philippine fulfills her dream of working with the native people of North America. She will be seventy-one years old.

~

As Philippine is replenishing her Vitamin C in New Orleans, Sophie's little Society is expanding eastward into the Kingdom of Sardinia.

Despite the wary eye he has been known to cast on those "formidable ladies of the Sacred Heart," Chambéry's amiable Abbé Curtet is beginning to change his mind. Perhaps because Savoy, free at last from Napoleonic domination, is now settling into its former status as part of the Kingdom of Sardinia. Perhaps because he has visited nearby Sainte Marie d'en Haut and been swept away by Thérèse Maillucheau. Whatever his reasons, he has decided there *must* be a Sacred Heart school in Chambéry, the old capital of the Dukes of Savoy that stands at the foothills of the French Alps. He and Thérèse have already procured a site.

Sophie is familiar with Thérèse's expansive if not always measured enthusiasms. A bit of the Bordeaux Artemis still remains, and Sophie wonders if Father Curtet is not perhaps a kindred spirit. For this reason, she decides to leave Paris and oversee the opening personally.

When she arrives in Grenoble, Thérèse greets her with a curious amalgam of joy and hesitation. "*Ma Mère,* welcome back into our humble community!" She ends with an awkward curtsy.

"My darling Thérèse!" Sophie answers, sensing already that something is amiss. "How wonderful to be back on Philippine's dear mountain!" The two embrace, and Thérèse explodes her grenade.

"I fear I have bad news," she says as the two of them sit down in her small office. Thérèse has headed the novitiate at Sainte-Marie d'en-Haut for over a decade.

Sophie steels herself for the information though nothing in her outward demeanor suggests it.

"It seems that Father Curtet forgot to receive the proper permissions from the Archbishop."

Sophie sits perfectly still. Finally she looks up and smiles, remembering once again that practicalities are not Thérèse's forte.

"If God wishes us to have a school in Chambéry, God will see to it that we have it, *non?*" Sophie replies lightly, though she is filling with a sense of dread. "If not, we shall spend many quiet hours among our beautiful acacias and pray that our Philippine has arrived safely in Louisiana."

The next day, the Abbé Curtet, flushed with victory and emanating an ebullient faith that even Sophie finds irresistible, arrives with the necessary documents.

"I have them, *chère madame!*" he exclaims, waving a sheaf of official-looking papers with one hand as he helps her into the carriage with the other. "You see how the Lord works in strange and mysterious ways! It is all arranged! It is all arranged!"

She and Thérèse take their places in his carriage; Joséphine Bigeu and a young Savoyard novice climb into another. Once they are outside the city walls, Father Curtet insists on changing places with the driver and lashes the horses into a high-speed trot, leaving Joséphine and the novice quite literally in the dust.

Sophie wonders again whether the worthy Abbé and Thérèse Maillucheau might not be twins separated at birth.

They pass through forests of chestnut trees and begin their way through a valley framed by the savage crests of the Chartreuse Mountains and the more gentle contours of the Belledonne. Despite their apparent difference in temperament, the snowy peaks of one seem to

sing their brilliance across the sky to the other, and at one point the Abbé shouts excitedly that from the eastern side of the Belledonne, one can discern the shape of a mother holding a child in her arms.

When they stop at a small village to rest and feed the horses, Sophie follows the animals into the stable. Moments later the groom arrives with a loaf of coarse bread and a large bowl of wine.

"Might I share a bit of your meal?" she asks briskly.

"*Mais oui*," the man answers, slightly taken aback, and offers her a large chunk from the loaf.

She breaks off a bite-size piece and motions toward his cup of wine. His face breaks into a smile, and they both laugh as he extends it toward her.

At this moment Joséphine Bigeu arrives breathlessly and out of humor. "At *last* I find you, Sophie! We are waiting for you at the inn! The luncheon is all prepared!"

"But we have already eaten, you see," she answers gaily, motioning to the horses and the groom and placing the wine-soaked bread in her mouth with gusto, as if to bring any further conversation to a close.

When they arrive at the old convent of St. Clare, they find that the Abbé's young seminarians have been cleaning and preparing the abandoned site for several days. Their host, whose excitement has not abated in the slightest, shows them proudly into the cloister garden at the end of the tour and serves them a *gâteau Savoyard* that he has had made especially for them.

"*Voilà, Mesdames!*" he cries as one of the seminarians arrives with a tall, golden cake garnished with a cheery rosebud. "To celebrate your foundation at Chambéry and the many graces you will bring to the region by your presence!" He punctuates his statement with a courtly bow, and the women's appreciative laughter mingles with the water flowing from a small fountain in the center of the garden. A white cat appears from nowhere and approaches the group as if to requisition cake that is rightfully hers.

It is only moments later that a messenger arrives and whispers something into the Abbé's ear. His smiling demeanor shifts, and he looks at his guests with a mixture of disappointment and concern.

"It appears that the Archbishop wishes to see us. He's just had a visitor from Rome. A Madame Anne Baudemont."

Sophie feels a collective shudder pass within herself and her companions. She knows that Saint Estève has not stopped operating in Rome, even after being exposed as a poseur and dismissed from the French Ambassador's service. She knows, too, that his house is struggling, and that Anne Baudemont has been trying with minimal success to recruit new members to their community. Sophie has no inkling, however, that she has been seeking postulants in Savoy.

Archbishop Irénée-Yves De Solle greets them courteously and asks to speak alone with Sophie. She follows him into his large, well-appointed office and ponders with practiced resignation the Cross.

"I am sorry to have to call this meeting," the Archbishop opens, motioning her into a seat across from his immense armchair. "But I received a visit from Madame Anne Baudemont just this morning. She is staying here with the Governor, whose wife escorted her personally to the palace this morning."

The Archbishop stops as if he expects Sophie to respond, but she only nods and waits for him to continue.

"She is seeking postulants for her order in Rome, and in discussing this with me, she related an interesting story about your Society of the Sacred Heart."

"Yes," Sophie finally speaks, "I am quite sure that she would have, given our lengthy association in Amiens."

"And what, if you please, was that association, madame?" he inquires politely, clearly uncomfortable with his mission.

Sophie proceeds to relate the story of Saint Estève and Baudemont's days in Amiens with as much generosity as possible, omitting anything that would cast a negative light on either of them and allowing for Anne Baudemont's perfect right to solicit members for her Roman community in Savoy.

When she has finished, the archbishop leans back in his chair and assumes a look that combines respect, relief and pleasure. "It is as I supposed, madame, but you surely understand my position. I must make

further inquiries, and indeed I have already sent messages to Paris and Rome so that I might understand the situation more clearly."

"I understand of course, your Excellency," Sophie responds, wondering if—like some Dark Angel—Saint Estève will forever stalk her work. "I shall remain here in Chambéry until the matter has been settled, and I thank you for coming to me directly for clarification."

The archbishop bows and watches with a certain wonder as his diminutive visitor rejoins her associates and disappears down the chestnut-lined drive.

Before another year is out, there will be, in addition to Chambéry, four more new foundations: in Quimper, Lyon, Bordeaux, and St. Charles, Missouri.

The Hôtel Biron

1820

AT AGE EIGHTEEN, CATHERINE ANTOINETTE SALINGUERRA DE Gayardon de Fenoyl was married in a sumptuous ceremony to Louis Charles René, the Count de Marboeuf. He—a general under three French kings and now military governor of the island of Corsica—was seventy-one. Rumor had it that in addition to serving as Napoleon Bonaparte's godfather, he had earlier served as something more to Napoleon's mother Lucrezia and was in all probability the boy's father. On the day of her marriage, Catherine could hardly have known that her unacknowledged stepson, then only fourteen, would be indirectly responsible for her own son's death. But she doubtless had other things on her mind as she knelt at the altar with a man fifty-three years her senior.

The good count had the good taste to die within three years, leaving her with an enormous government pension and an infant son and daughter. Laurent-François moved quickly up the ranks of Napoleon's military, and when he perished in November of 1812 from wounds received on the march from Moscow, the Emperor made her a Baroness

of the Empire and doubled her income. This did not compensate her for the loss of her child.

A few years after Laurent-François' death, in an act designed to counterbalance his lack of the final sacraments, the Countess de Marboeuf entered the Society of the Sacred Heart under an assumed name. She was fifty-two years old.

When Sophie summoned me to attend a "critical finance meeting" on the rue de l'Arbalète, I was unprepared for the presence of the woman whose decision had been the talk of Parisian society for months. Enrobed in black but veiled in the white of a novice, she sat regally on one of two large fauteuils that faced Sophie's desk in the Mother House. Sophie introduced her only as Sister Catherine, adding that she was "our newly appointed ambassador to King Louis." Moments later I realized I was in the presence of the famous countess, whose family traced its ancestry back to fifteenth-century Brittany. The lively charms that had allowed her to dazzle both the *Ancien Régime* and the Empire had not diminished under Sophie's tutelage.

"So what might be the nature of this particular embassy?" I asked, noting a complicit smile that passed between the two women. It was clear that I was there as a functionary whose stolid presence would assure that legal protocols were followed. The imaginative piece was entirely theirs.

"We have an idea that might help us to purchase the Hôtel Biron," Sophie replied.

I groaned aloud at the mention of it.

Since the establishment of the Mother House in Paris four years earlier, the number of students and novices had grown exponentially. Within two years, the first house on the rue des Postes was bursting at the seams. The purchase of a second building on the rue de l'Arbalète had allowed the novitiate to move into separate quarters. But crowded conditions persisted, and the death of several students and novices during a recent epidemic made it clear that larger, airier quarters were needed.

"Monsieur Lorrain," the white-veiled countess responded graciously, "Madame de Charost is offering it to us at a very low price, surely you must see that."

"Madame," I bowed in her direction. "Seven hundred thousand francs is not what I consider a 'very low price' within the overall financial scheme of the Society."

"She understands that, Guy," Sophie interrupted, "and in fact Madame de Charost has just lowered it. But hear us out, please."

I was shocked to hear Sophie argue in favor of the acquisition, given her initial response to the building and its price.

"How will the world view our little Society if we move into such a setting?" she had asked weeks earlier when the Hôtel Biron was first forwarded as a possible location. Indeed I wondered how Parisians would reconcile a vow of poverty with an establishment whose opulence was legendary—and whose recent owners included a dissolute young aristocrat whose gatherings had lent the place a whiff of scandal.

We had spoken at length about the impression such surroundings would create, one that implied an intimate link between the Society and the corridors of wealth and power. Among other drawbacks was its physical setting. The Hôtel Biron was situated in the Faubourg Saint-Germain, a bastion of Ultra-royalists, many of whom still held fervently to the Divine Right of the King of France to rule his mortal subjects.

"I thought you were against acquiring the property on the grounds of its being too lavish," I protested. "How will this appear to outsiders?"

Sophie dropped her head and clasped her hands together on her desk, squeezing them together as if to wring patience from her weary palms.

"Guy, we've been over this already. Several times. And while it of *course* matters to me what outsiders will think, we *cannot* allow public perception to drive our decision." She clenched her fingers together several more times and then looked up. "I've spoken with the entire community. I've consulted several bishops. We have weighed the pros and cons and find no other solution. If you have an alternate location to offer us, please let me know what it is. I am *more* than ready to consider a reasonable alternative."

I'd been looking at properties for several months and could only shrug my shoulders.

"We *must* have more space and fresh air for the children," she continued. "I know the dangers we are running, Guy, and yes, even with the reduction, it is an enormous amount of money, but—"

At this point, the White Countess intervened. "Monsieur Lorrain, you know that we've already received one hundred fifty thousand francs from families and individuals who would like to see the school established there."

"Of *course* they would!" I shot back. "The Hôtel feels just like *home* to them!" I knew that the Countess's dowry alone had been in excess of 50,000 francs, and the school was attracting more and more members of the old aristocracy who had returned to France, their fortunes largely intact.

"It is more than that, monsieur," she demurred, speaking with a voice that mingled wisdom, persuasion and infinite tolerance of my social naiveté. "The Society needs to be successful in Paris. It sounds superficial, I know, but an establishment such as the Hôtel Biron will attract both students and novices. Sophie is making a new start in Paris, and there are many people here who want to support her work." She tilted her head and smiled in a way that promised our imminent agreement. "You know that a school which attracts the aristocracy and the upper bourgeoisie will enable her to open more establishments for the poor. And surely *all* of these children have a right to the immense spiritual gifts the Society has to offer them. They are all, even the little countesses and princesses, the children of God, *non*?"

Rather than answer her I glanced over at Sophie, who was giving me the kind of look generally bestowed on me by my sisters.

"So what great plot are the two of you fomenting?" I asked, knowing defeat when it stared me in the face.

Sophie smiled and said "We're sending Sister Catherine to King Louis to ask him for a hundred thousand francs!"

It was not without surprise that I heard the news: the White Countess, in the company of her son-in-law, caught Louis in a jocular and open-handed mood and accomplished her mission with relative ease. I helped arrange a low-interest loan for the balance due, and on the Feast of Saint Francis the religious moved into the servants quarters and stables. Two weeks later the students moved into the Hôtel's grand apartments—but only after Sophie had ordered every mirror, every mural, and (except for the chapel) every ounce of gilding removed from the premises.

Eugénie de Gramont

1820

WHEN EUGÉNIE DE GRAMONT ARRIVES IN PARIS FOR THE GENERAL Council of 1815, she is twenty-seven years old and still in thrall to Louis de Sambucy de Saint Estève. While Sophie has selected her as an official representative from Amiens, Eugénie has little affection for her Superior General. In fact, she has not yet fully abandoned her plan of joining Saint Estève's community in Rome.

Despite the deformity that has twisted her upper spine since birth, she is a young woman of enormous charm—provided one is of her class. This personal magnetism is coupled with a strong capacity for leadership, and Sophie believes that these qualities, accompanied by her illustrious family name, will serve the Society well as it attempts to establish itself in Paris. She decides, despite advice to the contrary, to name Eugénie head of the new school.

Geneviève Deshayes and Félicité Desmarquest remember Eugénie's behavior in Amiens and fail to understand how Sophie can trust her with such responsibility.

Father Perreau warns Sophie to keep the novices away from Eugénie's worldly influence.

Joséphine Bigeu, who has been charged with the novitiate in Paris, asks herself how she and Eugénie will ever be able to work together effectively as colleagues: Joséphine is resolutely middle class.

When Eugénie is finally installed in her new position, Thérèse Mailluchau becomes increasingly concerned about the many hours Sophie and she are now spending together. "People are gossiping in the other houses, Sophie," she writes. "You must not show her such preference."

Others watch and say nothing.

Sophie, however, finds herself in thrall to the young aristocrat, a woman whose inner contradictions bespeak a complexity that both fascinates and repels her. She is almost ten years younger than Sophie, but exile and loss have lent her a strange sort of wisdom that belies her years. Her religious vows clash with the glamour of her worldly connections, and Sophie often wonders what residual memory of monastic life before the Revolution might have motivated her decision to join the Society. In spite of (or perhaps because of) her own petit bourgeois origins, Sophie is fascinated by the aristocracy and enjoys her relationship with all the de Gramont women. But there is something special about Eugénie. Perhaps it is that coexistence within her of deformity and allure. Sophie has always been drawn to woundedness as an exemplar of Christ's suffering, and in Eugénie she finds, perhaps, an avatar of her Beloved. What Eugénie finds in Sophie remains to be seen.

The two of them will eventually develop pet nicknames for one another, and at times Sophie feels she may have found a new Célestine: another human soul with whom she might share her deepest aspirations and secrets, but who has also reawakened an inner spirit of playfulness that Sophie thought had died with the Revolution.

Having drawn her first breath at the Palace of Versailles, Eugénie de Gramont feels perfectly at home in the Hôtel Biron. One might imagine that a tiny sigh escaped her lips when she saw the gilding disappear from its walls and ceilings. The magnificent building, designed in 1728 for a financier who wished to build the most magnificent house in Paris, sits on the rue de Varenne, close to where it intersects the Boulevard des Invalides. Formal gardens surround it on three sides, and only steps

away the Esplanade des Invalides, complete with its golden-domed edifice, extends majestically to the Seine.

Here Eugénie is surrounded by the world into which she was born. Her uncle, the Duc de Gramont, lives in a vast hôtel not four blocks away. The school is visited almost daily by the highest members of the aristocracy, most of whom Eugénie welcomes personally and with all the affectations of the mistress of the manor.

On a blustery day in late November, 1820, the young Duchess of Berry, widow of the king's recently assassinated nephew, arrives at the Hôtel Biron along with Marie-Antoinette's daughter, the Duchess of Angoulême.

"*Soyez les bienvenues, majestés,*" Eugénie says in greeting, sinking to the ground in a deep curtsy.

The duchesses express their wish to visit the temporary chapel, and when they arrive in the Salon de la Rotonde, they find Sophie there alone, lost in prayer. The women cross themselves and kneel before the makeshift altar, and it is only when they get up to leave that Sophie notices their presence. She rises with an imperceptible air of annoyance and follows them out of the chapel, where Eugénie formally introduces them.

"I congratulate you on the recent birth of your miracle child," Sophie says to the young duchess. She refers to Marie-Caroline de Bourbon's newborn son, born seven months after her husband was stabbed outside the Paris Opera House. The infant—Henri Charles Ferdinand Marie Dieudonné d'Artois—is now third in line to the French throne, and the French Ultra-royalists consider him a gift from God.

"*Merci, madame,*" Marie-Caroline responds in a low voice, curtsying slightly in deference to this tiny woman about whom all Paris is talking. Eugénie grimaces. The duchess is known for her lack of ceremony—she is rumored to have swum in the ocean and is famous for breaking into operatic arias at the slightest provocation. Such departures from protocol make Eugénie nervous.

After paying her compliments to the Duchess of Angoulême, whose dour temperament appeals to Eugénie's sensibilities, Sophie proposes that they all take a stroll through the gardens. As they move between hedges of clipped boxwood and allées of graceful linden trees, Sophie and Marie-Caroline at one point lose themselves in the beauty of a small bed of asters, still flowering at this late date. Marie-Caroline—born in Sicily and raised in Palermo and Naples—lives up to her reputation and bursts into an aria from Rossini's *Barber of Seville*. Sophie, whose taste in music does not extend to comic opera, is nevertheless struck by the duchess's mezzo-soprano voice as she runs down the scales of "*Contro un cor che accende amore.*" And the notion of a heart flaming with love, though its object in Sophie's case is worlds removed from a Spanish barber, is something she profoundly understands.

A group of little girls suddenly emerges from one of the classrooms to see who is breaking the silence of the garden. One of them recognizes the younger woman, whose recent tragedy has made her an iconic figure for all of Paris, and as if on cue each child places right foot in front of left, gracefully lifts the sides of her skirt, bends her left knee all the way to the ground, and bows her beribboned head.

Eugénie smiles in spite of herself at the courtly perfection of her young protégées.

Before the two women leave, they pledge to contribute to the building of a permanent chapel.

That night after dinner Sophie calls Eugénie to her room.

"I am pleased, *ma chère fille*, at the work you are doing here," she opens. "The children's behavior in the garden today was one more example of the high standards you are developing within them, and it is clear that our two duchesses went away with nothing but positive feelings."

Eugénie, who has seated herself in one of the two chairs Sophie has brought into the tiny room, nods her head to acknowledge the compliment, wondering what she really wishes to discuss. "I believe they will do what they say regarding the chapel," she offers in response, "and I suspect they will stimulate other donations. They told me the king may even donate an altar."

"Indeed," Sophie replies, "and this is all to the good."

She chooses her next words with care.

"But I must open my heart to you, *ma chère.*" She feels Eugénie stiffen. "While these visits do much to draw attention to our work, I am fearful about their possible consequences."

"What do you mean?"

"You know what I mean. We've discussed it many times. And I am even more fearful of these consequences since moving into such elegant surroundings."

Eugénie pauses a moment to look at the servants' quarters that surround them. The sign over Sophie's doorway still says *Baker;* Eugénie's reads *Blacksmith.*

"People are identifying us with reactionary politics. With the Ultras. Such a political connection, as you well know, has *nothing* to do with our Society's vision or intention." At this point, Sophie's face loses its composure and assumes an expression of intense sorrow. Despite her growing love for Eugénie, she has little faith that she will understand her feelings—or that if she does, she will wish to modify such a perception.

"People believe what they wish to believe," Eugénie responds evenly.

"But we must do everything we can *not* to encourage such a belief, Eugénie!" Sophie responds quickly, her grief giving way to exasperation. "Surely you see that!"

"So what do you want me to do, *ma mère?*"

The question is simple, but beneath its simplicity are layers of resentment, anger, and aristocratic entitlement that are fairly blooming in their new surroundings.

"There are several things, *ma fille*. Let us begin with the instruction itself."

If Eugénie was rigid before, she now becomes a marble statue.

Sophie continues. "You know that we've just ended another General Council whose primary purpose was to discuss our Plan of Studies."

Eugénie nods her head sullenly. All efforts to camouflage her feelings have ceased.

"Monsieur Loriquet was quite firm about the curriculum we must maintain if the schools are to uphold their reputation."

Father Loriquet, who consulted on the Society's first Plan of Studies in Amiens, has designed the curriculum now followed in all Jesuit schools in France. He has been a key presence at the recent Council.

"I have noted," Sophie goes on, "that the school in Paris is lacking in many of the areas taught elsewhere. Perhaps too much time is being spent on dancing, music and drawing? Perhaps we could do without so many charades and tableaux vivants and other such elaborate theatricals? Perhaps more time could be devoted to spelling and mathematics and the sciences?"

"We spend a great deal of time on religious practices, *ma mère*. Our masses, devotions, processions, confessions—all of these are at the center of our educational program."

"I am aware of this. But I am speaking of studies. These young women need to learn to *think*—to develop their sense of logic and *reason*!"

"We also need to prepare them to live in the world of high society which they will soon inhabit," was the icy reply.

"Precisely! They will be moving in circles where great ideas are shared, and they must be part of the conversation! They are not fixtures to stand beside their husbands and fondle their ropes of pearls. This may have been Napoleon's program, but it is *not* ours."

At this point, Sophie's eyes are shooting cinders, and Eugénie knows better than to argue back. She also knows that she has arranged to meet with two bishops and the Vicar General of Paris the next morning, and that three countesses of the House of Orléans are coming for afternoon tea. She wonders when she will ever have time to train teachers.

"And there is one more thing, *ma chère*."

"*Oui?*"

"It concerns the nieces of Philippine Duchesne and Félicité Desmarquest, both of whom are seeking admission to the school here."

"*Oui?*"

"It seems that you have suggested the girls will not be welcome because of their bourgeois origins?"

At this point Eugénie refuses her even the monosyllable.

"If you recall, I am the daughter of a barrel maker." Here, Sophie stands and draws herself up to her full four feet ten inches. "Our schools are not sanctuaries for the elite, Eugénie, despite the grandeur of our current location. Please arrange for their admission at once."

"*Oui, ma mère.*" The ersatz Countess of Gramont d'Aster moves out of her chair with as much dignity as she can muster and walks out the door.

As she sits alone in her baker's quarters, Sophie wonders once again what her life might have been as a Carmelite. Never has she been so surrounded by people—and never has she felt so alone.

Intrigues

1820

WHEN THE BOURBON MONARCHY WAS RE-RESTORED IN 1815, Joseph Fouché saw little reason to resign his post as Minister of Police, despite a lifetime of service to the king's enemies. During the first several months of his reign, Louis XVIII, needing Fouché's knowledge and expertise, overlooked the fact that the man had voted to guillotine his older brother. Fouché took the king's seeming approbation of his violent methods as license to unleash a period of "White Terror." For several months, anyone suspected of Republican or Bonapartist sympathies was at risk of imprisonment, assassination, or worse. The ultimate irony of the Minister's position, coupled with the pitiless ferocity of his tactics, finally caused Louis to dismiss him.

Joseph Fouché retired to Trieste and was never heard from again.

Denis Marmaton, whose lower profile and endless files of blackmail combined to make him more tolerable from the Royalist point of view, maintained his position in the newly christened Ministry of the Interior. After Fouché's departure, he became top assistant to Fouché's replacement, Elie Decazes—the exquisitely handsome young man who was rumored to be the king's lover.

Though Denis and I hadn't seen each other for several years, our paths crossed at the Opera, resituated in the Salle de la rue Louvois since the Duke of Berry's assassination. The king had ordered the previous Opera House demolished after his nephew's murder. Denis entered my box during the first intermission of Mozart's *Marriage of Figaro* with two glasses of champagne. We spent the first few minutes discussing the inferior acoustics of the new space, and then I saluted his having hung onto his position in the wake of Decazes' recent resignation.

"The man is a fool," he answered.

"But you don't *really* believe he could have engineered the Duke's assassination?" I asked. This was the theory that had provoked the Minister's demise, but it seemed absurd.

"Entirely possible," was Denis' quick response. "He's a man filled with liberal ideas, just like the king. The assassin claimed to be a Bonapartist acting alone, but I see no reason to believe that Decazes wasn't capable of some level of involvement. I've always questioned his devotion to the Restoration, though clearly His Royal Majesty was *slavishly* devoted to him."

I ignored the suggestive tone of his final remark. "That's what the Ultras are putting about, I know, but it makes no sense."

"At the very least his carelessness made it possible," Denis answered curtly. "I warned Decazes that an assassination could happen, but he insisted that bodyguards weren't necessary. That the people of Paris 'adore the royal family.'"

"And yet," I quipped, "I doubt that you yourself lament the good Duke's demise. He promised to be as liberal a force as Louis—perhaps even more so with that free-thinking Italian wife at his side."

Denis merely grunted.

"The assassination ensures that Charles is next in line for the throne," I continued, "and by all accounts the man is a complete throwback to the *Ancien Régime*."

"He's the kind of man who will keep order among a population that is by its very nature incendiary and violent," he retorted sharply. "Surely the past thirty years have taught us that much!"

I often asked myself what unspeakable wound was at the source of Denis' bitterness. Or if he'd simply been born that way, crippled in soul rather than body and seeing only the darkest side of human nature. If anyone had helped to unleash the forces of violence and darkness over the past three decades, it was he.

At my failure to take the bait, he changed topic. "So how goes Marie and her motley ménage, now that I'm no longer admitted beyond the threshold?"

"Héloïse has just entered school at the Hôtel Biron," I responded warily. "The boys are doing very well with tutors at home."

"Ah. The famous Hôtel Biron," he said with an unpleasant laugh. "Good thing the child's family name suggests a connection with the *noblesse d'épée* or she never would have been admitted. One has to marvel at how Mademoiselle Barat has risen in the world, *non?*"

I wondered if the irony ever left his voice.

"And how in the world does my widowed sister manage to pay the tuition?" he continued. "I understand it's enough to keep even many little countesses outside the walls."

"You know that Célestine helps her. Marie's family has been her only concern since Alex died."

"Indeed," he replied, loading his syllables with innuendo and finishing his glass of Veuve Cliquot.

"And you, Denis?" I asked quietly. "Still no progeny of your own to fill that enormous house of yours?"

"Ah, I thought you might ask, though I might well ask the same of you, Guy."

I smiled and waited for him to continue.

"At the age of fifty-two, *oui*," he continued, "it's time to think of leaving one's biological mark on the world." Here he chuckled. "As it happens, I'm at this very moment in what we might call 'nuptial conversations.' With a family that has found itself in straightened circumstances."

I wondered how much his secret files had to do with the family's destitution.

"So who's the lucky woman?" I asked, expecting him to name any one of several well-connected Parisian widows still young enough to give him children.

"I can't reveal her name at the moment; negotiations are still in progress," he said with malignant deliberation. "Suffice it to say that she's at the Hôtel Biron with Héloïse and has just celebrated her seventeenth birthday."

Héloïse and Marie

1820 – 1821

JUST DAYS AFTER HER FIFTEENTH BIRTHDAY, MARIE DE FLAVIGNY arrives at the Hôtel Biron from her grandmother's home in Frankfurt. Several days later, a grand piano is delivered to the spacious rooms that Eugénie de Gramont has assigned her, followed by an Alsatian music teacher the day after that. Eugénie allows him entry but insists that the bi-weekly lessons be chaperoned by one of the novices.

Marie's lineage is mixed. On her father's side, she descends from the old French aristocracy. Her mother, Maria Elisabeth Bethmann, is the daughter of an enormously wealthy German banker. Marie has spent much of her childhood in Frankfurt, where her family is famous for entertaining the intellectual lights of Europe. Among others, Marie has dined with Goethe, Chauteaubriand, and the young folklorists Wilhelm and Jacob Grimm. As a result she brings a curious mind and high expectations to her school in Paris. She also brings a romantic spirit that will one day cause her to abandon her husband and daughters and run off with Franz Liszt.

When Héloïse de Beixedon hears the second movement of Beethoven's *Pathétique Sonata* wafting from the room next door, she thinks she is perhaps already dead and ascended into heaven. When she meets Marie that night at dinner, she knows it.

The two girls immediately discover their mutual love for Germany and its language, a fact that causes Eugénie de Gramont to consider them a common enemy. The girls reciprocate by becoming inseparable, speaking German at every opportunity, and dedicating themselves to making her life miserable.

"You *know* who she is," Marie states one night after the girls have escaped into Marie's roomy quarters.

"Who?"

"She is the wicked witch of *Hansel and Gretel*! You *know* she must be fattening up little girls *somewhere* in this colossal house!"

When Héloïse looks at her blankly, Marie repeats with theatrical fervor a story Jacob Grimm recently told at the Bethmann dining table. As she narrates the children's arrival at the gingerbread cottage, she introduces a witch who bears a striking resemblance to their headmistress. "She has *bony* hands and a *hunch* back and a *hoarse*, rasping voice and *cold* grey eyes that practically *hypnotize* any child who comes near her!"

Héloïse claps her hands in recognition, and the two of them shriek with malicious delight at the image of Eugénie de Gramont preying on children abandoned in the Black Forest.

"I don't see how Antoinette can possibly be her sister," Marie says when the story is over and the witch is cooked in her own oven.

"I know. She's so lovely and so kind." Héloïse, homesick and chafing under the stringent rules laid down by Eugénie, has come to identify Antoinette de Gramont with her own mother.

"I shall always consider her the Eternal Feminine," Marie says dramatically. She is in thrall to the tempestuous swells of German Romanticism and hopes to write novels one day. "Antoinette shall be one of my heroines. A beautiful nun locked away in a convent because her parents refuse to let her marry the man she loves!"

"No!" Héloïse retorts. "Because her evil sister is jealous and wants to marry him *herself*, even though she's so ugly no one would ever want her!"

The girls collapse in laughter once again, reveling in the dark pleasure provided by a common enemy, particularly when one is fifteen and the enemy is one's warden.

"Do you know what I just learned?" Héloïse suddenly asks. "Tomorrow is Antoinette's birthday! What shall we do for her?"

"Let's buy her the most *beautiful* bouquet in Paris! Herr Ludècke comes for my lesson in the morning, and I can send him out afterwards to buy flowers!"

Marie is already discovering that men will do almost anything she asks of them.

The girls spend the rest of the evening picking apart their schoolmates and critiquing the level of studies they have found at the Hôtel Biron. Héloïse's continuing sojourns in the ducal palace of Eugène de Beauharnais bear a strong similarity to Marie's life with the Bethmanns, and neither child has found at the school the intellectual ambiance she had anticipated. They blame this, too, on their headmistress, who has become a lightning rod for every disappointment in their young lives.

The next day, just before afternoon classes are to begin, Eugénie finds Marie and Héloïse reading Goethe's *Sufferings of Young Werther*. After confiscating the book, she demands that Marie follow her to her private offices.

"Mademoiselle de Flavigny," she opens, motioning the girl to remain standing as the syllables suspend themselves in the air like a hangman's rope.

"*Oui*," Marie responds, knowing full well that she is meant to remain obediently silent.

"You will *not* present my sister with the insulting bouquet of flowers that arrived this morning, and you will furthermore apologize to the entire school for indulging in an affection and a behavior that are *entirely* inappropriate!"

Marie looks directly at her headmistress and replies with a single syllable.

"You dare to defy my authority?" The voice shrills through the room, and Marie begins to smile in spite of herself, thinking of gingerbread and the Black Forest.

"Take that grin off your face!" Eugénie makes a move toward her but Marie stands her ground.

"I will not apologize, for I have done nothing wrong." Marie's voice is even, and she looks Eugénie directly in the eye.

"Then you will have no meals until you do."

As events unroll, Marie de Flavigny eats nothing for several days, not by Eugénie's directive but by her own choice. Within hours, she falls into a fever worthy of any Goethe heroine and stops sleeping. At the end of a week she receives a visitor in the school infirmary. It is the Reverend Mother Barat.

"Good evening, my child."

"Good evening, *ma mère*." Marie waits for the verbal reprimand and feels her body tense up under the sheets. She stares at the decorative plasterwork on the ceiling and tries to allay her anxiety by tracing out the geometric shapes above her.

After a few moments, Sophie speaks again. "It would seem that we have made a mistake, and that you have been punished for no good reason."

Marie turns her head toward the woman at her bedside to see if she is joking. When she looks at her face, she sees only a pair of dark eyes looking into her own with an inkling of self-recognition.

"I know what it's like to be punished for an act of kindness." Sophie can still see her brother's shirts—a gift she had made Louis for his feast day—dissolving in flames as she was roughly berated for her vain frivolity. She had been just about Marie's age. "I assure you Madame de Gramont simply does not understand what was behind your gesture."

Marie, who is no longer so sure about the purity of her own motives, simply stares.

"What Madame de Gramont fears, I believe, is the development of an attachment that is too strong." Sophie pauses for a moment to let the idea seep in. "While a powerful affection might seem perfectly harmless, one must learn to exercise moderation, *ma fille*. Such passions can be dangerous, though you cannot be expected to see that now."

Marie stretches out one of her hands and places it in Sophie's. Sophie holds it gently and allows the young girl to confide her thoughts on love and desire and friendship and truth for over an hour. When she finally tiptoes away from her bedside, Marie is asleep.

Reinventing the Past

1824

LOUIS XVIII DIED IN SEPTEMBER OF 1824 AFTER A LONG ILLNESS whose gruesome conclusion could hardly be matched for horror. The gargantuan body—riddled with dropsy, gout, diabetes, and arteriosclerosis—had spent most of its last years in an oversized wheelchair and at the end was literally devoured by gangrene. The stench of decaying flesh kept Louis' family away from his deathbed, and when a pair of valets attempted to move the body, pieces of his feet came off in their hands.

It was a death unmerited by a king who had tried to steer a moderate course between Ultra-royalists on the right and strident Republicans and Bonapartists on the left. His refusal ever to have himself officially crowned was a signal that his return to the throne would not be a return to 1789.

Such liberalism did not continue when his brother Charles X assumed the throne. An elaborate coronation in the cathedral of Reims, following a medieval tradition going back to Joan of Arc, was scheduled for the following spring.

I visited the Hôtel Biron with Marie shortly after Louis' death. Eugénie had draped the parlors with black crepe and decreed that the boarding students wear no bows in their hair for a month.

"I often wonder that she ever lets us wear anything that isn't black and dismal," Héloïse grumbled. "The woman makes a cult of death!"

"Héloïse!" her mother remonstrated.

"It's true, *maman*! I think she loves the fact that the king is dead! Marie and I are convinced she's a necrophiliac."

I smiled in spite of myself. The child had a point.

"She positively *hovered* around me when Uncle Eugène died last winter. Ask anyone."

Eugène de Beauharnais, Grand-Duke of Frankfurt, Duke of Leuchtenberg and Prince of Eichstätt, had died the preceding February of a heart attack at age forty-two, leaving behind six children, a grieving widow, and adoring subjects throughout Bavaria. Célestine had gone into seclusion for several weeks.

"So what do you hear from *la belle* Mademoiselle de Flavigny?" I asked. Marie had left school the year before, preferring to receive private tutoring at her mother's home in Paris.

"Her family is arranging a marriage," she replied. "She's already rejected several possible husbands, but they seem to have found her a docile count who will fit the bill nicely."

"At least they're giving her a choice!" Marie responded, her voice tinged with horror.

We knew what she was referring to by this remark, and the room fell quiet. One of the impoverished young countesses that Eugénie had admitted—a timid, unprepossessing child of seventeen—had left the school several months earlier to marry Denis Marmaton. His enormous fortune had allowed the family to reposition themselves, and Denis could now claim direct connection with the nobility.

It was Héloïse who broke the silence. "The poor girl comes often to visit Aunt PhiePhie." She paused for a moment and then continued. "The last time she came, she had covered her face, but I saw the bruises."

"*Le salaud*," I said under my breath and then looked up to apologize to the women. At that moment Sophie appeared on the threshold.

"*Ah, c'est ma famille jovinienne!*" she said with delight, overlooking the expletive that had christened her entry and embracing each of us. "When you've finished your visit, Guy, I need to see you for a moment! Eugénie kindly told me you were here."

A half hour later, the two of us were closeted in her office.

"I have something I want you to think about," she said briskly. "But first I have a question that needs to be answered by someone from"— here she spun her hand in the air—"outside."

"I'll do my best," I responded with a grin. "Just what kind of outsider information are you seeking?"

"I hear that our new king is making preliminary plans to offer 'full legal recognition' to any religious order of women that submits an application."

"I've heard the news as well," I replied.

"What are his motives, do you think? And do you think submitting such an application is wise?"

"On the surface it looks as if he's moving to ratify the many congregations that have sprung up since the Revolution."

"'On the surface,' as you say, yes." She looked at me to continue.

"My guess from your expression is that you hesitate to tie yourself any more closely than necessary to the French government," I added.

She delayed her response for a full minute and wound her fingers through the chain of the large silver cross she wore around her neck. "To submit such an application," she began, "implies a first loyalty to France rather than to Rome. Whether it is or it isn't, Rome will see it that way. In addition, we have houses in three countries now. What will our houses in Savoy or Turin or Missouri or Louisiana think if we make such a move?"

"What will it look like to the king if you refuse his kind invitation?" I was used to playing devil's advocate in situations like this, but I fully understood her concern. We both knew that Charles X was a zealous Catholic whose zeal had political motives. He and his Ultra-royalists longed for the halcyon days when Church and King formed an indivisible, insuperable, and absolute union. Whatever "full legal recognition" Charles was offering stank of Gallicanism, and she was right to anticipate a negative response from Rome.

"So what does your council say, Sophie?"

"They are leery of such a move, as am I. It seems one more way to throw us under the yoke of the French bishops. All the bishops with whom I've spoken are of course in favor."

"Of course!" I replied with a knowing laugh. "What does your new friend Father Favre think?"

Joseph-Marie Favre had become Sophie's spiritual friend and counselor since the death of her beloved "*Gran'maman*," Jean Montaigne. The two of them shared a powerful belief in the gentle, healing power of the Sacred Heart and rued its appropriation by the Ultras.

"He is wary as well. But Favre is seen as a hopeless ultramontane, and I worry that *not* to submit an application identifies us firmly with Rome."

"So once again you are trapped, *ma chère* Sophie. My feeling, however, is that you should submit the application regardless—if, in fact Charles follows through on his plan. At this point, it's only talk."

"Which brings me to my little piece of news." Her voice was loaded with mystery, and her eyes sparkled in the way I remembered them in the vineyards, full of excitement and just a tinge of mischief. "What would you think if I told you that we're seeking—*quietly*, mind you— full Papal Approbation for our little Society?"

"And you're worried about submitting an application for legal recognition?" I looked at her with a mix of incredulity and wonder. "You don't think this act on its own will throw you, whether you intend it or not, into the ultramontane camp?"

"This is why we are proceeding so carefully," she answered. "I have only mentioned it to one person in Rome, Father Rozaven. But he is very enthusiastic and believes we'll be able to obtain it."

Father Jean Rozaven, the Jesuit Assistant General for France in Rome, had become a staunch ally of the Society. Sophie counted other allies in Rome as well, and I fully understood why she would seek Approbation: it would protect her from French bishops whose internal rivalries and power struggles with the Vatican had returned to pre-Revolution levels and could threaten Sophie's ability to move the Society forward.

"Then perhaps," I suggested, "if the king moves forward with his plan, you should consider submitting the application. Such a move could free you from the suspicions a Papal Approbation will surely engender, at least among the French bishops!"

"This is what I'm thinking, *mon ami*," she said with a large smile. "I just wanted to verify my position."

Part 8

Rome

The Russian Princess

1828

THE DISCOVERY THAT HER MOTHER HAS CONVERTED TO CATHOLI-
cism leads Elisabeth Alexeievna Galitzine to swear an oath in blood that
she will hate the Catholic Church in general (and the Jesuits in particular) for the rest of her life. She already hates her mother.

Since her father's death when she was only four, Elisabeth has
watched her mother slide into grief-induced madness. Eventually the
young Russian widow hands her strong-willed daughter off to a series of
tutors who are given carte blanche to beat the child into submission if
she doesn't behave. Elisabeth will later call it an *éducation à la Tartare*,
and her childhood in St. Petersburg is, to say the least, an unhappy one.
She believes—because this is what she is told—that she is an intrinsi-
cally bad person. Using a gurkha knife once given to her father by a
Nepali prince, she repeats her bloody vow nightly, opening small veins
and capillaries in her forearm and upper thigh as she recites her prayers
according to the rituals of the Russian Orthodox Church.

At age sixteen she begins to study Italian with an ancient priest who
has lived in Russia since the Jesuit expulsion from Europe. When he
dies, she walks into his Requiem Mass and experiences a miraculous

conversion. The next day her mother consigns her to a Jesuit confessor—and Father Jean-Louis de Rozaven knows he has found the child of his heart's desire.

Two months after Elisabeth's first communion, the Jesuits are banished from Russia, and Rozaven leaves for Rome. Here he is appointed Jesuit Assistant General for France, but the fifteen hundred miles between himself and his spiritual daughter do not prevent him from knowing everything that goes on inside her head and heart. Once a week a package containing Elisabeth's journal leaves St. Petersburg for Rome. Every thought, every desire, every notion that passes through the young girl's head is recorded and becomes Rozaven's property. He sends her letters directing her what to think, what to say, how to conduct herself.

In point of fact, he is the first person ever to have shown any interest in her.

Eventually she tells her mother that she wishes to join a religious community. Her mother responds that she must wait until she turns thirty. The day after her thirtieth birthday, in a move choreographed entirely by Jean de Rozaven, Princess Elisabeth Galitzine is secretly entered into the Sacred Heart novitiate at the Hôtel Biron.

It is with Jean de Rozaven that Sophie has been so very quietly communicating about the possibility of Papal Approbation for her "little Society"—an association that now numbers almost twenty schools. With Rozaven's help and with the redoubtable presence of Sophie's emissary Joséphine Bigeu (dubbed *la furia francese* by the Vatican officials who must deal with her), the Society is finally awarded official papal approval in 1826. Soon afterward, Pope Leo XII—despite his initial apprehension of these *Madames* of the Sacred Heart, who have slipped the nets of papal enclosure and display a mettle that makes him slightly edgy—presents them with an exquisite architectural treasure.

And it is toward this treasure that Elisabeth Galitzine now moves in the autumn of 1828. Toward it, and toward her beloved "father."

La Trinità dei Monti

1828

IN 1475, BY ORDER OF CHARLES VIII OF FRANCE, A MONASTERY WAS built atop the Pincian Hill for the friars of St. Francis of Paola. Situated at the top of the Spanish Steps, it neighbors an elegant Renaissance church, La Trinità dei Monti, whose twin bell towers overlook the city of Rome like two saffron angels. Centered between them, at a measured distance from the central doors and down a short flight of steps, a granite obelisk thrusts itself into the Italian sky, the fleur de lys at its top a not-so-subtle reminder that both church and monastery are the property of the French government. A long, circular double staircase winds its graceful way down to the Piazza di Spagna, where Bernini's Barcaccia Fountain flows over the bow and stern of the sunken ship it is meant to represent.

This was the treasure that Pope Leo XII bestowed on the Society of the Sacred Heart with the understanding that it would house a school for daughters of the Italian nobility.

"Voilà the legacy of our purchase of the Hôtel Biron!" Sophie exclaimed, delighted with the property but unhappy with the condition that the school cater exclusively to the aristocracy.

I looked at her quizzically, remembering the conversation we'd had eight years earlier with the Countess de Marboeuf and wondering what, exactly, she wanted me to say.

"I know what you're thinking, Guy. Don't say it," she said with a peremptory wave of her hand. "But we did not *seek* this position. It's been foisted upon us, you know that."

I only shrugged my shoulders, knowing that she was thinking aloud and not yet ready for commentary.

"I feel once again as if we're sparrows whom fate has landed in an eagle's nest," she continued, her voice echoing a baffled recognition of the power of events to recast one's intentions. She shook her head as if to dismiss what was passing through her mind. "And yet there's nothing to be done. *C'est fait.*"

I recognized my cue in her final words.

"You need to take a deep breath and consider what this offers you, Sophie," I counseled. "It's what you've wanted for a very long time, no? A school in Rome with a novitiate to follow soon after? And with politics the way they are in France—"

"Yes, of course." She waved her hand in the air once again as if to ward off hearing me state the obvious. Then she stopped and thought for a moment. "It's a trade-off, isn't it? The king is allowing us to have the Trinità in exchange for closing down the Jesuit schools."

"The timing *is* rather coincidental," I conceded, certain that she was right. By a recent order of Charles X, all Jesuit schools in France had been either closed or taken over by secular institutions. And while Pope Leo had offered the Trinità to the Society, he needed official permission from the French king to do so.

"Perhaps the pope expects our schools to be shut down next?" she said.

I knew she was giving voice to her own fears. Anti-clericalism was on the rise as Charles's Ultra-royalist policies became more and more repressive. The French population was coming to view any religious community as being in bed with the monarchy, and educational orders were particularly suspect. The move against the Jesuits represented Charles's attempt to pacify the increasingly hostile voices of a parliament that wondered what was happening to its constitutional monarchy.

"You need to be careful, Sophie. It doesn't help that you're centered in the Faubourg Saint Germain—and that the Archbishop of Paris and half the royal court are frequent visitors here!"

"Archbishop de Quelen is Eugénie's special friend," she replied loyally, though I knew his abject allegiance to the Bourbons provoked her. "And I don't know how we can shut the door on the king and his family!"

"Of course. I didn't mean that. But I go back to my earlier remark. Focus on what this Roman school will offer you rather than worrying about the implications of its clientele."

She sat there quietly, looking beyond me.

"Who will head the new foundation?" I finally asked.

"Armande de Causans," she replied quickly, turning her gaze back to me. "Cardinal Lambruschini has requested her. She's led the school in Turin for the past two years, she speaks beautiful Italian, and she gets along well with the *Piemontese*—including their rather testy archbishop. Hopefully the Romans will love her, too."

"And who will accompany her?"

"That I haven't decided, though Elisabeth Galitzine will surely be among them. Father Rozaven has lobbied on our behalf for over four years now, and he's *insistent* that she be brought to him."

Because of Rozaven's unceasing interference in the particulars of Elisabeth's dowry, I was well aware of the control he exercised over his protégée. I could only imagine what would happen when they found themselves together in the same city.

"I'm sure he is," I replied drily.

She didn't seem to notice my reaction.

⁓

A few months later, Sophie was writing a letter to Henriette Grosier from her office at the Hôtel Biron. After remarking on the sudden chill that had descended on Paris, she clambered onto a table to close a window. The letter remained unfinished for a week while she recovered from a fall that left her crippled for almost four years.

I visited her when the leeches had been removed and the doctor was no longer concerned for her life. He was clear, however, that if Sophie put any pressure on her foot, it could end up in a jar with the rest of his specimen collection.

"I don't know how I can possibly do what needs to be done from a horizontal position!" she exclaimed. "Just *look* at the contrivance they've created for me to ride in!"

I looked over at the basket in which she was to be dragged about for the next several months. Featuring several small wheels instead of runners, it looked like a bastardized sled but allowed her to keep her injured foot raised as she was hauled from place to place. I tried not to smile, but the vision of the Mother General Barat conducting business from such a contraption overcame my reserve. When she saw my expression, we both exploded with laughter, which stopped abruptly when Eugénie walked in to announce the arrival of a bishop.

For the next several months, Sophie found herself occasionally dropped on the floor by an inept porter or left at the top of a flight of stairs until someone remembered to bring her down. Her happiest hours were spent when she was forgotten in the chapel. Here she could pray undisturbed and meditate on the dark clouds that were gathering over Restoration France.

La Marseillaise

1830

ON MAY 25, 1830, FOUR HUNDRED FIFTY-THREE WARSHIPS BEARING more than thirty thousand French troops leave the southern coast of France for Algeria. The invasion is a last-ditch attempt on the part of Charles X to salvage his monarchy by drawing attention away from his failed domestic policies. For a few short weeks it works. But on July 25—after having already dissolved the popular Chamber of Deputies, broken up the National Guard, and effectively overturned the French Constitution—King Charles suspends the liberty of the press. When his police move in to shut down a defiant newspaper, they are greeted by an angry mob, and the July Revolution is on. Amidst familiar cries of "Down with the Bourbons!" and less familiar shouts of "*Vive la Constitution!*" the mob slowly evolves into a street riot and the riot into a full-fledged revolution.

At the Hôtel Biron, with gunfire and the roar of cannon in the background, parents are pulling their daughters out of the school and fleeing across French borders. Eugénie de Gramont is convalescing from an illness in nearby Conflans, where Archbishop de Quelen has lent them a small house next to his summer palace. Sophie, who is now limping about on crutches, is finally convinced to join her there. On the night of her arrival, the Archbishop's palace is sacked, and a band of students singing *La Marseillaise* tries without success to set fire to the little house where she and three companions are praying.

Two days later a gardener from the Hôtel Biron arrives breathlessly to say that the revolution is over. Charles X has abdicated in favor of his unpretentious cousin Louis-Philippe, and the Paris streets have quieted.

Eugénie reacts with an epithet that causes both Sophie and the gardener to stare. "*Le salaud!*" Eugénie repeats the word, heedless of their reaction, her voice filled with hatred. "His family are Jacobin scum! His father voted for King Louis's execution—Louis' own *cousin!*"

Sophie tries to calm Eugénie's rage, reminding her that political neutrality is key to their survival. She engages the gardener's help in camouflaging their appearance, using whatever they can find in the house. Draped in an assortment of brightly colored shawls and sporting large straw bonnets on their heads, the women journey back into Paris in a rickety two-wheeled cart. As the frazzled driver maneuvers around uprooted trees and torn up cobblestones, a man who's been celebrating events in a neighborhood tavern leaps into the seat beside them.

"*Vive la Constitution!*" he reels and shouts. "Long live the Constitution!" he yells again, turning to stare directly at Sophie. "Long live whatever the hell makes you happy!" he bellows louder, leaning in suggestively toward the startled Eugénie and howling with amusement at the expression on her face.

The two women, recovered from their initial alarm and realizing he's their passport to safety, laugh along with him—Eugénie between clenched teeth.

"*Et madame,*" he says, noticing Sophie's crutches, "I see you've got problems with your legs! I have a feeling this rattletrap won't go much farther, but wherever you are going, I'll carry you on my *back* if I have to!" He belches loudly as if to seal the promise, and Sophie has the impression that he's seen through their disguise.

Stopped at a barricade in the rue de Varenne, Sophie manages to trade her copy of the most recent daily newspaper for permission to pass through. Eventually, when it becomes impossible for them to continue on in the cart, their buoyant companion proves true to his word and carries Sophie into the courtyard of the Hôtel Biron.

Once they've sent their new friend on his rollicking way, Sophie gathers together the few remaining students and nuns and leads them into the stables, where the novices have established their community room.

"*Courage,* my daughters!" she exclaims, almost believing it. "We are safely together in this humble space, and we know we are the children of Christ's loving heart. Let us give thanks with a beautiful song!" They've not sung four measures when they hear someone breaking into the next room.

Sophie again whispers "*Courage!*" though at this point she feels the last ounce of it drain through the soles of her feet.

The children are rigid with fear, the novices' faces ashen. Before they know what's happened, a man crashes through the door. He is wearing an enormous overcoat and the tricolor cockade, emblem of the French revolutionaries.

When he pushes his hat back to reveal his identity, Sophie recognizes Joseph Varin.

It is clear that Paris is no longer a safe setting for the school or the novitiate, and Sophie spends the next several months wandering about a continent that is exploding with violence. She sends the Paris novices to Besançon and Lyon, then travels to Switzerland. Here the father of three former students in Paris has offered her a place to live while she tries to establish a novitiate in Montet. When Charles X's Swiss Guards return battered and bruised from Paris, public opinion turns against anything French—particularly if it has clerical connections—and Sophie is advised to cross the border into the relative safety of Savoy. Here she reinjures her foot and spends the next eight months in a chaise longue in Chambéry, travelling occasionally to take the healing waters in nearby Aix-les-Bains.

Secrets

1831

WHEN I RECEIVED THE MESSAGE THAT MARIE DE BEIXEDON MIGHT be on her deathbed, I rushed across Paris to the comfortable home that she and Alex had bought on their return from Milan. It was Célestine and not the butler who greeted me at the front door, her face lined with exhaustion.

"She's running a high fever and experiencing horrible cramping. I'm terrified it's cholera."

"I'm here, *ma chère*," I said, kissing both her cheeks and steering her back into the house. She had passed the entire night at Marie's bedside. "The cholera epidemic is still far away in Germany," I reassured her. "Not one case has been reported in Paris or anywhere else in France." But I knew even as I said it that the disease was stealing its way westward from Moscow, leaving tens of thousands of violet-blue corpses in its wake.

"It's only a matter of time," she responded, her eyes darkened with fatigue and her voice close to breaking. "*Someone* in France has to have the first case!"

"May I see her?"

"Not just now. She's finally fallen asleep. Come into the salon. Héloïse and Jean-Marie are here, and they'll be so happy to see you. Alexandre will be here soon."

Since their father's death, "Tante Célestine" had been the emotional mainstay of the de Beixedon family. Without Marie's knowledge, she was also the financial angel whose fortune had allowed Héloïse to attend school at the Hôtel Biron and the two boys to attend the University of Paris. Jean-Marie was finishing his studies in law, and his younger brother, Alexandre, had just entered the school of medicine. For the past several years, Célestine had also been supporting a school for disabled children that operated on the property of the Hôtel Biron. But her life was centered on the de Beixedon home, and all three children adored her.

"Uncle Guy!" Héloïse exclaimed when I entered the room, and in a motion recalling her exuberant childhood, she threw herself into my arms.

Jean-Marie, who at age twenty-two exhibited the dignified reserve of his father, stepped forward politely. Both their faces revealed shock and worry, and it was obvious that Héloïse had been crying.

An hour later Marie was still asleep, and Célestine convinced us to follow her into the dining room. "It might seem sacrilegious to eat at a time like this," she said, looking straight at Héloïse and Jean-Marie, "but it won't help anyone, least of all your mother, if you don't keep up your strength."

Célestine took her meal upstairs to be near Marie, but the children and I, in one of those surreal moments that validate the adage "life must go on," sat down to share a hearty dinner. Jean-Marie spent a fair amount of time questioning me about recent revisions in the inheritance laws, and by the end of the meat course we'd decided that he would do an apprenticeship in my office during his school vacation.

"And you, *ma belle?*" I turned to look at Héloïse, now twenty-five, whose luminous beauty had been turning heads in Paris for years. "What are you doing now that the latest attempt to marry you off has failed?"

She rolled her eyes. "Oh la!" she exclaimed. "Always, *always* the marriage question!"

"What was wrong with *this* poor fellow?" I asked, an indulgent smile on my lips.

"Nothing more or less than the last one," she replied with a tone of intense boredom and pursing her lips as if to blow away the noxious and seemingly inevitable cloud on her horizon. "And what if I choose *not* to marry?"

Jean-Marie drilled a look of exasperation across the table. "And then what? You plan maybe to turn *nun* on us?"

Héloïse glared back at him and I intervened. "Married life seems to agree with your friend Marie de Flavigny, no? I hear she's just had a second little girl."

She burst out laughing and earned another scowl from Jean-Marie. "Ah yes. The ever-so-contented Countess d'Agoult. Deliriously happy with husband, household, and two tiny daughters!"

"For God's sake, Héloïse," Jean-Marie snapped, and I looked at them quizzically.

"I think I'm missing something," I said.

"The woman is bored out of her mind!" Héloïse exploded. "All the man does is hunt. What kind of husband is that for a woman like Marie!"

"And what do you mean by 'a woman like Marie'?" I asked tentatively.

"You've heard her play the piano, Uncle Guy—do you even have to ask? She's seething with passion and imagination. She wants to talk about art and politics and music with people who are at the *center* of things. Like she did with her own family in Germany! She wants above all to write, and now her life is filled with babies and horses and a husband whose favorite pastime—whose only pastime—is to shoot things!"

"I've heard she manages to do all kinds of fascinating things in spite of her husband and children," Jean-Marie interjected with a snide expression.

"Of course you have! I'm the one who told you!" Héloïse shot back. "What he really wants to tell you, Uncle Guy, is that Marie and I see each other occasionally, and he doesn't approve. She's invited to interesting gatherings. When her husband allows it, she sometimes even hosts such gatherings. And in order to assure myself that I'm still *alive*, I tag along." She glared at her brother one more time and then looked to me for support.

"I can understand Marie's desire to mingle with this world," I responded. "Who wouldn't?" I'd heard that Rossini himself had recently played at her palatial home on the left bank. "I just hope she doesn't lose her bearings."

Héloïse settled into a full-body pout, and Jean-Marie quietly excused himself to go check on his mother. When he'd left the room, I sat patiently in my chair and waited for her to resume the conversation.

"You *see* what it's like for me here!" she finally exclaimed. "Why is it that nobody in this family understands me? *Maman* sounds just like Jean-Marie when we get on this subject." Here she stopped and bit her lower lip, suddenly remembering that the woman she still believed to be her mother might be dying on the floor just above her. As tears of exhaustion, guilt, and confusion welled in her eyes, I pulled out a hand-kerchief.

"What is it you want from life, Héloïse? If not marriage, then what?"

"I don't know, but I *do* know I can't survive a life like Marie's."

I looked at her tear-streaked face and thought about how to answer her. To insist on marriage was to trivialize her argument, and—aside from her brother's suggestion, which seemed unlikely—I had no alternative to offer.

I was spared the effort, for at that moment Jean-Marie ran into the room, a joyous smile on his face. "*Maman*'s fever has broken!"

Célestine appeared behind him and verified his statement with a nod and a look of unspeakable relief. "She would love to see you now, Guy."

I rose from the table, but before I could leave the dining room, a scuffle erupted in the entry hall. The butler's voice was drowned out by the shouts of a man who insisted on entering.

"She's my *sister*, God damn you, and I heard she's dying,"—we heard the sound of shattering glass—"and I have every right to see her, you fucking little *bastard*!"

We heard another crash as the butler was shoved into a collection of Chinese porcelain, and before anyone could stop him, Denis Marmaton stood weaving in the arched doorway. He stumbled crabwise into the

room and looked around with a dazed expression, as if wondering suddenly where he was. His face was puffy beneath a two-day beard, his eyes were rheumy and yellowed, and his expensive clothing looked as if it had been slept in for several days. Jean-Marie and I moved quickly to keep him from approaching any further, and as we forced him back toward the front door, I could smell the acrid combination of alcohol and sweat coming off his skin. He began shouting again, this time a series of profanities mixed up with his sister's name and something else I couldn't decipher, and then vomited in the entryway. From the corner of my eye, I saw Héloïse trying to support Célestine, whose face had drained of color and who was groping for anything to keep her from collapse.

Waterfall

1831

SOPHIE LIES ON A CHAISE LONGUE IN AIX-LES-BAINS AND READS her latest letter from Eugénie de Gramont. It is full of news from Paris, including the fact that Eugénie has invited Archbishop de Quelen to occupy the guest apartment at the Hôtel Biron.

"I'm having him move into the Petit-Hôtel in view of his current situation," her final paragraph begins. "His palace remains in a catastrophic state, and we *surely* can't expect his Excellency to keep shuttling from place to place like a homeless vagabond!"

Sophie stops reading and flings the letter down with an exasperated cry that brings her young attendant, Sister Annette, out into the garden.

"What's the matter, *ma mère?*" she asks with a worried look. "More attacks on the school in Paris?"

"Indeed," is Sophie's cryptic reply. "It seems we now have the archbishop living among us, and I have a hunch the man might never leave."

In fact, Monsignor Hyacinthe-Louis de Quelen will stay in his sumptuous lodgings at the Hôtel Biron for nine years, until he's carried out feet first.

"Madame de Gramont continues to make our establishment a hub of political intrigue," Sophie continues, "and such a move will only add to this reputation!"

She is furious that her instructions to Eugénie have been ignored. She knows that Eugénie and Archbishop de Quelen feed each other's perpetual state of fury against the upstart "Citizen King." Louis-Philippe's shameless audacity in placing his unsanctified derrière on the sanctified throne of France challenges their most deeply held beliefs.

Another letter is from Perpignan, where pillagers have broken into the school, chased out the children and the nuns, and converted the building into a factory. In Autun and Niort, anticlerical mobs have stormed the Society's schools but eventually allowed teachers and students to repossess the damaged structures. The Chambéry newspaper reports ongoing upheavals in Belgium, Poland, Germany, Italy, and the Netherlands. In every case, revolutionary fervor is connected with violent opposition to the Catholic Church.

Sophie, overwhelmed by this latest round of events and by Eugénie's defiance, asks Annette to help her into the garden, where a waterfall spills down from the Alpine foothills.

"I love this waterfall," she says, her voice turning slightly dreamy and belying her depression. "Sometimes I think I can almost hear the voice of Arethusa." She turns to see if her companion recognizes the allusion. "Do you know the story of Arethusa, my dearest Annette?"

When the young woman shakes her head, Sophie settles herself into a large, cushioned chair, motions for Annette to do the same, and assumes the role of a storyteller.

"It is a story from Ovid, a Roman poet who loved to write of magical transformation." Her eyes glow with the memory of reading his *Metamorphoses* in her little attic room in Joigny.

"Arethusa is the daughter of an Arcadian river god," she opens, "a young nymph who loves nothing more than to roam the hills and valleys of ancient Greece. She worships the untamed beauty of nature and has vowed to devote herself to the goddess Artemis and thus to a life of chastity."

Sophie waits for Annette's eyes to register a glimmer of self-recognition and then continues.

"One day it is so very hot that she goes to bathe in a river whose clarity and stillness draw her to its bank. She places her clothes on a curving willow branch and dives to the bottom, not realizing that she's plunged into the silvery depths of the river god Alpheus. Feeling her body fall into his and marveling at her great beauty, he wraps his watery essence around her and declares his undying love."

Annette's eyes have become large brown disks.

"Arethusa escapes his embrace and begins to run. She flies across the vale of Maenalus and as far as ice-capped Erymantus in the western Peloponnese, but still he pursues her—now in his human form. Unable to maintain her pace, and sensing Alpheus' breath panting over her narrow shoulders, she calls out to Artemis for protection. The goddess hears her cry and sweeps her up into a shimmering white cloud. Still the god persists, stalking her aerial hiding place and promising eternal fidelity."

Annette's eyes darken as she leans forward, mesmerized by Sophie's cadenced delivery.

"The young nymph begins to perspire from fear. Moisture trickles from her brow and larger drops begin to fall from her feet and hands. A stream begins to spill from her braided hair and then the braids themselves become liquid. She realizes she is turning into water, and when she looks down, she discerns a glowing cleft that Artemis has opened in the earth below her. She cascades into the opening and, free of her pursuer, flows under the earth until she raises her watery head in Ortygia, a small island off the eastern coast of Sicily.

"The stream continues running to this day in honor of the island's sacred goddess—Artemis."

The sensuous coils of the ancient story wrap themselves around both women. Annette stares at the waterfall and wonders what Savoyard goddess might lie at its source. Sophie simply stares.

The water tumbles from a height of almost thirty feet, falls onto a rocky ledge at the elevation of the garden, and then plunges into a canyon far below. As she listens to the roar of its descent, she imagines the small pieces of uprooted matter being swept along with the surge and is overcome by thoughts of impermanence.

"Vanity of vanities," she whispers after several minutes, the lines from Ecclesiastes sidle into her brain from nowhere. "All is vanity."

Annette, snatched out of her reverie, watches as Sophie gets up on her crutches and moves close to the edge of the ravine. The raw surge of water holds her in thrall, and Annette places her left arm tightly around Sophie's waist. Without seeming to notice her presence, Sophie finds herself once again dreaming of Carmel, lamenting the life of constant activity and motion into which she has fallen, and wondering how she has ended up where she is. She ponders the resurgence of violence in Europe, Eugénie's stubborn willfulness, the recent deaths of Joséphine Bigeu and Lydia Chobelet, Philippine's endless struggles in North America.

She stares into the rushing water and knows that all of this, too, will wash away without a trace in the current of time. And she weeps.

La Trastevere

1832 – 1833

BARTOLOMEO ALBERTO CAPPELARI, AN ITALIAN PRINCE FROM THE region of Venice, is elected Pope Gregory XVI in early 1832 after sixty-four days of contentious voting. He wins by default—not because the College of Cardinals wants him in the position, but because they cannot decide between their two favorites. Once on the papal throne, he rules with a monarchical fist. In an effort to retain control over the vast area of the Papal States, Gregory does everything possible to keep his subjects living in the past. He forbids gas lighting and the building of railroads because he fears such projects will advance commerce and give too much power to a rising bourgeoisie. He drains the papal treasury for projects that flatter his ego and promote reactionary causes. In concert with other Church authorities, he issues a public reprimand of Sophie's spiritual advisor, Joseph Favre, because of his liberal views—most notably that of a God whose loving accessibility would encourage frequent, even daily, communion.

As Gregory works to turn the clock back to the preceding century, Giuseppe Mazzini, from his place of exile in Marseille, is methodically organizing the revolutionary group *Giovine Italia*—Young Italy. Its purpose is to unify all of Italy into a modern nation state.

~

After receiving considerable pressure to do so, Sophie decides to travel to the Eternal City. In addition to visiting the school at the Trinità dei Monti, she hopes to establish a novitiate open to Italian women and to found a second school that will serve the poor. En route to Pope Gregory's fiefdom she visits Avignon, where she oversees the opening of a new foundation. In nearby Aix-en-Provence she negotiates the fusion of an existing school with the Society.

Here, too, she learns of the death of Marie de Beixedon.

"A childhood friend has died of cholera," she says softly to Annette, setting the black-bordered envelope on a table. "Her daughter Héloïse was at the school in Paris." The epidemic has indeed found its way into France, and Marie is one of its first victims.

For several minutes she stares out into the brilliant Provençal sunlight and thinks of the eleven-year-old Marie shrieking through the vineyard during the vendange of 1791, a stick in her hand and violence in her mouth. She remembers racing down the hill with Célestine and dancing the little dance they loved to do when they were so full of life and joy they didn't know how else to release it. And the chilling expression on Denis' face when he'd looked at Célestine. How little any of them could have imagined then what the world held in store for them.

"This news on the heels of Eugénie's letter is almost more than I can bear," she finally says, closing her eyes and leaning her head back in a large wicker lawn chair.

"Paris has become a city of death."

Eugénie writes that the disease is ravaging Paris. Over thirteen thousand men, women, and children have died within the first month, and by the time the epidemic runs its course in France, it will have killed over one hundred thousand people. The streets of the capital crawl with hearses. Archbishop de Quelen—in an act that allows him a temporary reprieve from Sophie's disapproval—has mobilized an effort in Paris' poorer neighborhoods to help the ill and the dying. Sophie has suggested that they house some of the city's burgeoning orphan population on the grounds of the Hôtel Biron, and within days fifteen children are moved onto the premises. Célestine Lorrain, in memory of Marie de Beixedon, offers to fund the entire operation and promises to see the little girls' education through to adulthood.

In May, the head of the school in Turin, Louise de Limminghe, insists that Sophie consult an Italian surgeon about her foot. The doctors in Paris have suggested a last attempt at a cure at Aix-les-Bains but are once again talking of amputation.

Louise is adamant. "You *must* see Dr. Rossi, Sophie! He's the official court doctor here in Piedmont and a gifted surgeon. You cannot go on like this for another four years!" Louise arranges to meet Sophie in Provence and accompany her south to Turin.

When they reach the Italian frontier at Nice, their carriage is stopped and surrounded. One by one, a series of uniformed men peer into the interior, and an animated debate ensues, though neither woman can decode the subject of the controversy. Eventually they are escorted to the offices of the chief of police. He stares at Louise de Limminghe with exaggerated attention and then scrutinizes her passport.

"There is something seriously out of order here, madame," he says peremptorily, taking the passport with him and hurrying out of the room. Another official, this one decorated with fringed epaulets, yards of gold braid, and rows of shiny buttons, enters the room with him a few moments later. He repeats the inspection, eyes moving suspiciously between Louise and the passport.

"We believe you are not who you say you are, madame," the official declares, caught somewhere between awe and indignation.

"And who might I be if not Louise de Limminghe?" she responds, bristling.

"The Duchess of Berry."

The women's jaws drop in unison.

"We are sending to the Consulate in Turin for verification of your papers. That is all."

The two men leave the room abruptly, lock the door behind them, and abandon the women to their own semi-amused stupefaction.

"The Duchess of Berry!" Sophie finally repeats, a twinkle in her eye. "I really had no idea, *ma chère!*"

The duchess's "miracle child" is now ten years old and the last hope of the Bourbon legitimists. She has escaped Paris with her son during the July Revolution and is rumored to be cruising somewhere off the southern shores of France, doing what she can to stir up opposition to King Louis-Philippe. All border towns have stepped up security measures.

Louise, simultaneously flattered and horrified to be compared to the dashing duchess, looks at Sophie with as much dignity as she can muster, gracefully extends her hand, and asks, "Aren't you going to kiss my ring?"

When the police chief re-enters the locked room several hours later, Sophie turns on her persuasive powers. Within less than an hour, she manages a diplomatic exchange of two eggs and a new passport for two bottles of wine and a host of prayers.

Wishing to avoid cities because of the cholera quarantines, the two women arrive in Turin via a series of narrow alpine passes. At one point their carriage is lifted off its wheeled chassis, and they find themselves whizzing through ice and snow on a sledge pulled by twenty men.

When the famous Doctor Rossi finally examines Sophie's foot, he realizes the ankle has separated from the other bones in her foot by over an inch and adjusts the dislocation. In three weeks she is, albeit gingerly, walking again.

It is October by the time she sets out for Rome. She and Louise, whom she teasingly calls *Addolorata* because of her perpetual look of sadness, pass through Piacenza, Parma, and Bologna and then swing east to visit the little town of Loreto on the Adriatic coast. It is here, so they say, that the Virgin Mary's house landed in 1294 after being swept off its foundation in Nazareth and flown through the air by angels. Their carriage next takes them southwest to Perugia and Terni and finally through the majestic Porto del Popolo and into the noisy streets of Rome.

"I don't know quite how to tell you this," Louise de Limminghe splutters at the door of Sophie's room at the Trinità dei Monti, "but the

Holy Father is here to see you. He has just pulled up—I am quite serious, Sophie—in a glass coach."

Sophie looks at her, dumbstruck, but there is no time to indulge in personal reactions. The words *"Subito! Il Papa!"* are flying through the house, and she can hear the clattering of horses in the street.

Sophie, whose accident-prone foot is now recovering from a serious burn (the result of an overzealous foot-warmer), attempts to kneel as the tall figure enters her chamber, preceded by a cross-bearer. He motions Sophie back into her armchair and sits down on a nearby couch, dismissing his attendant with a regal wave of his hand.

"You are still so very young!" he exclaims, noting the animation in her expression and the quickness with which she has flung herself on her knees before him.

"On the contrary, I am very old, Your Holiness, and feeling older with this injury that has become my cross and constant companion," she responds. "Without it, I would have come to call on you by now."

"But you must know how much pleasure it gives me to see you safe within your convent walls," he answers with a byzantine smile. Gregory's disapproval of the Society's lack of strict papal enclosure is well known. She nods and returns his smile, syllable for syllable.

"I believe we've found a location for your novitiate," he continues, noting her unrepentant response and wondering again what the world is coming to. "It is in the Trastevere, very close to the Vatican, on the Janiculum Hill. A wealthy widow, the Marquise of Andosilla, has offered to pay for the repairs and the decoration, and I give it to you on the condition that you establish a school for the children of the neighborhood. "

Sophie, who has already been in correspondence with both Armande de Causans and Jean Rozaven about such an establishment, is now beaming.

"Such a school would be a great blessing, Your Holiness," she responds with a dazzling smile, this one devoid of double-entendre.

"It's a ferocious population," he explains. "They believe themselves to be the only true descendants of ancient Rome. They are poor but faithful and last year defended their pope with knives against that unholy group of Italian nationalists."

Sophie remembers hearing this story from Armande: of the papal palace's being besieged by Carbonari, and of the *Trasteverini*—in the wake of their victory over the "infidels"—unhitching the horses from Gregory's carriage and pulling it themselves through the city, singing victory songs and attracting a procession behind them that stretched for over a mile.

Three weeks later Sophie visits Santa Rufina, accompanied by Armande and Louise and the redoubtable marquise whose fortune is enabling its refurbishment. It is Sophie's first excursion since arriving in Rome, and the marquise is determined to show her a bit of the city's splendor before visiting the monastery. They travel from the Trinità northwest along the Via Sistina until they reach the Piazza del Populo, where the driver maneuvers them through hordes of pedestrians, carts, and carriages. He turns left toward the Tiber, and Sophie shifts her gaze from the vine-covered walls of the Borghese Gardens to the river itself. At the Lungotevere, they turn south and are confronted with the massive circular ruin of Caesar Augustus' tomb and then, further down, the looming hulk of the Castel Sant'Angelo. When they finally cross the Ponte Sisto to the other side of the Tiber, they find themselves in another world.

Narrow, winding streets present an impenetrable labyrinth to the unfamiliar visitor. Sophie breathes in the aromas of garlic, oregano and unidentifiable foods frying in olive oil, and revels in the sight of children running barefoot through the streets with an energy and spirit that she's encountered only in Provence. Vines bursting with flowers creep up the sides of buildings and fall in cascades from upstairs balconies, their riotous tangles of greens, pinks, and purples at times even leaping across the street to a neighboring balcony or rooftop, forming a sort of floral bridge. The buildings themselves, most of them three stories in height, are painted in shades of peach and melon, amber and apricot, whimsically punctuated here and there by a door of scarlet or sapphire blue.

They finally arrive at the old monastery and walk through empty arcades and corridors, some bearing evidence of a languorous process of restoration. The building, though in serious need of paint, is a lemon yellow, giving everything within its walls a warm glow. They stop in a cloister whose garden has long since collapsed into compost, but whose central fountain splashes with unexpected vigor and augments a tranquility that has already seeped into Sophie's bones.

"I feel already like Rome is the city of my soul," she says to no one in particular. "If I were a Hindu, I'd say I must have lived here in another life," she says, smiling now at the marquise, who puffs up like a pleased parrot. Sophie looks around the courtyard and imagines throngs of children playing amidst the arcs of tumbling water.

"I'd love to attach you here with a golden chain," is the marquise's reply. Neither of them notices the look that passes between Louise and Armande.

By this time Sophie has met her long-time correspondent Jean Rozaven, whose assertive presence at the Trinità is becoming increasingly worrisome to Armande.

"He meddles, Sophie," she says one afternoon as they are sitting in a large meadow behind the school. "There are times I think he'd like to annex us to the Jesuits altogether."

"Without him I doubt that we'd ever have received Papal Approbation," Sophie replies, though her antennae are picking up disquieting evidence of his intrusion into the internal affairs of the Society.

Eugénie de Gramont, for one, is livid. "He *insists* that Natalie Rostopchine be reprimanded for verbal indiscretions," she writes from Paris in a hand clearly shaking with rage. Natalie Rostopchine is a member of the Society in Paris—another Russian convert, whose uncle is supposed to have given the order to set Moscow afire in the winter of 1812.

"His beloved Elisabeth," Eugénie continues, "claims that Natalie has been reckless with information about certain Russian families in St. Petersburg, and that the Tsar has become suspicious. But the two of them are overstepping their bounds, Sophie. Rozaven in particular. How *dare* he tell me from his lair in Rome how to handle my personnel?"

"I fully understand your irritation, my darling Topina," is Sophie's measured response, invoking one of her favorite nicknames for Eugénie in an attempt to mollify her anger. "But I wonder why such irritation is directed at Fr. Rozaven and not at the Russians!"

And yet Sophie is aware of Rozaven's impolitic behavior—and of his increasingly obvious attachment to Elisabeth, the topic of mounting gossip in Rome.

Before she returns to Paris, she makes a courtesy visit to Anne Baudemont, whom she has not seen in over twenty years. Madame de Baudemont and Teresa Copina, who left Amiens with her at the time of their defection to Saint Estève, are living at the Convent of Saint Denis, where together they continue to run a small school for young women. Saint Estève has long since abandoned them. Sophie invites them to visit the Sacred Heart establishments in Rome and promises them support should they ever need it.

As she leaves the women, now both in their late seventies, in the doorway of their dilapidated building and rides back to the Trinità dei Monti, she relives those early days of anguish in Amiens and wonders if she is once again headed into such a storm. She is aware of the criticism mounting against her. That she never should have allowed Eugénie to assume the ascendancy she has in Paris. That she is allowing the same thing to happen in Rome with Rozaven and Elisabeth Galitzine. That by refusing to assert herself, she is allowing the entire Society to become something it is not. That she cannot connect with the younger generation of religious.

"I watch, I listen, I pray," she murmurs to herself as the carriage rolls over the cobblestones, surrendering herself to the intuition that has sustained her for over thirty years. "Do not force a conflict," her inner voices tell her. "Believe that time will lead to discernment, and discernment to consensus."

But there is no doubt in her mind that the rapid expansion of the Society is causing her to lose the personal connection with each school that has been its strength.

The horses turn into the Viale della Trinità dei Monti that crests along the Pincian hill, and Sophie looks out the carriage window at the golden city of Rome. She is both fortified by its eternal grandeur and haunted by the knowledge that, seen in a certain light, it's a vast city of ruins.

Part 9

Paris and Rome

The Artist and his Muse

1833 – 1835

THOUGH HER BIRTH CERTIFICATE CLAIMS THAT SHE OPENED HER eyes to the world at four a.m., Marie de Flavigny (now the Countess d'Agoult) insists to all that she is Midnight's Child: born at the stroke of twelve on December 30. Perhaps this is why she agrees to her lover's latest romantic fantasy—that the two of them gain secret access to the Cathedral of Notre Dame at midnight. He will play the organ and she, dressed as a man, will sit quietly in the archbishop's chair and listen to his performance. Because her lover is Franz Liszt, one can only imagine the rendezvous' rhapsodic splendor.

It's the latest chapter in a love affair that has taken on all the trappings of a Romantic novel.

⁓

"He's the most magnificent human being I've ever encountered!" Marie writes Héloïse the day after meeting the Hungarian pianist at one of the Marquise du Vayer's musical evenings. "If human being *is*. For he seems so very beyond human. Divinity animates every note, every silence, every gesture. He's as close to a god as one can get, my darling Héloïse! Tall, astonishingly thin, as if his body is a refraction of light—so pale, pretending to be flesh and yet spectral! His eyes are luminous orbs of green that stare into your very *soul*. And then to hear him play—it's as if one has connected to the heartbeat of the universe. If he isn't the godhead itself, he's its most eloquent priest!"

Héloïse is beside her when she writes him a formal invitation to play at her own salon. It takes three attempts before she feels the letter is worthy of sending. She assures Liszt that in her home—unlike those of her fellow Parisians—musicians do not enter through the servants' entrance. "Had I a separate doorway," she ends the letter, "for those who transcend the limitations of our frail humanity, it would open for you."

He comes, and then he comes again—not just to play music, but to discuss literature and philosophy and the rising currents of utopian socialism that are flowering from the pens of the Saint-Simonians. Liszt shares with Marie the radical egalitarian writings of Félicité Lammenais, a Catholic priest whom he considers his spiritual father—and whom Pope Gregory XVI is threatening to excommunicate. Marie shares with Liszt her readings of Goethe and Shakespeare and Chateaubriand. They revel in the decade's rising theme of the artist as humanity's savior: a living representative of God on earth who will free human beings from the bonds of servitude and reconnect them to their natural roots.

The relationship veers swiftly into an exchange of love letters written in French or German or English, depending on the writer's mood and the capacity of each language to relay what the other two cannot. Héloïse becomes a favored courier, carrying letters between Liszt's apartment just off the rue de Rivoli and Marie's home on the nearby Quai Malaquai.

~

"He's awakened something within me that's been smoldering for my entire *life!*" Marie cries, as if experiencing physical pain at the mere thought of him.

It is early spring, and she and Héloïse are sitting in her home's garden room, a many-windowed conservatory that faces directly across the

246

Seine. Héloïse stares across the river at the endless façade of the Louvre Palace and wonders if she'll ever be capable of such emotion. At twenty-eight she still has no idea what course her life should take.

"He's made me see that the ideas we've been brought up with are an illusion," Marie continues. "That the old social and religious ideas and constructs are no longer valid. That God resides in Nature alone and we forget this at our peril."

"And what about your marriage?" Héloïse asks, shifting her eyes from the river to her friend of almost fifteen years. "What about your children?"

It is Marie who now stares out the large windows. "Father Enfantin says that marriage is a tyranny. That men and women should be free to love one another at will."

"Yes, I've read Enfantin, and I agree with much of what he says about marriage, especially the way it works in France." In Germany, both women know, Marie would be able to attain a divorce and retain full control of her dowry. "But I don't understand how you can risk your daughters. If you leave your husband, you could lose them forever."

"I'm aware of our medieval custody laws," Marie responds sourly, twirling one of the golden curls that fall in front of her ears. "But try to understand what I'm *feeling*, Héloïse. There are times I think I've been chosen by the gods to be Franz's muse—a kind of martyr on his altar."

"And this doesn't strike you as a kind of tyranny?" Héloïse raises an eyebrow.

"To be a saint of *love*, to be the mediator of Franz's *genius*—what greater purpose could possibly shape my life?"

Héloïse remains silent, waiting for her friend to see the logical flaw in her own argument.

"Have I ever told you about my evenings with the Duchess of Angoulême?" Marie asks in a voice now empty of passion, though her eyes are begging for Héloïse's approval. Because of her husband's royal pedigree, Marie occasionally serves as lady-in-waiting to Marie-Antoinette's aging daughter. "We sit in a perfect oval doing needlepoint. Depending on our rank, we are assigned a place closer to or further away from our lugubrious hostess. There's no conversation—only a series of superficial questions, initiated by the duchess according to a code of etiquette whose origins nobody remembers. At one end of the room the king plays whist. At the other, the duke plays checkers. None of them ever speaks a word. The clock ticks loudly in the corner, and I think I will go *mad*."

"I understand," Héloïse replies, smiling at the thought of her lively friend sitting with mindless docility in a sewing circle. "Sounds ghastly. But let's return to your children. What is your plan for them? And what will you do for income?"

"Why do you think I haven't already run off with the man?" Marie snaps back, her eyes directed once again across the river.

~

Several months later the two women are returning from a party given by Paris's most prolific hostess, the Princess Belgiojoso. The evening's guests, among others, have included the Polish composer Frederick Chopin, the painter Eugène Delacroix, and the infamous writer George Sand.

"The woman's *incredible*!" Marie almost shouts out the carriage window. "Can you imagine anyone else getting away with wearing men's clothing and smoking cigars in public—"

"And managing a legal separation from her husband, personal assets intact—including children!" Héloïse interjects, still astounded at this episode of Sand's growing legend. "She reminds me of the women Aunt Célestine used to tell me stories about when I was little—her 'Amazon friends from the Marais,' she liked to call them."

"I remember you talking about them back at school. Wasn't Reverend Mother Barat one of them?"

"I don't think so!" Héloïse sputters, widening her eyes and looking at Marie as if she's spent too much time under the full moon. "She might have *met* some of them once—she and Aunt Célestine were both living in the Marais when they were in their teens. But these were singers and actresses and political activists—women of the Revolution"— she paused for a moment and lowered her voice into its most suggestive register—"and none of them leading a life of chastity as I recall."

"I sometimes think about the Reverend Mother Barat," Marie mused, ignoring Héloïse's last remark. "She was very kind to me once. I've often wondered what she was like as a young girl."

"Aunt Célestine says she was the most delightful child in Joigny—passionate, imaginative and *terrifyingly* intelligent!"

"Maybe that's why she never married!" Marie snaps back, and the two women burst into laughter, feeling as if they're fifteen once again and back in boarding school.

But as she laughs, Héloïse looks out the carriage window at the lights along the Seine and begins to think deeply about Sophie Barat—what factors motivated her to take the path she chose, whether the reality of that life has come anywhere close to her original vision. She wonders, too, why Sophie might not in fact be considered one of those "revolutionary" women Célestine still loves to talk about.

When she looks back at Marie, her friend is watching her with a fixed expression, as if waiting for her full attention.

"I made a decision tonight. I'm leaving for Switzerland with Franz."

Chessboard

1834

At the fifth general council of the society of the sacred Heart, held in Paris at the end of 1833, Elisabeth Gatlitzine and Louise de Limminghe moved into positions of considerable power. As Secretary General, Elisabeth was now responsible for all official communication within the Society; as Admonitrix General, Louise would serve as Sophie's confidential advisor. Félicité Desmarquest and Eugénie de Gramont were voted First and Second Assistants General, respectively. Sophie left the Council uneasy, not because of any specific occurrence, but because of recurring doubts about her capacity to lead.

She called me to the Hôtel Biron several days after it had ended. We sat in her office, looking out into gardens that extended for a half kilometer along the Boulevard des Invalides. Even in late November, they tranquilized the eye and spirit with their sculpted hedges, graveled paths and stark allées of leafless trees. The weather was mild for this time of year, warm enough for a group of students to be out sketching beside a small fountain. Their teacher, a young novice whose great-grandfather's paintings hung in the Louvre, resembled a black and white swan as she motioned her young charges to translate what they saw onto large sheets of paper.

"I feel as if things are slipping through my fingers," Sophie said softly, "as if clusters of power are growing here and there, leading all of us away from our common center." She turned her gaze toward me and held the large silver cross that hung from her neck. "*Cor unum*—One heart. These words are engraved on our crosses. *One heart and one soul in the heart of Jesus.* And yet I feel as if our hearts are splintering in every possible direction."

"My dear Sophie, your 'little Society,' as you like to call it, has doubled since the Constitutions were written," I answered. "How could any single person possibly administer thirty-five separate houses? They're not even all on the same continent!"

"But it's more than that, Guy. Father Rozaven says that in Rome, Félicité Desmarquest is spoken of as the *real* superior. And it's hardly any wonder—she's been training most of our novices for the past thirteen years while I don't even *know* some of them! And you know what's happening in Paris." Here her voice began to rise into an unwonted shrill. "It's a scandal! Our chapel has become the fashionable setting for society marriages and christenings and whatever other manner of ceremony Eugénie and Archbishop Quelen decide should occur there. Even his business meetings are held on the premises!"

I nodded reluctantly. Her concern was well founded, and criticism of the worldliness of the Hôtel Biron was rampant in Paris. In addition, and to Sophie's growing consternation, the school was increasingly identified with the most conservative politics in France as the Archbishop pursued his ongoing cold war with King Louis-Philippe.

"And one more thing. I've just received a very disturbing piece of news." Her voice quavered slightly, and her eyes narrowed. "They've refused to allow my brother to serve as the school confessor."

I looked at her in disbelief. Louis Barat had spent much of his career serving as confessor at his sister's schools, and while he continued to harbor some of his Jansenist inclinations, his professionalism and dedication had never come into question.

"Eugénie asked the Jesuits to send someone to assist our chaplain with his duties," she continued, "and when the Superior recommended Louis, she said no. I received a letter from him this morning."

I whistled softly and remembered another piece of Paris gossip, this one regarding the current chaplain's easy familiarity with the older pupils. "I suspect it may have something to do with your dashing young Father Jammes. He may not want Louis' austerity cramping his style with the young ladies."

"But this is *outrageous*, Guy!" Her eyes flamed with indignation.

I knew it was outrageous, but I also knew that Eugénie had overstepped Sophie's boundaries so many times that she now felt invulnerable.

"So what do you propose to do about it?" I finally asked her. "You've been bemoaning the situation for years, but things keep cruising along at the same pace, at least to the outside observer. It would appear that you need to make a move—probably *several* moves. But are you prepared for an outright break with Eugénie?"

She looked at me with an expression that mingled frustration and fury. Then she looked again into the garden, where the little artists were rolling up their drawings and getting ready to move into the house. The sun had sunk to the level of the Invalides dome, and it seemed as if two globes of light balanced precariously in the late autumn sky.

"It's obvious that changes need to be made," she finally responded. "Not just in Paris but within the entire Society. As you suggest, our administrative structure no longer fits our reality."

"Your Society is like any other group of people, Sophie—a live organism that must adapt or self-destruct. You've done a pretty fair job of adaptation up to now, but this time your crisis points appear to lie within the organization. In some ways, fighting off Napoleon's secret police was easier!"

She laughed wearily, and then her expression changed into one of resolve. "I'm leaving soon for a lengthy trip—but it will give me time to think. I should tell you that I've been in correspondence with Father Rozaven in Rome regarding all of this. He's suggesting we move toward a model that's closer to the that of the Jesuits, with separate provinces and provincial heads. When I return, I should be ready to make some major changes. I've been thinking about this for many months, but I needed your wise voice, old friend. It helps to have advice from the outside world once in awhile."

I smiled at her choice of words, thinking of the small perimeter of my world compared to her ever-widening one.

"Before you leave, Sophie, I need to ask you a small favor."

"Anything, of course."

"I'd like you to speak with Célestine. She's worried about Héloïse."

Book of Revelation: Part I
1834

CÉLESTINE LORRAIN ARRIVES IN THE SWEEPING CIRCULAR DRIVE of the Hôtel Biron at twilight, that magical juncture wherein time and light hang in a state of mutual suspension. It is a moment she loves, when the sky is lit only at its uppermost edge and endows everything below with a bluish cast; when the world waits with hushed voice and bated breath for darkness to descend once again. She remembers Eugène once explaining to her that early twilight—when the sun has sunk only three or four degrees below the horizon line but still casts its light into the upper atmosphere—mirrors the radiance of the full moon. They had climbed onto the roof one evening just before he left for Moscow and watched the sun set together. She sighs deeply and longs for Eugène, even now, ten years after his death. He would have approved her arrival at this "blue hour," when things appear to be what they are not, and reality itself shifts shape in the darkening gloom.

She is heavily veiled and descends from the coach with help from a footman, who leads her up to the entry. A young novice, serving as portress, leads the mysterious figure down a corridor and into Sophie's office at the back of the building. Through the windows, the garden is a maze of curves and shadows—black, grey and dusky indigo. Seated before them, looking into the maze, is a small figure in black, who turns her own veiled head as the figure enters the room. Célestine lifts off her wide-brimmed hat to reveal her identity. Sophie stands up and opens her arms.

"My beautiful friend!" she exclaims, folding Célestine into her embrace. "You've come." Her voice ripples with emotion.

She steps back to look at her, seeking the child she remembers beneath the elegantly coiffed matron whose slowly whitening hair is swept up into an Apollo knot. She offers the chair next to hers, and Célestine removes her cloak, revealing a dress with enormous gigot sleeves and a wide pelerine collar.

"I'm sure you know why I'm here," Célestine opens awkwardly, pressing her gloved hands together and leaning forward in her chair.

"Your brother only told me that it concerns Héloïse," Sophie replies gently. "That you are worried about her."

Célestine leans back and stares into the garden's violet darkness.

"She's begun to ask me questions, Sophie. Questions I don't know how to answer."

"What kind of questions?" Sophie asks after a long silence. Her voice is filled with that boundless optimism Célestine remembers from their girlhood. It seems, as it did then, to sweep everything away before it, leaving only simplicity and trust.

"About who she is." She twists her hands and clasps her fingers tightly together. "You must know I've been waiting for this. They say the truth always finds its way to the light."

Sophie waits for her to continue.

"Something happened when Marie was so ill the first time. When we thought she was dying. We were all at the house, and Denis arrived. Drunk. Screaming."

She halts briefly to reassemble the fragments of a scene she's tried to repress for the past three years and looks directly at Sophie. "He shouted something that Héloïse picked up. I didn't think she heard it. She waited until almost a year after Marie died, but she finally went to visit Denis's wife. His wife went to school with her here, if you remember."

Sophie bows her head and laces her own fingers together as if to pray away a marriage she'd prefer to forget. Instead, she sees the young countess as she appeared to her not long after the wedding—the bruises that had covered her face and neck. The eye that was swollen shut. The terror that had informed her every word.

"At first the girl refused to speak. But then she admitted Denis had said something odd once. About Héloïse. It was during one of his drunken rages, so she didn't give it much credence. And Denis said he'd kill her if she ever repeated it."

"What did he say to her?"

"Héloïse wouldn't tell me. But she asked me if there was anything about her birth that I thought she should know." Célestine's pupils have dilated so that her eyes appear almost black. She looks back out the window, where the last vestige of light has disappeared. "Sophie, this was several weeks ago. And I don't know what to do." Her voice is barely audible, and she begins to rock slightly in her chair.

Sophie leans forward and takes Célestine's hands in her own. She can feel their chill despite the gloves, as if her friend's blood had stopped circulating entirely.

"I've known you all my life, and yet I've never shared with you my own deepest secret," Sophie opens. Célestine pivots her head back toward Sophie, and the rocking stops. "It's the secret that keeps me going when I feel utterly abandoned. When I hold my life up to the light and think about how I've used it, how I've lost my way, how I've betrayed all the hopes and passions of my youth."

At Célestine's incredulous expression, Sophie nods her head and squeezes her friend's hands. A full minute passes before she continues.

"When I was a little girl and Louis sent us those images of the Sacred Heart—you must remember seeing them on our wall in Joigny—I used to stare at them for hours.

"And when Louis was in prison and my mother was out of her mind with grief and my father had lost himself in his work to forget that he was losing his family, I could look at those pictures and know there was something outside of our little world that could give me strength. Not through fear or self-denial or self-affliction, but through love. Ah—the power of that heart!"

To mark her words, she takes Célestine's hands, still folded in her own, and moves them toward the large silver cross hanging over her own heart. "You *do* believe in love, Célestine?"

Célestine looks back into the darkness and nods her head listlessly, believing at this point only in its fragility.

"If you can't use my image, then think of the power of love as it works in your life. Especially of its power to heal. There is no stronger power in the universe. You know it as well as I, especially as it resides in your love for Héloïse. But you must trust it—and know that it will survive anything, even the truth. Especially the truth."

She feels Célestine's hands grow rigid in her own. "If I tell her, I could lose her."

"What makes you think she won't love you all the more when she knows who you really are?"

"To discover she's been deceived about her entire life? To know she isn't who she thinks she is? That she owes her existence to—" her voice breaks and she pulls her hands away. When she is again able to speak, she says dully. "It's like a trap that has finally snapped shut."

"Or a trap that has just sprung open," Sophie counters. "She's your daughter. Whatever you have done you did out of love for her. You must trust that she will understand that."

Knights and Castles

1834 – 1836

As the first snows began to fall, Sophie travelled due north from Paris to visit the foundations in Beauvais, Lille and Amiens. After Christmas, she began moving in a large arc, journeying southwest through Le Mans, Poitiers, Niort, and Bordeaux and then eastward toward Lyon. When she arrived in France's second-largest city, she found herself in the midst of bloody street riots. The city's silk workers were in open revolt, protesting the cutting of wages and the repression of their right to form trade unions.

"We're surrounded by the endless rumbling of cannons," she wrote to me in mid-April. "The military has occupied the town and the bridges leading into the city, and we hear the crack and fire of rifles day and night. Whole sections of the city are in flames or have been leveled by cannon fire. Troops are firing on the unarmed crowds, and hundreds have been wounded or killed. It's worse than anything I remember from the July Days of 1830."

A similar letter followed. "The leaders of the uprising are on trial, and the workers are all on strike. We all pray that the violence will end soon. I was surrounded by poor children at the school two days ago.

No wonder there are so many! Lyon is home to thousands of weavers, as well as tens of thousands of apprentices and assistants. They all live in the most squalid of conditions—and now the owners talk of cutting wages!"

I heard the voice of the barrel maker's daughter and smiled in spite of the letter's grim news.

A month later, Sophie's carriage pulled into the gates of the Hôtel Biron. The building was ablaze with lights, despite its being almost midnight on a Sunday, and when she entered the main hall, the room was teeming with students, clerics and religious, all of them there to celebrate Archbishop de Quelen on the Feast of the Good Shepherd.

"She's lost her *mind*, my poor Eugénie!" she exclaimed, outlining for me the scene that had greeted her. We were seated at a small table in a hidden corner of the garden, now exploding with color.

"There was a band of musicians—" she continued, leaning forward and opening her eyes wider to accent her point, "hired musicians!— playing at one end of the room. Tables were loaded with sweets. Japanese lanterns were strung everywhere across the ceiling. We might as well have been at the Tuileries Palace!" Here she leaned back in her chair, as if the account had exhausted her descriptive powers. "If I needed one more piece of evidence to tip the scales—"

"But you don't."

"No. I don't. This settles it."

"So tell me the order of our business this afternoon." I took out my pen.

She replied in a voice that rang with an authority I'd not heard for some time. "I plan to reopen the novitiate in Paris. You are going to draw up a contract with the Marquis de Nicolay, who has offered his home in the rue Monsieur for use as our new Mother House."

She waited a moment for me to grasp the importance of this point before continuing.

"It will be the center of operations for the entire Society—a place where I shall reside, along with my Assistants General, and where our novices will come for formation. It will be *completely* separate from the

school and house all of our offices, including the treasury, the secretariat, and the archives."

I knew that all of what she suggested lay well within the bounds of the Constitutions, but her implementation of it—and, more important, her removal of herself and the novitiate from the rue de Varenne—would send a direct signal to Eugénie and Archbishop Quelen that things were moving in a new direction. I tipped my head slightly to acknowledge my approval and began writing.

When I'd finished with these notes, she continued.

"I'm also relieving Félicité Desmarquest as Mistress of Novices. It's too much responsibility for her to hold that position and function as First Assistant General. I'm naming Eulalie de Bouchard to replace her. She is thirty-two years old, gifted in spiritual guidance, and the perfect person to train our next generation of religious, despite her youth. Perhaps because of her youth."

I sat back in my chair and whistled softly in admiration. With two swift moves, Sophie had seriously undercut the power of her two top lieutenants.

~

In June, she sent a circular letter to the Society explaining the new changes.

"This little Society, still in its infancy, has already made considerable progress. To achieve continued success in fulfilling the plans that must complete our institute, we have decided to establish our own residence, which will be the Mother House or headquarters of the Society. This house will be the very center of the Society and consequently the source from which the true spirit should spring forth and spread, and which must inspire each and every member who makes up this great family."

Whatever reaction Eugénie had to the new plan was not in evidence when the Mother House opened in July. Archbishop Quelen paid a formal visit to the new establishment and evinced not an atom of angst to the casual observer.

I could only imagine his glee at being free of Sophie's constant presence.

"Eugénie has requested that I let her know ahead of time when I plan to visit the Hôtel Biron," she shared with me on my next visit.

It was obvious that Eugénie was making a show of the authority that remained to her, and in fact, the proximity of the Mother House—just steps away from the school's southern border at the rue de Babylone—made frequent visits from the Superior General not unlikely.

"Thus far," she added, a mischievous twinkle in her eye, "our good Archbishop has been curiously absent when I've taken the liberty of intruding."

"It was a good move, Sophie," I responded, chuckling at the thought of Hyacinthe de Quelen hurriedly summoning his carriage at Sophie's heralded approach. "And long overdue."

She nodded in assent and motioned for me to sit down.

"So what's the next order of business? I know you've brought me here for reasons other than sharing the Archbishop's new predilection for travel."

"Rome," she replied with a smile, as if the mere thought of it lifted her out of the political convolutions of Paris.

"It's time for us to open a new establishment in Rome. The Villa Rufina is proving far too small to house both the school and the novitiate. Father Rozaven suggests, among other things, that we separate the novitiate and move it elsewhere."

"What else does Father Rozaven say?" I asked, trying to keep the cynicism out of my voice. Despite our many differences, Eugénie and I shared a deep concern about Rozaven's tendency to micromanage the Society's affairs. His location in Rome and close connections with the Vatican did nothing to mitigate that concern.

"He wants me to travel to Rome immediately to talk about a new administrative structure. I've told him that I must remain in Paris for several months to consolidate the position of the Mother House."

I nodded a quick assent, acknowledging her need to stay in Paris and wondering what new "administrative structure" Rozaven might have in mind. I fought off the impulse to inquire further about his plan and waited for her to continue.

"In the meantime, we may have found a property for the novitiate."

I held my pen poised in the air. "And this property is?"

"The Villa Lante, on the Janiculum Hill. The Borghese family wants to sell it and is offering us a good price if we reach an agreement quickly."

Sophie stayed at the Mother House for the next eight months, fluttering over her novices like a mother hen. Joseph Varin, showing visible signs of his almost seventy years—including a heavy limp owing to his youthful military wounds—visited occasionally to share his dramatic narration of the Society's birth amidst the fire and blaze of the Revolution.

"I was there this afternoon," Varin said as we enjoyed a quiet dinner at my home in the rue de Rivoli. "When I arrived, they were all gathered around her at the far end of the garden—an attentive circle of white veils under a grove of linden trees. She was telling the tale of a monk who goes into ecstasy upon hearing the sound of a bird; when he comes back to consciousness, a hundred years have passed."

I smiled, remembering as if it were yesterday my eight-year-old sister in thrall to Sophie's stories.

"And what great wisdom did she pull out of this for her young protégées?" I asked.

"Something about her desire to be present at the end of the world," he replied, "to share stories about the Society's beginnings that no one would ever believe." His face wore the expression of a proud father who marvels at the distance his child has traveled even as he wonders at the years that have flown by.

"She's happiest doing this work," I said softly.

The old Jesuit nodded. "She spoke a great deal today about Poitiers. About Lydia Chobelet and Joséphine Bigeu and the woodland nymphs from Bordeaux. She still calls it her Manresa."

We both knew she was headed into a storm, and I hoped she was storing as much energy from this interlude as she could. Varin's next words gave voice to my anxiety.

"I received a letter from Rozaven three days ago," he said. "He's railing for her return to Rome and wants me to throw her into the next carriage south."

"She's told me as much," I replied, feeling my neck muscles tighten at the mention of his name. "Our good father in Rome doesn't seem to understand the need for her to strengthen what she's just founded in Paris."

"I'm not at all convinced that he's *happy* with what she's just founded in Paris," was Varin's quick reply. "I strongly suspect he wishes the Mother House were located near the Vatican."

Book of Revelation: Part II

1835 – 1836

WHILE SOPHIE REVELS IN THESE QUIET MONTHS WITH HER NOV-
ices, she is also receiving a steady stream of visits from Héloïse de Beixedon.

The young woman, who arrives at the new Mother House only days
after its opening, is now thirty years of age and bears a striking resemblance to her mother. Her ash blond hair, parted in the center, falls over
her ears in two braids that sweep back and upward to encircle a knot at
her crown. She dresses with far more simplicity than Célestine, however,
and wears no ornament except for a narrow gold bracelet—a gift from
Eugène de Beauharnais when she'd turned eighteen, the year before his
death. As she enters Sophie's new office, she curtsies in the way she was
trained to do at the Hôtel Biron.

Sophie, who greets her with the open arms she generally reserves
for her novices, notes Héloïse's self-consciousness and suggests that they
walk through the gardens.

"I saw the way you looked at me," the young woman says, staring
intently at the gravel path as they move away from the building. "And

I know what you must be thinking." She forces her eyes away from the ground and offers Sophie a shy smile.

"Tell me what I was thinking, my darling girl," Sophie responds with a playful grin. "I'm always so interested to learn what's going through my mind."

Héloïse's smile widens and they take several more steps before she speaks. "That I look just like her." Here she looks directly at Sophie, and her smile disappears. "I don't see how I could have missed it."

When she realizes that Héloïse is waiting for a response, Sophie takes her arm and steers her toward a bed where lavender and roses spill over a low stone border. "Most of us see what we're trained to see, Héloïse. It's only the rarest person who can push past those fundamental truths she's been taught to accept for her entire life."

"But I've *always* felt like the outsider in my family. Somehow I should have known."

An edge of self-reproach has crept into Héloïse's voice, as if a lifetime's clues have somehow eluded her and now heaped themselves at her feet, mocking her inattention. "When I was little and behaved badly, my brothers always said I'd been left on the doorstep by gypsies. Jean-Louis still thinks I come from some wild place he'll never understand."

"Your uncle Guy has shared a bit about your struggles in this regard," Sophie responds, imagining the storm that would have broken if Louis Barat's visions of her future had not coincided with her own. "We're not all meant to have husbands, you know."

The two women exchange a sly smile, and Héloïse pauses to take in the scene before her, feeling her body begin to relax. The perfume of roses hangs heavily in the air, and she drops Sophie's arm, leans into the flowerbed, and breathes in the fragrance of an opening rosebud. On a neighboring bush, two butterflies flit about in a frantic dance of courtship, finally losing themselves in the folds of a large crimson blossom.

"I've always felt so much closer to Aunt Célestine than I did to my—" She moves to a nearby bench and falls into it heavily. "Listen to me. I don't even know what to call anyone anymore!"

Sophie remains standing, a vertical slash of black amid arabesques of surrounding color. The frill of white that encircles her face illuminates her expression and enhances the darkness of her eyes.

"How *is* your mother?"

Héloïse's expression slides through a series of emotions, finally landing somewhere between grief and disorientation.

"One of the strangest things is waking up in the morning to find oneself no longer an orphan."

The butterflies zoom out of the rose and fly off into another bed, to be replaced by a hummingbird that hangs in the air, its wings a blur of motion. Héloïse stares at it transfixed, and Sophie turns to see what has captured her attention.

"What happened to my mother, Aunt Sophie?" she finally asks when the bird has flown away.

The question drops into the silence, and it is Sophie who now shifts her gaze to the gravel. She twists the gold band that she's worn on her finger for almost forty years and joins Héloïse on the bench.

"I don't know," Sophie replies gently. "She's never told me, though I'm certain she was violated in some way after she moved to Paris."

Héloïse closes her eyes and wraps her arms tightly around her shoulders as if to protect herself. "How do you know this?"

"Because it's the only logical explanation for what happened later. And because she knew that I knew it without ever having to tell me. We always read each other's minds as children, and that doesn't change with time."

Héloïse begins rocking sideways on the bench and then slowly opens her eyes, turning them on Sophie in expectation of something more.

"What has she told you?" Sophie finally asks.

"Only that she broke down. That she was in some terrible abyss for many months, and that my mother—I'm sorry, that *Marie* and other women took care of her."

"That's all Marie ever told me," Sophie responds. "But there's only one event I can imagine that would send a woman into that particular darkness where your mother ended up. When she finally emerged, I think she wanted to kill herself. And doing what she did seemed a way to do it."

Another minute goes by before Héloïse responds. "And yet she's survived. And in many ways, she seems far stronger than Marie ever was."

"We can never know what the two of them endured during that first year or so in Paris. We were all living through one kind of horror or another, but something happened that broke their spirit. I suspect it started with the factory. That kind of slavery can be death to the soul. But in your mother's case it was more than that. And while Célestine's life might appear far more broken on the surface, I would agree that it was Marie's spirit which was utterly crushed."

When the hummingbird zooms off to find another bed, the two women get up and resume walking.

Héloïse visits several more times over the ensuing months. They discuss her mother's childhood in Joigny, the stolid Lorrain family's inability to understand their youngest child, the women she fell in with during the final years of the Revolution.

"I met some of those women!" Sophie recalls, clapping her hands together at the memory. "Your mother and I walked all over the Marais one afternoon not that long after the Terror had ended. I remember drinking hot chocolate and feeling like a country bumpkin in my Burgundian clothes. They were a colorful group indeed!"

Héloïse laughs aloud, remembering Marie d'Agoult's suggestion that Sophie had been one of these revolutionary *amazones*. When she explains the source of her laughter, Sophie asks what has become of her delightful young friend.

"I thought you might have heard," Héloïse responds with a note of surprise and suddenly becomes serious. "She's left her husband and is living in Switzerland with Franz Liszt. A daughter was born to them last December."

Sophie leans back in her chair and stares at an image on the far wall of her office.

Héloïse continues, filling with a strange sense of guilt on Marie's behalf. "Before you judge her, you should know that she struggled for many months before abandoning her family."

"I don't judge her, *ma chère*," is Sophie's gentle reply. "That is God's work, is it not? Or perhaps better said, that is our work—to judge ourselves, I mean, when we have a moment's grace to feel God's presence working within us."

"You know, of course, that I have a great deal of difficulty with your notion of God," Héloïse responds with unaccustomed shortness.

"And what is my notion of God?" Sophie asks, looking at Héloïse with a mix of indulgence and genuine curiosity. "And before you answer, perhaps you might share with me your own sense of God."

Héloïse squares her shoulders and answers with a question. "Do you know the writings of Félicité Lammenais?"

Sophie nods and looks again at the engraving on the wall. "Indeed I do. There are parts of his thinking I find quite compelling."

"How can you *not* find it compelling? How can anyone? His belief in the power of the Church to regenerate society—it's so obvious! I don't see how the pope can condemn him."

"I suspect he's rather unnerved by some of Lammenais' anti-royalist remarks. And he didn't condemn Lammenais himself—only some of what he has written."

"What? That the working class is entitled to a life of dignity? That the Church should be free of the power of the State? If anything, his writings defend the pope against the kings and bishops who are constantly undermining him! Don't you find that a bit ironic?"

Sophie smiles at the rising passion in the young woman's voice, and she also remembers Lammenais' persuasive opposition to Charles X's veiled command that women's religious orders apply for full legal recognition. She is still apprehensive about the signed document that lies quietly in the Society archives. "You seem to know his writings well."

"I've met him," Héloïse responds quickly, and Sophie raises her eyebrows. "He's Franz Liszt's spiritual advisor. Marie and I have read almost everything he's written."

"People are afraid of some of the ideas he presents," Sophie explains.

"But these are truths of the Gospel! How can you deny them?"

"You cannot force the future, *ma chère*. It takes time for people to understand new ways of thinking, even when they are just. It is difficult, I know, but we must exercise patience." Yet she applauds the young woman's intensity and feels a glimmer of self-recognition. "Now tell me what you think about God."

"What I do know is that my God has nothing to do with the Church." Héloïse responds after a long silence.

"In this I think you are very much like your mother," Sophie smiles. "And your uncle Guy, for that matter."

"My mother says she's always been an outsider. Maybe even more than I am. And we're both very skeptical of groups. We see them as dangerous. They can make us do things we wouldn't otherwise do. All you need to do is look at recent history to know that!"

"In some cases, yes. But not all groups are harmful, and many people need their support. It takes a great deal of strength to sustain one's outsider status, don't you think?"

"Maybe," Héloïse responds a bit sullenly. "But I'm leery of falling into patterns of behavior dictated by men with impure motives."

"Ah. Purity of motives," Sophie answers with serenity. "And where do *you* find purity of motives?"

Héloïse pauses a long time before answering. "In art. In music."

Sophie looks across the room at the painting on her wall—the one item, the scarlet Madonna, that she retains from the secret chapel in the Marais—and wonders what personal or political agenda might have colored the artist's vision of Mary and Jesus. Or whether she agrees with Dante that art is indeed the unsullied grandchild of God.

Héloïse's final visit occurs just days before Sophie's departure for Rome.

"I'm leaving next week for Germany and Sweden," she announces. "To visit two of my cousins."

Eugène de Beauharnais' six children have, to put it mildly, all married well. The eldest daughter, Joséphine, is now Crown Princess of Sweden and Norway; the second daughter, Eugénie, is Princess of Hohenzollern-Hechingen. Both have adored Héloïse since her childhood visits to Munich; neither will ever know that she is their half-sister.

"We'll both be on the road then, *ma chère*. Tell me what you will be doing in these exotic northern places."

"Cousin Eugénie is gathering a large group to celebrate the birthday of her cousin—of *our* cousin." She smiles an odd smile. "Louis-Napoleon, Hortense's son. They were born on the same day and have been celebrating their birthday together since they were children."

"And what is the young Napoleon up to?" Sophie asks with just a shiver of nerves.

"He spends most of his time in Italy."

Sophie hears the reluctance in her voice and suddenly grasps that this young Napoleon—son of Hortense de Beauharnais and Napoleon's brother Louis—is also Héloïse's first cousin.

"And how does the young man occupy himself in Italy?"

She waits a long time for Héloïse to answer and is relieved when she answers frankly. "He associates with the Carbonari."

Sophie stays abreast of political events in Italy through Louise de Limminghe, Father Rozaven, and Armande de Causans. She knows the young Bonaparte is now first in line to assume the imperial throne, should the Bonaparte faction ever succeed in overthrowing King Louis-Philippe. She knows that he is involved with the Carbonari, and she is well aware that the Carbonari, in their drive to unify Italy, bitterly oppose the pope—and religion and its hold on the Italian people in general.

"And why do you go to Sweden?" she finally asks, shifting her mind away from the tangled consequences of a revolution in Italy.

"My cousin Joséphine has asked me to come. Her husband, Crown Prince Oscar, is having an affair with an actress."

The two women exchange a look and continue walking in the garden.

Desire and Forgiveness

1835

IN THE SUMMER OF 1835, I TRAVELLED TO JOIGNY FOR THE CHRIStening of my sister Véronique's first male grandchild, born to her son Christophe and to be named after me. Christophe had married his second cousin Jeanne, daughter of the young Nicolas Guillot who had so gallantly offered a bouquet of pink and white roses to Sophie forty years before. The young couple had taken over the running of the extensive Guillot vineyards outside Joigny.

As I rolled out of Paris, news of yet another attempt on the life of King Louis-Philippe greeted me in the morning headlines. It was the seventh assassination attempt that year.

A native Corsican named Carlo Fieschi, described in the article as an "anarchist, soldier of fortune, adventurer, and vagabond," had constructed an "infernal machine" comprised of twenty-five gun barrels that fired simultaneously as the king passed in the street below. His accomplices claimed membership in the radical Republican Society of the Rights of Man. All went according to plan except that the weapon failed in its primary target—giving the king a harmless flesh wound but killing eighteen people and injuring forty-two others. Among its victims was Denis Marmaton, who lost both legs and his left eye to the explosion.

"Sounds like a fitting punishment for the dreadful man," Véronique exclaimed with an unusual degree of passion; she had inherited our grandmother's Swedish calm.

We were gathered around the family dining table after the baby's baptism at Saint Thibault.

"It's a miracle he's survived as long as he has," her husband Alain responded. "You can't help but marvel at his ability to stand for absolutely no set of principles and yet wriggle his way into the bosom of whoever's in power at a given moment."

"I believe they call it soullessness," was Véronique's icy rejoinder.

"Whatever we may think of Denis, he's managed to keep the assassins at bay for the last several decades," I replied. "The miracle is that Louis-Philippe has survived the past five years."

"He's a tyrant!" Christophe barked from his place at the table. "He may claim to be our 'Citizen King' but he's as autocratic as his Bourbon cousins—and as murderous as they were, if not worse!"

Christophe had been in Lyon at the time of the *Semaine sanglante* the year before, when hundreds of silk-workers were killed by the army. Thousands more were later deported after hasty trials. "At least the Bourbons didn't pretend to be friends of the people!" he added.

"One does wonder how long the man will stay alive," I acknowledged. "This plot was engineered by Republicans, probably in connection with a Carbonari cell. But the Ultra-monarchists are rumored to have organized the last one, and the Bonapartists are muttering that Louis-Napoleon is organizing an army in Strasbourg."

"You call him a man? He's an imbecilic *poire*!" Christophe exclaimed through a mouthful of *terrine de porc*. His young wife shot him a look at his use of language, reminding him with her eyes of the presence of their two small daughters.

The rest of us chuckled at his allusion to the political cartoon that had captured the heart of the nation—and landed its artist in jail: a four-stage caricature showing the face of Louis-Philippe turning into a pear. The image, complete with its disparaging and lewd implications, had become a powerful allegory of the deterioration of the King's popularity.

"If the income gap continues to widen, most of France will welcome *any* change from the current mess," interjected Véronique's son-in-law Antoine. He taught history and economics at the Collège Saint Jacques and tended to side with the Republican and Bonapartist elements. "I almost wish the young Bonaparte would make his move."

"There are more than a few Joigny families who are struggling to hang onto their homes or businesses—or both," Alain added, wishing to steer the conversation away from Louis Napoleon but agreeing in principle with his son-in-law. "I've never seen anything like it in my forty years as a solicitor." His profession was allowing him to witness first-hand the downturn that was threatening the entire French economy.

What Alain didn't know was that I'd recently floated a large loan to Christophe in order to keep him from losing his wine business.

"So, Uncle Guy," Antoine's wife Marie-Claire interrupted, reading her father's discomfort and determined to head the discussion away from politics. "You must bring us up to date on other events in Paris. How is the lovely Sophie Barat? She's not visited Joigny in such a very long time, and we get very little information out of Marie Louise."

"She's right," Véronique concurred. "How goes our town's favorite daughter? And what's the latest news on Marie's children? Has Héloïse found a husband yet?"

I filled them in first on the de Bexeidon family and then offered the short version of Sophie's current political crisis. "She'll be off to Rome soon to try to relieve the tension between the Gallican and Roman factions. I'm afraid that the group in Rome is every bit as hard-nosed as Quelen and the rest of the French bishops."

"And by extension the French king!" Alain interjected. "Does she have any idea what she's up against?"

"Trying to undo seven hundred years of history in one fell swoop?" Antoine commented with more than a tinge of cynicism. "This I can't wait to see!"

"If anyone can do it, it's Sophie," Véronique responded. She chafed at her son-in-law's liberal politics. "You've never even met her!"

Marie-Claire kicked her husband under the table, and he tucked dutifully back into his *terrine*.

"This may be more than even she can resolve," I responded. "Church politics at their worst. It could mean a serious break within the Society."

Several hours later, when the guests had all gone home and Alain had retired for the night, Véronique and I found ourselves alone together. I poured us each a glass of brandy, and we sat in the salon of the home in which we'd been raised.

"You have a rich life, Véronique," I observed, thinking of her sitting at the large dining table that afternoon, surrounded by her children and grandchildren.

She smiled shyly and waved her hand as if to minimize the compliment. "Not as glamorous as your life in Paris, Guy. But God has been good to us. I cannot complain."

"I'm honored that Christophe and Jeanne have given their son my name, you know."

"They love you very much." She looked at me oddly before continuing. "I think they figured it was the surest way for your name to continue. It's a matter of much speculation among us all why you never had a family of your own."

I stared into my brandy, stunned that my older sister would break through her normal reserve and ask such a question.

I shrugged my shoulders in response and swirled the liquid in my glass. The light from the fire had died down and given the room the appearance of a dark cave.

"I remember when we all used to joke about Germont Fouffé," she continued, "following her around with that dejected expression. *He* never married either." Her pointed reluctance to speak Sophie's name was the only vestige of her usual restraint. "Has it satisfied you, this life of devotion to a woman who will never be yours?" she continued.

I shrugged my shoulders again, annoyed by my sister's tactless questions. "I suppose in the final analysis one's state of satisfaction depends entirely on one's self," I responded. "Much like forgiveness."

Now it was Véronique's turn to stiffen.

"If I'm satisfied," I continued, "—and I *am*, by the way—it's because I've put an end to my desire for whatever it was that I once wanted and reshaped it. It's entirely within my power. It's within anyone's power, you know."

She stared into her glass.

"Véronique, it's been almost forty *years*." I took a deep breath before continuing. "How much longer can you hold on to your rage?"

"*You* weren't here to see father sinking into an early death!" she hissed. "Or mother living on for twenty more years in a misery of grief and shame!"

"Mother's been dead for a decade," I retorted. "Father for over thirty years. When do you finally let it go? She's your only sister."

"She's not my sister! She gave that relationship away when she left home. And again when she took up that life."

I waited to frame my response.

"I understand, Véronique. I saw what her actions did to mother and father. But neither you nor I have any idea what her life was like when she first arrived in Paris. I don't think either of us can possibly imagine. And she went there in order to support Marie, remember—an act of incredible kindness, even if it almost destroyed her own family."

I could see that my words were getting nowhere. These were old arguments, and time had not made them any more persuasive.

"I've also seen what she's done since Eugène left her," I added. At the mention of his name I saw her flinch. "It took me time, but I came to understand (and it was Sophie, you might be interested to know, who helped me get there) that I could release my self-righteous fury and see her for what she is. Whatever you may think, Célestine is a remarkable and generous woman."

"Remarkable and generous woman!" She spat out my words and moved to the fireplace to stir the remaining embers. "Remarkable and generous woman indeed! She's a—"

My sister's inflated sense of decorum prevented her finishing the sentence, and I marveled at how an inability to forgive can harden the human spirit.

"Think, if nothing else," I added gently, "about what this is doing to you. I said you had a rich life, Véronique. Think about making it richer."

When she made no response, I stood up and kissed the top of her head before going upstairs to my room.

275

Part 10

Rome and Paris

Our Lady of Sorrows

1837 – 1838

SOPHIE REENTERS THE CITY OF ROME ON A COLD BUT SUNNY AFTER-
noon. She has been on the road for over eight months, visiting foundations in the south of France, Chambéry, Montet, Turin, and Parma.
When she reaches the Villa Rufina, where a boarding school has now
been added to the free school and the novitiate, women and children are
tumbling over one another like everything else in the Trastevere.

"My novices are withering away before my eyes," she says to Louise
de Limminghe, who has travelled with her from Paris. "We must find
them space in which to *breathe!*"

L'Addolorata, who is always happiest when looking on the dark side,
agrees that the need for another building has reached the crisis point.

The next day the two women leave La Rufina early to visit the Borghese property. A carriage takes them up the hill and along the road that
winds its way along the crest of the Janiculum Hill. Their driver helps
them to dismount, and all three of them pause to look at the dazzling
panorama spread out beneath them. Across the city on the Pincian Hill,
the towers of the Trinità dei Monti, wheat-colored in the morning light,
nod in their direction. Below them to the left, St. Peter's Basilica lifts

its golden dome, the baroque curve of Bernini's piazza just visible to its right.

The villa is a gem of cinquecento architecture, designed, they discover later, by Raphael's favorite pupil, Giulio Romano. A graceful sweep of stairs curves upward to the large front door from either side of the facade, and cream-colored pilasters and wrought-iron balustrades stand out against the villa's pale apricot walls. On either side of the building lemon and orange trees, bearing blossoms and fruit even in the Roman winter, share space with vineyards and vegetable gardens that spill down the eastern slope of the Janiculum Hill.

"It's beautiful," Sophie exclaims, finding herself once again falling in love with the city and breathless at the acres of natural beauty around her. "But it's far too small, Louise!"

Louise enters the building ahead of her and reemerges almost immediately. "You must come inside," she beckons with a degree of agitation. "Wait before you make any decision!"

Still in thrall to her surroundings, Sophie obediently mounts the curving staircase and allows Louise to lead her over to a fresco.

"Our Lady of Sorrows," Louise almost whispers, as if afraid to disturb the woman depicted on the wall. "Just look at her!"

The fresco is in need of restoration, but Sophie is struck by its profound sadness. It is a Pietà, but unlike any she has ever seen. Mary sits alone, a bare foot emerging from under her robe, her arms encircling only a crown of thorns, her palms open and utterly bereft. Three empty crosses stand on a hill behind her. The body of Jesus is nowhere yet everywhere, and that eerie physical absence causes Sophie quite literally to catch her breath.

Louise smiles inwardly at her reaction, but Sophie holds to her objection.

"She's beautiful, my darling *Addolorata*, but we'll be hardly better off than we are already. It's quite impossible!"

The two of them walk into villa's main salon where five floor-to-ceiling windows reach up two stories and give onto the spectacle of Rome below.

Sophie looks down the hill at the terraced vineyards and orchards and notices an enormous structure below. Even from this distance, its state of dilapidation is evident, but it boasts three large wings and glows with the color of golden ocher.

"What is that building down there?" she asks the driver, who has wandered in with them to investigate the villa's interior.

"Ah, *signora*, that is the ghost palace!" he answers quickly.

"The ghost palace?" Sophie exclaims, shooting a curious look across the room to Louise.

"*Si, signora*," he responded with a slight bow and explained. "It is haunted. It was last used as a tobacco warehouse, but the workers claimed it was full of ghosts. It, too, is owned by the family Borghese."

Sophie looks again at Louise. "If we can have that building, too, I'll take them both!" she snaps, her expression suddenly all business. "It's highly unlikely the locals will want to buy a haunted house!"

Two months later, both properties belong to the Society.

While repairs are made to the ghost palace, she and her band of young women retire to the hilltop villa, where they farm the extensive terraced gardens, tend the grapes that they will harvest in the fall, listen to Sophie's endless stories, and revel in their seeming proximity to the stars.

In July, when the heat bears down with Mediterranean intensity, cholera strikes.

"The pope is leading processions through the streets, and the churches cannot hold all the supplicants," she writes Eugénie. "So far, no one here at the villa or at Santa Rufina has been taken ill, but we wait with grim anticipation. This area of Rome is so very crowded, and many have died outside our walls. Orphans wander in the streets; we are working to create a shelter for as many of them as we can. All appears to be well at the Trinità, but the general quarantine makes it impossible to travel across the city. It's difficult for us even to receive their letters."

In fact, contact with the Trinità dei Monti is virtually cut off for reasons that go far beyond the cholera quarantine.

"Relations between the schools grow increasingly strained," she writes to Philippine Duchesne. "Santa Rufina has its third superior in as many years, and she's finding the job to be more than she can handle. In addition, she doesn't get on with Armande de Causans, whose leadership of the Trinità is under much criticism. Armande has run the school since its opening ten years ago. She has many powerful friends among the clergy and the Roman aristocracy. But many, including those at Santa Rufina, criticize her for laxity and worldliness. We must keep in mind, of course, that the Italians would love to see us all fully cloistered and back behind grilles! To complicate matters further, the Jesuits, fearing further entanglement with our problems, are now refusing to send their priests to the Trinità. How must this look to those on the outside?"

When seven novices at the Trinità die of cholera, Sophie is not informed. Louise de Limminghe, knowing Sophie's physical frailty, keeps the information from her, fearing she'll find a way to maneuver across the quarantined city and—in ministering to the young victims—fall prey to the disease herself. Armande de Causans, receiving no word of support from Sophie in the face of such catastrophe, believes she has been abandoned.

Sophie is finally told of the deaths all at once, and she writes to Eugénie de Gramont. "The Trinità has been shaken to its foundations. I cannot describe to you how bitterly shocked I was. They believed that they were sparing me several shocks at so many deaths, but this was too much I think! As Louise read the list of names, one by one by one by one, it nearly killed me."

Two more novices die in agony before Sophie can travel to the Trinità. She describes the meeting between herself and Armande as painful, and indeed relations between the two women will never fully recover. Many in the Society, including Eugénie de Gramont, attack Louise de Limminghe for keeping Sophie from knowing the truth; others agree with Louise's judgment and lash out at her detractors.

Meanwhile Eugénie is furious with Sophie for a series of letters she has sent to Archbishop Quelen, imploring him once again to recognize the unseemliness of his residence at the Hôtel Biron.

"You must be aware of the shameful and derisive rumors concerning your residence at the school," Sophie has written him most recently. "They circulate everywhere and confront and depress me wherever I go. The gutter press has carried these rumors as far as Rome. The reputation, even the very existence, of the Society is seriously compromised as is your own."

To punish Sophie for her most recent assault on the Most Reverend Archbishop, Eugénie refuses to answer her letters. When she finally breaks her silence, it is to rebuke Sophie for her impudence. To others, she suggests that Sophie is devious and dishonest.

From America, Philippine writes that the Society there is suffering its own litany of grievances. The houses in Louisiana have become deeply estranged, and local newspapers accuse one of the Superiors of "highly offensive Jesuitical gravity," exposing the fact that she has borrowed money from the local Jesuits and is now unable to pay it back. Sophie knows from several sources that the community in St. Louis feels deserted and that they are resentful of her perceived neglect of the American foundations. A Jesuit priest working in Louisiana suggests to her that a schism is imminent.

Sophie leaves Rome just after Easter, knowing she can no longer delay in calling a sixth General Council. The carriage rumbles its way toward Paris, and she is consumed with grief and apprehension. Never had she imagined, when Joseph Varin thrust her into this position so many years before, the complete isolation in which she would find herself. Regardless of what she does or writes or says, people are waiting to twist her words or actions into something unintended. Her attempts to be generous with one group inevitably lead to bitter accusations from another. Even those women with whom she has shared the very essence of her soul fail to understand, attributing—explicitly or implicitly—callous motives to decisions that she has made out of compassion. As she ponders her current position, she sees the edge of self-pity creeping in to muddle her thinking but is too tired to fend it off.

When she is brave enough to hold her little Society up to the light, she sees nothing but cracks—ready to break open and shower a thousand fragments into the wind.

Ill-Gotten Gains
1838

I WAS CALLED TO DENIS MARMATON'S BEDSIDE SEVERAL WEEKS after his legs were blown off by Giuseppe Fieschi's infernal machine.

He was once again alone in his cavernous home, his wife having died four years before. A stillborn son, delivered breech, finished the work Denis had begun over ten years before on his child bride. It took her twenty-three hours to die as the infant attempted to push himself, buttocks first, into the world—their first and only child to make it to term.

Finding himself deprived of his object of abuse, Denis had offered his services to Louis-Philippe. The first attempt on the Citizen King's life had provoked within His Majesty an understandable desire for increased security, and Denis—effectively retired since the July Revolution—was only too happy to reenter the brutal world of espionage. He was instrumental in uncovering three plots on the king's life in 1832, and it was he who convinced the king to call out the military against the Lyon silk workers two years later.

He was operating as part of the king's covert entourage when Fieschi loosed his angst and his weapon in the rue du Temple. It was the fifth anniversary of the July Revolution, and Louis-Philippe, accompanied by his three sons and a colorful royal entourage, were doing a pass in review of the National Guard. A bullet grazed the king's forehead, but others killed his horse, his top general, and sixteen other people. When Denis Marmaton recovered consciousness two days later, he was missing one leg from below the knee, another from below the hip, and his left eye.

"You never change," he muttered as I approached the large four-poster bed where his mutilated body had been confined for the past several weeks. An infection had set in at one of the amputation sites, and two nurses had just finished changing the bandages and were opening the large mansard windows to air the room. He grimaced with pain as they shifted his position in the bed.

"They're bleeding me like a stuck pig, the sadistic bitches," he said, motioning to the jar of leeches and other bloodletting devices that sat on a neighboring table.

I could only shake my head in response to his situation and took a seat near his bedside. The skin had tightened over his face, rendering it already a mask of death. His single eye fixed me with an expression mingling hatred and envy, and I looked over at the nurses to avoid its effect.

"So you have no words of sympathy for your old friend?" he asked. Even in the face of mortality, his voice seethed with insincerity.

"I'm sorry for your suffering, Denis. Truly." I shifted my gaze back to his face. "But I'm certain you didn't invite me here to engage my pity."

His face assumed its usual leer and then twisted into a ghastly expression of pain. When it had passed, he continued. "I called you here for your professional services. As you see, I'm about to die."

I looked down to unbuckle my briefcase to avoid responding to his last remark. "And you want to get your financial house in order, I presume," I said in as businesslike a tone as I could muster.

"My financial house," he laughed softly. "Yes. My financial house, if that's what you choose to call it." Here he shouted for one of the nurses to give him more morphine.

"What do you want me to do?" I asked, once she had administered the drug.

"Adjust my will."

I removed my copy of his will from the briefcase, unscrewed the top of my pen, and waited.

"I wish to leave all of my assets to the fair Héloïse de Beixedon."

I looked up from my notebook and tried to decode his expression. Whether it was the morphine, the heavy bandage that covered his eye socket and forehead, or the vast moral emptiness at his core, his face was an indecipherable mask.

Bishops, Castles, Knights, and Pawn

1838 – 1839

EN ROUTE BACK TO PARIS, SOPHIE LEARNS THAT POPE GREGORY, AT the instigation of Fr. Jean Rozaven, has sent a priest to investigate the quality of religious life at the Trinità dei Monti. Now firmly allied with Louise de Limminghe, Rozaven is doing all in his power to unseat Armande de Causans. The "inquisitor," as Sophie terms the visiting cleric, has been directed to assess the observation of cloister within the community there, and she is irate at Rozaven's intervention.

"I assure you that while our friends the Jesuits render us services," she writes to Louise, "they also cause us enormous problems. Through lacking more patience and forbearance, they will destroy everything."

Sophie is hoping to name Armande de Causans the new Secretary General at the upcoming General Council, a promotion that would allow Armande to leave her position as head of the Trinità without losing face.

Meanwhile, Cardinal Lambruschini, the Vatican Secretary of State who personally negotiated the acquisition of the Trinità on behalf of the

Society ten years before, is also stalking its corridors. He is a staunch ally and friend of Armande de Causans—as are several other influential cardinals. "We must tread carefully," Sophie writes again to Louise. "Cardinal Lambruschini has never had the habit of going so often to the Trinità, and it is clear he is lining up people in Armande's defense."

Sophie has originally hoped to call the Sixth General Council for the end of 1838, but serious problems with her health defer her arrival in Paris for several months. An infection of her chest and throat leaves her bedridden for weeks in Turin and almost costs her the use of her voice. She feels increasingly isolated, and news that her beloved spiritual advisor, Fr. Jean-Marie Favre, has died in Chambéry leaves her spirit as bereft as her body.

In early August she is strong enough to resume her travels, but she nears Paris with a growing sense of dread. Two enormous decisions lie before her: how to resolve Archbishop Quelen's continuing residence at the Hôtel Biron, and where to hold the Sixth General Council. She knows that whatever setting she chooses will be loaded with implications and consequences. She writes Louise from Autun, "Sleep is difficult and rare. The nerves in my head are frayed and my stomach is upset with anxiety. Worst of all, I find myself almost unable to pray."

When she arrives in Paris, she sees that nothing has changed. The archbishop is as ensconced as ever in his sumptuous quarters, and he refuses to meet with Sophie even to discuss the situation. Eugénie remains icily aloof. Félicité Desmarquest's dominance over the Society in Paris has continued to grow, and Sophie realizes that she and Eugénie will instinctively oppose any significant changes to the Society's power structure.

"It's clear that Paris offers an unsuitable setting for the Council," she writes to Elisabeth Galitzine in Rome just before Christmas. "Archbishop Quelen's presence and the general climate here would make it impossible to move ahead with our proposed changes. Besides that, Armande de Causans refuses to attend if it takes place in Paris." Elisabeth has remained behind in Rome to work out final details of the revised structure with Louise de Limminghe and Fr. Rozaven. No one else in the Society knows anything about the proposals.

On Christmas Eve, Sophie receives the news that Armande de Causans and her top assistant have left the Trinità during the night of December seventh without a word of explanation to anyone in the community. Their official statement to the French ambassador is that Sophie has summoned them to Paris, but in reality the pope—through the mediation of Cardinal Lambruschini—has quietly dispensed them of their vows. They hope to join a community of Visitation sisters in Rome. Joséphine Coriolis, who has authored the letter to Sophie and is now temporarily in charge of the Trinità, has every intention of following them.

In mid-January Sophie receives a glacial letter from Armande's brother, who states that he has taken his sister home to Aix-en-Provence "for the sake of her health." Rumors fly about Rome as Sophie tries to smooth over the women's departure as travel to the upcoming Council.

"I foresaw the indiscretions of the Jesuits," she writes to Louise, barely containing her fury, "but had hoped the situation could be held in check until our meeting. Now that they've pushed the situation to conflict, we must repair the damage. They have done us much harm, and I'm frankly beginning to ask myself who's really running our Society." Louise knows that within Sophie's "they" is a pointed reference to herself and Elisabeth Galitzine, both of whom Sophie has repeatedly begged to heal the rift with Armande.

By now it is clear to her that the Council must occur in Rome, and Sophie hurries there to calm the growing sense of unrest. Her thoughts at this moment are of an even darker cast than those she experienced travelling back to Paris the preceding spring. Armande's defection has put Sophie in a position where lying seems to be the only option. The need to offer an explanation for her sudden disappearance and cover the current brokenness of the Society has eclipsed the value of truth, and Sophie ponders the awful implications of this fact. She asks herself these days whether she is slowly losing her soul in order to hang onto the vision. And in her moments of deepest depression, she asks herself what kind of vision is worth lying for and, worse yet, covering over with a smooth, smiling veneer of hypocrisy. Surely Armande's defection is a marker of either the failure of that vision or her own, personal failure to keep it alive and whole. Louis' voice inevitably whispers in her ear at times like this, and she fears that his angry God will damn her soul to perdition.

She arrives at the Villa Lante on a sunny afternoon in mid-April and calls for an immediate meeting with Louise. The two women sit before the vast expanse of windows that stretch across the villa's western exposure. They look out over acres of red-tiled rooftops, punctuated here and there by a Renaissance church tower or the open space afforded by a piazza. Sophie chooses her words with care.

"I find it astonishing that Pope Gregory would dispense two of our members of their vows without consulting me."

Louise, momentarily relieved that Sophie's criticism is not directed at her, concurs. "I couldn't agree with you more, Sophie. We were all enormously shocked and don't know what he could have been thinking!"

"While I understand that the Vatican may still hold to the monastic model," Sophie continues evenly, "the pope should surely understand that Armande—even in her position as Superior at the Trinità—is subject to *my* authority as Superior General. Our schools, as you well know, are not autonomous."

Even as she speaks, however, Sophie knows that the old ways of doing things die hard—especially at the Vatican, where the mental frameworks that underpin them stretch back many hundreds of years. After a short pause she looks directly at Louise and adds what the other woman has been dreading to hear. "And as you know better than anyone, Louise, I had hoped so very much that a confrontation such as this could have been avoided in the first place."

Louise shifts her eyes to the rooftops and determines how to answer, finally able only to murmur, "I know."

"I've sent several people to Aix-en-Provence to speak with Armande, asking her to reconsider her decision to leave," Sophie continues. "We must all pray that she returns to the Society, whether her work is at the Trinità or elsewhere. But she must not become the scapegoat for larger problems that exist here in Rome. Do you understand?"

Louise nods almost imperceptibly, knowing that she is part of that larger problem but unable to acknowledge any responsibility for the rift.

She answers Sophie with another question. "Who will run the Trinità if she goes somewhere else?"

Sophie, frustrated at her old friend's stubbornness, replies with an unusual degree of impatience. "I will take it over temporarily, though this will only strengthen the perception of many here in Rome that it is I who have forced Armande to resign."

Louise now looks directly at Sophie, seeing in her eyes the anguish of having to suppress the truth in order to preserve the illusion of a larger one.

In May Sophie sends out the invitation for the Sixth General Council of the Society. Because of the enormity of the issues to be discussed, she decides not to include an agenda. Eugénie de Gramont categorically refuses to attend, stating that events in Paris will prevent her from leaving the Hôtel Biron. Two other delegates, Geneviève Deshayes and Henriette Grosier, find themselves unable to travel such a distance because of their precarious health. In a highly unusual move, Sophie asks that they sign a declaration agreeing to abide in advance by the decisions of the Council, a request to which all three agree.

The Council opens in June with ten of the council members present. The only people besides Sophie who know the agenda are Louise de Limminghe, Elisabeth Galitzine, and Jean de Rozaven. It is Rozaven whom she has placed in charge of introducing the proposed changes to the Society's administrative structure—Rozaven, whose tone will inform the entire proceedings.

"I wish it to be known that my presence here enjoys the full approval of the Jesuit Superior General," Rozaven begins, bowing to the assembled women. Catherine de Charbonnel, though she is effectively blind and deaf, later believes that he has clicked his heels in a quasi-military salute. "I have been working for the past several years with Madame Barat on a revised plan for the structuring of the Society of the Sacred Heart, one that is modeled on the Constitution of the Society of Jesus and will more fully serve the needs of your expanding community."

The silence in the room is deafening. Félicité Desmarquest looks across the room at Thérèse Maillucheau, whose eyes have widened into a mystified stare. Elisabeth Galitzine and Louise de Limminghe survey the room to gauge the general reaction and are relieved to note an unusual level of passivity. Sophie notes the same passivity and is filled with foreboding.

Over the next several days, Fr. Rozaven presents forty-seven decrees to the assembled delegates, all of which pass with little or no debate.

"The Society will henceforward be divided into provinces, each with its own provincial to be appointed by the Superior General," Rozaven summarizes on the final day. "The Superior General, the Assistants General, and the Admonitrix General will be elected for life, and the Superior General and her assistants will reside in Rome."

The women disperse and return to their communities on July 5, 1839. Eleven days later Sophie visits the pope, accompanied by two of her religious and Father Rozaven.

"We shared with him the outlines of our new structure," she writes to Eugénie in Paris. "He was interested, of course, but we are not yet ready to ask for his formal approbation. We must wait and see how the new decrees are received by the Society as a whole."

She knows that Eugénie, in particular, must be won over to the new ideas, or they will have no chance of being accepted in France. Eugénie, whose absence from the meeting has cost her election to the General Council, does not answer her letter, preferring to indulge her enraged reaction with Archbishop Quelen.

When, in her official capacity as Secretary General, Elisabeth Galitzine writes up a summary of the new articles for distribution to the Society worldwide, she strongly implies that the pope has already given them his official approval. Sophie writes a follow-up letter several days later, attempting to soften the aggressive tone of Elisabeth's report and pointedly neglecting to state that she will reside in Rome.

As the letters are received, a crescendoing groundswell of opposition rumbles throughout the Society. A growing number of people, including Joseph Varin, Father Loriquet, and many of her oldest associates, believe that Sophie has allowed herself to be manipulated by Louise de Limminghe and Elisabeth Galitzine—both of whom are considered to be the puppets of Jean de Rozaven. As word gets out to the French bishops, centuries of Gallican suspicion are shaken awake, rekindling their fear of Roman power and causing them to interpret the new decrees as a frontal attack on their own God-given authority.

The Jesuit Superior in Rome, recognizing that Rozaven's high profile at the Council poses a potential threat to the Jesuits' survival in France, demands that his men—including Rozaven—distance themselves immediately from the Society of the Sacred Heart.

By the end of 1839, it is clear that Sophie's desire to restructure has opened up a battleground whose perimeters extend far beyond the world of her little Society.

She finds herself dreaming of tornadoes, seeing herself as some tiny speck at the center of a powerfully moving vortex. A still point with eyes that can see the violent air whirling with ever-increasing speed, ripping out everything in its path as it moves mindlessly along, and leaving behind it a trail of destruction.

Book of Revelation: Part III

1839

HÉLOÏSE DE BEIXEDON DID NOT RETURN TO PARIS UNTIL THE SUM-
mer of 1839. Her cousin Eugénie's joint birthday celebration with Louis-
Napoleon never occurred because of the latter's attempted invasion of
France, but she remained at Eugénie's new palace at Hechingen for over
a year and a half. She then spent an equal period of time in Sweden,
consoling the young crown princess Joséphine over the infidelities of her
husband and reveling in the company of the painter Sofia Adlersparre,
who was at that moment painting Joséphine's portrait.

"They are remarkable women, both of them," Héloïse exclaimed to
me shortly after her return. "When Eugénie isn't out hunting deer with
her husband or designing a new palace or musical extravaganza, she's
founding orphanages or homes for the elderly. Meanwhile Joséphine—
who's unofficially separated from the faithless Oscar— surrounds herself with artists and garden designers and her five beautiful children.
And she's reopening Catholic churches in Sweden and Norway for the
first time since the Reformation. The Lutherans don't know quite what
to do with her!"

I had invited Héloïse to my home for dinner not just to catch up on her travels, but to inform her of her recent inheritance—information I wished to deliver in person.

"It sounds as if the two of them have settled into domesticity rather well—or some version of it at least," I replied.

"Royalty does confer its privileges," she responded quickly, "though Joséphine suffers greatly from Oscar's infidelity, and Eugénie mourns her lack of children."

"Still no thought of marriage for yourself then?" I asked, trusting she would take my question as a mark of simple curiosity and not a judgment.

"No. None. It's not that I don't love men or their quirky ways"— here she shot me a look that recalled her mother—"but tie my entire life to one? Never. Perhaps I can become your surrogate daughter and take care of you in your feeble old age!" A smile played around her mouth, and I realized in that moment that I could think of no one with whom I'd rather spend my final years.

She took advantage of my silence to satisfy her own curiosity. "I might ask you the same question, Uncle Guy. Why didn't you ever marry? Surely the women in Joigny must have lined up in droves for the privilege of becoming Madame Guy Lorrain!"

Her tone was mischievous, but I could see in her eyes that she wanted a serious answer.

I made a lengthy exercise of cutting my *boeuf en daube* before responding. "You can't possibly imagine what those days were like, Héloïse. When we were at the age to marry, it was a terrible time to bring children into the world. Of all my childhood friends, only Alain Guillot and Étienne Dussaussoy took the plunge."

When she failed to respond, I added, "And of course, with the economic ravages of the Revolution and everything that followed, my own family needed my financial support."

She remained silent for a moment longer, tracing a circle with her finger onto the tabletop; finally she looked me in the eye with more than a fair amount of skepticism. "Are you sure there wasn't a certain young woman whose hand you would have taken if it had been available to a mortal bridegroom?"

I took a large mouthful of beef and chewed it well past the time required, staring at the flames of the candlelabra that sat between us. Héloïse refused to rescue me from my silence, and I finally requested that we leave the past and talk of her current plans.

She gave me a piercing look and shook her head in mock despair before giving in to my request. "I don't really know what to do next. I realize after this last trip how much I want to go out and see the world," she said a bit ruefully. "I even think of going to America. Louis-Napoleon lived in New York for a short while, you know, right after his foiled coup. I saw him when he came back to see his mother."

Hortense de Beauharnais Bonaparte had died in October of 1837, and Louis-Napoleon had managed to slip back into Switzerland to be with her at the end. The facility with which he had avoided the security nets posted all over Europe didn't bode well for Louis-Philippe's continuing reign.

"What would you do in America?" I asked.

"I have no idea. I don't know anyone there, though Louis-Napoleon would certainly give me some letters of introduction. But I don't see myself just traveling around from hotel to hotel. I'd want to be accomplishing something. And my English is rather sketchy, though Marie and I still try to read English novels together. We're both reading Jane Austen at the moment." Here her voice quickened, revealing a level of enthusiasm absent from her earlier remarks. "Have you heard of her?"

I shook my head. "I don't read fiction."

She pulled a disapproving face. "You should. It holds life's greatest truths."

"I'll stick to history, thanks. And how is the Countess d'Agoult these days? She seems to have evaporated entirely from the Paris social scene."

"I haven't seen her since I left on my travels. We write to one another, of course. Endless letters. But I gather that domestic life, even with a towering artist to whom one is not married, is fraught with peril. She and Franz have had two more children, another girl and a boy. They're still in Switzerland, though Franz spends most of his time performing all over Europe."

Rumors of the Liszt ménage had, of course, reached my ears, but Héloïse filled me in on the growing strains between Franz's insatiable need for public adulation and Marie's desire that he live the secluded life of a composer. I'd also heard vague murmurs of his philandering.

We moved into the salon for an after-dinner brandy, and I brought out the sheaf of papers that had motivated my invitation.

"I have some startling news for you, Héloïse. Good news, I think, but startling."

She set down her glass and looked warily at what I held in my hands.

"I must tell you that no one knows what I'm about to tell you, not even your mother. And we can keep it that way if you wish."

She stared at me, anxiety flickering about her eyes as she waited for life's next bombshell to explode in her lap.

"Someone has left you a great deal of money."

A look of relief momentarily erased the anxiety, and her blue eyes seemed to brighten in hue. "Praise the gods. You have a new relative to reveal to me?"

"No," I smiled. "No new relatives."

"So who is this mysterious benefactor?"

I breathed deeply before answering, still unclear as to why Joigny's most notorious son had landed his vast fortune on my niece.

"Denis Marmaton."

She looked at me quizzically, as if she barely recognized the name.

"Denis Marmaton?" she repeated slowly. "Marie's brother? The man she banned from visiting our home?"

"The very one."

"But why? He didn't even know me. He wasn't allowed near me—near any of us for that matter!"

"Probably because he still believes you to be his niece. Why would he think otherwise?"

"But why not give his money to all three of us? Alexandre and Jean-Marie are his nephews. Truly his nephews. And from what I know about his marriage, he hated women. I don't understand."

"I agree, Héloïse, it's a mystery. But he's left you an enormously rich woman." After a long silence I added, echoing her earlier comment, "Great wealth, too, confers its privileges, my dear."

"And its responsibilities," she whispered, her voice shaking with disbelief and an inchoate sense of dread.

Awakening the King

1840 – 1842

IN THE CHILL OF AN EARLY JANUARY MORNING IN 1840, ARCH-bishop Hyacinthe Louis de Quelen finally makes his exit from the Hôtel Biron in a gilded casket. His funeral cortege from the rue de Varenne to Notre Dame Cathedral is the largest Parisians have witnessed since the assassination of the Duc de Berry. Eugénie initiates a cult dedicated to his memory, claiming for him a series of miracles and cures, and begins to write a reverential treatise on his life. It is clear that his hold over her in death will be stronger than it was in life.

As the wave of opposition to the forty-seven new decrees grows, Sophie writes two circular letters to the Society, acknowledging the growing anxiety and attempting to dispel the fear and anger that have gripped many of the houses—particularly those in northern France. The only opposing force she can call on with any level of self-assurance is love. "The greatest assaults on the Society have been repulsed by this bronze wall, this impregnable bulwark of divine love," she writes from Rome. "I cannot hide the fact that this wall has been weakened at the time of the decrees."

She takes Eugénie's suggestion that the decrees be given a three-year trial period, after which another General Council will be called to decide their ultimate fate. She meets with Pope Gregory, who advises her to return to Paris as soon as possible. She prepares Elisabeth Galitzine to travel personally to the foundations in America and invite them to test out the new decrees. Tactfully.

Her last act before leaving for Paris is to consecrate the Society to Our Lady of Sorrows, a decision she reaches after several days of prayer before the fresco at the Villa Lante—as if she knows what lies ahead.

She gazes into the grief-stricken face of Mary, who, she realizes, must have been approaching her own age at this moment of her life. Mary's face is canted upward, as if to question some vast force that she fears might not be there after all. She holds the edge of what must have been her son's white robe in her left hand. The sky behind her has darkened to a terrifying charcoal, all but blocking out the sun that looms as a pale white disc in the background. If Sophie looks at it a certain way, the disc appears to be the ghoulish face of an angel of darkness, whose dark grey robes sweep almost to the ground. When she looks at it again minutes later, the charcoal cloud appears to be a cyclone, moving toward the grieving mother as mindlessly as the crucifixion had moved toward her son.

As Sophie's carriage moves north in early June, Denis Affre, the newly appointed Archbishop of Paris and a long-time critic of Eugénie's autocratic style, evicts the elegant confessor Fr. Jammes from the Hôtel Biron, where he has remained in the wake of Hyacinthe de Quelen's death. She is hopeful that in the new Archbishop she will find an ally. She spends two weeks at the Mother House in the rue Monsieur and then moves into the Hôtel Biron, though she knows she will find herself ostracized and watched from all sides. What she doesn't know is that this state of siege will endure for the next three years—and that her circle of detractors will eventually widen to include all of those in whom she has placed her greatest trust.

"I watch, I listen, I pray," she writes to *Addolorata* in Rome. "I ask others to pray."

At the end of the year, in a pattern of self-preservation that will hold for the remainder of her life, Sophie falls ill and is confined to her room throughout the winter. When allowed to leave her bed, she spends as much time as she can in a hidden passageway between the sacristy and the chapel. Sitting on a small bench in its quiet shadows, she can peer through a grill into the sanctuary. From here the comings and goings of the Hôtel Biron are virtually invisible. More to the point, she is invisible to them.

Today she is caught up in a silent dialogue with Philippine Duchesne, whose most recent letter has arrived that morning from America. Philippine has sent back an account of Elisabeth Galitzine's recent visits to the schools in Missouri.

"People are in awe of her," Philippine writes. "Most have never seen a Russian, much less a royal one. Her self-assurance and gift of eloquence quickly win people over to her cause."

Sophie suspects that Philippine's frank opinion of such eloquent self-assurance is tinged with more than a soupçon of skepticism. She tries not to read unintended significance into the words "her cause," though she knows that Elisabeth has already overstepped her careful instructions and is proceeding with her own agenda. Sophie has heard from sources in Louisiana that her delegate's manner is viewed as highhanded, and that she is asking the American communities to sign petitions in favor of adopting the new decrees. She knows, too, that one of Elisabeth's first moves was to relieve the stalwart Philippine from her position as Superior at St. Charles.

Philippine also writes that she is finally leaving to fulfill her dream of living with the Native Americans. "I depart for Sugar Creek in June. As you know from my earlier letters, the Jesuits have been there for many months, helping the Potawatomi tribes to resettle. The United States government has now pushed them out of Indiana—as they did earlier from Michigan—and hundreds are still on the move. Many have died of typhoid, especially children and elders. The Potawatomi call it the Trail of Death."

Sophie folds the letter, places it on the bench beside her, and closes her eyes, imagining children dying in droves during an endless march westward. To erase these visions, she tries to conjure images of those idyllic months with Philippine at Sainte-Marie d'en-Haut, but she cannot pull them forward.

Eventually her thoughts turn back to the urgent challenges posed by her ever-expanding network. Sugar Creek is only one of seventeen schools that have opened since 1839 in America, France, Alsace, Canada, Italy, Ireland, Poland and Algiers. The total number of houses is now approaching fifty.

"And yet everything is unraveling," she says aloud into the stillness, her right hand moving to touch the silver cross she wears over her heart. She listens for a response but hears only silence.

Another letter from the morning's delivery reports that the Bishop of Beauvais, furious with Sophie's decision to close a struggling boarding school there, is petitioning Pope Gregory to allow the school to separate from the Society. She knows that if the pope approves his petition, other French bishops—unhappy with the decrees and their perceived anti-French bias—will soon follow.

Jean de Rozaven writes her a scathing letter from Rome, berating her for failing to enforce the decrees in France and insisting that she assert her "rightful power" as Superior General. Sophie knows that she must at all costs retain his support—despite his utter failure to understand the situation in France.

At night when she cannot sleep, she imagines Eugénie de Gramont and Félicité Desmarquest lining up on one side of a mist-covered battlefield beside Archbishop Affre and all the bishops of France. On the other side, barely discernible under their standards, are Elisabeth Galitzine, Louise de Limminghe, Jean de Rozaven, and the entire church hierarchy in Rome.

In early September Sophie summons all her strength and decides to visit the disaffected houses in northern France in an effort to win them over to the new decrees.

"I shall visit Lille, Beauvais, Amiens, and Jette," she tells Eugénie. "If I can sustain my health and my energy, I hope to travel to Autun and Lyon as well."

She sees the wariness leap into Eugénie's eyes and decides not to reveal that her final destination is Rome.

Before she begins her peace-weaving odyssey, she travels to Joigny to visit her sister. Since her husband's death almost twenty years before, Marie-Louise Dussaussoy has found herself in an increasingly precarious economic situation. Sophie has done everything possible to help educate and find situations for her children. Several of the girls have joined the Society, and Louis-Étienne is a priest. Zoe, the second youngest, is now engaged to be married.

"It's still strange to be home and yet not be *home*," Sophie says to Zoe as the two women stroll along the banks of the Yonne. The summer heat has not abated though it is mid-September, and the flowering meadows along the river open themselves to the ripening vineyards on the hillsides above. "Perhaps you and Pierre can one day buy back the old family house!"

Zoe smiles. It has been years since her grandmother's death. Years before that, old Madame Barat, going blind and deaf, had sold the house in the rue du Puits Chardon and moved in with Marie-Louise. "Perhaps," she answers shyly.

"Are you happy with your young man, Zoe?" Sophie has stopped walking and looks directly at her niece, who has always been in awe of her aunt and worries that Sophie disapproves of her fiancé.

Zoe feels a blush steal slowly across her face. In fact, Pierre Cousin's temper frightens her at times, but she is thirty-five years old and fears a lifetime of loneliness if she doesn't marry him.

"Yes, Aunt Sophie. I am happy with him."

"Then that is all that matters," Sophie responds, watching a peacock butterfly flutter out of the next clearing, and remembering a day forty years earlier when she'd walked along the river with Zoe's brother.

One of her last stops before she arrives in Rome is Turin, where the young Anna du Rousier greets her with the warmth and enthusiasm that have catapulted her into the position of Superior at the age of only thirty-three. "You look tired, *ma mère*. Come quickly inside to meet your daughters who are so very eager to welcome you."

Exhausted from two months on the road, Sophie gives Anna a weak hug and allows herself to be led into the large community room where the novices have gathered.

After dinner the two women spend several hours discussing the mounting crisis. Sophie shares her hopeful sense that the French schools might be opening their hearts and minds to the new decrees. Anna, who has lived and worked in Piedmont for over fifteen years and feels strongly allied with the houses in Italy, listens to Sophie's report and camouflages her pessimism.

Sophie arrives in Rome in late November and meets with Pope Gregory and Cardinal Lambruschini.

"We have no desire to reawaken the French bishops' fears of Rome," the

Pope Gregory responds when Sophie has finished her summary of events. "Whether you reside in Rome or somewhere in France is not an issue for us."

"I know this, Your Holiness. And I've attempted several times to communicate this to Elisabeth Galitzine, though she continues to insist that you wish for me to reside here."

"I suspect that there's more than a touch of the fanatic in the woman," Gregory answers, and Lambruschini nods an energetic assent. "I wonder at times if the Princess Galitzine's defection from Russian Orthodoxy hasn't somehow addled her reason."

"And her relationship with Fr. Rozaven doesn't help," Lambruschini adds quickly. He has just issued yet another order to the Jesuit Superior General, Jean Roothan, to disentangle his men from the Society of the Sacred Heart. "If she and Rozaven aren't careful, they'll see the Jesuits expelled from France. Again."

Sophie nods in assent but waits for one of them to continue speaking.

"Under the circumstances," the pope finally says after clearing his throat, "I suggest that you fix your primary residence in France. I have no need to worsen relations between myself and the Archbishop of Paris."

And neither he nor I will benefit from the breakup of your Society and the chaos within the schools that would surely follow."

Sophie leaves the Vatican somewhat comforted.

When she arrives at the Villa Lante, however, a disturbing letter awaits her from Elisabeth Galitzine. "I have just finished a retreat with Father De Theux here in Grand Coteau," she writes, "and a miraculous idea came to me in the midst of prayer!"

Sophie leans back in her chair and breathes deeply before reading the next sentence. She must concur with the pope's earlier suggestion that Elisabeth harbors a fanatical streak, and that streak seems to be widening with each day she spends in North America.

"In order to save the Society," the letter continues, "you must—like St. Ignatius—make a special vow of allegiance to the Holy See in Rome. All of your General Council should make this vow *personally* to the Pope and offer the Society to his Holiness so that he can deploy us for whatever mission he designates."

"Deploy." Sophie sits before the fresco in the Villa Lante and whispers the word into the silence. "Such a word, Elisabeth. What does the Sacred Heart of Jesus have to do with the positioning of troops? Why must you always see a battle?"

What Elisabeth does not put in her letter is a second idea that has "come to her in prayer": that the Society's entire leadership, Sophie included, should submit themselves immediately to the Jesuits' authority. Before her retreat has ended, Elisabeth makes a solemn vow before the Reverend Father De Theux that she will offer her life to see the new decrees implemented.

Whether or not she signed it in blood has not been recorded.

Sophie meets with Louise de Limminghe, Jean de Rozaven, and Félicité Desmarquest in Rome soon after her meeting with the pope. They reluctantly agree that she must abide by his desire that she fix her residence in France. They also agree that a General Council to discuss and resolve the issue of the decrees must be called for the summer and that it should occur somewhere in France.

Sophie writes a Circular Letter in June announcing that the Seventh Council will be held at the end of July in the diocese of Lyon—midway between Paris and Rome. She feels that such a setting will provide a neutral space within which to discuss the decrees and move toward a final decision on their acceptance or rejection.

In Paris, Archbishop Affre, receiving word of the upcoming Council, writes an incendiary letter to every bishop in France. In it he accuses Sophie of failing to submit to his authority by calling the Council without his approval. He roundly censures the Archbishop of Lyon for allowing her to host the proposed Council and forbids any of his bishops to host such a Council. In a separate letter to Sophie, he threatens to destroy the Society in France if she fails to recognize his authority over her. Her attempt to clarify that she is subject only to the Society's Cardinal Protector in Rome falls on deaf ears.

What Affre fails to realize is that his letter has now aroused the attention of the French Government—and by extension the King of France.

Mothers and Daughters

1839

Despite the fact that she has moved out of the de beixedon home and now resides with her mother, Héloïse waits several weeks before revealing the news of her financial windfall.

She and Célestine are returning home from an afternoon at Saint-Lazare, a prison that doubles as a hospital for prostitutes and a detention center for young women whose husbands or fathers have found them to be intractable. Another section houses young girls, some as young as seven or eight, whose families wish to remove them from an "undesirable" domestic situation.

"I don't see how anything could be more *undesirable* for a child than living in that awful place!" Héloïse exclaims. She has spent several hours with the youngest of Saint-Lazare's inmates and is railing against the irrationality of a legal system that would confine them there.

Célestine remains silent, looking out the carriage window as the horses trot south along one of the wide boulevards leading to the Seine. She has spent the afternoon with the city's registered prostitutes and knows that greater degradation is possible.

"Most of these girls are simply being prepared for a life on the streets!" Héloïse continues.

"And what, exactly, are their options, *ma chère*?" Célestine replies. "They have no family—or their families are unfit to raise them. They have no skills. Many of their mothers or sisters are prostitutes themselves."

"Sounds pretty cynical, *maman*. What's the point of all your visits if you're so fatalistic?"

"Empathy," she responds after a long pause.

They arrive in front of a pair of gilded iron gates on the rue Saint Honoré, and a porter admits the carriage into the cobblestone courtyard. The women enter the mansion through one of the side doors and walk into a small sitting room. Exhausted, they throw themselves into a pair of armchairs that face into a shaded garden. A fountain in its center—one of Eugène de Beauharnais' last gifts to Célestine—features a statue of Arethusa. They stare silently at the water as it falls from the river nymph's inclined head and splashes gently into a pool below. Two blackbirds stand at the water's edge, ducking their heads into the water and flapping their wings with delight.

"How do you go there every day?" Héloïse asks her mother.

"Since you and the boys grew up, those women are my family."

"We are still your family, *maman*—all three of us."

Célestine gives her a look of indecipherable sadness and returns her gaze to the blackbirds.

"Don't misunderstand me," Héloïse responds quickly. "I value your desire to extend sympathy and help—truly I do." She knows that her mother has set several young women up in small business ventures that have allowed them to escape a life of prostitution. "But it all seems so futile. The whole system needs to be overhauled."

Since returning from Sweden, Héloïse has reconnected with the Saint-Simonians whom she and Marie d'Agoult have met through Franz Liszt.

"I can't help agreeing with my friends here in Paris that women will *never* succeed in achieving their rightful place until the working class has achieved theirs," she continues.

"They may be right, Héloïse. But until that day comes, I can only do what I can, one person at a time. Is that so very bad an idea?"

Héloïse looks at her mother and smiles. Célestine is now sixty and is one of those women whose beauty only increases with age. But this afternoon she looks unusually tired, the lines around her eyes and mouth etched more deeply than usual and her eyes lacking their usual sparkle.

"I had dinner with Uncle Guy a few weeks back," Héloïse says softly, "when you were away in Aix-les-Bains."

Something in Héloïse's voice puts Célestine on alert. She picks up a small jade figurine from the table beside her and turns it around in her hands for a moment before raising her eyes to meet her daughter's. "He must have been interested in hearing about your travels," she responds tentatively.

"Yes. He's always interested to hear about the 'Bonaparte brood,' as he calls them. Especially Louis-Napoleon."

"I think there are more than a few of us who are interested in that one," Célestine answers quickly.

Héloïse doesn't respond, trying to find a way to broach her real topic.

"*Maman*, Uncle Guy had some surprising news for me."

Célestine places the figurine back on the table with exaggerated care and braces herself.

"It seems that Denis Marmaton has left me a rich woman."

Héloïse waits for some response, but aside from a quick intake of breath Célestine does not move. Her eyes are riveted on the piece of jade.

"Can you think of any reason why he might have done so?" Héloïse asks, still waiting for her mother to say something. "Uncle Guy had no idea."

Célestine exhales softly and sinks back into the depths of the chair. She shifts her eyes back to the fountain and, as if they sense a brewing storm on the other side of the windows, the blackbirds fly off, leaving Arethusa to her watery fate.

"Why was he never allowed into our home, *maman*? Why did his own sister not receive him?" A tremor has crept into her voice.

Finally Célestine responds. "Because he had done things—during the Terror and then later on, under Napoleon, and then again under

308

Louis and Charles. Things that ruined people's lives. Blackmail. Secret arrests. And worse."

Héloïse has heard many of the stories as a child when no one thought she was listening. But she also remembers the look on her mother's face the day a drunken Denis Marmaton burst into the house to see Marie, and she knows there is something beyond his secret police work that has caused her family to keep him at bay.

Part 11

Paris, England, and Rome

Chant

1842

IN 1842 THE KING OF BURMA WROTE TO SOPHIE ASKING HER TO open a school near Rangoon. "Please," she read aloud to me from the letter, "send me not two nuns, lest they die, but seven or eight. No. On second thought you had better send ten or twelve."

She and I were sitting in the gardens of the Hôtel Biron. She looked up for a moment to gauge my reaction then continued, her voice rippling through the air like a brook tumbling over stones in sunlight. "They *must* bring a lot of gold thread for embroidery, and a present for the Queen, such as a cushion or a handbag, all in gold. If anyone should be wanting in respect to the nuns it would cost him his life."

She removed the silver-rimmed spectacles she now used for reading and awaited my response, her eyes dancing with a delight that was rare in them these days.

"My, my, Sophie," I responded. "Ten to twelve nuns. Several of whom, it would appear, are not destined to survive—for lack of respect or otherwise."

Her mouth widened into an enormous smile. "Not that I wouldn't love to send them, my friend! Imagine! Burma! The far side of India!

And he promises us a large house with gardens and the education of his nieces!" Here she got that dreamy look that always overcame her when she imagined the love of God's heart pouring into new corners of the world.

"But you have no such personnel at the moment," I reminded her.

"I know. It's all we can do to staff the schools we have already." Her voice became businesslike and she replaced the spectacles on her nose.

"Mother Chavroz has just arrived in Algiers, speaking of personnel," she continued, "and she hopes to open the school in Mustapha within a month. She writes that when they sailed into the harbor, they were met by the admiral himself—in a boat hung with garlands of white flowers." She looked up, her left eyebrow arching slightly. "A bit much, don't you agree?"

I shook my head, knowing Sophie's aversion to fanfare and imagining her own horrified reaction to such a reception. She had finally opened a school in North Africa, but only because the local bishop had agreed that it might serve the children of Muslims and Jews as well as Christian colonials.

Despite the controversy swirling around the Society, she currently had three times as many requests for schools as she could fill.

"Now you must hear Philippine's latest." She pulled another letter from the stack of mail at her side and the twinkle returned to her eye. "She wants to travel to the missions in the Rocky Mountains. Listen!" She shuffled through several pages of spidery handwriting and cleared her throat. "'They say that in the *Rockis* people live to be one hundred years old. As my health has improved and I am only seventy-three, I think I shall have at least ten more good years to work. Will you now authorize me to go further west if they want me to do so?'"

Renewed wonder at the woman's dogged perseverance struck us both. But contrary to what Philippine had written in the letter, Sophie knew from her sources in Sugar Creek that her health was deteriorating quickly.

"You know what the Potowatami call her?" she asked.

I shook my head.

"*Quahkah-ka-num-ad.* The woman who prays always. They say that children creep up behind her at night and place acorns or tiny stones on her robes to see if she has moved. Apparently she doesn't. All night long she prays."

I could hear the longing in her voice.

"And here I am," she continued, throwing up her hands and wiggling her fingers, "waiting to be excommunicated or accused of treason—or both!"

It was one of the rare times I'd heard her speak lightly of the crisis that had been stalking her for over three years. The discord within the Society showed no sign of abating, and at times I feared the bright light that animated her being was in danger of going out. Her face was showing evidence of her sixty-two years, and creases of worry and self-doubt had begun to win out over the laugh lines that lent her face an expression of perpetual hope and optimism.

A commotion at the back of the building signaled the approach of someone forcing her way into the garden. It took us a moment to recognize Héloïse. Trailed at a distance by the portress, whose ability to run was hampered by her heavy black robes, she arrived before us in a state of complete disarray.

"It's *maman*," she cried, throwing herself into my arms and sobbing uncontrollably. "You must come at once! I've brought a carriage!"

The portress, arms flailing and breast heaving, finally caught up with her quarry and apologized for allowing the visitor to arrive unannounced.

"It's all right," Sophie responded gently, motioning the young woman back toward the building. "Héloïse is practically my niece. Please tell Reverend Mother de Gramont that I have been called out on an emergency."

The three of us hurried to where the carriage stood waiting in the courtyard. The driver lashed his horses across the Seine and into the Faubourg Saint-Honoré as Héloïse recounted the details of the last twenty-four hours.

"She returned from Saint-Lazare yesterday afternoon with chills and a very high fever. You *know* how much sickness there is in that horrible place! She hasn't really felt well for weeks, but she kept insisting it was nothing serious. By last night she was delirious, and when the doctor finally arrived, he discovered a pink rash on her chest."

"Typhoid," I said quickly.

Célestine nodded frantically, and Sophie's eyes met mine across the carriage.

"Today she's been mostly unconscious, and the doctor doesn't think she'll last the night."

Here Héloïse collapsed in tears, and Sophie, who had taken the seat next to her, cradled her in her arms. A few minutes later the carriage burst noisily into the courtyard, and we ran through the main entryway and up the sweeping staircase.

A nurse had just finished administering a series of cold compresses when we walked into the room, and Héloïse rushed to her mother's side.

"Aunt PhiePhie and Uncle Guy have come to see you, *maman*," she said, smoothing Célestine's hair and searching her face for any sign of awareness. "They want very much to speak with you, *maman*. Please wake up." She continued to stroke her mother's forehead and temples as Sophie approached the bed, placing one arm over Héloïse's shoulder and taking Célestine's hand in the other.

Célestine's hair was loose on the pillow, the golden curls of her youth now heavily shot through with silver. Her face was ashen, but her cheeks were flushed with fever, and I could hear the rattle in her chest.

I moved over to speak with the doctor.

"Her spleen is twice its normal size," he whispered, "and her lungs are filling with fluid. She's probably been walking around with typhoid for weeks without knowing it, and now pneumonia's set in."

"I'm here, *ma chère amie*," Sophie said softly. "Squeeze my hand if you can hear me."

I could see my sister's fingers tighten slightly around Sophie's, and then her eyes opened slowly. They focused first on Héloïse and then shifted to the black-robed figure beside her. Despite the extreme dilation of their pupils, her eyes conveyed a quiet sense of joy, and I thought I saw a slight upturn at the corners of her mouth before she once again closed them. Sophie moved into a kneeling position beside the bed and took out her rosary.

We stayed at her bedside for the entire night while her temperature ranged wildly up and down, climbing at one point to over 106 degrees. A priest arrived just before midnight.

"How strange," Héloïse said to me not long after the priest had left. Grief had rendered her voice almost robotic. "It's the third time you've waited with me for a mother of mine to die."

When the morning sun lingered just below the horizon, at that twilight hour she loved almost as much as its penumbral evening twin, my sister's labored breathing finally stopped. Sophie placed her rosary on Célestine's breast, marked her forehead with the sign of the cross, and took each of our hands in hers. For the next few minutes she sang *Requiem Aeternum*, a centuries-old Gregorian chant. I'd never fully realized how beautiful her voice was, and as it filled the mystical space around my sister's deathbed, I knew that somehow—wherever her lovely soul had flown—Célestine could hear her.

The Queen Victorious

1842 – 1843

SOPHIE CALLED ME TO HER OFFICE IMMEDIATELY AFTER THE ARCH-
bishop had left. She was still shaking when I walked through her doorway.

"What *happened*?" I cried.

Her face was drained of color, and her eyes had the look of a trapped
animal.

"Affre has struck, this time with the backing of the Minister of Justice and Religion," she replied quietly. "They were both here this morning, and they effectively accuse me of treason if I refuse to sign *these*."

She thrust a pair of official-looking documents across her desk.

The first demanded that Sophie reside in Paris and abide by the
Statutes of 1827—the edict she and virtually every other order of religious women had agreed to abide by sixteen years earlier at the behest
of Charles X. I remembered her anxiety at the time. I also remembered
Félicité Lammenais' impassioned editorials against such a blatant knot-
ting together of church and state, for the statutes placed religious orders
under the technical jurisdiction of the French government. Most of her
advisors, myself included, had been in favor of her applying for official

government recognition, preferring not to attract the wrath of the king and the possible suppression of the Society if she refused his invitation.

But now it was coming back to haunt her.

The second required that Sophie convince the pope to agree with Affre that the Society's 1826 Constitutions must be made to accord with the Statutes of 1827.

"And this, of course, places you under Affre's control rather than the Cardinal Protector's," I said, pointing to the second document.

"Of course," was her reply, and I heard more than a shadow of anger beginning to creep into her voice.

"What was your response?"

"That I couldn't possibly sign such statements without having time to reflect and consult with others on the situation."

"They must have *loved* that," I responded with an appreciative smile. I imagined her tiny frame standing up to the stately Minister and the relentless Archbishop, whom many were now calling "*Affreux*" behind his purple-soutaned back.

"Monsignor Garibaldi warned me this might happen," she snapped, shaking her head and walking over to the windows to stare at the November rain that was pounding the gardens.

Antonio Garibaldi was the Papal Nuncio in Paris, one of the few people Sophie felt she could trust in the current crisis. Several months earlier, when Affre had forbidden her to hold the Council in Lyon, Sophie had written Cardinal Lambruschini requesting that the pope investigate Affre's claims of authority over the Society. A special commission of Cardinals, personally appointed by Pope Gregory, handed down a decision affirming Sophie's independence from the Archbishop of Paris—and sending the zealous prelate into a fury.

"Affre doesn't understand your vision, Sophie. He can't *afford* to understand your vision. From his point of view it undermines his power completely."

"How can I administer an international Society if I'm under the thumb of a French bishop? Why can't he *see* that?" Sparks were now leaping from her eyes, and I sensed with relief that all would be well.

"Because he's blinded by a mindset that has existed in this country for hundreds of years," I answered, "and he trusts the Vatican about as

much as he trusts an adder. It's been this way since the middle ages—you know that!"

"Our only hope is Bishop Mathieu," she responded, referring to the Archbishop of Besançon, who had been encouraging her to stand firm in her resistance to Affre. "He claims this is a cross we must carry with great calm and perfect trust, but he agrees with me that both sides can eventually be brought together. And he thinks Affre has made a serious tactical error in involving the government."

"He's right," I answered. "If Affre isn't careful, they'll secularize the schools and he'll lose whatever influence he and the bishops *do* have. And remember—the king and his ministers don't like their bishops' communicating with one another without their knowledge and blessing. Affre is putting his own bishops at risk with his incendiary letters."

Sophie stared into the rain-drenched garden.

~

For two months Sophie refuses to sign the documents. To protect herself she engages in a strategy of seclusion: she eats alone, she walks alone, she prays alone, she avoids all community meetings.

All of her Assistants General have abandoned her, aligning themselves with one side or the other and writing to tell her so in graphic and judgmental detail.

Eugénie and the Gallican lobby at the Hôtel Biron record her every movement. Her mail is monitored and sometimes intercepted. Archbishop Mathieu must engage a personal courier to ensure that his messages reach her unopened.

Elisabeth Galitzine, inspired by her vows and her visions, warns Sophie that she will be excommunicated and the Society suppressed if she fails to live in Rome. She refers to the Hôtel Biron as "a house of mad and angry women."

Archbishop Affre pens another letter to the French bishops reasserting his authority over the Sacred Heart schools in France. He threatens to expel the Society unless Sophie signs the two documents.

Louise de Limminghe, in tones even more ominous than usual, hints at an impending schism of the schools in Italy.

The French ambassador to the Vatican assures King Louis-Philippe and his Ministers that the pope would *never* insist that the Superior General of the Society of the Sacred Heart live outside of France.

Jean de Rozaven mutters that she is a demon.

Monsignor Garibaldi and Archbishop Mathieu whisper that she is a saint.

Finally, during a series of meetings in the dead of the Parisian winter, Sophie and Minister du Nord begin to work out a solution. The cool-headed Minister of Justice and Religion has no desire to see thirty French schools collapse—a situation he knows will alienate many if not most of the most noble houses of France. He also knows that Archbishop Affre's increasingly strident letters are beginning to make other bishops, especially those with schools in their dioceses, more than a bit nervous.

They decide that she will write a letter stating that she has no intention of not abiding by the Statutes of 1827. She will suggest that the pope himself formally request that the new decrees be abrogated—but that the French bishops be the ones to petition the pope to do so, thereby drawing the two sides together in common cause.

Three French bishops craft such a petition and gather the signatures of their peers. Archbishop Mathieu delivers it to the pope during his annual visit to the Vatican. Superior General Roothan warns his knights-at-arms that if they do anything whatsoever to block the proceedings, the Jesuits in France will surely be proscribed.

After several meetings in February and March, a committee of eight Cardinals rules that the decrees of 1839 be annulled and that the Society of the Sacred Heart revert to the Constitutions of 1826. The king, his ministers, and his bishops, including the temporarily chastened Affre, agree.

The Society is safe for the moment—but Sophie now faces the greater challenge of bringing the two factions together so that no one appears to be the loser.

Mater Admirabilis

1843 – 1844

"The challenge is to keep everything from becoming personal," Sophie said to me wearily, her face showing the strain of the past several months. An infinite sadness had now blanketed her features and stripped her body language of its characteristic ebullience.

"One group wants me to get rid of Eugénie de Gramont," she continued. "Another insists that the Italian faction be purged. But what happens to us *all* if the Society's leadership is cast out? What do I prove by such a move—and just *where* am I supposed to find qualified people to replace them?"

We were in one of the Hôtel Biron's large parlors, sitting in a pair of armchairs that looked out into the front courtyard and across to the Hôtel des Invalides. It was late January, and a somber rain fell on the cobblestones. The golden dome of the Invalides, now a constant reminder of Napoleon Bonaparte's renewed presence in Paris, glistened in the damp. Louis-Philippe, in an attempt to heighten his foundering popularity, had recently brought the Emperor's remains back to Paris amid much pomp and fanfare. Sophie still worried that a hidden fire burned within the body lying in state just across the boulevard.

"*Courage et confidence*," I replied, quoting Joseph Varin's mantra. "Your instincts have proven right so far, Sophie. No need to start pointing fingers now."

We were interrupted by the portress, who came hurrying into the room with a letter marked "*grande urgence*." It was bordered in black. Sophie slowly extended her hand.

"It's from Louisiana—the school at St. Michael's," she said, looking with dread at the envelope. She scanned the first page and drew in her breath sharply. "Elisabeth Galitzine. She has died of yellow fever."

When she'd finished reading it, she set the letter down in her lap and folded her fingers around the cross at her neck, her eyes filling with tears.

Elisabeth had begged Sophie to send her back to the American province so that she might explain the cardinals' decision about the new decrees. While I and others worried that, despite the Vatican's decision, she would continue the ultramontane lobby and counseled her against it, Sophie had given her permission to return, trusting that Elisabeth would follow her better instincts and work to bring the houses there into alignment.

"It seems she suffered horribly," she said finally, shifting her gaze from the wintry scene outside and bringing herself back from wherever it had taken her. "She spent days nursing the nuns and children at St. Michael's and then fell victim to the disease herself."

She handed me the letter, and I read the description of the Russian princess's final days—lying prostrate in the one-hundred-degree heat, suffering agonizing muscle and back pain, and bleeding profusely from her eyes, nose and mouth. I wondered which had constituted her greater torment: the pitiless hemorrhaging or dying with an unfinished agenda.

"She told me once when she was very angry with me," Sophie said gently, "that she would offer up her life in exchange for seeing the decrees implemented. What strange ways providence finds to twist our desires into shapes we could never have imagined. May she rest in peace, *ma pauvre fille*."

I bit my lip and said nothing.

Several months later, after requisitioning Elisabeth's correspondence and papers for the archives, Sophie learned that her delegate had, in fact, been lobbying heavily to retain the new decrees.

"So once again I'm proven to be a fool," she said, after reading me a particularly incriminating passage from a letter Elisabeth had written to one of the regional superiors.

"Not so much a fool, Sophie, as a generous observer of human nature," I countered. "Perhaps *overly* generous at times," I added with a smile, knowing there were many who agreed with Sophie's self-assessment.

She didn't answer me, keeping her eyes fixed on the letter she held in her hand.

"Come on, Sophie," I remonstrated. "How are any of us really supposed to *know* what another is thinking? We barely understand ourselves. You believed Elisabeth to be capable of something, and perhaps at the time she agreed to do it, she was. Eventually she fell short, though she may very well may have *wanted* to follow through with your desires."

"I'm losing confidence in my instincts," she replied softly. "How can I possibly exercise my authority if I can no longer trust my instincts?" She looked at me with eyes that were utterly bereft.

"You're tired, Sophie. And you're overcome with bad news. So Elisabeth deceived you; it's a minor miracle to me that she performed as well as she did, given her background. Give yourself some credit for her achievements. And try to remember what you said to me once. 'We should do as few stupid things as possible—'"

"'But to wait for a time when we would do none,'" she interrupted, finishing the quote herself, "'would be the stupidest thing of all.'"

"*Voilà!*" I responded, relieved to see some vestige of her sense of humor return.

Within the week, Sophie announced that she was assuming temporary leadership of the now thoroughly confused American houses. She began a tireless correspondence with the two regional superiors, Aloysia Hardey and Maria Cutts, and slowly began to untangle Elisabeth's intrigue. Before long, she had won the full confidence of the Society's growing foundations in Louisiana, Missouri, New York, Pennsylvania and Montreal.

"I'll be traveling to England later this month," she said to me in mid-May. Spring had invaded the gardens, and we were in one of her favorite spots, a secluded corner bounded by boxwood hedges and featuring three large peony bushes whose glamorous blossoms were just opening. From here the Invalides dome was nowhere visible.

"Crossing large bodies of water now, are we?" I asked, pulling back in feigned astonishment. "Let me guess. It has to do with Cannington."

A certain Lord Clifford had badgered Sophie into opening a second school in England despite her reluctance to do so. I knew that the two new British establishments—Berrymead near London and Cannington in the western county of Somersetshire—were proving to be an economic drain: she and I had recently spent an entire morning reviewing the Society's accounts.

"How did you guess?" she answered, the playful light finally returning to her eye. "We can't possibly sustain two schools there—at least not yet. I've decided to travel to England personally to decide which one must close. Bishop Morris is coming from London to escort us across the Channel from Abbéville."

I remembered her amused description of the tactics used by Lord Clifford to lure the Society to his favored setting, an old Benedictine Abbey on the Severn River. The *pièce de résistance* was a garden he had planted in the shape of an enormous heart—a prickly holly bush at its center meant to invest the overall design with profound theological symbolism.

"And you'll *never* guess how we shall travel to Cannington, my friend!" she exclaimed, clapping her hands and showing the excitement of a child. "In a *train!*"

⌒

As Sophie makes her way across the English Channel and into the island country where a twenty-five-year-old queen is beginning her legendary reign, a young French novice is painting a fresco into an alcove at the Trinità dei Monti.

Pauline Perdrau has been studying in the Roman atelier of the German Romantic artist Maximilian Seitz. Inspired on the first of May to paint a fresco of Mary, Pauline receives reluctant permission to do so from her superior. Utilizing the prayerful technique of byzantine iconographers, she spends weeks channeling the Virgin Mother of God. Little girls from the junior school cluster around her, handing her brushes and bowls of rainwater as they are needed.

While she paints, Pauline remembers her childhood nurse Jacquine—saddled with a charge whose willful stubbornness eclipsed even her artistic impulses. When Pauline refused to learn to spin, Jacquine described a Madonna she remembered from her youth, hoping to encourage the child's domesticity. "Imagine her, *ma petite Pauline*," she would proceed in fairytale tones, knowing that stories were a way into her heart. "There she was on a wall near the altar, sitting in silence with a spindle in her hand, dreaming of the beauty of God."

It is this Mary who emerges slowly from the wet plaster. A girl of fourteen or fifteen, eyes cast down, spindle lying idle in her right hand. A lily curves out of a bright blue vase at her right; a distaff stands resolutely to her left. In the painting's lower corner a book lies face down upon a wicker workbasket. Twelve golden stars encircle her head and a thirteenth hovers above in the violet tones of a late afternoon sky. In a shocking deviation from tradition, Pauline—remembering a favorite party dress from childhood—drapes her subject in pink.

The colors scandalize, and the fresco—called *The Madonna of the Lily* until its rechristening two years later—is hidden behind a curtain.

Moderato Cantabile

1845

SHORTLY AFTER HER RETURN FROM ENGLAND SOPHIE TRAVELS TO Rome. There are several reasons for her journey. Archbishop Affre's continuing wariness of the Society makes the calling of a Seventh Council a potentially divisive step, and in its absence she wishes to consult directly with the Society's Cardinal Protector—a position now filled by Cardinal Lambruschini himself. She feels the need to visit her houses in the south of France and Italy and to assure them personally of her love and support. She wishes to reconnect with Louise de Limminghe, who remains as Superior at the Trinità but has resigned her position as Assistant General in the wake of the cardinals' decision. And she yearns to see Pope Gregory for what she fears will be the last time; he is now in his eighties and rumored to be in poor health.

She falls ill en route, takes to her bed at the Villa Lante upon her arrival in January, and is not well enough to visit the Trinità dei Monti until March. The first thing she does upon her arrival there is to shove into the corridor the rug, the firewood, and the furniture that has been placed in her room to enhance her comfort.

When she is well enough to wander through the surrounding meadows, she prefers to be in the company of children from the junior school. They gather around her amid the wildflowers and alfalfa, and—to the delectable accompaniment of fresh ricotta, strawberries, and cookies swirled as if by magic from puff pastry and almonds—listen wide-eyed to her endless stories.

"And just look who's come to join our beautiful feast!" she will exclaim as a pair of resident lambs—blessed and given over to the community's care on the preceding feast of St. Agnes—amble up to the gathering and nibble from Sophie's hand.

One night a baby goat is stabled with a full-grown donkey, which kicks it nearly to death. Sophie sits down beside the creature in the corner of the stall, speaking softly in rhythmic patterns and eventually rousing him from his comatose state. For days afterward, he will eat a mash of bran and milk only if it's offered from the hollow of her hand. "Bichette must be hungry! I'll be right back!" she will cry suddenly in the middle of business, looking at her watch, dropping her pen in mid-sentence, and dashing out to the stable to feed him.

Atilio, the ferocious watchdog from Villa Lante who feels abandoned when Sophie moves to the Trinità, makes a daily excursion across the city and up the Spanish Steps. When he sees his opportunity, he scrambles through the open gates and into the cloister garden, seeking out his tiny friend in black. He is reputedly frantic until she appears to give him a biscuit and a reassuring pat on the head.

She meets Pauline Perdrau.

"Your little Blessed Virgin isn't half-bad," Sophie tells her one afternoon. "I often turn aside to look at her when I'm praying in the tribune."

By now the offending colors have softened into the plaster, and when Pauline makes her first vows just after Easter, she asks her Madonna to hold the thread of the Society in her hands and spin its history. A year later, the newly installed Pope Pius IX will visit the painting and rename it *Mater Admirabilis—Mother Most Admirable.*

Sophie has an unanticipated final audience with Pope Gregory when he drops by unannounced at the Villa Lante one afternoon in late May. The next day he sends twelve live partridges to the Trinità. To thank him, Sophie instructs the Trinità to send his Holiness a large square of house-made French butter.

～

Georgino Albertazzi loves his horses more than any other thing on this earth. At this point in his life he categorically refuses to believe in heaven. When Sophie hires him as a driver for her circuitous journey from Rome to Turin, he accepts the job for one reason only: her willingness to pay extra for a pair of oxen to pull the heavy carriage over the Apennine Mountains.

"*Questa donna*, she understands you, my angels," he whispers into the horses' ears as he loads the carriage with passengers and luggage. He watches Sophie climb into her seat with the admiration of one earth-loving creature for another.

It is June, and Georgino has placed large branches over the carriage windows to ward off the sun's merciless heat. There are four of them in addition to Sophie— her secretary Adèle Cahier, her attendant and nurse Marie Patte, Louise de Limminghe, and Pauline Perdrau. After an hour or so on the road, Sophie reaches into her traveling bag and pulls out a well-worn French translation of Dante's *Divine Comedy*.

"Adèle, *ma chère*," she asks, "please read to us from Signor Alighieri's *Commedia*. My brother had me read it when I was a teenager, and it still delights my mind and heart!"

Louise, whose dolorous disposition has only darkened over the past three years, pulls a long face. Sophie watches her eyebrows knit themselves together with increasing fervor as Adèle reads. She smiles inwardly, realizing that the work's title must suggest to Louise an unseemly frivolity.

"Don't frown so, *carissima Addolorata*," she exclaims when Adèle comes to the end of a canto. "I once heard a cardinal say that the poem should be considered a fifth gospel!"

Louise's eyebrows contract even more fiercely.

Georgino sees to it that the women never miss daily mass, timing their arrival in the little villages and towns to coincide magically with the pealing of church bells.

Pauline has hoped they might stop to visit a community of contemplative *Poverelle* sisters in Assisi whom she's befriended on a pilgrimage to Giotto's frescoes, but Sophie decides against the visit. "I fear if I walk into their life of solitude and prayer, I will never leave," she explains to a heartbroken Pauline.

The young artist writes to the *Poverelle* Superior, explaining Sophie's decision—but sharing their itinerary. As the carriage skirts its way around the fabled city, the women stare up at the enormous basilica that enshrines the body of St. Francis. Suddenly Georgino pulls up the horses: their way has been blocked by a large wagon full of women.

"It's the *Poverelle!*" exclaims Pauline, and as Sophie throws open the door of the coach to receive the Superior and two of her nuns, Pauline, Adèle and Marie hop into the wagon. The women travel in caravan to a nearby inn where they celebrate a mid-day meal in the midst of the Umbrian countryside. Before the afternoon has ended, they've locked themselves into a declaration of mutual solidarity.

Two days later Georgino turns the carriage east toward Porto Sant'Elpidio. They cross the Appenines over a series of steep and narrow mountain passes, eventually descending toward the Adriatic Sea. It is evening when they reach the coast, and the water glitters under a full moon the color of canteloupe. The evening is warm, and Sophie proposes a stroll along the beach. As the moon rises higher overhead, she begins chanting *Ave Maris Stella,* a centuries-old evensong invoking starlight, the sea, and the Virgin Mary. The other women join in, their long travelling skirts brushing softly along the sand and lending the song an ethereal percussive quality.

When the last note fades into the stillness, Sophie picks up a small flat stone and skips it across the water. *"Little stone go to Greece!"* she cries, picking up another and encouraging her companions to join in. As she watches the pebbles skim across the water, she remembers the Homeric poems she so loved as a child.

They approach Modena, and Sophie draws her new friend aside. *"Georgino, amico mio.* We must avoid going through the city if at all possible." Her voice is conspiratorial. "I fear a meeting with the duke, who continues to ask for a school—and to whose regal self I continue to say no."

Georgino has a friend in the city's outskirts, and the women spend the night in his little home, far from passport control and the threat of a royal audience. They do their morning meditation in the stable.

In Parma, there is no way to avoid an audience with the Duchess Marie-Louise, Napoleon's Austrian widow who has presided ably over the duchy since 1814. But when a scarlet carpet is unrolled at her feet, Sophie asks politely that it be re-rolled immediately. The saving grace of her visit is a convivial magpie that takes up residence in her windowsill. She greets him daily with a robust *"Buongiorno, Gazza!"* and requests that visitors salute him in like fashion before any morning business is transacted.

Georgino drives them safely into Turin in early July. It is the end of his contracted journey, and tears spring to his eyes when Sophie places a heavy gold watch in his hand. "To thank you for your troubles and your care, dear friend," she says affectionately as she presses the gift into his palm.

Turning his beloved horses south toward Rome, he thinks he might now believe in heaven.

Reprise

1846

"I WASN'T ABLE TO DO IT IN MY BROTHER'S LIFETIME, BUT IN SOME way his death has finally given me the courage to take action. You know how much he hated the school here."

"I'm so very sorry, Sophie," I responded. It was our first meeting since her return from Italy.

Louis Barat had died before she could get back to Paris, but I had managed to see him several times during his last tortured months when, overcome by dropsy, he was forced to spend day and night in a large armchair. On my last visit, his calves and ankles had ballooned to three times their normal size.

"He was a complicated person," she replied softly, "and I know he was working against me during our recent troubles." Louis had remained a fanatical ultramontane to his death, and Sophie knew he had engaged in correspondence with Louise de Limminghe and Elisabeth Galitzine that was highly critical of her. "But he loved me. I never doubted his love, even when his methods of showing it might have seemed cruel to some."

I remained silent, feeling that in many ways I knew Louis Barat better than she. I'd seen the silhouette of cruelty emerge in our boyhood games, and his tenure at the Collège Saint Jacques had not been without criticism of his severity with the boys in his care.

Never had a brother and sister seemed so very different in temperament, and I asked myself once again—as I had for decades—how love could possibly dress itself in the dour and merciless forms with which Louis imbued it. Surely his sister must have asked herself the same questions. Surely at times she must have hated him—and then hated herself more for hating him.

"One by one," she finally spoke, her voice weary, "we're losing our founding voices." Over the past three years, six of her closest companions, including Lydia Chobelet, Henriette Grosier, and Antoinette de Gramont had died. And now she watched another piece of her childhood disappear as Louis took with him his memories of the child she had been.

"So," she said brusquely, tearing herself away from her personal musings and forcing her voice into a more businesslike key. "We were speaking of Babylon."

I smiled at her nickname for the Hôtel Biron.

"Cardinal Lambruschini writes me endlessly on the topic," she continued, a new energy flooding her voice. "He seems to think I can just toss Eugénie into the streets without unraveling the entire social fabric of Paris—not to mention the school! I continue to write her letters, but to no effect. So I've decided to move in."

For the past few years, the Mother House had been relocated at Conflans, a quiet suburb northwest of Paris. The setting, a large rambling chateau on a low bluff overlooking the Seine, afforded the novices a healthy separation from the worldliness of the boarding school and Sophie a quiet space within which to work.

"We'll be crowded, I know. But I know of no other way to make my point."

"And that point *is*, just for purposes of review?" I asked, inviting her to catalogue the grievances that were launching her back into the worldly corridors of the rue de Varenne.

"No more society weddings. No more use of the school for any kind of social activities the Faubourg Saint Germain might wish to hold

there. In short, no more fodder for the rumor mill that sees our vow of poverty as a joke."

"A 'Restoration' of your own, if I understand you correctly."

She nodded once and then held up her right hand to emphasize her next remark. "And another object of restoration—point two on your list if you're keeping track. Our academic reputation. It has suffered here in Paris over the past several years. If we don't want to incur the attention of the university inspectors, we'd better start strengthening our teaching."

"So how do you plan to proceed?"

"I've already let Eugénie know that I'm replacing the headmistress of the boarding school. I've told her that the new head and I will be making a formal visit in July. I hope to move in at the end of the summer."

I whistled softly. For over twenty years Eugénie had been virtual queen of the Faubourg Saint Germain, and I didn't imagine she'd take her dethroning lightly.

"I don't intend to make any formal announcement about the change. I shall simply do it. In this way Eugénie can save face. But I can no longer worry about her face when our own is in such disrepair."

We were meeting in my offices on the Champs Elysees, very near the Place de la Concorde. From my window, we could see the Egyptian obelisk that Louis-Philippe had erected on the spot where the guillotine had once bled endlessly onto the cobblestones. At this moment, as sometimes happens at the end of February, the winter clouds lifted, and sunlight flooded the room. We looked out the window at the obelisk whose red granite, etched with hieroglyphs tracing the glories of Ramses II, now appeared a rosy pink. Since its installation ten years before, I'd often asked myself how it must feel to stand exposed in the midst of a modern French city after having spent three millenia before a temple of Amun Ra.

As if she read my mind, Sophie asked what an obelisk would have meant to the culture that created it.

"An Egyptologist once told me that it's a variation on the Djed Pillar—the backbone of the god Osiris," I explained.

"Who is he, the god Osiris?" Sophie asked.

"God of the dead. God of the afterlife. Also the god of love, interestingly enough. A very benign figure."

Sophie nodded.

"In this interpretation," I continued, "the obelisk offers stability as well as hope for resurrection. The fellow I was speaking with explained it as a conduit for divine energy, moving upward and downward between heaven and earth."

Watching the expression on Sophie's face, I wondered whether she was trying to pull in some of the obelisk's celestial energy—or saw in its displaced isolation an image of herself as she moved through the gates of Babylon.

~

Just as there are people who, when faced with their loss of power, sit tightly in the saddle and dig the spurs ever deeper into their mount, there are others who hand over the reins as if they've been waiting forever for someone to relieve them of their terrible burden.

Eugénie de Gramont proved to be of the latter persuasion.

Three months after Sophie took up residence in the Hôtel Biron, she lay on her deathbed. The spinal deformation that had crippled her from birth now bent her over double in her wheelchair, and the sudden weakening of her body echoed a simultaneous weakening of the iron will that had troubled her friendship with Sophie for over forty years.

She spent many hours of her last weeks of life begging Sophie for forgiveness—something for which Sophie, of course, insisted she need not even ask.

"I knew she was virtuous, but I did not know to what extent," Sophie wrote to me the day after she died, choosing as she almost always did to overlook Eugénie's faults and insist on her religious devotion and love for the poor. "Her soul was strong and her heart was full of joy and devotion. More than anyone she taught me how to love."

Here I believed her, for years before I had watched the woman awaken a passion within Sophie that no one else ever had. How two women of such different backgrounds and affinities could have touched one another so deeply remained a mystery to all of us who knew them. But I knew that despite their stark differences, Sophie had lost a friend whose absence would never be compensated for.

Eugénie's funeral, however, served as a sharp reminder of the tension that had strained their friendship. Without Sophie's knowledge, the de Gramont relatives had smuggled a small orchestra from the Paris Conservatory into a side chapel at the Hôtel Biron. The requiem mass rang with music that could only be described as theatrical.

Sophie refused to attend the reception in the parlor, where the illustrious descendants of Duke Antoine de Gramont, Peer of France, enjoyed their last gasp of notoriety within the convent walls.

Renaissance

1846 – 1848

OFELIA PLISE IS RUMORED TO BE A DIRECT DESCENDANT OF THE last Inca king. While she is a devout Catholic and has been raised in Mexico, at night she dreams of the Peruvian goddess Mama Quilla and frequently sees her own face engraved on the moon's silvery surface. Her widowed father has told her endless stories of his boyhood travels on horseback throughout Panama and Guatemala, inspiring within her an incurable wanderlust. He has left her at the Hôtel Biron while he conducts business in Paris, and Ofelia is so happy there that she asks to be left behind as he readies himself to return to Mexico City. She has fallen in love with Madeleine Sophie Barat.

Tatiana Fyodorovna Pushkin claims to be the niece of the Russian poet and wears a pendant of black onyx beneath her blouse to commemorate his death ten years before in a duel. She recites long passages of *Eugene Onegin* by heart, and Sophie Barat—who speaks no Russian but loves the melody of poetic verse in any language—encourages her. The two of them once spend an afternoon picking walnuts as Tatiana relays the passionate convolutions of the poem's plot to her fascinated listener.

Her best friend at the boarding school is Ana Isabella Ramos de Tagle from Santiago, Chile, who recites back to Tatiana the poetry of Sor Juana Ines de la Cruz. In Spanish.

Julia is a beautiful dark-eyed child, picked up off the streets of Marseille by a Russian countess who adopts her and delivers her into Sophie's care. The child speaks a language no one can decipher and baffles everyone with behavior whose oddities mirror her linguistic otherness. When this behavior begins to border on criminality, Sophie devotes herself to saving her soul. Ignoring the reasoned counsel of those who have given up on the child, Sophie adores her until the day she dies and will write her over two hundred letters.

"You want to go on the foreign missions?" Sophie asks her novices, most of whom dream of traveling to the Americas. "All the world is already here!"

~

As the school's reputation for excellence reestablishes itself and the daughters of international diplomats, bankers, and entrepreneurs increasingly populate its hallways, another group finds its way to the back door.

Those who arrive in need of money are given alms from a special box located in the bursar's office.

"We have only five francs left in the box?" Sophie asks, echoing the concern of the dutiful nun charged with the accounts. "Then give them to the poor so that it will fill up again!" The accountant, who spends sleepless nights worrying about the profligate charity of her superior, shakes her head and empties the box into the palm of an unemployed father of six.

A young woman stumbles through the door on a rainy winter afternoon, shivering from exposure and exhaustion. When Sophie discovers that the supply of warm coats has temporarily run out, she orders her own chapel cloak to be cut up and tailored to fit her while the woman eats a hearty meal beside the fire.

A bearded vagabond named François appears weekly to receive a pouch of tobacco. "He has a right to his pleasures," Sophie retorts when criticized for encouraging his habit.

One night very late an old woman arrives raving at the kitchen door. Sophie, unable to sleep and hearing her cries, runs to the kitchen and fixes her a cup of hot chocolate. For the next several hours she sits beside the visitor on a wooden bench, holding her hand until the sun begins to rise. Neither of them speaks a word.

When the young bursar shares the information that someone has wasted the alms given him on drink or gambling, Sophie is quick to counter her disapproving tones. "How many times has God forgiven you, *ma chère fille*? The poor are the blessing of this house. I am at peace because they are well received here."

Part 12

Jubilee

Bouillabaisse

1847

"Franz won't allow marie even to visit the children," Héloïse exclaimed over a dinner of bouillabaisse. She had prepared it for us herself in the small but elegant apartment on the Île Saint Louis, where she had lived since her mother's death. "He, of course, hasn't seen any of his offspring for the past two years."

"Are they still living with his mother?"

"Technically yes. They reside with Madame Liszt. But they're all locked away in boarding schools."

"So the children see neither of their parents?"

"That's right. Franz has settled in Weimar with his latest paramour, and the last time Marie tried to visit the girls at school, she was turned away—by order of their father!"

"I guess there are many ways to be orphaned," I responded, shaking my head.

"The headmistress," Héloïse continued, stabbing a large chunk of monkfish with her fork and suspending it in the air for effect, "told the girls they really shouldn't see their mother anyway because she writes for the *newspapers!* Can you imagine? It's 1847, for God's sake!"

After publishing a pair of novels, Marie d'Agoult—now writing under the pen name Daniel Stern—had turned her attention to philosophy and politics. In addition to studying German philosophy and the American Transcendentalists, she continued to explore Lammenais' radical Christianity. Much of her writing was devoted to reforming the laws on marriage and child custody—views that flew in the face of the Church and tended to make other segments of the French population nervous.

"I read her recent piece on Emerson in the *Revue indépendante*," I responded. "Very intelligent."

Héloïse nodded enthusiastically, swallowing the fish and following it up with a robust sip of white burgundy. "He's promised to come visit her salon when he's in Paris next year."

"This is delicious, by the way," I said, spreading a round of toast with the creamy *rouille* and dropping it into the broth. "Where did you learn to cook?"

"This dish I learned to make in Marseille, on my way home. Come over next week and I'll make you some couscous!"

I looked at the woman sitting across from me and smiled in amazement. Since Célestine's death, she had been shuttling all over Europe and North Africa, doing whatever she could to support Sophie's free schools and orphanages. Her most recent trip, to Algiers, was at Sophie's personal request—one whose subtext, I suspected, was a desire for Héloïse to extend the foundation some much-needed financial assistance.

"I learned to cook at the orphanage in Algiers. One of the women there taught me everything there is to know about Berber cuisine," she explained.

"If it's anything like this," I said, holding up a large spoonful of broth-soaked crouton, *rouille* and shrimp, "I'll be back tomorrow night!"

She smiled and speared another piece of fish.

"So tell me about the school there," I asked. "Tell me about North Africa!"

"Algiers is unbelievably beautiful. When you sail into the bay, a city of white seems to rise out of the sea to meet you. Honestly! The old town is up on a hill behind it, crowned by the Casbah and looking much the same, they say, as it has for centuries. That was my favorite part—walking up, up, up through the winding old cobblestone streets and looking out onto the Mediterranean. From the citadel, you'd never know the French are there. The orphanage lies just at the base of the hill."

"And the school?"

"It seems to be doing well enough, despite its critics. There are those, of course, who don't like the fact that it's open to non-Christian students."

I nodded my head, knowing that one of those critics was the archbishop of Paris.

"Did you hear what Sophie said recently in response to one of them?" she queried, a playful gleam in her eye.

"No."

"In making them better Muslims, we become better Christians."

We smiled at each other across the table, and Héloïse reached over to refill my wine glass.

"Archbishop 'Affreux' must have loved that one! So tell me all about the orphanage. Everything." As I was moving up in years, I found myself relying more and more on Sophie and Héloïse to remind me of the world beyond Paris.

"Amazing," she replied, her smile enlarging to an almost childlike grin. "With the new building, we should be able to house and educate at least twenty more girls. Most of them are Arabs, but occasionally a Berber child will find us. They're incredibly imaginative—full of stories of the Casbah and the Barbary Coast pirates!"

She hesitated for a moment and then added, "I must admit that I ask myself more and more what in the world we're doing there."

I knew Sophie was asking herself the same question as the moral implications of France's colonial presence in Africa continued to unfold.

"Our former king's dubious legacy," I growled. "God forbid that we should be left out of Europe's ongoing game of empire-building."

Paris newspapers were full of the recent capture of the Abd al-Qadir, the Algerian military and spiritual leader who had been harrying the French army for over fifteen years. At one point his Muslim state had controlled two thirds of the Algerian territory, and the French army had prevailed only after sending in tens of thousands of reinforcements—and inflicting unspeakable terror on the civilian population. This the French press had reported as well.

"So what's the latest with your sister-cousins?" I asked, suddenly wishing to leave the topic of Algeria.

"Eugénie's very ill," she replied, becoming somber. "They've diagnosed tuberculosis, and she's barely allowed to see her husband. She's off to Badenweiler for a cure, but we're all terribly worried."

"My God, Héloïse, I'm sorry," I responded. "She's so young."

"Thirty-eight. Three years younger than I am." Héloïse picked up her spoon and swirled it absently in the broth. "She's a lovely, generous person. The people of Hohenzollern adore her. In a way she reminds me of *maman*."

It had been five years since Célestine's death, but I could hear the catch in her daughter's voice.

After a short pause, she continued. "She wrote in her last letter that Prussia will undoubtedly swallow their branch of the Hohenzollern dynasty, given their lack of children. She thinks her husband will be quite happy to relinquish power and let his cousin Frederick deal with what's coming."

The winds of change were sweeping across the kingdoms and principalities of Germany, as they were throughout the rest of Europe. Marie d'Agoult, whose salon regulars included several German writers, had authored a series of articles on revolutionary activity in Prussia and the growing movement for a German nation-state.

"You know, I'm sure," I responded, "that the new Swiss government has closed Sophie's house in Montet."

Héloïse picked up a mussel and began to loosen the meat from its shell. "I know. It's already happened there."

A short civil war in Switzerland had just dissolved the *Sonderbund*, a loose confederation of Catholic cantons, and established in their stead a strong central government. All Catholic schools were being closed and the religious expelled from the country.

"And it will happen in Paris before much longer," I mused and picked up another round of toast. "Louis-Philippe and his cronies would do well to heed your friend's articles."

She nodded but was momentarily lost in the succulence of the mussel.

"In the meantime," I asked, "how goes our lovely queen of Sweden?"

Héloïse brightened and set down her spoon, a look of triumph in her eyes. "You *must* have read about the recent changes in the inheritance laws there?"

I nodded, this being the kind of thing that one in my profession keeps close track of. "Yes indeed. Equal inheritance for men and women."

"Joséphine's behind the entire thing." She excavated another mussel from its shell. "We all love dear old Oscar, but this is *her* vision at work, not his."

I sipped my wine and refrained from asking about her cousin Louis-Napoleon, who was now lurking in England and waiting for events to explode in Paris.

"Have you seen Sophie since you've been back?" I asked.

"I was just there last week—to give her an update on the orphanage. And oh my. I meant to tell you. We were strolling through the gardens and encountered the most *extraordinary* young woman. I think she's from Mexico, but Sophie says her mother was Peruvian. A group of little girls had gathered around her, and she was recounting some amazing story about an Incan goddess who cries tears of silver."

"I'm fairly sure I who you mean," I answered, immediately reminded of my sister at age ten, utterly lost in Sophie's tale of Abélard and Héloïse. "Sophie's mentioned her. Her name is Ofelia Plise."

Barricades

1848

When king louis-philippe's government, fearing an out-break of violence, decides to forbid a fund-raising banquet in the working-class section of Paris, Alphonse de Lamartine states that he will attend even if accompanied only by his shadow.

"Whether the organizers are terrorized into canceling or not," the poet-activist tells his dinner hostess Marie d'Agoult, "*all* the vital energy of France is behind it!"

The banquet—part of an ongoing series of veiled political meetings that have brought together anti-government activists of every stripe—collapses. But on the evening of February 22, disgruntled workers begin filling the place de la Madeleine. The French Revolution of 1848 has entered its opening phase.

Two days later, the Citizen King Louis-Philippe flees Paris in a curtained coach, headed for England. As the next days unroll, parents of the local students begin to remove their daughters from the Hôtel Biron.

"Just ignore what's going on outside," Sophie briskly instructs her teachers, hiding any anxiety she might feel under a playful smile. "Proceed with your classes as if all the students were present."

As the sounds of gunshot and shouting move closer to the rue de Varenne, she sends to the chapel those whose nerves are frayed and suggests a game of hide-and-seek for everyone else—novices included.

"When the game is over, send the winners to me so they can tell me all about their clever hiding places," she says, her eyes dancing. "Then give everyone a delicious *goûter*. I've instructed Sister Patrice to bake her most irresistible cakes and prepare a vat of hot chocolate!"

The games begin, and the only casualty is a bed of tulips, whose nascent heads lie trampled in a flowerbed near the designated home base.

Several nights later, as bullets zing off the shutters and explosions echo in the darkness, several men break into the courtyard, carrying on their shoulders a mortally wounded comrade.

"Take him upstairs and call for the doctor!" Sophie orders and then invites them to sit down and enjoy a hot meal. Instead of dying, the young man makes a full recovery, stays two months, and learns to walk again leaning on Sophie's arm.

Another evening, a ragged brigade pounds violently on the outside gates just as the community is about to eat supper.

"They're starving," Sophie explains when she and the portress have returned to the white-faced gathering in the refectory. "I've invited them to help themselves to our supper, knowing that no one here will mind."

The women nod their veiled heads in obedient agreement, though more than one looks longingly at the plate before her as they abandon the table.

When the group of twenty men pours back out into the night, each has a bottle of wine under his arm and a loaf of bread skewered at the tip of his bayonet. For several days afterward, the Hôtel Biron becomes an impromptu soup kitchen until the police, suspicious of any kind of gathering in the streets, shut it down.

As Alphonse de Lamartine and the provisional French government work to establish the Second Republic, competing forces are at work. In addition to royalist, republican, and socialist factions, Karl Marx's fledgling Communist League issues its *Manifesto*, and re-emergent women's clubs are demanding the right to vote. A worsening economic depression is accompanied by a rise in property taxes. Marie d'Agoult

publishes a scathing series of letters, describing the increasingly conservative Assembly as "defiant of the power that created it, defiant of the People to whom it owes its existence."

In June, working-class Paris finally detonates, arming itself with guns and knives, throwing up barricades, and waiting for the inevitable counter-attack from the government.

"Archbishop Affre is offering to meet the people at the barricades," Sophie tells her community. "They've turned back the minister of the Navy and even Lamartine himself. But the Archbishop hopes to convince them to avoid bloodshed and wait for the Assembly to devise a peaceful solution. The workers trust him."

No one ever discovers who fired the shot, but Archbishop Denys-Auguste Affre, who has worked tirelessly for workers' rights during his short tenure as Archbishop of Paris, is shot behind the barricades on June 25 and dies two days later. On his deathbed he sends a message of regret to Sophie, who immediately forgives him the seven years of grief he has caused the Society.

The streets of Paris run again with blood.

~

Six months later, on December 10, Louis-Napoleon Bonaparte, who has promised everything to everyone and is considered by most voters to be the least of all possible evils, is elected President of the Second Republic.

Héloïse and Anna

1848 – 1849

"You'll *love* ANNA, UNCLE GUY!" HÉLOÏSE EXCLAIMED TO ME ONE gorgeous mid-summer evening in early August. Paris had quieted down, and in honor of my eightieth birthday, she had prepared the promised couscous dinner. The weather was warm, and we were out on her balcony, finishing a dessert of small, diamond-shaped almond cookies called *Makroud el Louse*. A crescent moon hung over the city, its silvery outline reflected in the Seine.

"Sophie has invited us both for a special lunch so that you can meet her," she continued, an excitement that I hadn't heard since her return from Algiers ringing in her voice.

"And who, pray tell, is this Anna?" I asked, imagining some form of Marie d'Agoult draped in a religious habit.

"She's just arrived from Turin, where she was Superior."

"Ah! One of the Sardinian vagabonds!" I replied, alluding to the stream of refugee nuns now pouring out of northern Italy. Mazzini's *Giovine Italia* was making its move to free northern Italy from Austrian occupation and begin the fight for Italian unification. Their unyielding anti-clericalism had caused all of Sophie's schools in the Sardinian

Kingdom, with the exception of Chambéry, to close in the past two months.

I met Anna du Rousier the following week. Sophie had arranged a small birthday lunch in my honor for the four of us.

"She lost her father when she was only eight," Héloïse explained to me on our way to the Hôtel Biron. "She was there when what remained of his body was wheeled into the courtyard of the family chateau in Poitou. He'd been tied by his feet to a galloping horse and quite literally shredded for political reasons that Anna never fully understood. Then or now."

I thought of Alex de Beixedon's death when Héloïse was only six. He, too, had been shredded by the political events of the day, though the beating was far more subtle.

Anna's bearing was that of an aristocrat, but her features were overlaid with the residual sadness that accompanies the early death of a beloved parent. Her wide-set eyes invited conversation and intimacy but at the same time held something back, as if to relinquish their reserve completely would leave her open to another scene of carnage and loss.

"I entered when I was seventeen," she explained in a voice reminiscent of Sophie's, "though I think I'd really decided to do so when I was a little girl." She paused a moment before continuing. "It didn't seem safe to tie my heart directly to anything that could die, so I tied it elsewhere." Here she locked eyes with Sophie in a way that made me feel like a voyeur.

"Though having tied your heart elsewhere hasn't always proven so easy!" Sophie responded lightly, her eyes on Anna's. "You must tell Monsieur Lorrain of your recent adventure!" Shifting her attention to me, she added, "Our Anna stood virtually alone against the entire Revolutionary Guard of Turin this past spring!"

I looked across the table at the young woman, whose face was reddening at Sophie's dramatic introduction.

"Don't be shy, Anna," Héloïse prodded her. "And don't forget to mention the part about the actress!" she added playfully.

Anna raised her eyebrows in mock protest, and then both of them started laughing.

"It wasn't funny at the time," she began, "but yes, I was impersonated on the stage in Turin. We were already being vilified in the papers and political journals as enemies of the Italian Republic. One afternoon a woman came to tea, pretending to inquire about sending her niece to the school. It turned out she was an actress—she'd come to study my speech and mannerisms so that she could more accurately caricature me in the theater!" After a moment she added, "I hear she was quite good!"

"I must say I wouldn't find such a thing funny even now," I responded.

"We're being demonized by every faction in Italy," Sophie interjected, her voice losing its lightness and betraying just for a moment the emotional exhaustion of a person whose entire life has been lived amidst violent political upheaval. "By Mazzini for being secret allies of Austria, by Catholics for being secret allies of France, by other Catholics for opposing Pope Pius' liberalism, by the working class for being hypocrites, by the middle class for sympathizing with the workers."

"And don't forget the anti-Jesuits!" Anna added. "There's another group that hates us for being some kind of secret female appendage of the Jesuit order. You know what they were chanting when they stormed the convent?"

When we shook our heads, she continued. "*Morte alle Gesuite*! Death to the Jesuitesses! When I saw that things were about to turn violent, I asked the king for protection, and he sent in members of the National Guard. But they turned out to be sympathetic to the Revolution and kept us up day and night doing their military drills in the parlors!"

"What about the children?" I asked incredulously.

"We'd sent them home by then, and when the actual siege began, I found places for the nuns to hide as well. We smuggled them out one by one, disguised in street clothes."

"And you?"

"I tried to remain in the building but was finally forced out by the guards. They marched me through the streets where people had gathered on either side to watch. They were not kind, but as you see,"—here she allowed herself a smile tinged with apologetic victory—"I made it to safety."

I looked at Sophie, but her eyes were riveted on Anna in a kind of flaming benediction. Héloïse, too, was staring at her in a way that mingled wonder, respect, and, I thought, a kind of envy.

Sophie broke the stillness. "It's so very odd. I always thought we'd be seeking asylum in Italy, not the other way around."

"It appears Mazzini now has his eyes on Rome," I responded.

Sophie nodded. "Louise de Limminghe writes that they're readying themselves for the worst." Then she suddenly brightened. "But you *see* what this all brings with it?"

We waited for her to answer her own question.

"More personnel for our schools here in France and abroad! Anna and I are already discussing possibilities in South America."

Here Anna du Rousier came fully alive, "The Archbishop of Santiago is requesting a foundation in Chile."

Next to me Héloïse's body seemed to inflate with a similar vitality. "We're both studying Spanish with one of the students from Mexico!" she said.

"Let me guess," I added. "Her name is Ofelia."

Now it was Sophie's turn to glow and expand. She looked at Héloïse. "Are you planning to join the child in her horseback adventure?" she asked, her eyes sparkling.

"Ofelia has this *idea*," Héloïse explained to me quickly. "When she finishes school here, she wants to return to Mexico, ride out into the countryside, and share her understanding of—wait! I can say it in Spanish!—'el amor infinito del sagrado corazòn.'"

"She claims she has no religious vocation," Anna added, "but she wants to give her life over to what she calls 'spreading the love.'"

"And I want to go with her," Héloïse stated, looking out of the corner of her eye to gauge my reaction.

"For the sake of Ofelia," Sophie said softly, her face lighting up at the thought of her Mexican-Incan disciple, "I would have founded the Society."

Garibaldi

1849

W‍HEN HIS MINISTER OF THE INTERIOR IS STABBED THROUGH THE neck on the steps of the Palazzo della Cancelleria, Pope Pius IX prudently decides to vacate the Eternal City and take refuge in Gaeta, a fortified coastal town in the Kingdom of Naples. Within three months, a popularly elected Constitutional Assembly proclaims the Roman Republic and in March names Giuseppe Mazzini to its ruling Triumvirate. Meanwhile, the charismatic Genoese adventurer Giuseppe Garibaldi, who has returned from Uruguay and Brazil to support the Italian War of Independence, gathers a military force on the Roman borders.

Opposition to the Republic arrives in an unlikely guise. President Louis-Napoleon Bonaparte, bound by an election promise made just months earlier to French ultramontanes, sends French forces to restore the Pope to power—this despite his youthful membership in the Carbonari. On April 25, the French army moves against Rome, and Garibaldi enters the city to defend the revolution.

Sophie watches events unfold from afar. Unable to send or receive letters, she depends on newspaper reports for news of her schools. Louise de Limminghe, firmly ensconced at the Villa Lante, waits confidently for doom to strike. Within four days, Garibaldi himself appears at the door, informing her that he wishes to occupy the building because of its strategic location atop the Janiculum Hill.

"I am sorry, sir," she responds acidly, "but the Villa Lante is not available to your men. As you see,"—she grabs her cross for effect and flourishes it in his direction—"we're running a novitiate here."

"Very well, Madame," the red-bearded soldier answers, clicking his heels and offering her a slight bow. "I shall return."

The next day he arrives with seventy men.

"We were loaded into large open carts," Louise writes in a letter that doesn't arrive in Paris until weeks later. "They drove us to the Trinità, where it seems every Frenchwoman in Rome has sought refuge! I need not tell you that the ride across the city was a terror such as I've never experienced—not even when you and I were stopped at the border so many years ago!"

"*Che donne sono!*" The Italian officer escorting the women across town is heard to exclaim. "I've never encountered such lion-hearted women!" he continues, riding beside his prisoners with a certain sense of awe. Despite the chaos in the streets, the crowd allows them to pass without incident.

When a delegation from the Constitutional Assembly bursts victoriously into Santa Rufina and advises the nuns that they are free from the bondage of their vows, the men are met with incredulous stares and a wall of ice that freezes them back out into the streets of the Trastevere.

Over the course of the next several weeks, as Louis-Napoleon's reinforced army lays siege to the city, Garibaldi's men subject the Trinità to a series of rigorous searches. On one occasion they claim to be looking for "Pius's spy," Cardinal Lambruschini. On another, they scurry all over the property seeking a supposed network of secret subterranean passages that they believe are connecting the Society directly with the French invaders.

At the end of June, when the French force has swollen to thirty thousand men and Rome has been under bombardment for four weeks, the Assembly votes to have the Republican army retreat into the Apennine Mountains.

It will be another eleven years before Giuseppe Garibaldi brings Mazzini's work to its inevitable conclusion.

Feast and Farewell

1849

BENGAL LIGHTS SPARKLED ACROSS ONE END OF THE ENORMOUS study hall at the Hôtel Biron, and the entire audience sat transfixed as Faith, Hope and Charity—draped in shimmering fabric and bearing lights of their own—mounted the stage and assumed their positions. Among her many gifts, Anna du Rousier, now Superior at the Paris school, could spin enchantment out of the most unlikely venues, and tonight was no exception. The three theological virtues, represented by girls from the senior school, passed behind a curtain of ivy and evergreen branches and emerged as if by magic atop a hanging platform. Behind them an image of the Sacred Heart, crafted entirely of flowers, had been suspended from the ceiling, and at a signal another set of sparklers burst from its center. When the applause had died down, the youngest children gathered around Sophie and performed a song they had written in her honor.

Poetry, dramatic dialogues, and more singing filled the next hour as students and community members acknowledged the feast of Mary Magdalene in this, the seventieth year of her namesake's life. Though averse to any kind of celebration of herself, Sophie sat obediently in a heavily decorated chair and patiently received the crowd's adulation. When the final tableau had ended and light from the last sparkler had ebbed into darkness, the children waited for the guest of honor to rise and extend her usual congratulations on a performance well done. But she was motionless, and her eyes looked out into some unidentified space beyond them all. When Anna du Rousier leaned over and touched her arm, indicating that the children wished to express a final wish for her feast day, Sophie remained catatonic. What was happening hit the younger woman with sudden force, and she turned to the students, whose expressions had moved from joy to alarm.

"Your performance, children, has so pleased Mother Barat that she's quite lost herself in prayer. She is grateful for your efforts and invites you to go enjoy your refreshments!"

Sophie sat without moving for the next forty-five minutes.

~

She visited me at my bedside the following week and described it all—except for the ecstatic finale.

"It seems quite impossible," she mused. "Almost seventy years on this earth!" Here she looked directly into my eyes and I could read the concern in her expression. "Who would have guessed that either of us would live to such an age?" I read her question as an exhortation.

She stayed with me for the better part of the afternoon. After relaying details of the feast-day extravaganza, she moved to business.

"I'm planning a final trip to Rome, now that the political situation there seems to be settling down. The minute the pope returns from Gaeta, I shall be on my way."

"I believe he's waiting for our resurrected Napoleon to stop telling him how he should run the Papal States."

"Indeed," she answered drily.

"What's on your agenda? The governance issues again?"

She nodded. "Of course! As you know as well as anyone, we're up to sixty-five institutions, and it's even more impossible than it was ten years ago for one person to administer them effectively. If something were to happen to me, the Society is at risk. We *must* come up with some form of provincial structure, and there *must* be a provision to ensure an immediate interim successor in the event of my death."

When I smiled at her final remark, she demanded an explanation.

"You were the child who was expected to die on the night she was born," I chided her. "You're clearly one of those people who spend their entire lives dying of one malady or another—and then go on to outlive us all!"

My laughter was interrupted by one of the agonizing pains whose source, according to my doctor, was "a tumor the size of a melon."

I waved away the nurse, who had left her seat in the corner of the room, and in response Sophie shifted her own chair closer, as if mere proximity to my failing body would mitigate its pain.

"I don't quite know what I shall do without you, dearest friend." It was her first explicit acknowledgment of my condition, and she reached out to touch my hand, looking as if she already doubted its material substance.

"You have an army of advisors, Sophie. And Jean-Marie de Beixedon is always there in the wings if you need an independent opinion. He's an excellent estate lawyer and has helped me with all the Society's transactions for the past twenty years."

"You know what I mean, Guy. You're the only one left who knew me in Joigny. Louis, Marie-Louise, Célestine, Marie—they are all gone now." Her voice broke, and I closed my eyes. "In some way you carry my entire life within you, and when you go, I feel like all those pieces will disappear forever."

As if we knew there might never be another opportunity, we spent the remainder of the afternoon lost in memories of our childhood. Of Louis with his academic brilliance, his austere faith, and his relentless demands on his little sister. Of Marie-Louise with her soft sensuality and easy laughter. Of Célestine and Sophie joyously shrieking through the medieval streets of Joigny. Of the way the river Yonne would glitter when viewed from high up on the Côte Saint Jacques. And of a particular *vendange* almost sixty years before when she and I had recited Andreas Capellanus' Rules of Courtly Love to one another amidst the blazing October vines.

The moment stood out for me as the centerpiece of my emotional life, that moment around which everything else had been spinning for eight decades. Sophie had forgotten the scene entirely.

Héloïse came by the next day, bringing several containers of food that we knew I wouldn't eat.

"I hear you had a visitor yesterday," she said with forced jocularity.

"Ah yes. She gave me an edited version of the celebration. And we talked about old times."

"She told me."

"What else did she tell you?"

"Nothing much," Héloïse lied, setting the food down on a table and pulling a chair up closer to the bed. "How are you feeling?"

"Great," I lied back. "What brings you here on such a lovely summer day?"

"I thought maybe we could talk about the Jubilee. It looks as if she'll be spending it in Rome, but you and I must do *something* to mark the occasion."

The Society's fiftieth anniversary was still over a year away, but I understood the need to discuss it now.

"So what do you have in mind, *ma belle nièce*?"

"I was thinking of an object," she responded. "A piece of sculpture. Something beautiful that could stand somewhere in the gardens, maybe just outside her window."

I nodded vehemently in agreement, trying to camouflage another one of the waves of pain whose visits were increasing in frequency. She wasn't fooled.

"Shall I get the nurse?" she asked.

"No," I gasped. "Just hand me that jar of morphine tablets."

"It's a perfect idea," I answered when I'd taken the pill and caught my breath. She nodded, rearranging the pillows and fluttering about the bed as if doing so would relieve my agony.

When the glazed expression had left my eyes, she spoke again. "I'd like it to be from the three of us—from you, me, and *maman*."

"And this sculpture would represent—?" I left the question hanging, knowing Héloïse had long contemplated the answer.

"Mary Magdalene."

"I thought so."

"But not for the reason you think."

"I know."

"What do you mean 'you know'?" The self-assurance in her voice suddenly disappeared.

"It's about your mother as well as Sophie," I answered.

There was a long silence.

"It's your paean to women," I continued. "A declaration of solidarity. Have I guessed right?"

She nodded her head, looking at me closely but still refusing to speak.

"What happened to *maman*, Uncle Guy?" she finally asked.

I merely shook my head.

"The money," she said woodenly. "There's no other reason he would have left it to me."

I nodded, still unsure as to whether Denis Marmaton's final bequest was motivated by guilt or malice.

Jubilee

1850

SEVERAL MONTHS LATER, AS LOUIS-NAPOLEON BONAPARTE IS LAY-ing the groundwork for the coup that will, in a blast of political déjà-vu, establish him as France's second Emperor, Sophie sets out for Rome. When she arrives at the Villa Lante, whose scarred exterior matches much of what she has seen as she passed through the city, Louise de Limminghe, wearing her most dolorous expression, comes out to greet her.

"Prepare yourself, Sophie," she exclaims, once they have greeted each other. "Garibaldi and his men were not kind to our little palazzo." They enter the building and Sophie exhales deeply. The once gleaming floors are scratched and broken, many of the polished tiles now missing and replaced with planks of wood or pounded dirt. The frescoes that once graced the walls and ceilings have been reduced to faintly colored ruins, their human subjects used for target practice. Windows, most of their panes shot out, have been papered over. All of the furnishings have disappeared.

"And here," Louise pulls herself up to her full height, as if offering physical resistance to the powers of darkness that had been there before her, "is the marble staircase where Garibaldi seems to have enjoyed riding his horse. You can see where the poor creature must have stumbled and kicked the walls."

Four days later, on November 20, Sophie speaks to the community gathered at Villa Lante. It is the eve of the fiftieth anniversary of the Society's founding, an event she has been dreading. Religious from all three Roman houses have gathered to hear her speak, and she is quick to deflect attention away from herself.

"Fifty years ago," she begins, "the Divine Heart of Jesus laid the foundation of our little Society. While other religious orders might study the spirit of their founders in order to attain some level of perfection, we are particularly blessed in that our founder is neither a man nor a woman, but rather the heart of Jesus itself." Here, she looks hard at the group assembled before her, as if challenging them to think otherwise.

"If God has used a small instrument now and then to further his work, this instrument is *nothing*. Its very smallness and nothingness speak to the real inspiration, which is God's very heart—that source of endless love and compassion that pours itself out for us with boundless grace. It is this action that we are meant to emulate above all things."

Louise de Limminghe notes the fire in Sophie's eyes as her voice—faint but vibrating with a peculiar force—fills the room. It is a voice, she muses, which has aspired to silence and self-annihilation all its life. She wonders that it emanates from such a tiny body and that such a body could have endured the upheavals and betrayals of the past decade—including her own.

The next morning the Jubilee celebration begins with a solemn mass at the Villa Lante. The Jesuit General, Father Roothaan, presides. On a stand to the right of the altar is a copy of the painting that hung above Sophie, Octavie Bailly, Marguerite Maillau, and Marie-Françoise Loquet when they first consecrated themselves to the Sacred Heart. Copies of the red-clad Madonna have been sent to every foundation in honor of the event. When she sees it, Sophie's imagination rushes back to her brother's secret chapel in the Marais. Joseph Varin, she remembers, had preached on the need for women to found a new social order in the wake of the Revolutionary Terror. She looks at the scarred walls of the

Villa Lante and wonders. In his homily, Father Roothan makes numerous allusions to Sophie as the Society's foundress, and she squirms in her seat, unhappy at his choice of words and telling him so after the service.

He ignores her protest and compliments her again, noting that no other founder of a religious order has lived so long.

"If anyone is the founder of our order, it is Joseph Varin or Léonor de Tournely," she retorts. "And your comment on my longevity is no tribute whatsoever. It merely proves that I spend way too much time taking care of myself!"

At an evening service, the officiating priest loads his final benediction with such effusive praise of Sophie that she slides out of her seat and leaves the chapel. That night, her eyes rolling with exasperation, she asks Louise that the man never be invited back.

"You objected to his calling you the 'veritable queen of the angelic multitude'?" Louise asks, her expression reflecting a levity Sophie hasn't seen in over a decade.

The two women burst into laughter.

Final Joust

1851

Sophie's annual winter flu strikes shortly after the Jubilee, and over two months pass before she is well enough to call on Pope Pius IX.

"So finally we meet, Madame Barat," he opens, his eyes curious but showing the strain of the past two years. The upheavals throughout Italy have caused him to desert the optimistic liberalism of his youth, and he knows that his safety in Rome hinges on the continuing presence of the French army.

Sophie goes down on one knee and kisses the ring on his right hand. "Your Holiness."

"I offer you my personal congratulations on the Society's recent Jubilee," he responds, motioning for her to rise and take a seat in the chair across from him. "You must know how much we value your work in these frightful times."

"You are young, Most Holy Father," Sophie responds with an upbeat smile. "Our Society has passed through many such upheavals, and yet the work goes on. We adapt to the times in which God's will places us and trust that God's grace will guide us through."

Pius wonders what, exactly, lies beneath her words and looks closely at the woman sitting before him. Despite her seventy years, she still radiates a childlike energy—a quality enhanced by the inability of her feet to reach the floor. Her eyes exude the same magnetic optimism that has captivated people since her youth, and whatever political subtext might have been buried in her allusion to "God's will," he decides to trust her.

"You can speak of grace when almost all of your schools in Italy have been closed?"

"In fifty years I've seen many of our schools come and go, for political reasons as well as others. But we go on."

Pius begins to ask questions about the recently opened schools in the U.S. and Canada, and Sophie deftly points out the increased administrative challenges these new foundations bring with them. "We hope to expand into Latin America," she continues. "But in order to do so, changes must be made to our governing structure."

He nods his head absently, the mention of Latin America reminding him of Garibaldi. Informants tell him that the swashbuckling adventurer is biding his time in Nicaragua and Peru. Meanwhile Mazzini, now in exile in London, is forming a new political group called *Amici d'Italia*.

The audience ends quickly, but several days later Sophie sends him a document she has drawn up on the advice of several ecclesial officials. Despite the political risk involved in any request to the Roman authorities, Sophie knows that the long overdue changes to the 1826 Constitutions can no longer wait.

⁓

"Why does Madame Barat send this request to me directly?" Pius asks Luigi Lambruschini.

"I do not know, your Holiness," Lambruschini responds, irate that Sophie has bypassed his authority as the Society's Cardinal Protector.

"Perhaps she was deferring to your recent ill health?" Pius suggests, his voice betraying just a trace of disdain.

The cardinal has finally returned to Rome after a nervous collapse. Loathed by the Republicans for his anti-constitutional views, he escaped from his palace only moments before Garibaldi's soldiers broke in and ripped his bed to shreds with their bayonets. He managed to slip out of the city disguised as a stable-hand and has been recuperating for months in Gaeta.

"Surely no reason for her to ignore Vatican protocols, Holy Father," he responds, bowing slightly.

"She doesn't seem like a person who would deliberately breach decorum."

"I shall speak with her, your Holiness."

"And you will please see to it that her request goes through the proper channels of authority?"

Cardinal Lambruschini, reading Pius' comment as a condemnation of Sophie's earlier maneuver, takes the document and bows again, giving his superior a meaningful smile.

On a beautiful morning in early May, Sophie—now staying at the Trinità dei Monti—receives two devastating pieces of news. First, that Joseph Varin has died in Paris after a long illness. Second, that an official Council of Bishops and Regulars has rejected her request.

She stares at the second letter in disbelief and falls heavily onto a nearby divan. The first she puts gently back into its envelope; Father Varin had been bedridden for many months, and the news is no surprise. In fact, she envies him his much-deserved rest. She wonders now how he would have reacted to the other document in her lap. She rereads it several times, asking herself what series of motives could possibly lie behind the rejection. After the initial shock has passed through her, she moves to her desk and calmly lists the three changes she wishes for the Constitutions—the organization of the Society into Provinces, the restructuring of the General Council, and the permission for the Superior General to nominate a temporary head to preside over the Society during the period between her death and the formal election of her successor.

She takes the list into the little chapel now dedicated to *Mater Admirabilis* and places it on the altar. For the next several days she sits alone with the rose-robed Mary, trying to emulate the young woman's perfect state of contemplation as she waits for she knows not what. She meditates on the nature of obedience. She ruminates in spite of herself on the allocation of power—and on what its possession does to those who wield it in its absolute form. She repeats to herself the advice she has recently given a young novice. "Go to the tabernacle. Be silent. Wait for the trouble to become nothing. Empty yourself before plenitude and remake yourself in the endless love of your Bridegroom."

When word of Sophie's unhappiness reaches Pius, he sends an emissary to the Trinità. She explains again what she has already asked for, and the man returns to the corridors of authority.

Days later a Papal Brief arrives by courier. This time she goes directly into the chapel before opening the document. She sits in the small pew before the altar and breaks the wax seal. "This affair was handled badly," Pius' letter reads. "Please accept our revised decision, and know that we are grateful for the good work you are doing."

Sophie looks at *Mater* and finds herself trying to catch the young woman's eye. She is filled with gratitude, but her attitude of thanksgiving mingles with one slightly less gracious. She finally casts her own eyes downward lest Mary look up and see the embers of exasperation glowing within them.

La Madeleine

1852

JUST BEFORE SUNRISE ON EASTER MORNING, SOPHIE AWAKENS IN her room at the Hôtel Biron. The sky outside her window is lightening at its upper edge, and she stays in bed for several minutes, watching the room come slowly into focus. Her lips begin to move, and silence invades the room like a shroud, enveloping the hush of her unvoiced prayer and rendering the entire space a kind of muted energy field. She closes her eyes and floats back into the dawns of her youth. Waiting as a child for the first rays of light to come through her window on the morning of the *vendange*. Praying all night with Philippine Duchesne in the chapel at Sainte-Marie d'en-Haut and then walking out into the blaze of an alpine sunrise. Sitting with Thérèse Maillucheau under the walnut tree in Poitiers, watching the great orange fireball come up over the Clain River.

There are times now when she can quite literally *hear* the silence, and within that silence every sound that she has ever heard. As if time has collapsed in on itself and delivered over the entirety of her life in sound waves, stripped first of any distinctness or intelligibility and then sucked up into a register that is inaudible to the human ear. In such moments she tries to discern the truth of her own life. Truth—that elusive creature that is so often buried in self-deception or self-pity, or in that frenetic round of activity that masquerades as reality. She is seventy-one years old and still wonders if she is the person God has wanted her to be.

When the song of a bird fractures the stillness, she opens her eyes and notes that the light has turned faintly pink. She gets out of bed and tiptoes to the window, hoping to glimpse the winged creature who appears to understand that this is a special morning. When she looks outside, a flash of white catches her eye beneath a large cedar tree. She squints to bring the scene into focus and catches her breath. A red-breasted robin has perched on one of the lower branches and calls her attention to the large block of marble below.

She can barely distinguish the figures of a man and a woman. As the light increases, she sees from his wounds that the man is the risen Christ. The woman at his feet, she knows, must be Mary Magdalene.

"*Noli me tangere*," Sophie whispers, citing John's gospel. "You saw him before anyone, Madeleine. You knew him when he called your name."

She meditates, as she has throughout her life, on this enigmatic apostle. She remembers her grandfather Fouffé promising to take her one day to the great abbey built in her honor at Vézelay. She thinks of the profusion of images the woman has inspired in the minds of artists. She ponders the tales that have been spun around her for almost two millennia. Sinner. Healer. Madwoman. Prostitute.

"I know you were his favorite," she whispers, a small smile playing about the corners of her mouth. Despite the chill of the morning, she opens the window and leans out to gain a closer view of the woman's features. She gasps, a glimmer of recognition sweeping over her.

Knowing that Guy's spirit is frolicking nearby, she pulls her head back inside the room and casts her eyes about the eaves. She smiles more broadly and leans back out the window just in time to see the sun's first rays illuminate the statue. There is no doubt. The face is that of Célestine.

Epilogue

- SOPHIE BARAT LIVED QUIETLY ON THE GROUNDS OF THE HÔTEL Biron for the remaining thirteen years of her life.

- She died there of natural causes on May 25, 1865—the feast of the Ascension. She was 85 years of age.

- In the wake of the legal suppression of religious education in France in 1904 her body was moved to Jette, Belgium.

- On May 24, 1908, she was beatified by Pope Pius X.

- On May 24, 1925, she was canonized Saint Madeleine Sophie Barat by Pope Pius XI.

- On June 19, 2009 (the Feast of the Sacred Heart), her body was returned to Paris. It lies in a glass coffin in the Sacred Heart Chapel of the church of Saint Francis Xavier—in the 7ème arrondissement, just across the street from the Hôtel Biron.

List of Recurring or Otherwise Noteworthy Characters

Numbers in parentheses indicate section in which each first appears. Asterisks indicate invented characters.

Affre, Denis-Auguste: Archbishop of Paris from 1840 to 1848 (10)

Agoult, Marie d': married name of Marie de Flavigny (8)

Angoulême, Duchess of: only surviving child of King Louis XVI and Queen Marie-Antoinette (6)

Audé, Eugénie: RSCJ who accompanies Philippine Duchesne to America (7)

Bailly, Octavie: religious associate of Sophie in the Marais (2)

Barat, Jacques: Sophie's father (1)

Barat, Louis: Sophie's older brother; priest, Father of the Faith, and eventually Jesuit (1)

Barat, Marie-Louise: Sophie's older sister (1)

Barat, Marie Madeleine: Sophie's mother (1)

Baudemont, Anne: early RSCJ in Amiens; former Poor Clare sister (3)

Beauharnais, Augusta Amelia: Princess of Bavaria; wife of Eugène de Beauharnais (6)

Beauharnais, Eugène de: son of Joséphine de Beauharnais; Célestine's lover (3)

Beauharnais, Eugénie de: daughter of Eugène de Beauharnais; later Princess of Hohenzollern-Hechingen (9)

Beauharnais, Hortense de: daughter of Joséphine de Beauharnais; marries Louis Bonaparte (4)

Beauharnais, Joséphine de: first wife of Napoleon Bonaparte (3)

Beauharnais, Joséphine de: daughter of Eugène de Beauharnais; later Queen of Sweden and Norway (9)

*Beixedon, Alexandre de: younger son of Alex and Marie de Beixedon (6)

*Beixedon, Alex de: diplomat under Napoleon; marries Marie de Marmaton (3)

*Beixedon, Héloïse de: daughter of Célestine Lorrain; adopted by Alexandre and Marie de Beixedon (4)

*Beixedon, Jean-Marie de: elder son of Alex and Marie de Beixedon (6)

Berry, Duchess of: mother of last Bourbon pretender to throne of France (7)

Berthold, Octavie: RSCJ who accompanies Philippine Duchesne to America (7)

Bigeu, Joséphine: early RSCJ met in Poitiers (5)

Bonaparte, Joseph: brother of Napoleon (3)

Bonaparte, Louis: brother of Napoleon; marries Hortense de Beauharnais (4)

Bonaparte, Louis-Napoleon: son of Louis Bonaparte and Hortense de Beauharnais; later Emperor Napoleon III (9)

Bonaparte, Napoleon: Emperor of France (3)

Capy, Claude: early RSCJ in Amiens (3)

Cassini, Cécile de: early RSCJ in Amiens (3)

Causans, Armande de: RSCJ who heads schools in Turin and Rome (8)

Charbonnel, Catherine de: early RSCJ in Amiens; long-time friend of Sophie (3)

Charles X: youngest brother of Louis XVI; second king of Restoration period (7)

Chobelet, Lydia: early RSCJ met in Poitiers (5)

David, Jacques-Louis: French painter (3)

Deshayes, Geneviève: early RSCJ in Amiens; long-time friend of Sophie (3)

Félicité Desmarquest: early RSCJ in Amiens; long-time friend of Sophie (3)

Duchesne, Philippine: early RSCJ in Grenoble; founder of first schools in North America; long-time friend of Sophie (4)

Ducis, Henriette: early RSCJ in Amiens (3)

Dussaussoy, Étienne: Marie Louise Barat's husband (1)

Dussaussoy, Jules: Étienne's brother (1)

Dussaussoy, Louis- Étienne: Étienne and Marie-Louise's son (2)

Dussaussoy, Zoe: Étienne and Marie-Louise's daughter (10)

Duval, Mademoiselle: landlord and religious associate of Sophie in the Marais (2)

Enfantin, Louis: Father of the Faith and charismatic preacher, met in Poitiers (5)

Favre, Joseph Marie: French priest who becomes Sophie's spiritual advisor after death of Father Montaigne (7)

Flavigny, Marie de: student at Hôtel Biron (later Countess d'Agoult) (7)

Fouché, Joseph: secret police agent; long-time associate of Denis Marmaton (3)

Galitzine, Elisabeth: Russian-born RSCJ; closely allied with Fr. Rozaven (8)

Garibaldi, Antonio: Papal Nuncio in Paris (11)

Garibaldi, Giuseppe: Italian patriot and soldier; key figure in the reunification of Italy as a nation-state (11)

Girard, Henriette: early RSCJ; first met in Grenoble (5)

Gramont d'Aster, Charlotte-Eugénie de: early RSCJ; Queen Marie-Antoinette's lady-in-waiting; mother of Eugénie and Antoinette de Gramont (5)

Gramont, Eugénie de: early RSCJ and close friend of Sophie; Charlotte's daughter (5)

Gramont, Antoinette de: early RSCJ; Charlotte's daughter (5)

Gregory XVI: Pope from 1831 to 1849 (8)

Grosier, Henriette: early RSCJ in Amiens; long-time friend of Sophie (3)

*Guillot, Alain: Louis' childhood friend; marries Véronique Lorrain (1)

*Guillot, Christophe: son of Nicolas Guillot and Marie-Claire Guillot; father of Guy Lorrain Guillot (9)

*Guillot, Jean: Alain's cousin; wealthy winegrower (2)

*Guillot, Marie-Claire: Alain's daughter; marries Nicolas Guillot (4)

*Guillot, Nicolas: Jean's son; marries Alain Guillot's daughter Marie-Claire (2)

Fouffé, Germont: Barat family cousin (1)

Gouges, Olympe de: woman of the Revolution (2)

Jugon, Adèle: RSCJ; long-time friend of Sophie (3)

Lacombe, Claire: woman of the Revolution (2)

Lambruschini, Luigi: Roman Cardinal who eventually serves as the protector of the Society of the Sacred Heart; Cardinal Secretary of State from 1836 to 1846 (8)

Lammenais, Félicité: radical Catholic priest whose writings were banned by the Vatican (9)

Leo XII: Pope from 1823 to 1829 (8)

Léon, Pauline: woman of the Revolution; chocolatière (2)

Limminghe, Louise de: RSCJ who headed schools in Turin and Rome for many years; nicknamed *Addolorata* (8)

Liszt, Franz: Hungarian composer; lover of Marie d'Agoult (9)

Loquet, Mademoiselle: religious associate of Sophie in the Marais and Amiens (2)

Loriquet, Jean-Nicolas de: Father of the Faith and (later) Jesuit; noted French educator (3)

*Lorrain, Célestine: Sophie's childhood friend (1)

*Lorrain, Guy: Louis' childhood friend; Sophie's property lawyer [also functions as narrator] (1)

*Lorrain, Hubert: Guy's father (1)

*Lorrain, Véronique: Guy's older sister; marries Alain Guillot (1)

Louis XVIII: younger brother of Louis XVI; after Napoleon's fall, the first king of the Restoration period (6)

Louis-Philippe: "Citizen King" of the French from 1830 to 1838 ["July Monarchy"]; member of the Orléans (younger) branch of the Bourbon family (8)

Maillot, Marguérite: religious associate of Sophie in the Marais (2)

Maillucheau, Elizabeth (later Thérèse): early RSCJ met in Bordeaux; lifelong friend of Sophie (5)

Marboeuf, Countess Catherine Antoinette de: RSCJ met in Paris; helps with purchase of Hôtel Biron (7)

Marie Louise: second wife of Napoleon Bonaparte (6)

*Marmaton, Denis: Louis' childhood playmate; secret police agent (1)

*Marmaton, Marie: Denis' sister; marries Alex de Beixedon (1)

*Marmaton, Olivier: Denis' father; Joigny winegrower (1)

Mathieu, Césaire: Archbishop of Besançon (11)

Mazzini, Giuseppe: Italian patriot instrumental in the unification of Italy as a nation state (8)

Méricourt, Thériogne de: woman of the Revolution (2)

Montaigne, Jean: priest in Paris at Seminary of Saint Sulpice; spiritual advisor to Sophie (6)

Naudet, Louise: member of Dilette di Gesù in Rome; early advisor to Sophie (3)

Paccanari, Nicholas: Father of the Faith; overseer of Dilette di Gesù in Rome (3)

Perdrau, Pauline: RSCJ who paints *Mater Admirabilis* in Rome (11)

Pius IX: Pope from 1846 to 1878 (12)

Plise, Ofelia: Mexican student at the Sacred Heart school in Paris (12)

Quelen, Hyacinthe de: Archbishop of Paris from 1821 to 1839 (8)

Roger, Pierre: Father of the Faith; charismatic preacher (4)

Roothan, Jean: Jesuit Superior General in Rome (11)

Rousier, Anna du: RSCJ who runs school in Turin for many years; founds first Sacred Heart schools in South America (10)

Rozaven, Jean: Jesuit Assistant General in Rome; mentor of Elisabeth Galitzine (7)

Saint Estève, Sambucy de: Father of Faith; early associate of RSCJ in Amiens (3)

Tallien, Jean: Revolutionary leader (5)

Tallien, Therezia: woman of the Revolution; marries Jean Tallien (2)

Varin, Joseph: Father of the Faith and (later) Jesuit priest; friend of Louis Barat; lifelong advisor to Sophie (2)

Constance Solari has taught English at Sacred Heart Schools in Atherton, California, since 1972 and serves on the Formation to Mission Committee of the U.S. Sacred Heart Network Board. Her academic areas of interest are French and Italian studies, Comparative Literature, and the Humanities. She lives in the San Francisco Bay Area.

Made in the USA
Middletown, DE
24 February 2017